I0564209

Daughter of Texas

Geron GA *& Associates*

Copyright © 2011 Celia D. Hayes

ISBN-13 978-0934955836
ISBN-10 0-934955832

All rights reserved. No part of this publication may be reproduced, stored in a retrieval system, or transmitted in any form or by any means, electronic, mechanical, recording or otherwise, without the prior written permission of the author.

Printed in the United States of America.

Geron & Associates
A Division of Watercress Press.
2011

Daughter of Texas

Celia Hayes

Daughter of Texas

Thanks and acknowledgements are due to a great number of people who contributed advice, feedback, editing, and all sorts of support to the writer of this novel, beginning with fellow members of the Independent Authors Guild, especially Al Past for the use of his gorgeous color photos.

Thanks are also due to Alice Geron of Watercress Press, for editing and encouragement, to long-time blog-fan Mary "Proud Veteran" Young for friendship and support in time of crisis, and to local historians like Vickie and Paul Frenzel of Gonzales, Texas, who very kindly gave me a guided tour of old Gonzales, and suggested a number of historical sources for further research. Thanks also to longtime fan Andrew Brooks of San Diego, California, who after reading various chapters of the *Adelsverein Trilogy* posted on online, suggested the humorous subtitle of *Barsetshire with Cypress Trees and Lots of Side-Arms* for my recreation of mid-19th century Texas. This has since turned out to be as apt as it is foresighted, since the interlinked adventures of the Becker, Steinmetz, and Richter families on the Texas frontier, as well as many of their friends and distant connections, are proving to be as rich and continuing a source of stories as the original Barsetshire ever was.

This book is dedicated with love to Mom and my daughter Jeanne, both of whom were supportive well and above the call of duty. Finally and most importantly – it is dedicated to the memory of Dad, who read every word of the final draft with interest and delight before being taken from us on the day after Christmas, 2010.

Celia Hayes
San Antonio, Texas
December 2010

Who can find a virtuous woman?
For her price is far above rubies.
The heart of her husband doth safely trust in her,
So that he shall have no need of spoil.
She will do him good and not evil all the days of her life.
– Proverbs 31: 10-12

Prelude – *In Margaret's House*

Over that winter, which was the fifty-third year of her life, and the last winter of the war that folk had begun to call "The War Between the States," a slow creeping paralysis at last confined Margaret to her bedroom. It was not her original bedroom, upstairs in the newer wing of a sprawling house in a park of meadows and fruit trees, which were all that was left of the farm that her father, Alois Becker, had established when the nearby hamlet and scattering of farms was called Waterloo on the Colorado. Cruelly, the paralysis had advanced, remorselessly taking control of her body and her life – she who had always appeared to be a domestic general in command of a small army, a whirlwind of activity in her vast, sprawling house; a hostess of no small repute, with many friends and the mother of sons. It was a particularly cruel twist of fate that her body should be first and worst affected, leaving her mind, her will and her memory unaffected. Margaret resisted being transformed into a helpless invalid, fighting as she had always fought, with resolute calm and by giving up as little as possible, every step of the way. When she could no longer climb the stairs, when she could no longer command her own lower limbs, and sat most of the day in a chair with wheels, in which her maids pushed her from room to room as she saw about the business of running a boarding house, she ordered that the room next to the private family parlor be cleared out, and that her own bedroom furniture and all her private possessions, her clothes and ornaments be brought downstairs and installed there.

"You and poor Daddy Hurst cannot be carrying me upstairs, morning and night," she said to Hetty, who was her cook and long-time friend.

"I wish you would do as the doctor advises, Marm," Hetty answered, "And take the water cure. Sure and 'tis the best thing."

"Too much trouble," Margaret answered, with indomitable cheer, intended to comfort Hetty as much as herself. "This way, I need not tire myself, and perhaps I may begin schooling Amelia in the art of keeping a large house full of guests and boarders as well as being a political hostess."

Hetty mumbled a Hibernian rudery under her breath, and Margaret sighed. Blunt, practical and Irish, Hetty had about as much in common with Margaret's daughter-in-law as a wild mustang from the Llano did with a pedigreed Kentucky racing horse.

3

"She is my son's wife," Margaret answered, "And the mother of my grandson. So I do have some hope of her. I want so much for her to take my place for her sake, as much as anything g else."

"An' them as are in Hell want ice water," Hetty riposted. Margaret sighed again and patted Hetty's work-worn hand.

"There are so few respectable avenues for a woman to provide for her children, for her family," Margaret said, momentarily distracted. Her hand felt numb, stiff and lumpish, as she moved it. There was a new chill striking her to the heart. So had her good friend Colonel Ford warned her – he who had once practiced medicine, who had worn himself ragged attending on the wife that he loved so dearly. So might her second husband have seen to her needs and to her care. Alas that he had been fifteen years older than herself, struck down by camp-fever two years ago. Margaret had mourned for him as she saw to the necessary rituals, for she had loved him – not as dearly and hopelessly as she had loved the husband of her youth, the father of her sons, but she had loved him well and he would have recognized and mapped the progress of her affliction. That was his way, for he was a logical man, who knew the vagaries of a human body as well as a musician knows his particular instrument. She took her hand from Hetty's and surreptitiously flexed her fingers. No, it was only a momentary, fleeting thing – but so had it seemed those many months ago, when she began to feel that numbness in her feet and ankles, began to stumble and falter.

In the end, as winter turned haltingly to spring, as the fortunes of the Confederacy began to falter, it seemed that Margaret's body, her strength – and her very will, as indomitable as the will of the men who fought for glory, for the bonny star-crossed flag of the Confederate States – all began to fail at once. Margaret privately found that ironic. She had always been a Unionist. In her secret heart, she was an abolitionist as well – a dangerous sympathy, which practically none in her wide circle of friends had ever suspected. Margaret had much skill and long experience in keeping her true feelings veiled. The old black fortune-teller had said as much, the conjure-woman who had looked into the lines of Margaret's palm and revealed the future mapped in them for her, sitting on a weather-bleached tree-trunk cast up on the muddy shore of the river. That very day that Margaret's father had brought his twelve yoke of oxen, his two heavy-laden wagons and his family across the Sabine, to St. Augustine and Nacogdoches, and down the old road to San Felipe on the Brazos, come to take up the land that had been promised to him by Mr. Austin and by Alois Becker's old friend, the Baron de Bastrop.

4

"I was just twelve years old," she remarked one chill day in February. A bitter cold wind stirred the bare grey limbs of the trees outside. The sun cast their eldritch shadows on the scrubbed pine boards at the foot of the French doors that led out to the verandah. Margaret's daughter-in-law Amelia had wanted to draw the curtains against the icy draft that seeped around the cracks. But Margaret had demurred, saying that she wished to see the outside, not be closed away like an invalid. Amelia did not say anything in reply, but Margaret read her thoughts, as she settled Margaret against the pillows. Amelia rustled away – even her crinoline sounded disapproving, Margaret thought.

"When were you twelve years old, Gran'mere?" asked her grandson. Little Horrie, just four years old; although the smallest, he was yet the most tenacious of her attendants these days; like a particularly devoted and affectionate lap-dog. He laid on his stomach on the hearth-rug among his toys, heels in the air and carefully setting up a row of painted tin soldiers.

"When we first came to Texas, Horrie," she answered. "And the conjure-woman told us our fortunes. Well, *my* fortune, for that day was my twelfth birthday. That is why I remember so well. My brother Rudi was just nine, and my little brother was four, a little younger than you are. The conjure-woman did not tell much of my brothers' fortunes – I thought that I was being especially favored, since I was the oldest. Later I began to think that perhaps she did truly see their futures and wished not to tell us of what she had seen." Horrie's eyes rounded in astonishment.

"Where did you live before then, Gran'mere?" he asked, breathless with curiosity. "And where did you meet the conjure-woman?"

"We lived in the North, Horrie," Margaret answered. "The conjure-woman . . . I don't know where she came from. We met her the day that we crossed the river into Texas. Only it was part of Mexico, then."

Horrie's eyes rounded even more. "You lived in the North, with the Yankees?" He breathed, as if this were the most horrible circumstance imaginable. "Gran'mere … was your papa a Yankee?"

Margaret answered hastily, "It was a very, very long time ago, Horrie, before the war was even thought of. There was no talk of Yankees and Rebs, then. We thought of all as one country, the United States." Margaret sighed a little, for Horrie's father had fallen on the first day of battle at Gettysburg, not fifteen miles away from where she and her parents had lived, long ago. "It seems a little unreal to me; that time before. Sometimes I think I was not really born until then, that all before we crossed the river were just dreams."

Chapter 1 – *Across the River*

The Sabine River flowed smoothly, as wide as an ocean, dark with mud in the shallows, but shining silver, in those places where snags and rocks did not interrupt the water's flow. The wagons had crossed that day, a train of wagons belonging to Mr. Sullivan of Georgia, and some other prosperous men, come to take up lands offered by the impresario, Mr. Austin. When the wagons had been all conveyed across, most of the folk in the party decided to make camp, for the traverse of the river had been muddy, exhausting work, both for the ox-teams and for their drivers.

Margaret Becker and her younger brother Rudolph were dispatched by their mother to gather firewood along the riverbank, within sight of the camp that had begun to blossom in a wide green meadow, a scattering of canvas tents and hastily piled brush arbors among the wagon tops and neatly piled harness and tack. "And take the baby with you," Maria Becker added. She spoke to the children in the language they used among themselves, the German of the district settled in during the last century. She mopped perspiration off her forehead as she set down a box of dishes. Two heavy wagons full of household goods and tools had come with them from Pennsylvania, a pair of long Conestoga freight wagons, with tall canvas covers sloping forward and aft. Alois Becker was a careful man, who had gone out to Texas two years before and returned to bring his family to his promised new holding in Mr. Austin's land-grant, along with all that he felt needful. Six yoke of draft-oxen pulled each wagon; the front of the largest was fitted out as a tiny cabin for Alois Becker's wife and three children. But still, unless they stayed at an inn or with friends and kin as they had earlier upon this road – they must set up a camp at night. Maria and Margaret must cook over an open fire, under a sky that might arc overhead, sequin-spangled with stars or drizzling with rain falling from cotton-wool grey clouds.

"Don't go far from the wagons," Maria added in warning, as Margaret lifted her littlest brother up and perched him on her hip, trying to do as her mother did so capably. But she was twelve years old, and had no hips, and not the strength to carry a heavy four-year old that way for long, especially not a sturdy child like Carl. He smiled tranquilly up at her, as she set him down and led his faltering footsteps, following after her brother Rudi, who carried a length of canvas over his shoulder. Margaret, like her brothers, had fair hair, as pale as sun-bleached wheat-straw. She had a firm chin, a face as oval as a bird's egg and serious blue eyes.

"Don't walk so fast, Rudi," she begged, as the three children picked their way among the rocks and drift, half-sunk on the muddy shore. She yelped as her right foot sank suddenly through a tangle of short grass and squelched in the mud underneath. "Mama said to not go out of sight of the wagons. There's plenty of wood, close enough."

"I want to see more, M'grete," Rudi pleaded, "We're in Texas proper now, Papa said." He was an adventurous child, nine years old and completely fearless, charming and the apple of their father's eye.

"It doesn't look any different from the other side," Margaret answered, firmly. Rudi scowled; he might be Papa's favorite, but Margaret was the oldest and utterly reliable when it came to remembering and minding what Papa and Mama said. Curiously, only Margaret could make him obey. Mama might try, but Rudi would then appeal to Papa, who would always let him do as he wished. "There's plenty of wood here."

Rudi spread out the length of canvas on a mostly-flat bank, packed tightly with tree-mast and litter brought down by the highest floodwaters. She and her brothers began to gather up armfuls of small branches, cast up far enough above the present shoreline to be well-dried, piling their finds onto the canvas. Margaret, trailing Carl by the hand, ventured a little farther along the bank, where a huge dead tree stretched whitened branches against the firmament; a skeleton of a tree, clawing at the sunset-apricot sky. A chorus of birds started up from the branches, cawing and cackling noisily.

"You chillun come from a far place," said a voice, in strangely accented English. Margaret started; how could she have not seen the woman, sitting as if on a throne on the tall knees of the bleached tree roots which reached into the earth at her feet. It almost seemed as if the woman had sprung out of the earth herself, "And be goin' to a farther place, so de loah tell me."

"Yes, ma'am," Margaret answered, politely and in English, "Our father has been granted lands in Texas, and brought us here to settle."

"'Gwine t'be Mexicans, hey?" The woman chuckled, a rich cynical chuckle, "Swear t'be the king's man, an' foller after de old church, make an 'x' onna piece o' paper." She shook her head, still chuckling, "What de blanquettes won' do for a piece o' lan'!" Margaret stared frankly at her; she supposed the old woman was a slave, for her skin was brown as polished walnut wood. Margaret had hardly ever seen a person with skin so dark, before leaving Chester County in Pennsylvania so many months ago, although she had seen many since. Mama had said such people were slaves, owned like Papa owned his cattle. She also had murmured to the children in German that such things were wrong. Margaret wondered many things in that moment of looking upon the old woman; if she favored being a slave and where had she appeared from? Some of the other settlers in their train had brought slaves with them, people with dark skins, of all colors from ebony-black to brown and the color of coffee with cream in it, but Margaret didn't think this woman was among them. She was too old. Her hands looked like stems of grass, with painfully knotted joints. She had a long cloth wrapped around her head, elaborately folded and tucked, covering every scrap of her hair. There was a cloth-covered basket and a long stick, like a cane made from dark wood at the woman's feet, as if she had been gathering greens and roots, or mushrooms in the damp places by the river. Carl tugged his hand out of Margaret's; he was always silent with strangers. Margaret saw that he was heading towards a pile of drift at the river's edge, where the water was muddy and shallow, with no current to draw in a small and adventurous child. Margaret shook her head solemnly at the old women's skepticism.

"Papa says that we will be left to our own ways and our own church, and that it is only an oath of paper, not an oath of the heart. All we need do is obey the laws of their government. Papa says the laws are very alike anyway."

The old woman chuckled rustily, "An' if dey laws change, who will yore Papa obey, den?"

"I don't know," Margaret answered, much puzzled, "That is a matter for Papa, I reckon. Carl!" She called after her brothers, "Rudi – don't let Carl get into the mud!" The old woman looked at the boys and smiled in amusement, watching Carl solemnly tugging a sodden length of tree branch out of the shallows. Rudi set down an armload of bleached dry sticks, and hovered at Margaret's elbow, clearly fascinated by the old woman's answer.

"Don't you fret, girl – de spirrets tell me dat chile wuz born under a sign. De hangman will chase arter, but de water protec' an' nebber do him harm."

"Spirits?" Margaret asked curiously, "Like angels?"

"No, chile," The old woman looked amused, "De loah, like Baron Cemetary, an' Erzuli, an' Ogun de warrier. Open yore heart to de sperrits, dey tell you tings. Dere be no secrets, when de loah ride dis ole Nigra. My mama, she had de power, look into a pool o' watter, a candle lit at mid-night, she know tings. An' so do I know dese tings, Missy Margaret Becker!"

"How do you know my name?" Margaret asked, startled out of all countenance. She knew she had not said her name to the old woman, and if she was not one of their companions in the wagon party – and Margaret was very sure she was not, for they had been together on the road to Natchitoches for many weeks and she would have noted the presence of an old woman like this – how did she know such things about the Becker children? Even if she

8

had ridden in a wagon all day – and who could endure the constant jolting of the wheels, over the ruts and rocks in the road – Margaret and Rudi would have noted the presence of a woman like this, around the evening campfire or at the privy pits, at any of their noonings or at hitch-up time in the morning.

The old woman chuckled, "Hain't you ben listenin', chile? De loah, de sperrits tell me! Dey also tell me you is twelve year ol' dis very day. Dey tell me more den de pas' ... "

"Are you a witch?" Margaret asked boldly. The old woman shook her turbaned head. "Not de kin' yo think, Missy Margaret. Hyer, give me yo han's." The old woman reached out her own hands, the long slender fingers with the joints like grass-stems knotted with age and rheumatics. Taking Margaret's hands, she turned them palm up, and drew them towards her. Margaret did not resist, as the old woman carefully scrutinized her hands, the lines and creases across her palm. Finally, she closed her own fingers, dry and papery-feeling, only a little paler on the palms than Margaret's own, closing Margaret's hands and enclosing them in hers. She looked into Margaret's wide eyes, her own eyes deep pools of ancient wisdom.

"I see de future in yo han's, Missy Margaret . . . a big ol' house, an' a man you gwine marry fo' love, anodder fo' friendship." Her voice went sing-song, and she closed her eyes, as if she concentrated on what she was seeing, "Yo will meet de fust husban' befoah de moon waxes and wanes agin. Count ten and ten and ten an' one day t'day . . . ten year an' one will you be blessed, Missy Margaret. Joy an' sorrow, will you have, an' always frien's, some o'dem pow'ful men – even doh mos' o' dem will nebber know yo heart." Her voice died away and she opened her eyes and hands, relinquishing Margaret's.

"What else did you see?" Margaret asked. She did not altogether believe the woman saw her future, but still, this was very curious.

"Cain't rightly say no more, Missy Margaret. Somp-times dey ain't no good in knowin' more. I tole you jus' what yo have de need to know."

"What about me?" Rudi chimed in, and the old woman turned her head, acknowledging him for the first time. "What do you see of the future for me?"

It seemed to Margaret that the old woman gazed at her brother for a long, long time, squinting against the low-falling sun. Finally, she replied, "'Cain't see nothin'. Dere be clouds, like smoke, dark black smoke."

"Is that all?" Rudi asked, disappointed. The old woman shrugged.

"Jes' dark smoke, like from a bonfire."

Margaret, looking into the old woman's eyes, wondered momentarily if that had truly been all. Could she have seen some kind of misfortune for Rudi, just as she saw a big house, many friends and two husbands for Margaret, but

9

did not think she should know any more than that? Margaret thrust that thought away from her mind. Rudi was Papa's favorite; Papa had brought them all to Texas, to make a secure future for all of them, but mostly for Rudi. The old woman made a shooing motion with her hands,

"You chilluns best be gwine back to yo mama. Be dark soon, an' yo papa, he in a hurry." She cackled richly again, "He in a big rush to be a Mexican. Don't he know dat America gwine follow him, no matter?"

Margaret would have asked more, but for a sudden splash of water from the river's edge.

"Carl!" she cried, for her little brother had wandered into the shallows and sat down in the water; he was thoroughly wetted and daubed to the waist of his shirt in sticky black mud. "Come out of the water at once, before you catch your death of cold!" She caught up the hem of her plain homespun dress in one hand, wading out in waters up to her knees towards Carl, who laughed with delighted unconcern, inching away from her with a mischievous look on his face. Behind her on the bank, the old witch-woman chuckled, "Doan you have a care foah dat chile, Missy Margaret – de watter be his savior!"

But Margaret paid her no mind. Children drowned in river water all the time; hadn't Mama often told the story of her little cousin, swept away in the Brandywine River, when Mama was a girl? She snatched Carl's hand with her free hand, but he pulled against her, already looking cross and mutinous. "Gather up the wood, Rudi," she gasped, "We've enough of it for Mama — we're going back to camp now." With her twelve-year old strength she wrested her little brother out of the shallows. He was wet through, and filthy with river-muck. "Oh, Carl! Mama will blame it all on me; I was supposed to look after you! Papa will give us both a licking, for sure!" He ducked his head into her shoulder, in apology.

"Wood," he muttered into her collarbone. Carl hardly ever spoke more than a few words at a time, and never to people that he did not know. Sometimes people thought he was a deaf-mute child, he was that quiet.

"Mama won't let him do anything of the sort," Rudi panted, struggling under the weight of the canvas-rolled bundle of wood, and the old witch-woman shook her head. She gathered up her basket and her cane, and came to her feet by slow degrees.

"I tole you, dat chile won't come to no harm by watter, nor you neither, Missy Margaret . . . you gwine back to yo Mama and yo Papa, you heah?"

Margaret barely heard the old woman, for Carl pulled sulkily at her hand. In exasperation, she hoisted him up and carried him a little way, his soaking-wet clothes shedding water onto hers. They had come farther along the riverbank than had seemed at first, and this made Margaret cross and unhappy. Now, in addition to her brother having dirtied his clothing, Mama would be worried and needing wood to add to the cook-fire, so that she might continue cooking dinner, and Papa would be unhappy because supper might not be ready when he was hungry for it.

"I wonder what the old woman meant," Rudi asked. "About the water?"

"I don't know," Margaret, and paused to hitch Carl higher. His wet clothing was now soaking through her dress and shift to her skin, and Margaret's heart sank. Mama would look sad at the extra work that wet and dirty clothes would make for her. She would worry that Margaret and Carl would catch their death of cold, and send them to bed early, in the wagon. Of course, her little brother would not mind so much: he would be half-asleep before supper was even over. But Margaret would mind very much. When she was finished with helping Mama with cleaning up after supper, she might like to linger at the edge of the circle of men around the fire talking of land and of governments and of the wonders to be seen in their new country. This was their first night in Texas, now that they had reached it at last. Although it did not look all that much different from the country they had traveled through; all piney woods and sloughs full of long-legged water birds and those enormous scaly lizards that Papa said jovially were called alligators. Margaret had wanted very much to hear more of this talk, especially on this night.

Overhead, it seemed as if the color was bleached out of the sky, fading from blue to something like the color of oyster shells, save where the sun set in a smear of orange and purple clouds edged with a line of silver. Birds clamored in the tree branches above their heads, swift dark shadows, darting here and there against the pale sky. With no little relief, Margaret and Rudi crossed one last stretch of pebbly shore and saw the wheel-rutted path up to the higher ground where they had come, where the wagons had been brought.

"It's not much farther, Rudi – run along and take the wood to Mama."

Obediently Rudi ran ahead of her, his bare feet flashing, towards the circle of wagons and canvas tents, glowing in the twilight like paper lanterns. Margaret could already smell a drift of wood-smoke. In the dusty blue twilight, the flames from cook-fires were as pale as the sky. A chill breeze wandered across the campfire, creeping out as the going of the sun drained away all the warmth in the world.

"Walk, 'Gret," Carl fussed to be let down, but Margaret hoisted him higher against her and sang a snatch of children's rhyme to sooth him,

"Sleep baby sleep . . . while Mama watches the sheep . . . you are growing too fast, Carlchen!" Margaret sighed; back in Pennsylvania, Opa

Heinrich, their grandfather, had told her the story of the farmer who became enormously strong by lifting a newborn calf every day. Eventually, so said Opa, chuckling behind his beard, the farmer could lift the full-grown cow over his head. Margaret could lift her little brother quite easily when he was a baby, so Opa solemnly insisted that she would be able to lift him just the same, when they were both grown. Margaret had agreed with him at the time, but only now was beginning to suspect that Opa had been having a gentle jest at her expense. Her arms and shoulders ached; no, there was no help for it, she would have to let him down. They were nearly to Papa's camp anyway.

Margaret's heart lifted, for she could see Papa, hers and Rudi and Carl's Papa, talking with some of the other men of the train, where the leaping flames of a new fire sprang up and gilded their faces and hands in the swift-falling dusk. The firelight shone on Papa's hair, as he pushed his wide-brimmed straw planter's hat back. Margaret could always pick out Papa, among the other men, for he was so much taller than most of them, his hair as pale as ripe wheat, and his beard like fine curls of gold wire. Back in Pennsylvania, the Quaker schoolteacher had once shown the children a book of ancient history, illustrated with engravings of heroes of old, gods and warriors and kings and such. Margaret secretly thought that some of them looked like Papa, so noble and fearless. She had wondered, looking at those pages, if any of those cloaked and helmeted men, holding their swords before them, or at their sides, were as outspoken and easily angered as Papa. To herself, Margaret thought it very likely, for they were gods and kings, not a farmer – even if Papa was the best farmer in Chester County and accounted to be a very good man when it came to doctoring cows and grafting apple trees.

She set her little brother down so that he could walk as he wished, but once his feet were set on the ground, he began fussing to be picked up again. Margaret sighed again, much exasperated. Like Papa, Carl seemed to want always what he didn't have. To her relief, Mama hardly seemed to notice how wet and dirty the two of them had become. Mama was chopping onions on a tin plate held in her lap.

"Did we bring enough wood, Mama?" Margaret asked, and Mama smiled through tears from the onions, "Yes, Liebchen, just enough for the fire tonight . . . will you mind the baby a little longer? Your brother has gone to remind Papa to fill the water-barrel . . . your Papa! He is as pleased as a dog with another tail tonight! In Texas at last."

"Is it all that much farther to go, Mama?" Margaret asked, wistfully. "To San Felipe on the Brazos?"

"Some more weeks, Liebchen," Mama answered, with a smile. Margaret thought that Mama was pretty enough, compared to other Mamas – but not as handsome as Papa was, compared to other men. She had a round face, and her hair curled into little tendrils around her face. Mama never lost her temper, and nothing ever seemed to bother her the way things bothered Papa. Papa's anger didn't bother Mama; Margaret was most sure of this, for she watched her parents. Sometimes Margaret felt like she had stepped outside of herself, watching Mama and Papa as if they were strangers – how they spoke to each other, how Mama soothed Papa's bad moods and how Mama took the edge from Papa's temper when he had spoken hastily and in anger. No matter what, Papa paid mind to Mama's soft-voiced admonitions. He would not be angry with Mama, or say harsh words to Rudi. He might speak so to Margaret, but curiously enough Papa's anger did not so affect Margaret, ever since Papa had returned from his first trip to Texas. He had been away for a year, leaving Mama and Margaret and Rudi to manage with Opa Heinrich and Oma Katerina's help. When he returned, it seemed to Margaret that he was a stranger – still her Papa, of course – but a stranger, whom she could stand a little outside from and watch, without feeling a pain from thoughtless words.

Mama had set her shawl aside so that she could step safely close to the fire. Margaret wrapped it around herself and Carl, sitting on the three-legged creepy-stool brought out from the wagon. Margaret hugged her little brother to her, sheltered in the heavy woolen folds against the evening chill crawling up from her bare toes. Papa and the hired drover, Rufe Tarrent, had set up a lean-to shelter of canvas on tall poles, facing the fire and offering some shelter from the wandering breeze. It would be so nice to have been inside walls tonight, Margaret thought – and to be warm. Here was Papa, with Rudi perched on his shoulders. Papa carried a water-bucket in each hand. Rudi had Papa's hat on his own head, with the brim of it falling well over his eyes. Both he and Rudi were laughing.

"What a day!" Papa exclaimed exuberantly as he came to the Becker's campfire, "It smells good, Marichen, whatever it will be! And we can do it justice tonight, can't we, lad?" He set down the buckets and swung Rudi down off his shoulders, deftly turning the boy upside down for a few moments, while Rudi yelped.

"Venison stewed with onions and juniper berries," Mama answered, while Rudi squealed and begged to be put all the way down. Mama and Mrs. Sullivan had traded with some wandering Indian women who came bearing baskets of pecans and golden-dripping combs of honey, as they waited to cross the river that very morning, and so tonight they would eat well. Papa leaned down and kissed Mama on the cheek, while Rudi tugged on the hem of his rough roundabout coat.

"Sublime, my dearest. Such a country! A garden of Eden it will be, Marichen, just you wait."

"And for how long will I wait for a proper house, Alois?" Mama wrapped the corner of her apron around her hand to shield it from the heat of the fire and stirred the sizzling onions with a long iron fork. "With a proper stove and bread-oven in it, so that I do not break my back, leaning over a fire, nor set fire to my petticoat?"

"Not for long, Marichen," Papa promised with great exuberance, while Rudi begged, "Again, Papa, again!" Laughing, Papa lifted up Rudi and holding him at the waist turned him upside down.

"I play!" Carl wriggled to be let down from Margaret's lap, for he was as eager as Rudi to be played with, to romp as little boys did, as puppies did with an indulgent older dog. But Papa looked down, saying in annoyance, "M'grete, the idiot child is filthy. Can't you have kept him away from the mud, if he doesn't have the wits to stay out of it himself?"

"He was helping us with the wood, Papa!" Margaret began to plead, for Carl looked as if he had been spanked and Mama answered swiftly, "It is of no matter, Alois. Children will become dirty, when there is naught else to play with save the dirt. Play with the boy, then."

But the bright interest had gone from Carl's face at Papa's words, and he scrambled back towards Margaret, taking shelter under Mama's shawl, hiding his face against her shoulder. Papa had been a stranger to Carl, having gone to scout out their new land in Texas when Carl was still a lap-baby. When he returned last harvest-time, to make plans to bring them all to Texas, Carl had been just old enough to walk, beginning to talk. He pulled away from Papa's attention, screwing up his little face in distaste and almost falling to all fours in his haste to hide behind Mama and Margaret. He did not cry, for Carl was of a sunny and placid nature, but he was sullen and silent around Papa. Papa was one of those strangers that Carl did not talk to; in one of those standing-apart flashes of insight that had increasingly come to Margaret, she realized this made Papa very unhappy. Papa had wanted little Carl to like him, to be as open and affectionate as Rudi was. But he was too impatient to coax Carl into the same sort of liking, so Papa ignored him, or spoke to him with distaste, calling him an idiot – and made much of Rudi. Margaret wondered if she might do anything to make Papa see this; but if Mama could not make Papa see reason and favor his younger son as much as he favored the older, there was not much that Margaret herself could do. And perhaps she didn't mind, too much – for that left her little brother to her, like her real baby-doll. She was one of the few people whom he did talk to, she and Mama, and Opa Heinrich and Oma Katerina.

"Sleep baby sleep," Margaret drew the shawl closer around them both, while Carl hid his face against her collar-bone, "Mama is watching the sheep," she sang to him softly. Across the fire, Papa settled himself on a chair brought out from the wagon, took out his knife and began to whittle, for the amusement of Rudi, crouching at his feet. The fire spat up tiny sparks into the sky, sparks that were red and golden, merging with the stars, winking into the dark-velvet sky, more and more of them as sunset faded away entirely. A pale sliver of moon appeared, rising up from the branches of the dark trees as if escaping from a net, a new moon and curved like the clipping of a finger-nail. Beyond the pale shape of the wagon-top, Papa's oxen lowed companionably to each other, pastured for the night within a rough circle of wagons. Voices of their other traveling-companions casually floated on the night air, the light of their fires casting a ruddy light on their faces and bodies. Across the wagon circle, a dozen voices rose in a rhythmical song, a work-chant to the sounds of an ax thunking regularly into wood – Mr. Sullivan's slaves, chanting as they chopped more firewood for the night.

Margaret rested her chin on the top of her brother's head, thinking her own thoughts, wondering how soon Mama would have supper ready. It smelled so fine, the scent of fat-bacon cooking with beans, and something spicy. Margaret sniffed, appreciatively – perhaps Mama had baked a special cake, since it was her birthday. She had presents already from Opa Heinrich and Oma Katerina back in Pennsylvania, a string of pretty glass beads pressed into her hand from Opa, as they bid farewell. "You shall be far away, on the day that you are twelve, Liebchen; wear these and think of us!" Opa had said, and Margaret thought that Opa's eyes looked to be shiny with unshed tears, as he embraced her. Oma had given her a new dress and bonnet for her doll. Margaret only recalled afterwards that Texas was such a long ways away that she would likely never see Opa and Oma again. Perhaps that was why Opa Heinrich had looked so sad Margaret thought, as she looked into the fire, and let her own thoughts wander where they willed.

This was what Margaret liked to do, to sit and patiently think about things which puzzled her; sometimes she could see an answer to the puzzle. It was like Mama carefully unknotting a tangle in a ball of yarn. Now she sat in the shelter of Mama's shawl, while the warmth of the fire gently toasted her toes. Opa had looked very sad, Margaret thought; she and her brothers, Papa and Mama were going from them, into the west – just as Opa Heinrich had done from his own parents and family, long, long ago. Margaret knew the story well; Opa had been a young man, made to serve in the Landgrave's army, hired by the English king to fight in America. At first chance, Opa had put off his uniform, and vowed to stay, when the regiments of Hesse took ship to return to the Old Country. Margaret considered this some more. Maybe Opa Heinrich had indeed been sad, at never seeing his parents or his brothers again, missing their home in a village near Darmstadt in the Old Country.

How careful he had been in speaking the old language, ensuring that she and Rudi said words in the proper way, so that Oma Katerina laughed and laughed, saying that the children sounded as if they had a broomstick up their backsides, so prim and careful with words and sounding like proper children of Hesse. Margaret had never thought that Opa had been sad about leaving his family, and his soldier comrades. The story of Opa and Oma had a rightness about it; of course young Opa Heinrich should stay in America and marry the young Oma Katerina. That was the happy ending which all fairy tales had. But now, Margaret looked at the sliver of moon, sailing into the sky, through a netting of silvery stars and golden sparks from the fire, thinking of the old witch by the riverbank, and how she prophesied two husbands for Margaret – the first being someone whom she would meet very soon, when the moon was a little curl of silver, like a shred of candied citron. She was twelve years old, practically a grown-up young lady. When she married, Margaret thought, she would go with her husband, just as Mama had gone with Papa. This was a good thinking-session, Margaret concluded; how many things she had realized, just sitting by the fire!

"I hope that he will not take me too far away," she said out loud, and in her lap Carl stirred, sleepily. Mama straightened from the cook-fire, her face rosy with the warmth of it, and laughed affectionately, "Liebchen, who do you think would take you away, ever? You are dreaming, and half asleep, and the baby is well asleep – put him to bed and come and eat supper, before you have any more strange dreams."

Startled out of that reverie, Margaret looked up. It was full-dark now; night had come down with velvet wings. Carl was heavy and limp in slumber, sucking at his thumb – another baby-habit which she had not the heart to make him stop doing, Across the cook-fire, Rudi and Papa were laughing also, at some joke between them – but just beyond, in the light of the Sullivan's campfire, Margaret thought she saw a bronze face reflected for a moment in the warm firelight flicker, an old woman with an elaborate turban tied over her hair. And then Margaret blinked, and the old witch-woman's face was gone.

Chapter 2 – *San Felipe*

"Papa," Rudi called from the wagon-seat, where he sat squeezed in between Margaret and Mama, "What matter of man is Mr. Austin?" The near-front wheel dropped into a deep and muddy declivity in the road. At that very moment Papa, walking by the lead team, snapped his long whip over the laboring backs of his six-yoke lest they hesitate in their pulling.

"A very kind one," Papa called back, in answer, turning his head to smile fondly upon his family. "As well as being generous and far-sighted. He went to Mexico, to deal with their authorities in securing our holdings. Imagine what a princely amount of land for each of our families; a tract for a farm, and a league in addition, to pasture herds of cattle upon." It was very wet today, having rained in the night. The tall fronds of grass bent over from the weight of water droplets still clinging to them, but the mid-morning sun edged every leaf with silver-gilt, the leaves of spreading oak trees scattered here and there, interspersed in meadows of that same grass – grass that grew thickly on either side of the muddy track, grass that was almost to Margaret's waist. That was why she, and her brothers and Mama rode today in the wagon – and a very bumpy and uncomfortable ride it was, too. Although not wet, Mama insisted that they all ride, to save their shoes and clothes from the muck and the damp.

It was more than two weeks since crossing the Sabine, some days since passing through a town of log houses called Nacogdoches; theirs and the Sullivan's caravan of wagons had passed from flat and open grasslands, to woods and long narrow lakes, into rolling hills, dotted with heavy-limbed oak trees. Some of the oaks spread out, leaves so thick on their branches that the shade underneath seemed too dark for the grass to grow. Between the oaks, the meadows were starred with flowers growing on tall, nodding stems. Where the grass was not so tall, pink primroses peeped shyly out at the travelers, and clusters of purple verbena.

"It is more beautiful than any garden," Mama remarked. More beautiful than any garden on earth and the rivers were like Margaret thought the rivers flowing out of the Garden of Eden must look; clear and green, edged with thickets of tall reeds, and grapevines tangling in the trees like some kind of green tent.

One afternoon, as the men prepared to cross the wagons over another river, at a wide bend where it ran shallow over a bed of gravel, Margaret and her brothers went wading in the shallows. They were chasing after tiny minnows which flicked a brief grey shadow and then were gone, while Mama had taken the opportunity to dip up a pan-full of water to wash some clothing in. A little downstream, Papa and Rufe, and Mr. Sullivan's drovers hitched up eight and nine yoke of oxen to one wagon and then another, after raising up the wagon-bed with a lever and placing blocks of wood underneath, so that the cargo within would not be wetted by deep water. One by one, each wagon was drawn across the river, each wagon-top swaying as if a sail in a full breeze.

"Doesn't seem like much of a river, hey?" Papa had remarked that very morning to Mr. Sullivan, "but we're lucky it's not in flood, otherwise we'd have the very devil of a time."

It would take all day to bring over the wagons; Margaret expected that they would make camp on the opposite shore, for it was well-past midday. Water splashed and chuckled to itself, around rocks in the shallows; Margaret heard nothing more than the voices of her brothers, and Mama chiding Rudi for getting his clothing wet. Margaret's attention was all on a large frog, which Carl was chasing after. The frog suddenly leaped from sandy back to shallow water – ungainly on land, but gone in a flash – and Margaret hastily snatched the back of her little brother's shirt, as he laughed gleefully and plunged toward the water in pursuit. And suddenly, they were there, barely a stone's throw from shore; a narrow boat hewn of a single timber log, appearing as silently as the frog had vanished. Three big, wide-shouldered naked men, with paddles or long bows in their hands were staring at them in equal astonishment. Margaret held very still, both hands on her brother's shirt.

"Indians!" Carl cried happily and pointed at them. Curiously, Margaret did not feel any particular fear of them, although they looked very strange with blue markings scrawled on their bodies, and what looked like short lengths of sharpened cane piercing the flesh of their naked chests and faces. They stared at each other – the Indians, with their paddles and bows in hand, and Margaret and her brother in the shallows – for what seemed a long time. Margaret's heart seemed to thump in her chest; Rudi's voice chattering to Mama came from a long distance, as did the sound of men and cattle, a little way downstream. Only the sound of the water, lipping at the rocks and around hers and Carl's ankles seemed loud in her ears. At Margaret's back she heard Mama gasp, and say very quietly,

"Children . . . come out of the water now. At once."

"But Mama," Rudi protested, and with that, the spell holding her fast in place was broken. Mama was there, snatching up Carl, who cried out in astonishment, and taking Margaret's hand. Rudi looked backwards, as Mama led them at a swift walk, then faster and faster until they were running, gasping for breath.

"They're gone, Mama," he cried, "What are we running for, there's no one there!"

"They might be hiding in the grass," Mama gasped. "Hurry, children!"

They were almost to Papa's wagon, to Papa, who turned around, face beaming in welcome. Then he saw Mama's face.

"Marichen, what is the matter, what has happened!"

"Indians, Papa!" Rudi had breath enough to shout. Margaret's heart seemed to be in her throat – she could not talk for it hammering so hard. Obscurely she wondered why she had not at first felt frightened at seeing the Indians, but now she was terrified. Instantly, the men with Papa sought out their weapons from wagon-box or saddle-holster. Mama was sobbing in German, her voice vying with Rudi's excited one.

"Where, child?" demanded Mr. Sullivan, urgently, "Where did you see the Indians. How many!"

"Three," Margaret answered, "They were in a canoe; on the river . . . they were just looking at us. I wasn't frightened, they did nothing at all."

"What did they look like?" Mr. Sullivan demanded again. Margaret looked at the faces, so many men with grim faces, all looking at her.

"They were big," she quavered, "And painted blue, with sticks of cane in their cheeks and lips."

"Too far north for Karankawa," remarked one of the men, and in some infinitesimal way the men seemed to relax, "Coushatta, maybe. A hunting party, most like." He chucked Margaret on the cheek. Offended at this, she stepped back. "Lucky for you they weren't Comanche, anyway."

"Still, we should double the guards on the cattle tonight, hey?" Papa looked relieved. When the adults talked of the Comanche, Margaret knew, they dropped their voices to fearful whispers. She thought the Comanche must be several times more ferocious than the three Indians in the wooden canoe. "And thank the powers it is only a short way to the Brazos and San Felipe. There'll be nothing to worry us then, Marichen, you'll see."

Margaret didn't know quite what to think of San Felipe, for at first there did not seem much to be seen; there was another river to be crossed, only for this there was a ferry – a great raft of timbers which crawled back and forth across the Brazos, guided by a long cable. The ferry advanced, half by the current of the river flowing dark and silent underneath, and half by the efforts of a dozen sweating Negro slaves, hauling away on a long rope. At first, the tall bluff on the opposite side of the river seemed to have only a few houses upon the edge of it, as Margaret could see from looking up from the riverside.

Papa and his team pulled the first wagon, while Mama and Margaret and the boys waited on the muddy bank for Rafe with Papa's second wagon. That side of the river bustled with people, men of all colors, unloading a pair of flatboats drawn up to a wood and stone jetty along the bank near the landing. The ferry itself rode very low under the weight of Papa's great wagon, and the six yoke of obedient oxen pulling it. They had needed to be unyoked and led to one side, while many hands rolled the wagon onto the ferry by pushing with their shoulders. Now, as Papa and Rufe re-hitched the oxen, she asked, in great curiosity, "It doesn't seem very large at all, Papa. Are you sure this is Mr. Austin's city?"

"Of that I am, little M'grete – and it is bigger since I was last here. There's more to be seen, at the top of the hill." Papa slapped the last of the oxen on the flank; he was as tired and rumpled as any of the workers, unloading the flatboats, yet as excited as Rudi. Mama looked very cheerful, in spite of her weariness.

"Oh, to have a house again, Alois – and to sleep indoors, out of the rain!"

Papa chuckled, "Oh, no one spends much time inside a house, my dear Maria. And although I do not have proper title to our home farm and league of pastureland, we will see about building a house at once."

"It is too late to begin planting for this year, Alois," Mama replied firmly.

Papa chuckled again, "I fear so . . . I will use this time to assure my own satisfaction with my league and *sitio*, which I was promised by Mr. Austin, establish my claim on it. These Mexican administrators can be slippery characters, given to say one thing on one occasion, and then to say another when it suits."

"How long will that take, Alois?" Mama asked, and Papa's own excitement dimmed a little.

"Weeks, perhaps months – Nothing done well is done in haste, Mariechen, remember. Now, I have made arrangements to rent a house here in San Felipe, a house for you and the children. There was talk of a school last year. So the boys and Margaret will have proper lessons . . . and we shall have time to properly plan everything. It will not be a home such as I thought at first . . ."

"But it will be sufficient," Mama nodded; she seemed quite gratified about a school, although Rudi appeared disconsolate. Mama even kept her countenance serene upon seeing the house that Papa had already rented, for it was all of logs, and bare of comfort within. In truth, it was only one room – half of a house, although with a loft over half that single room, a generous covered porch along the front, and an open breezeway – almost another room in between the two little log rooms on either end. Several young men lived in the other side of the house who made friends of the boys almost at once.

There was no room for Rufe in such a tiny house: he would have to sleep in the wagon, although Margaret did not think Rufe would mind very much. He was the youngest son of one of Opa Heinrich's neighbors, a lanky and moon-faced young man who had never much to say unless he was spoken to directly. Opa Katerina had often 'tisked' to herself and said he was 'lacking' but she did not explain to Margaret exactly what that meant. Margaret thought that it must mean that Rufe was not very clever. But he was agreeable to Papa's orders, a very hard worker, and he had come all the way from Pennsylvania with them.

Mama, after taking one good look at the inside, sent Margaret for a broom, and basins and cleaning cloths. She inquired of the young men of where good water was to be drawn from.

"There is a well, my dearest Maria," Papa pointed out in amusement.

"Good," answered Mama firmly. She handed Papa and Rudi several buckets, and she and Margaret set to work with a will. "It is not a home," she said at last, after a good sneeze, "But it will do very well for one – and certainly better than a wagon! There is room for my loom on the end of the porch – that I will set up tomorrow!"

Margaret certainly agreed; once the bedstead for Papa and Mama was brought in and set up, and pallets for herself and the boys in the loft overhead, the little wooden room already looked more welcoming, if not very much more cheerful. Mama clicked her tongue and hung some patterned cloth over the single tiny window – where some previous tenant had pounded in a pair of nails with a length of string between – and ordered Papa to bring in the box of kitchen things, and the chairs and benches from the wagons, although by then it was already afternoon and hot within the room.

"I did say that one did not spend too much of the day indoors," Papa reminded her, "but rather on the porch, or in the space between – one only has need of walls for a little time in the winter, or if Indians come calling."

"Like the Indians at the river?" Rudi asked. Boy-like, he had spent much of the day while Margaret was helping Mama set up housekeeping in trying to evade such tasks as Mama had set him, by hanging around with the three young men who were their neighbors. He was not pleased at having school again; Papa finally brought himself to be stern, and told him that he must go with Margaret on the next day: he had already been to talk to the schoolmaster and to pay the fees that the schoolmaster had asked.

"He's an ambitious young man," Papa chuckled, seeing the look on Rudi's face. "From Boston, he said – and very proper with it too. Besides letters and numbers, he offers instruction in history, rhetoric, composition, natural and moral philosophy. Oh, and languages, also – Spanish would be most useful, but I do not see that Greek and Latin have much use."

"Must I, Papa?" Rudi's face fell even farther, upon hearing that daunting list of subjects to be taught and Papa laughed.

After supper that evening, Margaret sat on the edge of the porch in the twilight, her arms wrapped around her knees and watching the stars wink into view as daylight faded from the west. She was considering the next day, having one of her thinking moods. She and Rudi would start at school tomorrow; she was wondering if school in San Felipe would be anything like the dame-school where she had learned to read, back in Pennsylvania. She thought not – save for the look of the oak trees, nothing much here in Texas was like Pennsylvania. Now, as she sat with her chin on her knees, she noticed that the moon had turned new again. The moon had gone on waxing and waning, during all those days they had come west, and then south after crossing the Sabine. Was this truly the thirtieth day after her birthday? As the witch-woman by the river had foretold, would she meet the man she would marry tomorrow?

Margaret considered this for some time. Likely it would be one of the boys at school. There would be all ages of school-children, with but the one school. She sighed: the boys would be rowdy and given to teasing, especially the older ones. They would not be like Rudi who if he did play pranks, never did so to hurt feelings. And if there were to be an older boy, or a young man like Rufe, Margaret hoped wistfully that at least he be clever. It would be so boring to marry someone like Rufe, who had no more conversation in him than one of Papa's oxen. It was a pity that the witch-woman had not said how she would know, how she would tell which of them would be her husband. How did one come to know – did one even know, at first?

"I expect I will just fall in love," She said out loud, and behind her, Mama laughed, fondly, "So you shall, Liebchen, but not for a long while."

Margaret started. She had not known that Mama was sitting there on a crude wooden bench set against the cabin's outer wall. Someone – Papa? – had hung a lantern from a peg overhead, but the light was too dim, and the daylight too long fled for Mama to work at picking apart the woolen Mexican blankets that Papa had bought from a traveling merchant. The wool of it was beautifully dyed red, but the weaving so loose and coarse that Mama turned up her nose at it. She commenced unraveling the first of the blankets at once, saying that she could draw out the threads much finer and re-weave the blanket. And all that the lantern did, now that the sun had dropped well below the far horizon, was to attract a constellation of little night insects with feathery wings. In the afternoon, Papa had brought the spinning wheel and the pieces of Mama's loom from the wagon where they had been stored, and he and Rufe had patiently assembled the loom frame, where Mama could sit and weave in the daylight under the shelter of the porch.

"Mama," Margaret asked, in serious tones, "When did you know that you would marry Papa? Was that something you knew when you first met him?"

Mama laughed, "I never did not know your Papa, since his father's farm was close by ours, and my older brothers were his friends. We always had a liking for each other, although he was stubborn, and with a temper."

"When did you first think to marry, then, Mama?"

"Such a question, little Margaret – I always thought that your Papa was much the handsomest of all the young men his age, but I did not know that he thought of me, until my father held a husking bee . . . that was the year that I was fifteen – old enough to think of marriage. And at that husking bee, your Papa found an ear of red corn, which allowed him to kiss any girl that he wished. And so he kissed me. Of all the girls that were helping to husk the corn, and there were a great many girls that I thought were prettier, or that he could have chosen – he had kissed me! Of course, my brothers laughed as if it were a joke, or as if he did so only because of his friendship with them, but some days later, he came to my father and asked for permission to court me; which my father gave freely, as they had been friends for many years. Our parents thought it would be a fine thing, such a bond between our two families, so your Papa and I were married within a year."

"Oh," replied Margaret. That was something more to think about. It appeared that Mama and Papa's example would not be a guide for her in this quandary. Now Mama stood up, and added chidingly, "It is late now, my little dear; time for bed, since you shall have school tomorrow."

In the morning, she and Rudi walked together with one of their young neighbors, Mr. Bayard, to where the schoolhouse was. Papa was gone early to meet with Mr. Austin, and Mama had much to do with sorting out what could be taken from the wagons into their temporary home.

"It's not a proper school, yet," confessed Mr. Bayard. "The schoolmaster holds lessons on the porch of his house. Of all the things left undone by the Mexican governor, schools for children are the lack most keenly felt. There is a school for boys, kept by the priests in Bexar – but as for the rest of it, I believe we must sort that out for ourselves." Mr. Bayard was a clerk in the general mercantile, opposite the schoolmaster's house. He and the other young men had already made much of Rudi, treating him as a smaller brother and promising to take him hunting. Just then, from a little farther down the rutted and dusty road between houses and shops made of sawn lumber or rough-squared logs, came the regular ringing of a bell.

Mr. Bayard said, "That will be the school-bell, now – better run or you will be late."

The schoolhouse looked as ordinary as any other, save for having nothing like a garden or a vegetable plot outside, only a large trodden patch printed with the marks of many feet. A number of children milled around the breezeway of the little house, where there were several rows of crude benches, neatly lined up, and a wiry young man in a blue broadcloth coat stood with a bell in one hand. He eyed Margaret and her brother with one eyebrow high-raised,

"I presume that you are the Becker children," he said to them. "I am Horace Vining, the schoolmaster – such as it is," he added wryly, and then continued. "Your father spoke to me yesterday. He told me that you both could read and figure. How old are you?" He looked at them both very searchingly, and Margaret answered,

"I'm twelve – my brother is nine."

"You look older," Mr. Vining commented. Margaret couldn't think of a proper reply to that, but in any case, it was not needed. "Sit down here, please. I will need to examine you both to see what you already know." He turned away from them, and towards the other children, about twenty of them, of all ages from a little older than Carl, to a tall girl who appeared nearly as old as the schoolmaster himself. The children settled onto the ranked benches, facing the schoolmaster's tall desk. Nailed to the cabin wall behind the desk were three wide planks, planed smooth and neatly joined together. The planks had been carefully painted black: the alphabet was limned in chalk letters along the top. All the children had slates, although some were merely sections of smooth plank, also painted black. Margaret couldn't help noticing that the other students were not all sorted by apparent age – there were some older children sitting on the front-most bench. Mr. Vining directed them all to begin reciting the multiplication tables in unison; under cover of the chorus of voices chanting "four times four is sixteen, four times five is twenty," he handed Margaret a heavy book and commanded, "Read this, please – beginning at the third paragraph."

Margaret took the book from him, stealing another glance at the schoolmaster through her eyelashes. Mr. Vining seemed even younger than he had first appeared, or maybe it was that he was so thin. He had light blue eyes, or perhaps hazel-gray, but very sharp and penetrating, and sandy hair that curled tightly. His face was as thin as the rest of him, but he dressed as fine as a gentleman dandy in one of Opa Heinrichs' old illustrated books. She supposed that his waistcoat must be silk, in shades of brown and bronze the color of autumn leaves, so beautiful that she longed to touch it.

"'Then said Christian," Margaret read, "'You make me afraid; but whither shall I fly to be safe? If I go back to mine own country, that is prepared for fire and brimstone, and I shall certainly perish there; if I can get to the celestial city, I am sure to be in safety there: I must venture. To go back is nothing but death: to go forward is fear of death, and life everlasting beyond it: I will yet go forward. So Mistrust and Timorous ran down the hill, and Christian went on his way . . . '"

"Very good," Mr. Vining interrupted her, smiling in approval. "Enough, Miss Becker; now answer me this – divide four hundred and sixty-seven by 18." Margaret decided that she liked the way he smiled – there were two long creases which appeared on either side of his mouth when he did so, as if he smiled widely and often. He had her diagram a sentence on her little slate, and answer some questions, which she thought fairly simple and easily answered, after which he directed her to sit on the second bench from the back. The tall girl slid a little aside to make room for her, and turning her head a little aside, smiled also at Margaret.

"I'm Edwina Brackett," she whispered, and would have said more but for Schoolmaster Vining's sharp eyes falling upon them.

"Make each other's acquaintance during recess, young ladies," he commanded, and Margaret flushed in embarrassment. She joined in reciting the multiplication tables, for the other children were up to eleven times twelve. She stole a glance at Rudi, who appeared to be making a wretched stumble of reading from *Pilgrim's Progress*. Mr. Vining did not look so pleased. No, Rudi did not think about things in the way that Margaret did: sometimes Margaret thought that her younger brother was almost like a young animal, impulsive and adventurous. All of his emotions and appetites were on the surface, transparent and easily divined by anyone who cared to look. Schoolmaster Vining's inquisition was soon finished: Rudi went to sit on the second bench, with children obviously smaller than he was.

Schoolmaster Vining continued with mathematics after the recitation: he wrote a series of mathematical problems on the blackboard, going from easy to quite difficult.

"Begin with the easiest, and show me each answer, before going on to the next," he said, with a smile, and for the next hour or so, the silence in the breezeway was broken only by the scratching of chalk on slate, and quiet murmuring. Schoolmaster Vining went from bench to bench, now and again sitting next to one of his pupils as he corrected, explained, and approved. In between writing out and solving the problems set, Margaret stole glances at the other pupils: besides Edwina, there were only three older boys, all sitting on the backmost benches industriously working problems. Those three older boys all looked very ordinary – none of them, she thought, showed any potential of being as handsome as Papa must have been that Mama would have singled him out, particularly. In all of the little school, there were only about fifteen scholars, the youngest of them a little boy who looked barely older than Carl, with his feet dangling clear of the rough puncheon floor of the breezeway schoolroom. Margaret felt a small tinge of disappointment: perhaps the witch-woman had been mistaken about the day. Or perhaps she would meet her future husband somewhere other than school. Considering that, her spirits rose. It was only mid-morning, after all.

It was just a short way between school, and home. Rudi and Margaret walked home for a dinner of bread and jam, and cold apple-pie. During the morning when they had been at school, Mama had begun the finicky task of threading the warp threads through the loom heddles. Now, as soon as she and Margaret had finished spinning out the red wool into finer and tighter threads, she would begin weaving. Mama was also working on unraveling the Mexican blankets: three baskets full of wool yarns sat at her feet, and Carl sat beside her, busily rolling the unraveled yarn into loose hanks. He jumped down from the porch as soon as he saw them, and ran to meet them.

"So what have you learned this morning, my dear little ducklings?" Mama asked fondly, "Have you made any friends? Your Papa has gone to see Mr. Austin – I thought that he would return by now. Never mind, you shall be able to tell him about the first day of school tonight at supper."

"I have a friend," Margaret ventured. "Her name is Edwina – she is fourteen: her father keeps a general store, and her mother rents rooms to boarders. The schoolmaster says I read very well, even better than Edwina."

"And of your reading, little man?" Mama turned to Rudi, who scowled.

"I have to sit with the younger boys," he answered, and Mama chuckled.

"That is what happens, when you do not pay the attention to your letters which you should – even Carlchen pays better mind than you do."

"Then he should go to school, rather than me," Rudi answered, sullenly. Carl looked up at them, suddenly alert.

"School? I like."

"You've never been to school," Rudi answered, "and you don't know any letters."

"Do too," Carl looked stubborn, as only he could. He crouched on his heels, and picked up a small stick from the dirt at his feet. With it, he carefully scratched a letter A, and then a large B. "M'grete, showed. See? Thenna D." He was concentrating so hard, that he was biting on his lower lip. Margaret realized that her little brother had actually succeeded in surprising her. After all, she still considered him as her baby, as her doll. All the long weary days of travel from Pennsylvania, when they must ride in the wagon, she had amused herself and distracted her brother by writing letters on the slate and telling him what they were in English, and the sounds that they made, when put together in words. She had never expected that he would remember them, exactly. He was normally so quiet that people just assumed the world flowed around him, like a rock in a stream-bed. Papa even openly spoke of him as an idiot, which Margaret did not think fair. One might not have thought that the rock had absorbed knowledge from the stream – but Carl had. Now, he was industriously drawing out a long line of letters in the dirt.

"Ah, my dear little ducking," Mama set aside the half-raveled blanket, and stepped down from the porch to look at them, her face lighting up with pleasure and surprise as she looked at the letters. Carl had gotten up to Q. "You have learned so very well, now – Do you remember all of the letters?"

Carl ducked his head, twice, and confidently scratched out the letter R.

"R is . . . is for rat!" he answered, very clearly. "S . . . sis . . . S is for snake . . . an' school. School, Mama? Wit' M'grete?" he looked up at Mama and Margaret, yearningly – and of course, Mama yielded,

"Then of course, you should go to school with Margaret and Rudi, if you want it so badly. Papa will be so pleased with you!" Margaret couldn't decide who looked happier, Mama or Carl. From down the road, she heard the faint clanging of the school bell.

"Mama, we must go now," she took Carl's hand, as Rudi took the other.

"Wait!" Mama commanded, taking the corner of her apron and daubing at the smudge of dirt on Carl's face. "Now then, as handsome as a prince! Tell the schoolmaster he does know his letters," she added. "Now, go!"

The three of them hurried down the dusty street towards the schoolhouse; Margaret pleased with herself and her little brother: he knew his letters, and he said the sounds of them very well. The clever schoolmaster from Boston, Mr. Vining, was patient and painstaking with the little ones. He was a good teacher. She had observed him all morning, through her eyelashes, as she and Edwina industriously did sums and multiplication and long division. Surely this would not fail to please and surprise Papa that Carl showed evidence of cleverness. Once it might have hurt her very much to hear Papa calling little Carl an idiot and a dunce, but of late it bothered her much more that her little brother might be taking Papa's disparaging to heart. Margaret had often had one of her 'thinks' about this, of how to make Papa proud of Carl, and to take as much interest in him as he did in Rudi. At the schoolhouse, the other children were taking their places on the benches, and the schoolmaster held the bell in his hand, gazing at the Becker children in some puzzlement.

"This is our little brother," Margaret stated, baldly. "He knows his letters, and Mama says that he should go to school, too."

"Ah," Schoolmaster Vining looked at them, very severely. "And being good children, you do as your good Mater says. Does he know his letters? Give me your name, then."

"Carl Heinrich – Carl Henry Becker." Carl met a strange adult's eyes, straight on. "M'grete taught me letters. Sir," he added, as an afterthought.

Schoolmaster Vining sighed, although he did not seem much downcast. "Miss Becker, Mr. Becker – take your places, please, while I see how much this young man really knows . . ." Carl looked apprehensive, as Margaret took her hand from his, and Rudi from the other, leaving him alone, facing the schoolmaster from Boston. "Don't look so frightened, boy – I do not eat small children. Sit here, on this bench. You do not have your own slate? Bring one tomorrow, if you can . . ."

Margaret took her place at the back, next to Edwina, who ducked her head and murmured, "We're supposed to answer the questions on the board from this book. Two brothers, Margaret? I should die! Boys are such awful teases!"

"It's not so bad," Margaret whispered back, "Carlchen is really like my baby-doll. And Rudi does what I tell him, unless Papa interferes . . ."

"Young ladies," Schoolmaster Vining's voice interrupted, and they both started guiltily at finding his sharp, hazel-eyed regard upon them. "Attention to your lessons, please – not the latest gossip over the teacups." Abashed, Margaret and Edwina bent their heads over the geography book, open between them. She waited for Edwina to finish reading that page, and then turned it over to the next page. There was a list of geography questions chalked on the blackboard – the answers to them all being buried in Schoolmaster Vining's heavy, leather-bound atlas of maps and descriptions. She spared some attention to Carl, swinging his feet like the other small boy, his legs too short to reach the ground while sitting on the school bench. It seemed to Margaret that the schoolmaster spent more time catechizing her little brother than he had with herself or Rudi – and that Carl did not seem particularly apprehensive about answering the schoolmaster's questions. Finally Schoolmaster Vining gestured towards the front bench. Carl flashed a happy smile in her direction and nonchalantly took a place, shoulder to shoulder with the other little boy.

"Papa will be pleased," she whispered to Edwina, who looked warily around before she replied.

Schoolmaster Vining's attention seemed taken up with the youngest students, so Edwina whispered, "I should think so! Your brother must be quite clever, if Mr. Vining would take him into the class."

"Papa doesn't think so," Margaret sighed a little. "He believes that Rudi is perfect and Carl is an idiot and nothing . . ."

"Shhh . . ." Edwina hissed a warning, for the young schoolmaster seemed to be looking suspiciously in their direction.

When their schoolday ended, the sun's rays were slanting golden through the tree branches on the western aspect of their open-sided classroom. The boys on the benches towards the front seemed especially restless, fidgeting and elbowing each other in the ribs whenever Schoolmaster Vining's attention was elsewhere. At last, he consulted a heavy gold pocket-watch, which he drew from his vest pocket, and dismissed the class. Most of the boys scattered immediately in every direction, like the seeds from a dandelion head in a sudden breeze, shouting exuberantly as they ran. Margaret and Edwina sedately gathered up their slates and put on their bonnets, while Rudi waited at the edge of the schoolyard, the very picture of impatience. Carl also waited, but watching with complete absorption a number of crow-birds coming noisily to roost in the lone spindly tree which shaded the schoolhouse. They screeched and chattered to each other, animating the leafless branches with their dark wings, and splattering the dusty ground below with their droppings.

"You should see that your little brother has a slate of his own," Schoolmaster Vining observed as Margaret and Edwina passed by him at the top of the three rough plank steps leading down to the well-trodden space between log house and the rutted street.

"I shall ask Papa," Margaret answered, confidently. "I am sure he will permit that expense, once we tell him that he did so very well at school. He did do very well, did he not?" Margaret looked anxiously at the young schoolteacher. "He is so very quiet, most times."

"Better to be silent and thought an idiot, than open your mouth and remove all doubt," answered Mr. Vining, with considerable asperity. "No, young Master Becker is possessed of the full amount of wits normally granted to a child of his years. In truth, Miss Becker, I find your brother rather a refreshing change from the other lads, in that he does not chatter away like one of those wretched birds. Tell your father that I shall gladly teach him as well."

"Thank you, sir," Margaret answered, but her attention had been already distracted. Across the schoolyard, Rudi faced two boys of his age; his hands were balled into fists.

"Yah, yah!" taunted one of the boys, "What a dummy, can't even read!"

"You take that back!" Rudi shouted, "You do! Or I'll make you!"

"With what! Dummy!" the boys taunted, making faces at him, until Mr. Vining called, "Master Sullivan, Master Foster! Let it be! Your own intellects are hardly more glorious, are they? I would not recommend poking fun at anyone else's lack of academic achievement unless my own were beyond reproach." Abashed, the two boys contented themselves with making faces at Rudi before running away down the street. Margaret caught her brother's arm just in time to prevent him from running after them.

"Why are you stopping me, Margaret? Didn't you hear them? They called me names, said I was as stupid as Carl!"

"You are the one sitting with the younger children for your lessons," Margaret replied, crisply, "because you had not paid attention to your lessons – and forgotten most everything of what you had learned in Pennsylvania. If you don't like being called stupid and a dummy – then don't be stupid."

Rudi thought about that for a moment, and the storm-cloud in his face lightened somewhat. "You won't tell Papa, will you, Margaret? About sitting with the younger children?"

"I won't tell him," Margaret answered, taking pity on his despondency. "But I won't lie, if he asks me."

"He won't ask," Rudi immediately looked happier. They walked along the streets between the schoolhouse and the little log house that was their home for now. Home – even small and temporary – stayed in one place and that was an improvement on the wagon; Mama could set up her spinning wheel and loom, Margaret could have a place where she could sit and think about things. At night, Papa could bar the door, close out the dark, and the night, and all the dangers that might lurk in this strange and beautiful country.

Chapter 3 – *The Quarrel*

Margaret knew that something was wrong, even before she and her brothers came up the steps to the little log house that Papa had arranged to rent as their temporary home. Papa was walking up and down in the breezeway: he was angry, Margaret could tell even at a distance. His thumbs jammed into his trouser waistband, he trod the rough plank floor as if he wished to squash insects under his boot-heel. Mama sat on the bench, with a bundle of red wool in her hands, and the spinning wheel standing idle. Margaret's heart sank. Papa must be really angry that Mama must pay her entire attention to him. Papa hated it when Mama was spinning or weaving or knitting while he talked. Margaret supposed that it made Papa feel that she wasn't really listening.

". . . Damn him for a liar and a thief!" she heard Papa say, all the way from the road, and Mama made a futile shushing gesture.

"Something has happened," Margaret told the boys. "Something to make Papa angry."

At that moment, Mama saw them coming, and she called out to them, "There you are my dear little ducklings. Go to the well and wash up for supper, while Papa and I finish talking."

"What has happened, Papa?" Rudi blurted. "You said you were going to talk to Mr. Austin about our land-claim and . . ."

"I did, damn his eyes!" Papa shouted; his lips twisted like a snarling animal, and his face was red with fury. Margaret quailed within; this was very bad. Papa's talk with Mr. Austin must not have gone well. From Papa's face and Mama's anxiety, it must have gone quite badly indeed, although Margaret could not think how. Papa's land-claim was all but theirs. He had gone out to Texas two years ago, just to pick out the land that he wanted. Papa had selected a house site on it and felled logs, so that the timber for their house might dry and cure. He had even planted a few apple-tree seedlings, so that the trees would be well-established by the time they came to live there. Surely someone else had not claimed the land which Papa had been assured would be his? Margaret's eyes went to Mama, who briefly nodded her head at her. She and Rudi set down their slates on the bench next to Mama. The well was at the back of the lot which their little house sat on. Someone had made a rough stand of unpeeled willow branches, which supported a tin wash-basin. Mama had brought down a clean towel, after seeing the threadbare gray rag which the bachelors in the other part of the house thought sufficient. Now, Margaret dipped up a bucket of water from the well, and she and the boys silently washed their hands and faces. What would happen now? She wondered how Mama would damp down Papa's terrible anger. Did Papa mean that someone else had taken their land? It seemed likely. Now what would they do? Could Papa find another land-claim quite as fine as the one which he had decided upon?

When Margaret and the boys returned to the house, Papa seemed calmer; he no longer strode up and down but sat next to Mama, who had returned to unraveling the red blanket once more. Margaret pulled up her little three-legged stool, and sat at Mama's feet, rolling the unraveled wool into loose hanks. Mama shot Papa a meaningful look, but it was Carl who spoke first.

"I went to school," he announced quite clearly. "I know my letters, Papa." Mama beamed approval at him, but Papa said only, "Good, and make the most of it while you can, for we will not say here long." Margaret waited silently for Papa to explain, but Rudi plunged right in.

"Weren't we to move to our land . . ." he began, and Papa's balled fist crashed down on the bench, frightening Rudi into silence.

"And so we were – but the title to the property that I selected over all the others – that has been given to another. And that . . . that . . ."

"Alois . . ." Mama said very softly. "Remember the children." Papa swallowed the words that he was going to use, although he sounded as if he was grinding his teeth, when he continued.

"Mr. Austin refused to make amends. Another settler has already taken full possession – and possession of those improvements which I had made, upon assurances by the Baron and of Mr. Austin that all that remained was a mere formality of filing my deed with the Mexican government! Now he claims that it was a simple mistake – pah! He offered me another holding – a gesture of insult, since it was one I rejected out of hand two years ago."

"What will we do then, Papa?" Margaret made her voice as mild and soothing as Mama's. With that detached, standing-apart vision, she noted that her words had much the same calming effect upon Papa as Mama's always did.

He made an effort to smile at her, saying, "We will not brook such an insult as this, my little M'grete – no, indeed we shall not. We will not remain in San Felipe for any longer than it takes for me to find an even better tract of land. And," Papa's anger seemed to fade just a little. "There are other entrepreneurs, you know – not only the high and mighty Mr. Austin! I have heard much of Mr. DeWitt, whose grant lies farther west." Margaret turned her head to look at Mama's face, whose desolate expression made words hardly necessary.

"Alois, must we? We are only just arrived in this and the children are in school," Mama said. "And I have just begun a new weaving."

"Then I will go myself to this DeWitt colony . . . and I will take Rudi with me," Papa answered. "It will be his land someday, so it's only fair that he should take part in the choosing of it."

"May I, Papa? Truly?" Rudi simmered with excitement, and it seemed to Margaret that Papa's anger had faded somewhat, in the face of Rudi's pleasure and anticipation.

"Of course," Now Papa beamed, anger forgotten now that he had seemingly decided in a heartbeat upon a new plan. "So that is what we shall do, Marichen; You and Margaret and Carl will remain here – at least, it is a settled place, and I will leave you with the wagons and sufficient to see to all of your needs. The boy and Rufe and I will search out Mr. DeWitt, and the lands granted to him, and by next year we shall be settled. Mr. Austin should think again before he carelessly insults someone who has come to Texas whilst taking great pains to do so . . . and now," Papa took Mama's hand, "Marichen, is supper ready? We must eat, and then make plans for tomorrow! I promise, my dearest, this will be just a temporary halt to my plans. We will have a home – a splendid home, and a bountiful orchard; it will just take a little longer than we had thought. Trust me always, Marichen, our new home will be everything that I promised."

"I have never doubted you, husband," Mama answered, and at her side, Carl piped up, saying, "Papa – I went to school. I know my letters . . ."

"Oh, very good," Papa answered, absently, "Then the tuition I paid will not be wasted."

Margaret lay awake for quite some time, upon being sent up to bed. Mama and Papa's voices drifted up from where they sat, in the breezeway, Papa's voice rumbling like a heavy cartwheel on a log road, and Mama's soft undertone – neither of their voices quite loud enough for her to hear their words. She knew that Rudi also was awake and restless, for she could hear the tick mattress rustling as he thrashed about. Finally she murmured,

"Rudi – stop that. They're not quarreling, you know."

"Are you sure?" Rudi sounded anxious. "Papa was so very angry. I hate it when he is angry and Mama disagrees with him. It's not right – it makes me feel sick inside."

"They are not quarreling," Margaret repeated. She rolled over onto her side, and reached out in the dark, across the gap between the tick mattresses laid on the floor of the loft. "Here's my hand, Rudi – hold on to it, until you are sleepy. I won't let go your hand until you are asleep. Papa and Mama do not quarrel. Haven't you ever noticed? Papa does speak hastily and harshly, but never to Mama or you, for he loves you both very much. And Mama knows this very well. She does not argue with him, she waits until his anger is past. Papa in anger – he is like a thunderstorm, Rudi. All flash and noise, and then it is over, and you can hear the birds singing. And that is when Mama speaks, soft and sensible words, and Papa will always listen to her."

"Are you sure, M'grete?" Rudi took her hand in the darkness. "About the quarreling? I hate fighting – especially when Papa is angry."

"I am sure," Margaret answered. "I sit and watch them – don't you, Rudi? Don't you sit and watch people, or things like the birds in the trees? You would know almost everything if you take the time to watch and sit and think about what you see. Now, go to sleep. Everything will be all right. We're in Texas now, and Papa always knows what to do – even if Mama must give him a hint, now and again."

"*I* watch, M'grete," said a second, sleepy voice. Out of the dark between their pallets, a second small hand grasped at hers.

"So you do," Margaret answered, fondly. "Now, both of you – go to sleep."

And just as she drifted off to sleep herself, she recalled what the witch-woman had said about meeting her husband, today. Of all the men or boys that she had met during the day, she would marry one of them. Perhaps it was not someone she had really met, Margaret decided. Maybe it was someone who she had only briefly seen, passed in the street and exchanged a 'good morning' or 'good afternoon'. . . or perhaps the witch woman had been mistaken, after all.

The next morning, Rudi happily packed some clothes; Papa had already gone from the breakfast table when Mama called them down for breakfast.

"He has gone to look for some horses to buy for the journey," Mama explained, "since we have only the one. Mr. Bayard says he has a friend with horses to sell. He will hire out the oxen and the use of one wagon, to haul freight from the coast, while he is away. You know your Papa – once he has made up his mind, he is in a great hurry. Rudi and I must pack supplies for the journey this morning, as your Papa wishes to depart at once."

"Mama," Margaret ventured, between mouthfuls of oat porridge, "What about the Indians?"

"Shush, then," Mama replied, "Your Papa and Rufe will take the road to Bexar, which is much-traveled and patrolled by soldiers. There should be nothing to fear from Indians in your journey." But Margaret thought that Mama's eyes were worried, and that there were shadows under them. Here they were new-arrived in San Felipe, hardly knowing anyone – and Papa now was resolved to leave them for weeks or months! When he had gone before to Texas, they were at home, and with Oma Katerina and Opa Heinrich – this was different. She and Mama and Carl would have no one but themselves to depend upon. When the school bell rang faintly from across town, she gathered up the two school slates in one hand, and Carl's hand in the other. Rudi, his mouth full of porridge, nonetheless seemed quite cheered. He swallowed, and said, "It's all right for you, M'grete, you love school!"

"You'll never learn anything, if Papa keeps letting you play truant," Margaret answered. Rudi stuck out his tongue while Mama's back was turned.

"I'll sooner learn everything I need to know from Papa, rather than some old stick of a schoolmaster!"

When Margaret and Carl returned at midday, Papa and Rudi and Rufe were already gone. So was one of the wagons, the barrels and boxes of goods it had contained carefully removed and stacked along the back of the house, covered with canvas. The precious apple-tree saplings, rooted in boxes of rich black soil, had been taken from their places in the wagon, and now were lined up along the edge of the porch, out of harm's way. The soil was wet, and there were darker marks where the water had seeped out. All of the saplings had tiny, tiny green leaves, just out of the bud; to Margaret, the saplings looked as if they were stretching out little green fingers towards the sunlight. Papa had chosen and grafted cuttings from the finest apple trees in the Brandywine region. He would, he insisted to Mama, have the best apple orchard in Texas when those trees were well grown. Those pieces of furniture that had been packed in the wagon were now set out in the one little room or in the breezeway. Margaret thought how strange it looked, to have all those chests and chairs which had been dispersed throughout their home in Pennsylvania crammed into one room and spilling out onto the porches. Mama worked at her spinning wheel, walking back and forth a few steps to send the great wheel – as big almost as one of the wagon wheels – turning as she drew out the red Mexican wool into thinner and finer threads. The spindle was already nearly full. Mama must have been working all morning.

She smiled at them, saying, "Mr. Robbins came for the wagon and team just now, for he is going to haul goods from Anahuac, on the coast, while your Papa is away. There is bread and cheese for you, my dear little ducklings – I have already eaten. Papa and Rudi and Rufe left at mid-morning. Come and sit out here while you eat, and tell me of today at school." So they sat on the edge of the porch, eating their dinner.

"You should read to me, while I spin," Mama said, "you know that it would take five spinners to keep pace with one weaver!"

"Mayhap there are other women who will spin for you," Margaret put her chin in her hands, considering. The little house felt very quiet without Papa and Rudi in it. The whirring of the spinning wheel was comforting to her, as the regular wooden rattle of the loom heddles and the regular heart-beat sound of the shuttle going back and forth soon would be. Presently, she and Carl must return to school. Her little brother leaned against her.

"What 'choo do, M'grete?" he asked.

"I'm thinking."

"What 'choo thinking 'bout, M'grete?"

"Everything," Margaret answered. "About Mama and spinning. About school, and if Schoolmaster Vining's waistcoat is silk. My friend Edwina. What our new house will look like. The crows that roost in the schoolhouse tree, and why they come there every evening."

"I watch de crows," her brother confided. "I sit ver' still, and dey come close."

"That's good," Margaret answered thoughtfully. "What do you think the crows are doing, Carlchen?"

"Making mess!" her brother wrinkled up his nose. "A big mess!" and both Margaret and Mama laughed.

That afternoon, when they returned home from school, there was a horse tied up to the fence railings, and a visitor sitting in the best chair; a slight gentleman in a plain hunting coat, over a tall stock and neck-cloth. He had dark hair curling around his high forehead, and melancholy brown eyes, so dark they appeared almost black in color.

"This is Mr. Austin, children," Mama said quietly in English, as Carl hung onto Margaret's hand. "Mr. Austin – my daughter Margaret and our youngest son, Carl Henry. He came to pay us a visit, hoping to speak with your Papa."

"Alas, I find that I am too late." Mr. Austin had a gentle voice, and his disappointment sounded perfectly genuine. He rose and bowed over Margaret's hand as gallantly as if she had been a woman grown, and a fine lady at that. Then he shook Carl's hand, with grave dignity, although his lips quirked slightly upward when Carl went to stand by Mama's chair, like a small, fierce watchdog. "I had hoped to mend your husband's quarrel with me. I am certain that we could have come to an agreeable compromise over the matter, given time enough. I had taken such care to bring into this grant only the most substantial of folk, with their families, and it now grieves me to know that Mr. Becker thinks himself to have been ill-done by."

"My husband is a very stubborn man," Mama answered. "And he will not abide a situation not of his choosing, once his mind has been made up."

"To our mutual loss – mine and that of our community, no less than your own, as temporary as that might be." Mr. Austin stood, and bowed over Mama's hand. He hesitated, looking closely at Mama, and at Margaret and their disarranged household, piled around all higgledy-piggely. "Forgive me for asking this of you, Mrs. Becker, but with no male in your household in San Felipe – you have not been left living . . . without comfort, or resources. Your funds and supplies are sufficient for yours' and the children's needs during your stay?"

"I thank you for your concern," Mama replied, "but my husband intends to return by midsummer, and in the meantime we are well provided for."

"I look after Mama an' M'grete!" Carl announced firmly, and Mr. Austin smiled a smile of particular sweetness; he was a man, Margaret sensed, who truly liked children, who was at ease and inclined to treat them with a courtesy and consideration which most men usually reserved only for adults.

"I am sure you will, little man – and I repose the utmost confidence in you. But nonetheless, should you be in need of any assistance, please don't hesitate to send for me. Your situation . . ." he hesitated, and looked straight at Mama, "is in part, at least something of my making. I can assure you that I will take every care with regard to your distressing situation. Please do not hesitate to call upon me – or if I am not immediately available, then on my secretary, Mr. Williams."

"You are very kind," Mama answered – and Margaret thought she sounded so proudly regal, in her plain calico dress, standing in the breezeway of the little log house, with all the furniture and goods scattered or piled up around her, and baskets full of red thread taken from the spindle. "Be assured, I shall not hesitate, though I doubt it will be necessary. You see, Mr. Austin," and she put her hand on Carl's shoulder, "I have our little man and all of my husbands' goods in my possession. He will return at midsummer or send me word, of that I am entirely confident."

"I am relieved to hear of this, Mrs. Becker." Mr. Austin took up his hat from where it lay on the table. "Your husband is a man of his word – of that I have never doubted. I would welcome any chance of conversation with him which might allow me to dissuade him from his stated intentions. I beg you, Mrs. Becker – please allow me any opportunity to converse with your husband upon his return to San Felipe. He is a person of quality and industry, of the substance that will make the bedrock of this community. I would regret his permanent departure most keenly! Still, may I call upon you and the children, now and again, to assure myself of your continued well-being?"

"We are only recently come to this place," Mama answered with careful dignity, "and so have very few friends. I do not wish that people would think ill of us by refusing, or that my husband take offense by my accepting."

"Ah," Mr. Austin put on his hat; he was smiling, a wry and self-deprecating smile. "The proprieties – I do understand, Mrs. Becker. I shall endeavor to visit at those times when others shall be present, and not give any purchase to gossiping tongues. Good day, to you – to Miss Margaret and young Carl Henry." He solemnly shook Carl's hand, bowed over Margaret's and took his departure.

As he settled into the saddle of his horse, Margaret said, "Oh, Mama, I so wish that Papa had not quarreled so with Mr. Austin. He is so pleasant."

"Your Papa is a difficult man," Mama acknowledged. "But he is a good man – but you must always remember, Margaret; a good and loyal wife must be guided by her husband in all things."

I don't know why that must be the custom, Margaret thought, rebelliously. *What if the husband is being stupid and quarrelsome? What then must a good and loyal wife do? Be a patient Griselda and allow herself and her children to starve?*

This very question took up her interest for had not the witch-woman said that she would meet her husband? He must be someone in San Felipe, Margaret reasoned – someone who had come to Texas, just like Papa. She wouldn't relish being married to someone with Papa's temper, Margaret knew. She didn't care how handsome and fair-spoken he might appear to be. After supper that evening, she had one of her 'thinks' – sitting on the porch of the cabin, swinging her feet over the edge, with her chin in her hands.

After Mama had finished washing up the supper dishes, there was enough light left for a while, so that Mama could begin her weaving. The young bachelors living in the other part of their house had partaken of their own supper. Now they sat on their part of the porch, talking of men's matters as they smoked their pipes, tiny coal-red sparks now and again glowing briefly. Occasionally, the scent of tobacco smoke wafted towards Margaret. She could hear their voices, but not what they were saying, over the thump and rattle of Mama's loom. Mama was not doing complicated weaving, so she might be able to carry on with it for a while until it became fully dark. A few swifts darted after invisible flying insects, dark shadows flashing against an indigo-dark sky. The chorus of crickets singing, invisible in the growing twilight, accompanied the slow unveiling of the stars. When she was very small, about the age of Carl, Margaret thought that the crickets' song was the sound of the stars as they wheeled in the sky, the creaking of the tiny gears that moved the stars. At church, they had talked of the music of the spheres, and Margaret had once been sure that was what she heard. It was only logical, since the stars and the crickets' songs appeared together in the evening. She was vaguely disappointed when she told this to Opa Heinrich, who had laughed and laughed. He had caught a cricket to show her, keeping it in a tiny chip-wood basket with a lid. It all seemed very prosaic, with the music of the stars being only the sound of a little black cricket rubbing it's hinder legs together. It seemed that the world became a little less magical, but when she said so to Opa Heinrich, he had only laughed again.

"Little Grete, the world is full of magic," he had said, and pointed out the flock of birds, wheeling together through the sky, "The birds – they have no leader, and yet they move together. They have no language, other than their songs, but they know, somehow – where and when to turn, all at once, in the same instant! Now that is magic!" Margaret remembered his words wistfully; Opa Heinrich was wise, the wisest man that Margaret knew. He might have been able to divine the true intent of what the witch woman had said. Now, she would like to marry a man as wise and tender as Opa Heinrich. Margaret ran her mind hastily over those men of her acquaintance in San Felipe – only the schoolmaster, Mr. Vining, seemed to possess anything of Opa Heinrichs' qualities. Margaret sat up a little straighter, and stopped swinging her feet. Mr. Vining! She had met him on the day that the witch woman had specified, but all this time, Margaret had been thinking she meant one of the schoolboys. Mr. Vining was old, but not as old as Papa. Although, Papa had been older than Mama . . . Margaret's chin dropped into her hands again, as she pondered this sudden insight. How much older was Mr. Vining? She was just turned twelve, surely not old enough to be courted and wed. Why, she had barely begun having the monthly courses of a woman – a peculiar ache in the middle of her body, which could only be comforted by a stoneware bottle filled with hot water and wrapped in a towel – and the little regular dribble of vivid blood, coming from that place between her legs. Margaret had been terrified upon discovering that, thinking surely that she would die of that bleeding. Oma Katerina had comforted her, saying that she was now a woman, but Margaret knew surely that Mama and Papa did not truly think so, not in the ways that counted. She might wed when she were sixteen at least. Four more years . . . and Mr. Vining was so accomplished and handsome, in a clever way. He might be long wed, by the time that Margaret was of an age, but somehow Margaret found confidence that he would still be free when she was grown. The witch woman had said so; she would meet her husband on the thirtieth day after her twelfth birthday. And of all those men or boys which Margaret had met on the first day of school, she liked the schoolmaster best of all. The witch-woman had known so many things, just like the birds of a flock, wheeling and turning in the sky. Birds had a way to know certain things – so of course, the witch-woman must have the same way of knowing. The schoolmaster would be her husband; Margaret could hardly fathom when, or by what means, since Papa was now so set upon leaving Mr. Austin's settlement. When Papa returned, he would take them all to Mr. DeWitt's settlement, far and away to the west. She and Carl would have to leave school. How would she continue a connection with Mr. Vining, after that?

Margaret sighed, a little wistfully, but at the same time, she took heart in realizing that the witch-woman had known truly so many things, even before looking at Margaret's hands. Whatever happened, when Papa returned in summer, she was very sure that she would marry the schoolteacher; events or fate, or even those spirits that the old conjure-witch spoke of – all would conspire to make it so. All she need do was to wait.

All that spring, the web of Mama's weaving grew on her loom, fine scarlet-dyed cloth, re-woven from the Mexican blankets. Margaret took Mama's place at the spinning wheel, drawing out the unraveled yarn for Mama, so that Mama could continue weaving. Mr. Vining explained the dye to them, one day when he came to discuss with Mama the progress of Margaret and Carl at their lessons. He took note of Mama's weaving, telling them how the brilliant red color came from a dye made from the crushed bodies of little grey insects, which fed on a kind of plant which grew farther west; a cactus, he called it, a peculiar plant with many fat greenish leaves which all grew together, without a stem or trunk, and was covered with sharp spines. Margaret studied him, looking through her eyelashes, as carefully as she studied her school subjects: yes, the schoolmaster was nearly as wise as Opa Heinrich, and interested in so many things. Margaret thought, upon more careful study, that he appeared very fine – not as handsome as Papa, but elegant, and finely-drawn, like a copper-plate etching, all graceful and curving lines.

"He's from Boston," Edwina whispered to her, when the schoolmaster and object of their conversation was engrossed with the younger pupils, "and he is not a settler of Mr. Austin's. He told my father he had no wish to work on the land, it was not his fancy to farm or herd cows."

"Then what did he come here for?" Margaret asked. Edwina looked warily towards Schoolmaster Vining whose back was still turned, as he seemed to be correcting one of the middle-sized boys.

"He told Mary Kincheloe and she told my mother that it was for his health. He has a weak chest, so he said, and his doctors told him he should travel to a tropical southern clime for fear of developing the consumption. The winters in Boston were so cold and damp, he said, the air so bad that he could hardly dare to take a breath of it. His doctors told him the winter chill would kill him if he spent another year in the North. My mother told him that he should drink plenty of sage tea with honey . . ."

"What did he say to that?" Margaret whispered.

"He laughed and said to Mama that sage tea and honey couldn't be worse than any other nostrum that the doctors in Boston urged upon him, and perhaps it might help somewhat. Then he lectured the company present about the efficacy of sage and other herbs at such tedious length that Mama vowed she was sorry to have even recommended it to him . . ."

"Miss Brackett, Miss Becker – I regret this is not a ladies' tea party," Mr. Vining spoke from across the breezeway, his sharp hazel eyes suddenly upon them. Both Edwina and Margaret jumped guiltily. They returned their attention to the mathematics problem which was set out on the large blackboard and fell to work, although Margaret continued to steal glances at Mr. Vining.

A weak chest, and at a hazard for becoming a consumptive? Margaret knew what that portended from overhearing whispered conversations between Oma Katerina and some of her friends; a person with consumption grew weaker, pale and frail, coughing up more and more blood, until finally they could not breathe any more and they died. Then Mr. Vining's journey to Texas and his residence in San Felipe must have done all the good that the Boston doctors had originally advised. Mr. Vining, although whip-thin and rather paler in his complexion than a man who customarily spent time in the out-of-doors, yet appeared hale and fit. Still, there was a winter, even in Texas, and Margaret recalled how cold it had been at night, even as the Beckers and the Sullivans had traveled deeper into Texas after crossing the river after Natchitoches. She had not seen snow since leaving Pennsylvania. It was warmer here in Texas than it had been there, but not anything like what Opa Heinrich had said of the tropics, even farther south, where the air was always as warm as blood. Margaret bent her attention to her schoolwork;

41

later, she must have one of her 'thinks' about all this. Mr. Vining had no one to look after him, as Mama did for Papa. And if he was the man who would be Margaret's husband, than she must contrive some way to look after him until she were properly grown up and the witch-woman's prophecy would be fulfilled.

Late in spring, Mama received a letter from Papa which said that he had come to an agreement with Mr. DeWitt and claimed a very pleasing tract of land, well-wooded and located on the bank of a deep river. He wrote about visiting the town of Bexar, far to the west, where the Mexican governor of those parts lived, a little town of houses built of hardened mud bricks, and roofed with rusty orange tiles.

Mama looked immediately more cheerful as she read the letter. "It is a good omen, as I am nearly finished with the weaving!" she said. Margaret's heart sank a little; this would mean leaving San Felipe and not seeing Schoolmaster Vining for some while.

"Mama," she ventured at last, "what are you going to do with the red weaving?"

"I thought to make some blankets with it," Mama answered. "Some to sell at the general store and some for us. One for your bride's chest, I think. You should begin your bride's chest now, my duckling."

"Mama," Margaret put her chin in her hands, "Rather than keep a blanket for my chest, I would rather make a gift of it to Mr. Vining. He has been very kind to us, especially to Carl, in taking him into the school. I would like to do a kindness for him. Edwina says that he came to Texas for his health, and the cold is bad for him. I would like to think that he might have it to keep him warm next winter. He would be reminded of us, and think as kindly of us as I – as we do of him."

"That is a generous gift," Mama looked amused and also rather knowing. "And from your bride's chest? Rather unsuitable, a gift from you to a young man, M'grete. Make it a gift from all of us." Mama looked at her loom, a thick roll of tightly-woven crimson wool rolled around the take-up beam, with an expression of intense satisfaction. "Yes, a gift from the family, from all of us. He did Carlchen a world of good, teaching him to read his letters."

Chapter 4 – *Gonzales*

Every evening, sundown lingered a little later and a little later more, and for a week, Mama had been waiting. Papa had said he would return and take them all into the far west to Mr. DeWitt's colony. When Mama finished reweaving the red-wool blankets, she did not start another weaving, for what would be the use of that? As soon as Papa returned, they would take apart the loom, re-pack the wagons, and resume the journey. For several weeks, she and Margaret had occupied their afternoons, when school was done and she and Carl had finished whatever studying had been required, by firmly stitching a narrow binding of calico cloth around the raveled edges of the blanket-lengths. After supper every evening, she and Mama picked up their sewing once again, until it was too dark to see and the swifts had begin their darting, almost unseen against the darkening indigo sky.

Margaret never forgot the day when Papa returned from the farthest west, cheerful and invigorated, as if all of his fury with Mr. Austin had been but a bad dream. He was still resolved upon moving to Mr. DeWitt's settlement, which news sent Margaret's heart sinking down into her toes. He and Rudi arrived on an early evening in late April in company with a handful of other horsemen. The trees had finally put out all of their tender green leaves, and the meadows around San Felipe were deep in rich grass, all touched with gold by the setting sun. Two of Papa's companions were Mexican; handsome young men clad all in black, their trousers and short jackets trimmed with many bright silver buttons, with sashes of brilliant silk knotted around their waists. There was silver on their horse's saddles and bridles too; the men all waved farewell from the roadway, as Papa and Rudi tied the reins of their own horses to the rough-hewn wooden fence rails which marked the boundary between the street and the dooryard. Margaret and Carl had just come home from an errand bearing a message to Mr. Robbins telling him that Papa would soon return. They were walking hand in hand from Mr. Robbins' store when they saw the three horses and the other men of a party departing, Papa rushing exuberantly towards the house and Mama, leaving the horses still burdened with saddles and blankets, although the third horse bore a large pack. Rudi was dismounting a little more slowly: he appeared tired, yet excited.

"Papa has a grant from Mr. DeWitt!" he shouted. "I have seen it, M'grete! It is truly ours. Papa has a brand for our cattle and all – the Spanish governor an' Baron Bastrop said so. It is ours, and Papa says we will live like lords . . ."

"We have missed you!" Margaret hugged her little brother and ruffled his hair. Boy-like, he made a face at her. "Your neck is filthy, Rudi. Didn't Papa ever make you wash the back of your ears?"

"What for?" Rudi answered, "Esteban an' Diego say that I am now a true buckaroo – that is what they call a *vaquero*, a horseman. I should see to my horse before I see to myself."

Margaret sniffed disdainfully, "Than your horse would be nicer to sit next to at dinner. And where is Rufe . . . did he remain at Papa's new holding?"

Rudi's face suddenly looked most somber.

"He's dead, M'grete. We were coming along the road towards Bexar – Papa had him ride ahead a little way to see if we were near to water for the horses. He was only out of our sight for a few moments. We heard a sound, as if he tried to shout to us. Then just silence. When we came upon him, he was lying in the middle of the way, with two arrows sticking straight up out of his chest and the hair skinned off the top of his head. The other men – the men with us – said they were Comanche arrows. They steal horses, you know."

Rufe dead, and so abruptly? Margaret felt a cold chill, as if a winter draft had suddenly crept up on her. Papa had said nothing of this in his letters to Mama. Rufe had uncomplainingly come with them as a drover all the way from Pennsylvania. He never had much to say for himself, but now he was dead. Obscurely Margaret felt guilty for never having paid much mind to him.

"What did you Papa and the men do then?"

"They put his body over the pack-horse saddle and took him to be buried in Bexar. Papa gave a priest a few silver coins, and Esteban swore that for all he knew, Rufe was a Catholic, so that he could be put into a grave in the proper cemetery." Rudi looked down at his feet, shuffling them wretchedly in the dust. "And then we came straight to San Felipe. Papa says he must hire another drover, of course – as if the Comanches killed Rufe just to spite Papa, or that Rufe was careless and caused Papa special trouble!"

"It wasn't your fault, Rudi." Margaret soothed her little brother with another hug, for he truly looked quite wretched, "And it wasn't Rufe's, either. Go to the well, and wash up – Mama will have supper soon."

"I must see to the horses first," Rudi answered stoutly and repeated, "A *vaquero* always takes care of his horse. Esteban said so." There was nothing else for Margaret and Carl to do but help Rudi to unsaddle the horses and turn them loose to graze behind the house where the grass had grown lush and tall in the months that Papa and Rudi had been gone. Margaret lugged the first of the two deep willow baskets to the log house, while Rudi and Carl dragged the other, full of the bedding and gear which Papa had taken with them. The packhorse had borne the baskets, lashed to the sides of a wooden frame which sat on its back atop a thick sheepskin pad cinched twice around its belly.

In the porch between the two rooms of the house, Papa was taking bites out of some bread and cheese as he talked excitedly to Mama about the new holding.

"Along the river, which runs deep and fast between tall banks," he was saying, "the bottom lands are rich and well-watered by small streams. I have found a good site for a house, for we must cultivate within two years. I have been advised to herd cattle on the uplands. Mr. Menchaca and his brother were most kind to advise me. Alas, the DeWitt grant adjoins the tracts where the Comanche are accustomed to hunt. I will have you and the children live in the Gonzales settlement for a time, as my lands are only at a short remove. Until some kind of peace can be made with the Comanche, as has been with the Karankawa and such – that would be best, I think, Marichen . . ." He appeared to notice Margaret and her brothers for the first time, embraced them with an absent air, as if he were already thinking of other matters. "M'grete, my angel! Are you ready to help your mother with the packing? We should leave by the end of the week, I think. I must speak to Robbins, for I sent a message that we would return and need our wagon."

Margaret kissed Papa on the forehead, saying, "Must we depart so soon, Papa? Carl is doing so very well at school that . . ."

"There will soon be a school established in Gonzales," Papa answered, his attention already on matters involving his holding in the DeWitt grant. "And now I must hire another drover – perhaps Robbins can recommend a man."

"What of Mr. Tarrant?" Mama asked, looking swiftly from Papa's face to Rudi's dolorous one. "I do not understand, Alois – did he return with you?"

"He's dead, Mama." Rudi answered first, and almost tearfully. Mama's mouth rounded into an 'o' of shock and sorrow, and she abruptly sat down. "The Indians killed him."

"Alois," Mama said then, sounding as stern as if she wished to admonish Papa and Rudi both, "you said nothing to me of this in your letters."

"I did not wish to worry you, my heart," Papa answered. "It was one of those sad things which happen if one does not take sufficient care. Of course, I shall always take care – the boy and I were never in danger. We saw that Rufe had a proper Christian burial – the very least that I could do for him."

"You should write to his father," Mama said at once, and her lips tightened. "You should tell him at once, Alois; before we depart this place."

"Marichen, my heart, must there be such a hurry to write this?" Papa remonstrated, "for it will take months for a letter to arrive back East!"

But Mama repeated, "You should write to his father at once, Alois. His family – his parents – are friends of long-standing to my family and yours."

Margaret's gaze went from her mother to her father; again, she felt that 'standing aside' feeling, as if she were a stranger watching them. Carl's hand crept into hers seeking reassurance, and Rudi looked as if he were close to tears. Mama was angry at Papa. Mama was almost never angry at Papa, but in this instance she was, not just for his thoughtlessness in leaving that intelligence out of his letters, but in appearing to regard Rufe and his death as a matter of little importance. Papa was, Margaret realized in a flash of comprehension, as hasty and careless about Rufe as Mr. Sullivan or any of the other slave-owners in San Felipe were concerning the least of the slaves they owned, as if they were nothing more than a not terribly valuable tool which once broken could be set aside without a second thought. She wondered, with a little flicker of foreboding; what kind of man would Papa be if Mama was not there to anchor him to his better nature, to remind him of what was good and right, and make amends when he had spoken hastily or in anger to men like Mr. Austin? Margaret tried to put this unsettling thought aside. Mama would always be there; she was the fire on the hearth, the calm presence that made this bare little log room their home, the center and core of the family.

"Shall we be returning to school, then?" Margaret asked.

Before Mama could answer, Papa said, "No, little M'grete, we will begin packing at once in the morning. You and the boy will not miss any lessons, as there will soon be a schoolmaster in Gonzales." Margaret's heart sank. She had expected something like this upon Papa and Rudi's return, and thus had taken care with the blanket that she had marked out as Schoolmaster Vining's special gift. She had nurtured some faint hope that Papa would not act so precipitously, or even that he would amend his quarrel with Mr. Austin. No, she accepted and faced the inevitable: they would leave San Felipe immediately – as soon as they could repack the wagons and Papa could hire another drover. Unconsciously, Margaret squared her shoulders.

"Mama," she said, "Then I should go to the schoolmaster's house and tell him of our departure. I should also take our gift to him; may I then?"

"Of course, my duckling," Mama answered, and it seemed to Margaret that Mama spoke with tender sympathy, "And take Carlchen with you also, to convey our appreciation for the schoolmaster's teaching, all these months."

"Yes, Mama." Margaret went to the large willow basket which held hers' and Mama's sewing. The blanket which she had stitched the binding around entirely by herself was on the bottom, carefully folded into a neat square and tied with a narrow length of woven cotton tape with which Mama secured all of her household linens. She tucked it under her arm, and took Carl's hand with her other. He went with her, although he looked back at Papa. Papa, now having stuffed the last of the bread and cheese into his mouth, was pacing up and down restlessly, as was his habit when deep in consideration. He did not spare any glance after them as they walked away from the little log hut.

"Choo sad, M'grete?" Carl asked warily in the English that they used at school, as soon as they were out of earshot.

"I am," Margaret answered, with a sigh.

"Why, M'grete?"

"Because I liked living here, even in a little house not our own. I liked our lessons and I very much liked the master of the school."

"I like too, M'grete," Carl confided, with the air of someone confessing a great secret. "He ver' nize."

"I will miss school here." Margaret hugged the blanket to her chest. Yes, she would miss it very much. She would miss Edwina, and walking to school with her brother every morning. San Felipe was safe. Mr. Austin had made a kind of peace with the Indians, all but the Comanche and they were far away in the west. This was, alas, where Papa was going to take them.

The schoolmaster's house looked very different when school was not in session in the breezeway. All the benches were moved to one side, and the doorway to Mr. Vining's parlor stood open. It was always closed during school hours, and so Margaret and the other children did not know what the schoolmaster's house was like on the inside. She knew that he had a horse in a corral at the back of his town-lot, for he rode as well as any other man in San Felipe. She walked through the school-yard, half eager and half-hesitant. It sounded as if Mr. Vining had visitors. There were several more horses in the corral and some saddles piled in the breezeway. The sound of men's voices and laughter came from within. She could see a little, through the opened window: a young man who looked like one of the Mexican men who had ridden with Rudi and Papa. With a firm hold on Carl's hand, she walked across the porch and stood for a moment in the doorway, thinking to herself that the schoolmaster's parlor looked quite pleasant. In one of her 'thinks,' she had considered very carefully the matter of what one could tell of a person by looking at their possessions, or conversely, of what you could expect someone to own, just by studying them. Schoolmaster Vining had the things she had expected of him. Although the furniture was no finer than any other household in San Felipe, there were elements that Margaret found most pleasing, chief among them a quantity of books. A very fine glass-shaded lamp stood in the middle of a round table in the center of the room, and the chairs in it appeared both capacious and comfortable. The lamp shed a good light on those books lying upon the table. Schoolmaster Vining and one of his friends were taking turns leafing through the largest of them, while the other friend leaned back in his chair with a pipe in hand. The schoolmaster looked up at the sound of Margaret's gentle rap on the door-frame, and sprang up from his chair.

"Why, Miss Becker," he exclaimed, in pleased surprise, "And young Master Becker, too. Good evening! I was not expecting a call at this hour. I thought your family would be enjoying your reunion. My friends tell me that your father returned from Bexar with them, and that he has a fine property now, in Mr. DeWitt's land grant."

"Yes, sir," Margaret answered, "Good evening, sir." Suddenly, those things that were proper for a young lady to say, went entirely from her mind. "Papa says that we will leaving soon, so we will not be coming to your school again. We brought you a parting gift – this is from our family, of my mother's weaving." She held out the blanket, miserably aware that she sounded childish. "We are grateful for your teaching, sir, especially for teaching Carl."

"Convey my gratitude to your family, Miss Becker." Schoolmaster Vining accepted the folded blanket, although he looked slightly puzzled. "I find teaching to be rather a pleasure, especially with willing and talented pupils."

At Margaret's side, Carl tugged at her hand, and whispered, "I t'ink school very nize, M'grete."

"I am gratified," Schoolmaster Vining answered. "May I present my friends? They are already somewhat acquainted with your father. Miss Becker, Master Becker – may I present Señor Esteban Menchaca de Lugo, and Señor Diego Menchaca de Lugo, gentlemen of Spain and San Antonio de Bexar. Esteban, Diego – Miss Margaret Becker and young Master Carl Becker."

"I am honored," replied the young man with the book, who set it aside. The spurs on his boot-heels jingled musically, as he came to the doorway. "And to make your acquaintance is my pleasure as well, señorita." He bowed over Margaret's hand very correctly and smiled as if it really was an honor and a pleasure. Carl stared wide-eyed as an owl. "We traveled with your father and brother. Diego, recall your manners," he added, over his shoulder to his brother, who took his pipe out of his mouth, and drawled, "My head remembers my manners. Alas, the rest of me is telling my head that it does not wish to move a muscle out of this chair. Consider that I also am most pleased, so on and so forth." Señor Esteban said something chiding in Spanish to his brother who laughed sardonically and puffed upon his pipe.

"Forgive my brother, señorita, for he is a lazy swine . . ."

"Who has ridden a very long way," Señor Diego retorted, while Schoolmaster Vining laughed, and confided to Margaret, "They are both very dear friends, but sometimes they put me into the mind of some of my younger pupils. I am most grateful for this gift, Miss Becker. It has been most rewarding, teaching you and your brother. I regret your departure from my school, and from San Felipe. If business or friendship takes me to Gonzales, and your father's holdings, might I presume to pay a call upon your family?"

"Yes, of course," Margaret answered, and immediately regretted sounding so hasty. She should have sounded dignified as Mama had in response to Mr. Austin. Mr. Vining smiled, so that the deep creases on either side of his mouth appeared; by that Margaret knew that he was quite genuinely pleased.

"Then I will look forward to seeing how you have continued with your lessons," he answered. Carl stared at the Menchaca brothers, rapt by the splendid display of silver buttons on their coats and trousers, and the pleasant jingling sound of the spurs on their boot-heels. "Good evening, Miss Becker."

"Good evening, Mr. Vining," Margaret did a small, and awkward curtsy, and fled, tugging Carl behind her.

That night, as she lay in her pallet-bed in the loft, she thought about that brief visit and concluded that perhaps it had not been all that disastrous. He had looked on her and smiled, and promised to visit them in their new home. Margaret reposed tremendous confidence in the witch-woman's prophecy. Mr. Vining was the man that she would marry. Philosophically, Margaret set aside what the witch-woman had also told her about having another husband – one that she would marry for friendship. She decided it would be enough to settle the question of that first husband, the one who would give her eleven years of happiness. That was nearly as long as she had been alive.

Out in the breezeway, on the porch, Mama and Papa were still talking. They would begin packing the wagons again in the morning. Mama had already taken down the delicate parts of her loom, the heddle frames through which the warp threads were threaded. It made Margaret sad to see that. When she considered her feelings she had quite liked living in this little place. She had a friend in Edwina, a comfortable place and rhythm to the day – school, and chores, helping Mama with spinning and weaving, supper, and then sitting on the porch of an evening, doing schoolwork or sewing until the light faded. The birds returned to their roosts, and the bats to their lair, and the stars wheeled in their orbit, white-silver in an indigo sky, the sun set in a smear of orange and purple, then the moon rose to take its place, pale and milk-colored as it waxed and waned. Margaret had decided regretfully, after having one of her 'thinks' about it; that she did not like days of constant adventure, of seeing a different aspect to every morning. She preferred a set place under the sky, the march of the regular seasons and days. There was a joy to seeing things unfold.

"M'grete?" Rudi lay awake also. She could hear him turning over. The straw stuffing the pallet upon which he and Carl slept crackled as he moved.

"Rudi – what is the matter?" she asked, for he sounded deeply unhappy.

"I've been wondering, M'grete. Do you think it would hurt to be dead?"

"You are thinking about Rufe," Margaret answered. Of course, he would have seen Rufe's body afterwards, seen everything but the Indians actually killing Papa's hired man. "I can't see how anything that happens after someone is dead can hurt their body. Their spirit is gone to heaven, anyway."

"Are you sure?" Rudi still sounded unhappy.

"Of course I am – do you think that the pig objects to being cut up at butchering time, after it is dead? Can you imagine the fuss about hanging up the hams in the smokehouse if the pig was still squealing and wriggling?" That coaxed Rudi into laughing, at least a little bit.

"He looked . . . surprised. Rufe did. As if he couldn't believe it had happened. Do you think that it hurts to die, M'grete?"

"I guess it depends on how fast it happens," Margaret answered, carefully. "It probably does hurt at least a little – but not for long at all. And then you go to heaven, if you have been good. I think I would like Heaven. Opa Heinrich said Heaven was like a garden where there were never any weeds."

"I wouldn't like to be dead," Rudi said, after a bit. "I would miss Mama and Papa, and you and Carl, and all my friends."

"And we would miss you too," Margaret replied. "But nobody else is going to die, Rudi. It's late – go to sleep, now. Here's my hand – hold it, and I'll hold on to yours. Remember, Mama and Papa will always keep us safe."

But, thought Margaret to herself – *Texas is large, Papa and Mama are only two, matched against it. Best not to say so to Rudi or Carl; my brothers are still children, and children must believe that everything will be all right. I am twelve and will marry the schoolmaster someday. I am all but grown up.*

* * *

Five Years Later – Gonzales, in the State of Coahuila y Tejas

"Mama," Margaret ventured one late summer afternoon, as Mama worked at the loom which now sat in the outdoor room of the house that Papa had built for them when they finally settled in Mr. DeWitt's colony. "There is a roof-raising for the Darsts, on Saturday. Mrs. Darst and their friends are planning to have a fiddler for dancing, afterwards. I promised that I should bring some pies and Benjamin said that he would like to dance with me."

"Young Mr. Ful-fulka?" Mama garbled his name, as she usually did. Benjamin Fuqua and his brother Silas had arrived a year or so ago. He held a quarter-league of land in his own name.

"But certainly, M'grete." She flashed a quick and impish smile over her shoulder towards her daughter, although her hands had never stopped their rhythmical motion, sending the shuttle flashing back and forth. "Since your Papa is not here to withhold his permission, I give it very freely."

Margaret returned the smile. She and her mother had grown ever closer in the years since coming to Texas, united in a gentle but usually fruitless conspiracy to bend Alois Becker towards more sociability with his fellows. Most recently, Mama had also worked to soften or thwart his dictates regarding Margaret and those young single men who had began flocking to the Becker household as soon as Margaret put up her hair and began wearing womanly longer skirts. His horror at suddenly realizing that Margaret had grown tall, as slender as a young willow tree, and gravely pretty – and of an age to marry – was almost comic, if somewhat embarrassing to Margaret. Suddenly, Alois regarded every single man who came to visit his household with wary suspicion, even if they were truly his own friends and had no intentions towards Margaret. But every admiring glance in her direction or word spoken to her, even on the most mundane matter, seemed to inflame his temper. Lately, Margaret was glad that Papa had reason to travel with his wagons, for he had gone into partnership with several merchants in San Felipe and Gonzales to haul goods arrived at the port of Anahuac upcountry, leaving Mama to see to household and social matters.

"How Papa can expect me to marry well yet never be courted or even converse with a young man!" she sighed. "I think Papa just expects a husband for me to grow on one of the apple trees. And that one day, he shall pluck it from the branch, present it to me and say, 'Here, M'grete – a husband for you to marry, this very afternoon.'"

"Your Papa wishes only the best for you," Mama answered. "Like all men, he thinks that only he may make a decision on such matters as affect the family." She smiled again over her shoulder, "I permit him to go on thinking that. It spares his feelings."

"And then you work on him, so that he will do rather what you wish," Margaret said, with another sigh. "But it takes such a long time . . . and the Darst's roof-raising is Saturday."

"Your Papa will allow it," Mama answered serenely. "I will see to that. Everyone will attend; how can we keep ourselves apart? He will see the sense in that. Do not worry, Margaret, he will not be able to keep you as cloistered as a nun. Your Mr. F-fulka may accompany us to the Darsts, of course."

"Thank you, Mama." Margaret bent, and kissed her mother's cheek. She had been seventeen for four months, having put up her hair on her sixteenth birthday. There were always more unmarried and adventurous young men in Texas than there were women of marriageable age. Margaret had begun to lose that conviction that she was destined to marry Schoolmaster Vining. The schoolmaster had passed through Gonzales once or twice with his friends the Menchaca brothers, on his way to Bexar. He had paid a call on the Beckers, although he had not done such in a year or so. Rudi had heard from one friend or another that the Boston schoolteacher in San Felipe had returned to the East, and there was another schoolmaster there now.

Margaret wistfully hoped that he had taken the red Mexican-wool blanket with him to keep him warm in the Eastern winters.

"I think the beans are ready for picking," she said to her mother. "I will go and tend the garden for a while." She took a wide straw hat down from a peg, and tied it over her head. The Texas summer afternoons were brutally hot, but she felt the need to be by herself for a while. Her father had bought several town lots besides the one allotted to him for the family home in Gonzales. He and the men he had hired had built a log house very like one they had lived in at San Felipe, save that it was larger – and of course, the Beckers had all of it to live in for themselves. It sat on a low rise of land a little east of most of the other houses and business concerns. A narrow creek watered what Papa had begun planting as an apple orchard. Most of the sapling trees were still only a little taller than Margaret. An open space between house and orchard was plowed and planted in garden vegetables, corn and squash and row after row of beans. From the veranda of Papa's house, Margaret could see nearly all of Gonzales – split-shake roofs either new and dark or weathered to silvery-grey, interspersed with trees and chimneys. A few threads of smoke rose into the sky; beyond town, a line of darker green trees marked the river. The river, pale green and deceptively placid, ran so deep and swift at Gonzales that it had to be crossed by ferry. Margaret had first grown accustomed to the town, and then to love it, for now it was home, and overflowing with friends. There were days when the sky was a pure, clear blue, arching overhead like a bowl.

In spring, the meadows were starred with flowers, of colors that dazzled eyes with their intensity – pure yellow or yellow and red with dark, coffee-colored centers, lacy clusters of tiny lavender florets, or those dark blue spires stippled with white that some of the other settlers called buffalo clover, or blue-bonnet flower. But now, the flowers had faded in the heat, all but the stubborn pale-yellow mustard, and the green meadows were burned dry by the summer sun, the grass laying brown and lank, unless they lay close to a water course, or a small spring bubbling out from the ground.

"Where are the boys?" Mama asked, and suddenly the shuttle paused in it's ceaseless back and forth journey, "They should be helping with the garden, instead of taking every excuse to play in the woods."

"Benjamin was talking of going hunting along the river today," Margaret answered, "He had seen a large herd of deer, so he and Silas and some of their friends were going. He talked of it to Rudi and I suppose they let Carl tag along."

"Those boys," Mama resumed weaving. "They should take care."

"Don't worry, Mama." Margaret stepped down from the porch. As soon as she moved from the shade, the hot sun struck a harsh blow. "They were going in a party, and they all have rifles and plenty of bullets. Rudi wouldn't let anything happen to Carl."

Her littlest brother had turned ten, just a few weeks ago. He was tall for that age, and so most took him for older. Rudi was tall now also; at fourteen nearly the height of shorter men, although still a stripling next to Papa. Carl was quiet, Rudi outgoing and lively – very different in character although still much alike in looks. Margaret wondered absently why Papa had not taken Rudi with him to Anahuac. She didn't think Rudi particularly minded not going with Papa on that journey, for he would much rather have gone hunting with the older lads and the young men. She looped up the corners of her apron, and tucking them into her waistband, began plucking ripe green beans for supper.

When she straightened from picking beans, she could see her brothers and Benjamin walking towards the house; the two older boys were ebullient, although covered with dust. Rudi had taken off his hunting coat, tying it around his waist by the arms. He and Benjamin carried a long pole over their shoulders, from which hung the carcass of a deer, already roughly cleaned and gutted. Carl followed after, with a large turkey-cock slung over his own shoulder, the head of it swaying limp and loose with every footstep.

"Dinner for tonight, and smoked jerky for winter," Rudi called, as soon as the three had come close enough to the house. He was smiling, jubilant, as if they had just experienced the most wonderful adventure. "And Little Brother made the most amazing shot! You should have seen it, M'grete! They all bet that he couldn't do it, but he did – a wild turkey, gobbling up old corn, clear across the creek it was."

"A regular Leatherstocking, ma'am . . . Miss Margaret," Benjamin added, with enthusiasm. "That's what he is. Natty Bumppo couldn't have bettered it, nor my grandfather in his young days – and he was a champion-shot. They say in the War he shot a British soldier right in the place where his belts crossed at a distance of six hundred yards."

Carl only looked pleased, half-smiling as he ducked his head. Margaret thought it was as if he were unaccustomed to such praise. Perhaps he was, as he certainly got little of it from Papa. Papa had never really warmed to his youngest son, for all of Mama and Margaret's efforts. Carl was still a quiet youth – and Papa often and cruelly upbraided him to his face as an idiot.

Mama's face had lit up, rapturously. "Such clever boys," she exclaimed. "And we thought to have nothing but a little bacon with our dinner tonight. Tomorrow, we will butcher the deer and hang it to smoke. As for the bird, we shall dine like the royalty do tonight and for several nights hereafter." Mama got up from her loom. "Come help me clean and singe it, Carlchen, Rudi – and then fetch water from the creek to clean yourselves with." She collected the boys with a meaningful look, leaving Margaret and Benjamin for a brief moment alone.

Benjamin touched the brim of his hat to her, saying hesitantly, "Miss Margaret . . . did you speak to your parents about dancing with me at the Darst's roof-raising? Have I their permission?"

"Most certainly," Margaret replied, and his countenance lightened immediately. "And you may escort us to the Darsts, as well."

"Thank you, Miss Margaret!" he made as if to kiss her hand as Margaret added wryly, "We will be bringing some dried-apple pies with us and you might have to help us carry them!"

"My duty and pleasure," Benjamin added, looking inordinately pleased with this development. Margaret rather warmed to him then, for he was a handsome young man, clean-shaven but for a generous mustache. Indeed, he was almost as handsome as Schoolmaster Vining had been – only now, Margaret thought with a pang of regret, Benjamin Fuqua was here, and Schoolmaster Vining had returned to his home in the East long since. And she did wish so much that she was not wearing a plain dress, and with a quarter-bushel of green bean pods bundled up in her apron.

"I will call for you on Saturday, then, Miss Margaret."

Chapter 5 – *Under a Dew-spangled Tree*

The Darsts were new-come to town, a family with a son a little younger than Margaret's brother Carl. All summer they had been living in a brush-arbor roofed with tent-canvas, while Jacob Darst and his friends cut and cured timber for their log house. Their home would be constructed as were other houses in Gonzales; a two- or three-room log house with an open breezeway and a generous porch. So temperate was the climate in winter and so hot during the summer that to Margaret it seemed as if all life was lived in the open, only retreating to the shelter of four walls at night, or during those few weeks when the cold wind from the north scoured the land and sunrise revealed the sight of a countryside all hazed over with thick white frost, the colors muted and the bare limbs of trees glittering as if cut from crystal. All that was needed was shade from afternoon's scorching heat and shelter from the ravenous and barely-seen mosquitoes, which descended with a shrill whine when the sun was setting or the air was still, to settle upon bare skin and bite. One of the first weavings Mama had done upon arriving in Gonzales was a length of loosely-woven cotton-thread gauze to cover the windows, and drape over their beds, so that they would not be bitten at night.

After the breathlessly hot summer all lived for the first temperate day of autumn, for then it seemed to Margaret that everything truly revived. More folk had come and settled in Gonzales; more and more of them restless young men searching for trouble and adventure, rather than sober men of family with a wagon full of goods and plans for a settled business. That so many young men had come of late was a matter of worry to Papa and the other settlers of long-standing, for it seemed they were more inclined to hot-headedness and to pick fights with the Mexican governor's officers. Because of this sobriety and serious interests, the Darsts had been particularly welcome.

In the very earliest days of the settlement, there had also been danger from the wild-riding, far-roving Comanche Indians, whose hunting grounds reached far to the south and east of those rivers; the Guadalupe, the Colorado, and the San Antonio, which watered these gentle hills and woodlands. Other tribes – the Tonkawa, the Lipan Apaches and the Karankawa – contested with the Comanche for possession. Gonzales had first been established close to the coast, so perilous had the current location on the Guadalupe River been in the earliest days. There were times when the men of the militia company were out on a long patrol that Mama and Margaret and the other women had put on men's clothing to make it appear to a watcher from a distance that there were plenty of men remaining to defend the village and homes. The little timber blockhouse and fortress with its surrounding earth trench could not now shelter all the folk of town, as it had to do at first. With so many new settlers come in the last year or two, dangers seemed to have passed them by, although there still was peril to those outlying single houses and campments.

That very spring, Colonel DeWitt had written to the military officer commanding the Presidio in Bexar asking for a cannon to defend the fortress. This was willingly granted, although to look at, the cannon was a small thing and hardly used for anything more than to make a loud noise to overawe the Indians. Margaret was secretly convinced that the Comanche and other Indian raiders now posed more of a danger to each other than they did to the settlers and to settlers' horses. Those who owned good bloodstock kept them in a stable at night – a stable with a solid plank door secured by an iron lock. Men both young and old formed the mounted militia company, a company pledged to be ready and able at all times to form within minutes in response to news of an Indian raid. Few men went anywhere beyond the sight of their own roof unarmed. It had been some time since Indians had been bold enough to raid at the edges of town. Still, the sooner that the Darst's house was finished the better. There would be a picnic laid out under the trees by the homesite for when the work was done. Maggie Darst had a quilting frame set up and a quilt-top all pieced together and ready to be sewn, so that women could work on that while men swiftly assembled the house, doing the construction that could best be done by a team of many. It promised to be a fine party – a large gathering, and Margaret's heart lifted, just to think on it.

Sunday dawned fair and mild, with a tantalizing hint of autumnal chill. Margaret and her brothers had barely taken of their morning meal and rushed through the necessary chores when Benjamin arrived, walking from town, carrying a rifle over his shoulder.

"Good morning," he called, cheerfully, "The sun's up and I can hear them working. We'd best hurry, if we want to have the roof up by sundown."

Margaret caught up her best bonnet. She had a needle case and some precious spools of thread brought from the United States in her apron pocket. The boys carried some of Papa's tools – hatchet, drill, shingle-knife, and saw. Rudi had one of Papa's shotguns, not from any fear of danger, with all folk gathered at Darsts; just that they would be walking home well after dark. Three baskets of freshly baked apple pies sat on the table in the breezeway.

Margaret took one in hand, Mama another, and said to Benjamin, "You said you would help with the pies."

"And so I did, but I thought it meant with the eating of them."

They walked briskly, anticipating a joyful gathering of many old friends, and making new ones. Benjamin strode along next to Margaret, and looking sideways at her, said, "It's a fair day for a house-raising, Miss Margaret. Mebbe I am hoping to have one for myself, someday soon. That might be something to look forward towards, wouldn't it?"

"I enjoy such parties," Margaret answered sedately. "Quilting bees and husking bees, and house-risings – for the very enjoyment of the company, and for the joy of seeing something grand accomplished by so many hands."

"Many hands do make the work less irksome," Benjamin answered.

"But to see the walls go up, where there was naught but a pile of planked timbers and then to see the roof being covered in shingles – a home complete and entire, and all in one day, by the hands of friends? That is a wonderful sight, Benjamin, a most wonderful sight. It says so very much about us, that we can do it in a day – all of us, working together to benefit one family."

"Miss Margaret, you wax poetical," Benjamin looked on her with admiration. "'There ain't no flies on us Texicans. We hold to our own.'"

"You are very kind to think so," Margaret returned, thinking that she would be quite pleased to dance with Benjamin, and for him to walk with her. If only Papa could see reason. Every other girl her age in Gonzales had an understanding to marry a particular suitor, if not already married to him. Even Mama had married Papa by the time she was the age that Margaret was now. There were even a few newlywed girls who were younger than Margaret.

The sun had already dried the nighttime dew from the trampled grass around the Darsts' homesite, and tall piles of planked timbers, roughly cut to measure. The meadow with Jacob Darst's two town lots in it where the house would rise was already as busy as an anthill. The rough-shaped stone pilings upon which the house and the verandah would sit had already been placed, as had been the massive sill-beams connecting those which would form the outline and foundation of the house. A young redbud tree had taken root nearby; in the spring, the tree would be covered with dark pink blossoms – a beautiful thing to see from the verandah, which as of yet was nothing more than a row of stone pilings ranged along the front of the foundation pillars. Even within town, Jacob Darst preferred to build in sturdy logs rather than a timber-framed house with walls of hand-sawn lumber planks, as others with houses close to safety in the blockhouse-fortress had chosen to do. In the shade of the largest oak tree, a small distance away, there had been set up a quilting frame, and a table for food, with many rough chairs and stools set around it. A little way farther a large cook-fire had already burned down to grey-flecked red coals. A whole side of beef and two suckling pigs roasted on two huge iron spits mounted over the fire. Little spurts of flame came up from the fire as droplets of fat rendered out of the roasting animals dribbled down on it. Two of the DeWitt's Negro household servants tended the fire and the meats cooking on it.

"I think all of Gonzales will be here today." Benjamin looked around, in complete satisfaction. "Miss Margaret . . . Ma'am Becker. We must get to work – a whole house to build and only a day to do it!"

"I am sure that the men of Gonzales are equal to such a task," Margaret replied, taking from him the basket of pies that he had carried. His fingers covered hers on the basket handle for a brief moment and he whispered with a roguish look on his face,

"May I hope that someday soon, they might build such a house for us?"

"I cannot say," Margaret answered, sedately, but her heart did lift a little. He was amiable, handsome, and had no unfortunate habits such as a taste for strong drink. He was not of German descent, but surely Papa would not hold that against him, and would approve him courting her. Benjamin had a strong affection for her. Margaret knew this with sure instinct, in addition having had several of her "thinks" about the matter of Benjamin Fuqua. She was still not entirely certain if his affections were bent towards her merely because she was pretty and amiable – and one of the few girls of marriageable age available in Gonzales – or that Benjamin felt true affection for herself, valuing her wit and those other qualities which men never seemed to appreciate until upon second and most careful consideration.

"You did not answer him, directly," Mama observed in a soft voice, as they carried the pies towards the table already piled high with bread, cakes, and biscuits, crocks of pickles, and jugs of vinegar shrub and water. "Does he please you, Margaret?"

"He does," Margaret answered, "But what of Papa?"

"If he pleases you," Mama said, in her firmest voice, "I shall assure you of Papa's approval, but only if you are certain of your heart, my dear little duckling."

"I am not certain yet, Mama," Margaret sighed. "But I shall consider his qualities for a little longer before I ask you to intercede with Papa."

"That is good," Mama sounded mollified, "to not decide in haste."

All morning, the new house walls mounted up, taller and taller. Men most particularly skilled with a hatchet or an ax stood at each corner, waiting for the next planked log to be carried up, swiftly cutting the intricate corner notches that locked each log into place, to that log below and to that at right-angles to it. As the walls increased, they mounted up on ladders to do that work. Jesse Davis, the carpenter, whose strength was guided with the skill of a barber-surgeon, and certain others worked with a whip-saw, cutting more planks for the floor, and to construct door and window frames, each man working in a blizzard of chips and sawdust. The smell of fresh-cut wood, and trampled grass mingled with the appealing scent of roasting meats, and now and again the wet-clay odor of lime-cement. Mr. Darst and his friends had cut roughly squared slabs of limestone for a fireplace and chimney-stack, although the upper part of the chimney would be built of twigs, well-plastered on the inside surfaces, which work would progress as soon as the walls were finished. Rudi and Carl, with Davy Darst, and the other boys, helped by holding tools, bringing canteens of cold water so that the men could drink without ceasing from labor. Margaret was again reminded of an anthill, or perhaps a beehive, every bee intent upon its own task. Overhead, the sky was dotted with clouds like handfuls of clean-washed wool ready for the spindle.

"You like watching my house grow," Maggie Darst remarked, in merry tones, as Margaret had been sitting with her needle in hand and an ignored section of quilt in front of her. Margaret was startled – she had not taken a stitch for some little time, so absorbed was she in watching the work advance. Mrs. DeWitt looked faintly disapproving – she was the wife of Colonel DeWitt, whose idea and ambition it was to take up a grant and form a colony in Texas. Mrs. DeWitt and her daughters Naomi and Evaline had joined the women around the quilt frame while her youngest, the baby Minerva, played and chuckled to herself on a blanket spread out in the shade.

"It is a joy to see all of our houses grow, but I lament that we sometimes must labor to do so on the Sabbath!" Sarah DeWitt said, and Maggie Darst answered, "I believe that our Savior makes allowances – and besides, today is no labor, but rather a pleasure. At least Margaret thinks so!"

"I do," Margaret answered, "It is pleasing to watch, and to see how fast your dreams advance."

"My dreams," Maggie laughed, "for living under a solid roof for once – and to have a proper cook fire. Today, I vow, will be the very last day that I bake bread by burying a covered pot in coals at the edge of a bonfire. I only hope that my husband has situated the chimney so that it will draw properly . . . and what a pleasant view of meadows and trees we shall have! And a floor of planks to sweep, instead of packed earth! I have looked forward to this day for months, my friends – months! There was a red sky at dawn this morning; my dear husband swears it portends rain before nightfall. How marvelous if the roof is shingled tight by then, that we might spend a night in shelter."

"There is an art to situating a house," Margaret mused as all the other ladies laughed in knowing sympathy with Maggie Darst. All had lived, at one time or another, in wagons or brush-arbors, in tents or crude cabins made of twigs and mud. "So that all is comfort within, and attractive without . . ."

"There is!" Maggie agreed. "I had heard there were those who have made a study in ancient times, but what a pagan would have to tell us of value . . ."

"My grandfather, back in Pennsylvania – he said that all knowledge is valued, no matter where it came from, or how little sense it might make at first." Margaret finished her thoughts. "There is an art to it all – more than just putting up four walls with a floor beneath and a roof over."

"Of course there is," Mama spoke up. "And that would be that there is a woman in it to make it comfortable!" All the other women around the quilt frame laughed in amity and understanding, although Margaret thought, rebelliously, *No, that is not what I meant. A woman in it can only patch up those mistakes, to cover them over as one covers over a patch in a plastered wall. What if the foundation is not solid, the windows and doors face all the wrong way – and what you look upon from the windows or verandah is all ugliness? Why cannot a house such as this be as fair to live in as our meadows are in spring? Hanging a pretty calico curtain is hardly a remedy!*

She looked out again upon the Darst's house, with the log walls now grown to the height above which men could not lift the logs. Now the men must slide them up plank ramps, assisted by ropes and poles, while the men cutting the notches worked high above, swinging their hatchets and axes as they balanced at the top of a ladder. The work of house-building now went at a slower pace.

"A window each side, to admit the air," Maggie said, happily, and Margaret nodded, for she had noted those places where the log – before the next was lifted atop it – was sawn halfway through in two places, so as to admit a saw-blade. When the walls were complete the men would pound in wedges to hold the logs in place. Then they could easily cut two or three of them through, to make an opening. When the window frame was fitted into the opening in the wall, it would then be securely pegged between frame and log-ends, and the wedges taken out. "Perhaps you may have glass in your windows, someday," she ventured.

Maggie laughed. "My dear, the Mexicans tax simply everything or they would, if that power granted to the government here would ever be enforced scrupulously! I expect we will make do as everyone else does, with oiled paper or scraped cow-gut to admit light, when necessary. How very ingenious we have had to become since arriving here!"

"If we cannot make it ourselves, or bring it with us, then we must then do without," Mama was stitching busily away at the quilt. Since coming to Texas, all of their clothing and much of their other household linen had been made of her own homespun. Mama had woven away at her loom for a greater portion of most days. Machine-woven cloth from the mills of New England or even all the way from old England cost so very much to ship and was taxed at such a rate as to make purchase of it prohibitive. Margaret had one dress – her very best – made from figured calico, which had been smuggled in; all else was of homespun, left plain or dyed in muted colors, as were Papa's and the boy's shirts, trousers, and jackets.

"A gathering of us in our very best clothing does look very odd," Sue Dickinson giggled. "I am thinking of the men; I cannot think of any other place on earth where one might see a man wearing a very proper tailcoat and top hat, but with leather leggings, a sash of silk around his waist with an enormous hunting knife stuck through it, and Mexican spurs on his boots. Do the men newly come here put on such things, hoping to impress? And aren't those whose Eastern clothes have been worn to rags and must wear them by necessity see them find them most comic?"

"I think that the gentleman adapt what is suitable, regardless," Margaret answered. She rather liked Maggie Darst, but was in two minds about Sue Dickinson, pretty and willful, already married even though she was a year younger than Margaret. Sue and her husband, who had a good trade as a skilled blacksmith, had also just arrived in Gonzales. From what Sue had let drop, they had eloped and run away from Tennessee together. Naomi DeWitt had murmured to Margaret that Sue was altogether too bold – and that Sue had stolen Almaron Dickinson away from another girl just as he was about to marry her, back in Tennessee. "She looks at every young man as if he was a sweetmeat and she were wondering how he would taste!" was how Naomi had put it, and Margaret had answered, "Well, she may look, but since she is a married woman, I can't believe she would be wicked enough to try and taste!" and at that, Naomi and Margaret had dissolved into giggles.

Now a ragged cheer went up from the men laboring around the Darst's house, and the women raised their eyes from the quilt-frame.

"It's the first rafter," Margaret observed with interest – two long slender poles lap-jointed together and lifted into place, with their ends anchored into the plate-logs which joined the two parts of the house together. The first rafters overhung the walls just a little – followed by another pair of rafters and another, lifted up by willing hands and pegged into place by the skillful. Then the men began handing up the connecting roof-laths from the ground to those working on top of the walls, and presently the roof stood skeleton-outlined against the deep blue sky, in which the sun climbed higher and higher, only occasionally seeing its light dimmed by an intervening cloud.

"Now, there's a gentleman who's having a lazy day of it," observed Naomi DeWitt. "See – the man in the blue coat."

"Where?" Margaret asked, but she could see him very clearly – although he had his back to her. He was the only man still wearing his coat; all the others had shed theirs and worked in their shirtsleeves; a young man, by the look of what she could see, of a slender and wiry built. He stood by one of the corners of the new house, talking animatedly to the carpenter, Jesse Davis. He had a sketch-pad in his hand and seemed to be making a drawing of how the angles were cut in the logs to lock them close together and make a weather-tight fit.

He looked somehow very familiar, and she said as much to Naomi, who laughed and answered, "He is only just arrived from the East, to be our new schoolteacher. He held a school in San Felipe for a few years. He gave it up to return East for a year or so, but now he has returned. Someone else took his school in San Felipe, so he came here, instead. You might know him, then . . . Mr. Horace –"

"Schoolmaster Vining!" Margaret said with a gasp, for of course it was he, it could be no other, and her heart leapt up in rejoicing. The witch-woman's prophecy would be fulfilled, she had seen the future right, and all those tentative hopes she had of Benjamin Fuqua's attachment were merely a passing fancy, a tinsel dream. "Then I must say hello. He was our teacher, and a very fine one, when we first arrived in Texas." She set down her needle and sprang up from her chair, hardly noticing the meaningful look which Mama exchanged with Mrs. DeWitt, or the amusement on the face of Naomi and Sue Dickinson.

"You should take a pitcher of shrub and offer him a taste, and to your young man, also," Mama suggested, "for the day is warm, and he may be glad of a drink."

Margaret took up a pitcher of vinegar shrub, made from the juice of berries and sweetened with honey, and a tin cup, and hastened towards the house where it appeared now that the pace of work had slackened somewhat, now that the roof was up and all but shingled. The men and boys were tired, their shirts soaked with sweat and powdered thick with sawdust, yet they were exuberant, having won such a campaign against time and that natural wilderness which favored house timbers remaining as unfelled trees. Most of them had set down their tools and drifted purposely towards the cook-fire and the tables of pies and breads, or cast themselves down to rest in the shade. Rudi and Davy Darst were tossing a ball in a game of catch, still full of energy. Margaret walked with purpose towards the man in the blue coat still speaking animatedly with Mr. Davis, his back towards her.

At the moment when she came close, Mr. Davis looked past him, straightened his lackadaisical posture, and exclaimed, "Miss Margaret, you're an angel unlooked for, as we perish from thirst!"

"My mother said I should bring you some shrub," Margaret answered, and the man in the blue coat turned, abruptly. It was indeed Schoolmaster Vining; as his eyes fell upon her, his own face lit with astonishment and another expression which Margaret could not at first recognize.

"Miss Becker?" He sounded disbelieving, "Miss Becker . . . it is you, is it not? I . . . perceive that you have grown, and into being a most lovely young lady."

"It has been five years since Mr. Vining taught Carl and me at the school in San Felipe," Margaret said sedately, by way of explaining to Mr. Davis. We were sorry to leave – or at least I was, for he was a very good teacher, especially for my brother. Would you care for some berry shrub?" Gravely she poured out a cupful for the carpenter and then for Schoolmaster Vining, who took it from her hands as if it were made of gold and set with precious stones.

"Ambrosial," was all he said, after drinking deep, but he looked upon her as if he were slightly stunned. "I see that . . . all of your family has prospered since leaving San Felipe, Miss Becker."

"And you, also? I was told that you had left Texas and returned to Boston," Margaret answered, "and only now are come here to teach school again."

"I am . . . I was. A short visit to my family. But I consider my home to be here, always." He held the empty cup in his hands, until Margaret took it from him, whereupon he seemed startled. "Thank you, Miss Becker. Most refreshing. Yes, I will open a school again soon. Colonel DeWitt has been most cordial. I will have a house for myself and my books very shortly."

"Do you still have as many books as you did in San Felipe?" Margaret asked, for she was curious, and Schoolmaster Vining flashed a quick nervous smile.

"More, even. My collection is ever-growing, Miss Becker," he answered, and Margaret felt obliged to explain to Mr. Davis.

"Mr. Vining had more books then I had ever seen. Even my Opa Heinrich back in Pennsylvania did not have so many."

"A man has his own tools," Mr. Davis drawled, "and a schoolmaster has books as his tools." He shot a humorous look at Schoolmaster Vining, "Good thing, too, for he is as unhandy with my sort of tools as any man I had ever met."

"True," Schoolmaster Vining agreed, "I was interested in the clever way in which these logs are cut so that each fits together so closely one could barely slip a piece of paper between. It is an exercise in practical geometry, as well as in the science of architectural construction . . . but alas, when I attempted it . . . well, to my good fortune there were no permanent injuries to myself or anyone with the misfortune to be standing close by."

"Like to have scared me out of a year's growth," Mr. Davis retorted, "I have plain never seen a person so unhandy with a hatchet. When you marry, Race – it will have to be your wife who cuts the firewood. If she has any sense she will not let you anywhere near a cord of wood."

"We all have our own skills," Schoolmaster Vining returned, equably. "While a wise man would stick to what he knows best, he should try other skills now and again." He looked at Margaret again, with that slightly dazed expression. "I have an interest in architecture, Miss Vining – possessing Vitruvius' ten books on the subject. He was a practical man as well as a scholar . . . so it only seemed fitting."

"But dangerous to bystanders," Mr. Davis added, as Schoolmaster Vining seemed once again to have lost the trail of his thoughts.

"I took an interest in the building," Margaret offered, suddenly feeling rather shy herself. "I was curious about how best to build a home which is comfortable and pleasant to live in. It seemed to me that there should be a practical reason – as well as for a pleasing appearance – in putting a window there, or a door here."

"There usually is," Mr. Davis answered, cheerfully, "but I don't bother my head about it. I just cut the wood and do what the householder tells me."

"The design of houses interests you, Miss Becker? Perhaps you should read Vitruvius on domestic structures," Schoolmaster Vining ventured. "He had a great many sensible observations. I do recall that you read very well, and being that my copy is an English translation, it should not present any difficulty for you. I would be honored to make the loan of it to you."

Mr. Davis made a snorting sound, which sounded uncommonly like strangled laughter, as Margaret said, "I should like to do that, sir." Then, sensing that perhaps she tarried a little too long at her errand, she turned and walked back towards the other women gathered around the quilting frame.

As she went, she heard Mr. Davis say with rough and humorous affection, "Close your mouth, Race, 'afore you catch too many flies!" and Schoolmaster Vining exclaiming, "Jesse, I have seen a goddess walking on this earth, the likeness of the fair Helen, I would swear an oath to it. She was but a child in San Felipe – I had no idea that she would blossom into such a rare flower!"

And Margaret was immediately content and confident in her heart, for now she knew without a doubt that the prophecy would be fulfilled. Schoolmaster Vining had looked upon her as a woman, not a schoolgirl, and been dazzled by that sight.

They feasted on the cooked meats in the early afternoon, and since it was late summer, the heat had alleviated to a degree so that the men could return to work in applying shingles to the steep angle of the roof and the shallower one of the verandah. The sky curdled with clouds, more and more of it being hid as the men worked on. A little breeze kicked up, rustling the leaves of the oak tree over their heads and causing the canvas awning to flap wildly.

"There's a storm blowing in," Jesse Davis sniffed at the air. "I can smell the rain on the wind – ladies, if you still have stitching to do, I think you should move your quilting traps to the shelter of the house – we have shingled half the roof and most of the verandah, which should provide some shelter."

"It is merely one of our Texas thunderstorms," Margaret murmured to Sue, who looked rather apprehensive. There was already a peculiar greenish cast to the sky. Out towards the west, there was a towering mound of cloud moving slowly towards them, flat and iron-grey on the bottom but as white as cotton at the top where the sunshine made it shimmer as if threads of mica were embedded within. Mama and Maggie Darst each picked up an end of the light quilt frame and carried it towards the house – which, as Jesse Davis had assured them, was now partially roofed. Indeed, all but one room and part of the verandah offered shelter, the remainder being open to the sky although the pace of work on that unfinished portion had increased.

Margaret and Sue, with the DeWitt's daughters following, carried those sewing baskets and chairs which were left, forlorn without the clutter of the quilting frame. At a word from their mistress, the DeWitt's servants followed, carrying the table, with the remains of the meal upon it. The quilt-frame fitted within the wholly-roofed room and the table under that completed part of the verandah. The servants set it down, just as the first grumble of thunder announced the approaching storm. There was sufficient room to shelter all from the rain, which now Margaret could see as a thin grey veil, hanging from the bottom of the storm. She watched from the breezeway, from which a goodly view to the west could be had, thinking that Mr. Darst had chosen his homesite well. The house sat tall on a slight rise above the street, and in coming days would be every bit as comfortable as Maggie Darst had hoped. A white-hot bolt of lightning crackled from the top down through the bottom of the cloud-column, a flash of unbearably bright light for the merest portion of a second, followed almost at once by a crash of thunder.

"Two miles and coming on fast," commented Jesse Davis. "You boys better come down off the roof now," he called. The ragged chorus of hammering ceased; two or three men clambered down between the unfinished roof-rafters, hanging by their hands before dropping to the floor. Margaret, looking around for her brothers, saw them sitting on the edge of the verandah with Davy Darst and some other lads, swinging their heels and watching the approaching storm with keen enjoyment, as if it were a special kind of firework exhibition created for their own amusement.

"Another half an hour, we'd have had it all done," Silas Fuqua complained, and his brother shook his head.

"Heck, Si – the storm will be over in half an hour, then we can get back to work." There was a queer kind of sizzle and popping noise, sounding as if it came from directly over their heads. Margaret knew instantly that was the sound of lightning dangerously close by. The crash of thunder shook the half-finished house, and Sue Dickinson cried out, more in surprise than terror. Margaret's own heart felt as if it had leapt into her throat. She stepped back, almost involuntarily, and bumped against another person, one standing close behind her.

"Miss Becker – you are not . . . I beg your pardon," Schoolmaster Vining made as if he would put his arm around her shoulders, as if to shelter her, but then thought better of it, as she looked into his face.

"I am not frightened, sir," she answered, quickly, "but it is . . . noisy, isn't it?"

"Surely it is," he agreed, "but moving fast, so I believe it will be soon over." He remained standing close to her though, as they watched the trees lining the riverbanks sway in a sudden gust of wind. The sound of rain came to them, first as a gentle rustle amid the tree leaves and upon the grass – then like a rattle of drums on the new-made roof just over their heads. It fell in a sheet of water from the eaves and splattered up as mud from the bare ground.

"A fine test of a new roof," remarked Mr. Darst. Jesse Davis answered, "It could have waited until tonight, I'm thinking."

"But it might then have spoiled the dancing," Sue Dickinson exclaimed, and her husband laughed fondly; big Almaron Dickinson with one of his well-muscled blacksmith's arms around her waist.

"It wouldn't dare," he said, and Margaret saw how they exchanged so affectionate a look – no, pretty Sue might look now and again at a man, but her heart belonged entirely to her husband. It might also be very pleasant, she thought with wistful envy, to stand so, in the shelter of a mans' arms – better even to stand so with Horace Vining! She wondered if he were going to be at the dancing when the roof was finished and all of the Darst's few pieces of furniture ceremoniously carried inside.

"Shall you be staying for dancing, after the house is finished?" she asked, on an impulse, and Horace Vining smiled at her, answering, "Of a certainty, Miss Becker – as long as you assure me that I will be able to dance a figure or two with you!"

From across the open breezeway she saw Benjamin, standing with his brother and some of their friends; he was looking towards her, and their eyes met. It seemed to Margaret that Benjamin had something of an expression of resignation on his face as he looked at her – as if he sensed that his chance to woo her had come and gone.

The rain passed on, the storm-clouds hastening eastwards leaving the tree leaves adorned with clear pendants of raindrops as the sun emerged. Margaret stepped down from the verandah: the rain had settled the dust and wakened a rich smell of wet hay from the trampled grass. Under the young redbud tree she paused and stood for a moment. Schoolmaster Vining had followed after her, and they stood facing each other for a breathless moment. An errant gust of wind rustled the tree branches, and a glittering rain of diamond droplets pattered to the ground, a shower of bright rain in full sunshine. Margaret caught her breath, as she looked at the schoolmaster's face. There was an effortless, voiceless communication between them, an acknowledgement that something of great importance to each was about to happen. As if in a dream, he reached for her hand, and raising it to his lips, he kissed it very gently.

Margaret said, "On my twelfth birthday, a witch-woman promised me that I would marry you, and that we would be happy."

"We will," answered Schoolmaster Vining. "Of that I am sure."

Chapter 7 – *The Marriage of True Minds*

Margaret and Horace Vining were married by Mr. Ponton, the alcalde of Gonzales – as the Mexicans termed the mayor-magistrate – some six months after Horace's arrival in Gonzales. To Margaret's secret relief, Papa gave his consent willingly, although it seemed to Margaret that he did so in a fit of absent-mindedness, as if he were already thinking of something else.

"He likes you, my love," Margaret confided to her affianced, on one of those afternoons when he came to spend time with her and to take the evening meal with the family after the school day was done. They sat very close, on the same long rawhide-covered settle, in the breezeway of the Becker's log house, the regular thump-thumping of Mama's shuttle and batten as she sat at her loom being a discreet reminder that they were properly chaperoned. "A relief, for I was afraid that Papa would find fault with any man who dared to come courting! Papa is a bit of a domestic tyrant, if you have noticed."

"Thank god for that, Daisy-mine," Horace Vining laughed. "I did indeed notice all of that and more. I would have hated to have asked for your hand without his liking and approval – he is quite formidable." His face sobered. "He may be all bluster, but for those of us of a quiet and retiring nature that can be an insurmountable obstacle. I am glad that he approves."

"He would not have frightened you off?" Margaret asked, and Horace's arm around her tightened most affectionately. He had taken to calling her Daisy, as a pet name, explaining that Marguerite was a fancy name for a plain garden daisy, and she reminded him of one, especially when she wore a white house-cap over her yellow hair. Margaret had at last begin using the name that his friends called him by – Race – when he confessed that he hated the name of Horace and preferred the shortening of it.

"No such fear! I would have done such labor for you as would have made Jacob's years of service to Laban appear a small thing in comparison – but I am everlastingly grateful that I did not have to brave his bad-temper . . . at least, no more than strictly necessary." Margaret laid her head against his shoulder, utterly content. They would marry the following week: her bride's chest was packed full. She had already begun making a home for the two of them in a tiny house of sawn lumber on what was called St. Francis Street. The town-lot opposite was intended to have a public school built upon it, when the fortunes of the colony permitted. In the meantime, her husband would hold his classes on the porch of their house or under the large oak tree in front of it, much as he had in San Felipe. She had already brought many of her own possessions, as well as gifts from Mama and from their friends, to make the tiny cabin truly a home. She walked from the Becker home to his every day to sweep the floor and to dust. It pleased her yet more that Race Vining was a fastidious man, so there was no need for her to wage an unrelenting campaign against bachelor squalor. The only male vanity he possessed – aside from his collection of books and a rather daintier wardrobe than most men in Gonzales sported – was a powerfully-built black gelding named Bucephalus. Race had bought him from a horse trader in San Antonio and already had won so many scratch races with him that no one who had ever seen Bucephalus run would bet against him more than once. Bucephalus, with a white blaze on his nose, had a great fondness for apples, so Margaret had made friends with him almost at once. She had been also been touched and amused to see that Race still possessed the red-wool blanket of Mama's weaving that she and Carl had brought to him as their gift.

"Papa is quite contented regarding our marriage," Margaret ventured at last. "But Carl is unhappy that I will be going from Papa's roof to yours."

"Is he?" Race answered, thoughtfully. "I had not noticed particularly. Has he said anything to you at all?"

"No, not to anyone, which is why I know that he is unhappy. If he would talk at all, he would talk to me," Margaret answered. "And he has been silent. Carl wraps silence around him and he goes away to the woods."

"I have taught many boys of his age in my time – some of them sulky and sullen, and others bright and biddable," Race mused, "and all of them, especially the ones of the age that your brother is – think to themselves that the world revolves around them. He'll outgrow it, Daisy-mine. After all, you are not going that far away."

"It's not that." Margaret relished again the thought that in acquiring a husband she was also gaining a sensible and rational confidant. "But in some ways, because of the years between us and Papa's disfavor of him, he is almost my own child. It's very curious and rather sad, Race. Papa favors Rudi, over and above Carl and me. We all love Rudi – he is a good boy, even if I think Papa favors him to excess. But Mama favors Carl, and I stand almost as a second to Mama. I have always thought of him as almost my own baby, and now that I am marrying you, I might seem to be abandoning him."

"No, you are not, Daisy-mine," Race answered, in robust confidence. "Your little brother only fears that this change in your station will mean a great change in his world – and it will not, for he will be as welcome in my house as he is to your father's, and possibly something more. I am a fourth son, and borne by my father's third wife to boot, so I am in perfect sympathy with your forlorn little brother."

"You were not cast out to find your own way in the world?" Margaret asked, in swift concern and Race laughed, comfortably.

"No, never think that! My father was a loving and attentive parent; it's just that my oldest brother is his heir. I was spoiled and petted all my life, as my mother was the wife of his elder years. There is one more thing that you should know, Daisy-mine. I will most likely not make old bones." He looked down at her, held in the curve of his arm, and Margaret felt her heart turn over in her breast. This was what the witch-woman had hinted at, and what Edwina had mentioned all those years ago in San Felipe. "My mother was consumptive – and the doctors say that I have inherited that weakness. I was in poor health from my schooldays on, so I was taught at home. I am fit now, and have been for some years, but the consumption or some other affliction of the lungs waits for me around every corner unless I take the greatest of care. Good health is not the natural and ordinary thing for me, as it is for you or your brothers or most other men; rather, it is doled out to me in teaspoonfuls. In time, my ration of it will run short. I thought you should know, Daisy-mine – I am most likely to leave you in sorrow and wearing widow-black."

"No, you will not," Margaret answered swiftly. "Yes, our time together may be short, or at any rate, no longer than that which others have. But other men do die untimely, especially here. They die of an Indian's arrow, or of the ague or accident, leaving wives and children. There is no telling what the future may hold, my dear love, and so I am content and happy for today."

"*Carpe diem,*" Race chuckled, approvingly. "Live for the day, Daisy-mine?"

"Yes," Margaret answered. *Ten years and one, the witch-woman promised her, all those years ago.* Silently, Margaret vowed to herself to make every day of every one of those years happy ones for herself and Race. And then she folded up the thought of the witch-woman's prophecy, folded it very small and tucked in into a corner of her mind, resolved to not think on it ever again, until she had to.

To the very end of her life, Margaret held the memory of the first years of her marriage to Race Vining as a precious talisman, as a time of quiet and undiluted happiness for them both, sharing their tiny but comfortable rough-sawn lumber house. She braided a rag rug for the floor and planted a vegetable garden on the sunward side of it, a garden in which she worked in the cool mornings of the spring and fall while Race taught school on the porch and Bucephalus dozed in the little paddock in back of the house. Her brothers were his pupils again for a time; Carl more than Rudi, for Papa often took

Rudi with him on his errands. Gonzales town grew, by fits and starts around them, as more and more settlers finished houses and establishments on their town lots. The tiny cannon on the gate-tower of the fortress built of standing timbers watched over theirs and other households, and the green river slipped past, noiselessly. Sometimes she and her husband spent their evenings reading by the firelight. She often felt that her schooldays had only just begun; there was so much she learned, now that she shared his library, as well as his life and name. She had read all of Vitruvius, guided by her husband; how marvelous, to have it explained how so many things worked, by a Roman engineer nearly two millennia in his grave! Race talked of Boston with such affection that she almost began to feel that she knew it as well as she did Gonzales, and of his family – the three older brothers, and the clever bluestocking spinster sister, the townhouse in a quiet cobbled street where he had lived as a boy. There was such a wide world out there – and brought to her through her husband's library and the talk of his friends.

At other times, friends came to visit; Esteban Menchaca rode in from San Antonio with his brother and their friend Juan Seguin who was tall and courtly in the Spanish fashion, the son of the *Alcalde* of Bexar, but who also shared the same political leanings. They desired to see Mexico as a federation of states, each more or less self-governing; indeed Esteban and Juan, and men like the neighboring entrepreneur Don Martin de Leon at Victoria, all hoped that Texas would soon form a separate state from Coahuila, with a provincial capital at Bexar instead of Monclova. They would stay up very late at night talking of this, of politics and history, of the natural rights of man and the lawful obligations of a government. Of an evening, sometimes Almaron Dickinson came to continue his study of Spanish and practice speaking the language with Esteban and Juan. Margaret would sit quietly in a corner, her sewing in her hands, and listening.

One afternoon, some time after Race and Margaret were wed, Esteban and Juan arrived with another man, an American. Their friend was a burly square-jawed man with long sideburns, who spoke English adorned with a soft Kentucky drawl, who bowed over her hand with the grace of a polished courtier. He was dressed in Mexican-style coat and trousers, a monstrously large sheathed hunting knife thrust through the silk sash at his waist.

"Here is Señor Bouey, who is affianced to wed the daughter of the Governor Veramendi," Esteban said, the very first time he introduced Margaret to him. Señor Bouey swept off his hat, at once.

"I am honored to make your acquaintance, ma'am," he said simply. His hands were very strong; looking down at them, Margaret noticed that they were knotted with old injuries and seamed with scars, as if he had often used his fists. He was not handsome, she thought, until she looked up into his eyes and felt something of a magnetic sense of attraction. That evening, she sat in the corner as was her habit, listening to the men converse; now and again her eyes went to Señor Bouey, whom the other men addressed familiarly as Jaime or James. There was something in him which drew their regard and hers as well, with the irresistible force of a needle pointing towards a lump of iron. She looked towards him and was utterly taken back when he met her gaze so boldly that it was almost as if he was touching her – touching her in a way that only Race had the right to do. Margaret dropped her eyes, aware that she was flushing pink. But in departing, the disturbing Señor Bouey was all gentle courtesy, which unsettled Margaret even farther.

That night in bed, she said to Race, "That friend of Estebans', who is to marry the governor's daughter – I am sorry for her. I think he is a scoundrel."

"Well, yes, he is," Race chuckled. "Famously so. Also a land-speculator, a slave-runner and bare-knuckle brawler; a mad, bad, and dangerous man altogether – and that is just what his friends acknowledge freely of him. What his enemies say, I can't even repeat to you, Daisy-mine; but scoundrel though he is, he has never been discourteous to a woman of any degree, or failed to defend an unarmed man against unjust attack."

"Famous?" Margaret asked, much puzzled.

"Of a certainty – had not you ever heard of James Bowie?"

"Oh." Margaret considered. "Yes, I had heard of him, but such tall tales as my brothers heard from other boys. Based on what they said I would have expected him to have been ten or fifteen feet tall with his hunting knife in his teeth and dragging a defeated enemy under each arm." Her husband laughed, in great amusement while Margaret thought how that was one of the delights of marriage, to laugh with each other, alone and privily in bed, under the patterned ivory and blue bedcover that Mama had woven especially for Margaret's bride chest. "So that was indeed the famous Mr. Bowie. What brings him now to Texas, do you think?"

"Land," her husband answered, wryly. "Of which Texas has in plenty – if you can wrest it first from the government in Mexico City, and secondly from the Comanche Indians. Bowie has none, and desires more; better yet, he desires a higher place in society, which heretofore has been denied him. I expect that is why he courted Veramendi's daughter – though I suppose it could be love on both their parts. Yet, he will be a son-in-law to a rich and able family, which will be to his advantage, even if no more new American settlers are allowed to purchase land or take up grants." His voice trailed off in the darkness. From the closed shutters on one side of their house, pale silver moonlight crept through the cracks, tracing a white shadow on the floor by the foot of their bed.

"Is that what is happening?" Margaret asked, with a sudden chill of foreboding. "There has been talk – Papa said something of the sort – about how the Mexican authorities seem suddenly less hospitable."

"Dearest Daisy," Race's arms tightened around her. "Yes, I see matters much the same as your father does. The first faint flickering of chill in their welcome of American settlers, and a sad thing it is, too. Settlers like Austin's and the Colonel's – all came at an invitation and with every honest inducement and in good faith to settle their un-peopled lands. With our labor and our lives we worked to build our houses and fight back the Indians, to do what they could not induce their own folk to do . . . that is, to venture into the farthest wilderness and make our homes there. We came in answer to their invitation and intent, to establish a buffer state against the marauding Indians and perhaps the French, with their own imperial ambitions, and make the northern border safer yet . . . and to demonstrate the manner of a responsible government chosen by free men. We are two different peoples, yet wanting much of the same things in life. Alas, my love – it seems that the central government in Mexico City has waked to the realization that they have invited a tiger over the door, to sup freely and settle by their fire – and now are regretting their former agreement.

"Which is frustrating," Race added, "for all of this land's beauty and utility – for them, the farthest reaches of Texas, beyond the Nueces and San Antonio was a desert until we came. Of no use at all, or so they thought. And having made the desert bloom, without much outlay of effort on their own – it strikes me, Daisy, that a central government out of touch and accustomed to wielding autocratic and unaccountable authority . . . would be like the Crown, attempting to rein in the rebellious Colonies and control them to the Crown's advantage. I do not like to dwell overmuch on this parallel, Daisy-mine, and have not voiced such of my misgivings which have come to me to any but my closest and dearest, but it seems to me that a crisis may soon come to pass."

Margaret felt the swell of his chest as he sighed, and thought, *How very clever of my dear husband, to see and sense such matters long before others see the same!*

"What do you see, of our future?" she asked, in some apprehension. Just this very day, her regular monthly course had not begun when it should – and Margaret kept a careful accounting of such, for she hoped for a child. Several children, if such were granted to her and Race.

"I think there is a curse upon me, being obsessed by history and the accounts of the deeds of great men," Race answered at last. "When I was a boy, I loved to hear the accounts of my kin – who were soldiers or some such, in the Revolution. I used to wonder at their tales and envy them their opportunities to perform such brave deeds . . ."

He fell silent, and at last, Margaret asked, "Why should you think that a curse, my love?"

"Because I fear that I may be asked to live in such times," he answered, in bleak and despairing tones. "To experience them at firsthand; I am a schoolteacher, Daisy-mine. I love peace and my books and a quiet life. I have never wanted to be involved in great things, only to read of them, at a safe remove and a long while afterwards. I want nothing to do with great men! If a trial is to come for us – my greatest fear is that I will be revealed as having nothing of greatness myself."

"Fear not," Margaret drew her husband towards her. "You are all the man that I want, and should such a trial as you fear come upon us . . . then I expect that we shall muddle our way through, day to day. You could never be less than an honorable man, in my eyes and in the eyes of your friends."

Race sighed deeply, and kissed her forehead, answering, "Every day, I pray that such a cup will pass from us, but between those hotheads and *filibusteros* newly arrived from the United States and the naked ambition of certain fools and factions in Mexico City – in the worst of times, I fear that we may have to drink deeply of it. Go to sleep, Daisy-mine. It is only my darkest fears speaking, now that I am married most lovingly to you."

Long afterwards, when she considered those happy years, Margaret wondered if that was the moment when the serpent first slithered into her perfect Eden, for even though their life continued much as before, her husband's words made her aware of that which was beyond the boundaries of her sight and experience. Very shortly after that conversation, Race received a letter from Boston telling him that his father and one of his brothers had died suddenly. It was necessary for him to return to Boston for some months to assist his surviving brothers in settling their affairs. Margaret nerved herself to accompany him, for she dreaded the thought of traveling all that way – but mercifully he did not ask that of her.

"'Twill be a flying visit, Daisy-mine." he explained. "No pleasure jaunt, I am afraid."

"I might like to know your family," she ventured wistfully, and it seemed that her husband's expression was suddenly a little bleaker.

"I don't know why you would wish to, Daisy-mine," he answered. "My brothers are good company, but their wives are very dull, and snobbish at that. I do not think you would enjoy their company in the least."

So he was away for some months in the East and Margaret missed him dreadfully. On his return, bringing another box of books and a tiny keepsake portrait of himself, painted on ivory – *'So that you might have it to keep me in your memory, should I ever be parted from you again, Daisy-mine'* – all seemed to slip into the same rhythm as it had before. But if she still lived in an Eden, she was reminded of how illusory and temporary such boundaries could be on the afternoon that Carl came running down St. Francis Street from the direction of Smith's store. It was early spring; the wildflowers were just beginning to adorn the meadows and hillsides.

"M'grete, you must come with me at once," he gasped. "Mr. Smith and Rudi have just come from Anahuac – but without Papa! Papa was arrested, and is being held prisoner by the commander of the Mexican garrison, Colonel Bradburn! Mama does not know what to do!"

"Oh, my God!" Margaret caught up her wide-brimmed hat and called to Race, who had been reading peacefully in the breezeway.

He set aside his book, saying, "Here, lad – catch your breath. Where did this news come from? Why has your father been arrested? Did Rudi say?"

"He was accused of helping to smuggle tobacco," Carl answered, readily. "Rudi says that Papa did nothing of the sort, they only loaded goods for Mr. Smith. Papa was in a great fury, saying that he knew nothing of tobacco that the soldiers found when they searched . . . please come, M'grete! Mama and Rudi are waiting at the Smiths!"

"We'll both come," Race answered, decisively. "Not to fear, lad. We are coming at once!" The two of them followed Carl towards Smith's general emporium – a plank-walled building next to their house, on the corner of St. Louis and St. John Streets. Mama and Rudi waited for them, much distraught, in the tiny office at the back of the store. Stephen Smith, the proprietor of the store and Alois Becker's sometime partner, walked up and down, as if he were in such a fury that only constant motion assuaged his anger.

". . . such an accusation!" he was saying. "I cannot brook such a lack of trust, that Mr. Becker would so readily assume my guilt in this matter!"

Oh, dear, Margaret thought, with a sinking feeling in the pit of her stomach. Her eyes met Races' – *It sounds as if Papa has quarreled again. What will it mean for Mama and the boys, when Papa loses his temper with everyone – and Mama cannot smooth it over!*

"What has happened," Race asked, in a deliberately calm voice. "No, don't speak at once; just one at a time. What crime has my father-in-law been accused of committing?"

"Of smuggling tobacco," Rudi answered, impatiently. "Concealed in a bale of dry goods. "

He looked wrathfully on Stephen Smith, who paused in his up-and-down pacing, and snapped, "Don't you start with that slander, boy! I have no need to cheat the Mexicans out of their duties on imported goods, and even less desire to try it under the very nose of that officious turncoat!"

"Enough, Rudi," Mama said, in German. "Then, what happened to your Papa – tell us, now in English, without further angering Mr. Smith."

Rudi looked from adult to adult, abashed at Mama's rebuke. "Colonel Bradburn's men searched the wagon after it was loaded, and Papa was very angry when they found the tobacco in a little cask – and what he said made Colonel Bradburn's soldiers so angry that they arrested him and confiscated the wagon and cargo. They put him in a little room with no windows and said he would have to stay until the duty was paid. Papa refused to pay."

"And I did not pay either!" Stephen Smith seemed just as angry as Papa would have been. "The tobacco was not goods that I had ordered, nor did I give anyone instructions to conceal it. Partner or not, that damned stubborn Dutchman can stay in the customhouse lockup until he takes back his intemperate words to me!"

Race cleared his throat, saying, "If you had no part in concealing the tobacco, and if Father Becker swears he did not, might I suggest that someone at Anahuac or perhaps among the ship's crew concealed the cask among your goods, intending to retrieve it at a later time? You did not place a heavy guard upon the wagon, once away from the harbor, did you?"

"No need," Stephen Smith answered, somewhat mollified. It looked to Margaret that he had not considered that a third party might have concealed smuggled tobacco among his merchandise, trusting to opportunity to retrieve it. "We have never had to guard against anything other than Indian raiders."

"What can you do then for my husband?" Mama asked directly, and Stephen Smith looked at the floorboards.

"I cannot return to Anahuac until next month – my business and my family require that I remain here – and my former regard for Mr. Becker is now at such a low degree, I care no more for his imprisonment than I would for a stranger. If it weren't for my part-share in the confiscated goods, I would not care even that little. I am sorry."

"Then I will go, Margaret and I with Rudi," Race answered. "And if need be, hire a lawyer. I might even pay such fines and duties as are required," and he smiled with special affection at Mama and Margaret. "And do anything within my power to restore my father-in-law to the bosom of his family. I am certain that once released – and if the matter came about as I suspected – that you and Father Becker will resume your mutual good regard."

"I doubt that, very much," Stephen Smith answered with considerable heat, "for accusations were made by him which I found to be intolerable. Nonetheless, I wish you the best – and I will go as far as make the loan of a trap and a pair of team animals for the journey."

Race and Margaret, and her family made their departure from Smith's store and walked to their house, making plans for the journey all the while. It would be but a swift and short excursion, in Smith's light trap – to San Felipe and thence to Anahuac. They would stay with friends and such acquaintances as Alois Becker had made in driving his wagons between such settlements along the road. Although Margaret did not particularly relish the thought of the discomforts attendant on a journey, she looked forward to traveling with her husband and to see how San Felipe had prospered in the years since her father had brought them away from there. And to see the ocean – Margaret had never seen the ocean, although Race laughed at her and allowed that she wouldn't see it from Anahuac either, since the town sat at the head of a long bay, which reached far inland.

Rudi was their guide, once they reached Anahuac – dusty and tired, and Margaret felt rather ill, she thought from the swaying of the trap. Still, there was a fresh salt-smell borne on the breeze, and gulls – great white birds with long wings, wheeling almost motionless on the updrafts, and crying in shrill voices. The customs-house citadel was a tall-walled brick enclosure on a tall bluff which overlooked harbor and town, huddled at its foot like a shawl spread out. They had a room at the boarding house where Alois Becker had always stayed before. Since her father had always insisted on a modicum of comfort, the boarding house was not the squalid and noisy place which many of the inns and boarding houses were.

"You should go see Lawyer Jack," the landlord advised. Anahuac was a small town and even newer than Gonzales, and rumors of Colonel Bradburn's high hand and ill-temper were everywhere. "Patrick Jack is the name he goes by. He's an ornery young cuss, argue the hinder leg off a donkey, and that partner of his – young Buck – he will back you up in a corner and lecture you about anything under the sun until you fair want to cut your own throat or his, just to get him to stop yammering at you. Rumor is that he abandoned a wife, back in the States. I think she left him, just to get away from being talked at, night and day."

"One might have any number of better reasons for abandoning a wife," Race said, with unaccustomed bleakness of expression, and the landlord hastily reassured him.

"Both of them good lawyers, though, Pat and Buck – they'll latch onto a case as if they were bulldogs, with jaws that just won't let go."

"Sounds like just the men we need," Race allowed, and something of cheer came back into his voice.

The landlord laughed, sourly, "As a bonus, they've both good reason to dislike Bradburn – could you believe that sorry piece o' dog squeeze Bradburn is an American, born 'n bred? Matter o'fact – Pat and Buck hate him so much they may just take your case merely for the pleasure of going after him yet again."

"Although, I don't know if that is a good thing or not," Race confessed to Margaret, as they were walking along the street towards Lawyer Jack's place of business. "I have a brother and other kin who are guilty of committing the practice of law. If they are moved to embrace your grievance as if it were their own – that is well and good, but to have special cause to make an enemy of the very person you are appealing to? That is a perilous affair to bring to law, Daisy-mine."

"Perhaps we should search for another lawyer," Margaret suggested, and Race shrugged,

"The only lawyers in this town are Americans. I don't imagine that any of the rest of them are any more qualified, or bear less of a grudge against Bradburn and the Mexican customs authority." He smiled very wryly at Margaret, as they walked side by side. "We'll chance our luck . . . after all, with your father's temper, they might very well let him go just to have a little peace and quiet. I don't image that he has been the easiest of prisoners."

"But if they send him to Mexico to be judged by their harsh law!"

Margaret shivered suddenly, and Race answered, "Mexico is so very disrupted with fighting between factions these days – between the Centralists and the Federalists – I do not think they would bother over the matter of a small cask of tobacco, of which the ownership is in considerable doubt. Bradburn is an American by birth. I cannot see that he would be so lost to reason and logic by long service to the Mexicans that he would condemn a fellow American to an unjust trial in a far place. Especially if the ownership of the tobacco can be cast in sufficient doubt."

"Tell me where a man earns his bread, and I will tell you where his loyalty lies," Margaret retorted, and Race smiled in great pleasure, "That has the sound of a quote, Daisy-mine, although I cannot bring to mind the source. But you are correct; Bradburn is in service to a master. With luck, he might be brought to consider matters of justice and proof of intent." He shrugged. "Well, let us see what Lawyer Jack and his single-minded partner can accomplish on your father's behalf."

They found Lawyer Jack's office easily enough, for the name of his practice and that of his partner were painted on a shingle hanging over the door, a door which stood open to the breeze that came off the bay and the salt-marsh beyond: *Jack & Travis, Att'ys at Law.*

"A very small and select firm, I see," Race observed quietly to Margaret, as he and Lawyer Jack conducted her to a comfortable chair – the only one in the room which was not piled with books, files of paper, or collections of clothing and horse-tack. Patrick Jack was a stocky and able-looking man, with dark eyebrows – the left one quirked upwards towards his hairline, which lent him a quizzical look. He had the grace to look apologetic about the untidy office, as his partner hastily removed a stack of newspapers from another chair. Jack's fellow lawyer was much younger, seeming hardly older than Margaret. He was thin and fine-featured, and might have been thought handsome but for the nervous intensity of his gaze, and the blunt directness of his speech.

"I hear you have come to Anahuac to see about the release of Becker the Dutchman," he said at once, even before Race could introduce himself and explain their purpose. Patrick Jack closed his eyes, briefly, in an expression of mild exasperation.

"Courtesy, Buck, courtesies before business," he murmured in reproof, as Race answered, "Yes, that is indeed our purpose – and we have come a long way in pursuit of it so we are amenable to dispensing with further courtesies. We understand that Colonel Bradburn has charged him with smuggling tobacco, and that my father-in-law refuses to pay the duty on it, as he insists that the tobacco is not actually his property."

"It was found hidden in his wagon," Buck Travis answered, "and therefore assumed by Colonel Bradburn to be his property." He himself took a chair, a wooden one, straddling the chair backwards and resting his arms and chin on the back frame. "We might make a case that the tobacco in question was the property of another party . . ."

"We have considered that aspect," Race nodded, "and truthfully we do not wish to quibble over who owns the tobacco, although I suspect that my father-in-law would sooner spend the rest of his days in confinement rather than compromise a single iota in this matter. We, however, being rather more open to practicalities, would rather pay the duties on the tobacco and whatever fine has been imposed, and secure his release – with, I might add, a minimum of fuss. We had hoped that you were in a position to do so."

"That might be within the scope of our capability," Patrick Jack admitted, thoughtfully scratching his jaw, and Buck Travis frowned.

"It is the principal of the thing, sir – these duties on goods are imposed illegally by a corrupt government – by god, sir, an injustice such as this ought to be resisted, and by any means at our command!"

"Perhaps another time," Race answered, while Patrick Jack cleared his throat, warningly. "We do not want to make a grand gesture over principals, gentleman. We wish only to free my father-in-law and his goods from detainment. The rest is a fight I will gratefully leave to others."

"The fight may come to you, sir!" Buck Travis retorted, and his eyes were lit with the gleam of single-minded conviction. "At a time and in a place not of your choosing! What will you do then? Will you tamely submit to tyranny, or . . ."

"Never!" Race insisted, and Margaret could see that he was exasperated – and so was Patrick Jack.

She placed her hand on Race's arm, just as Patrick Jack held up his own hand, saying, "Enough, Buck. Enough politics for the day; our client has made it plain what his desires in this matter are. Our duty with regard to this matter is quite plain. Mr. Vining and I will endeavor to meet with Colonel Bradburn within the hour."

"I thank you, sir," Race answered, grateful to have the discussion steered back to where it belonged. He and Margaret rose. "My wife will wait for us at the boarding house." He nodded to Patrick Jack, and to Buck Travis, who once rebuked now appeared to be brooding and barely acknowledged their departure.

"What an uncomfortable young man," Margaret said, as they walked away. "Is he one of those fire-eaters that you spoke of once when you talked to me of your fears for the future?" Race nodded in assent, and with a touch of laughter.

"Yes, Daisy-mine. Not him specifically, but of his ilk, men who thirst to perform great deeds and are fixed upon a grandiloquent vision of themselves. Very discomforting for the rest of us, I assure you!"

Lawyer Jack worked a miracle, as far as Margaret was concerned; by a combination of his skill and Race's money, Papa, his wagon, and his goods were released that very day. Papa seemed hardly grateful for those efforts taken on his behalf, and refused to accept the disputed cask of tobacco. He put it out of the wagon, and stood with arms folded stubbornly.

"What would I want with such a thing?" Race exclaimed, and Papa answered,

"I care nothing, for it is not my property."

Race gave the tobacco to Jack and his partner in part-payment for his fee. Margaret thought the matter was resolved to everyone's satisfaction. But when they returned to Gonzales – and she was happy to be at home once again, since her courses still had not resumed, and she thought she might be with child – Papa quarreled again with Mr. Smith, and with Colonel DeWitt, who took Mr. Smith's part. Before Margaret even was certain of her pregnancy, Papa had resolved to leave Gonzales. In a fit of temper, he sold his town lots, the house and orchard. Dry-eyed, Mama disassembled her loom, speaking not a word of reproach to Papa. To Margaret's secret horror, when Papa first spoke of his intentions, he appeared to think that Race and Margaret would also accompany them.

"We'll build a house big enough for us all," Papa said, "or a separate house adjoining. As a married man, you may have as large a property as you like – as long as it matches to mine."

Race shook his head, sounding at least properly regretful, "Father Becker, I remain quite content here, with my school and my pupils. I do not look to disrupt our lives or theirs, so I must decline your invitation."

"Very well, as you think best." Papa frowned, his face thunderous.

It seemed to Margaret there was a chill in his manner to Race from that time on. When she mentioned this to him, her husband answered, "Daisy-mine, your father is an autocrat in the old Roman manner, whose children, when they marry, do not go forth from the shelter of his roof. Instead, they bring their wives and husbands under his. Lord help them when Rudi and Carl establish their own households. Father Becker will be loath to allow them leave."

Hearing this, Margaret shivered a little. "I am glad that you did not wish to join him. Mama did not want to go from here, but she did not say a word against his plans."

"She would not," Race agreed. "Your mother is the most nearly perfect domestic saint that I have ever known. Still, I am sorry that you will be deprived of her company, Daisy-mine. Your father's choices seem to put sorrows in the path of everyone else but himself."

Within weeks of his decision to depart, Papa had found a tract in the hills, far to the north on the Upper Colorado, in a tiny settlement called Waterloo. Before mid-summer, he and the boys had packed the wagons, even going so far as to dig up the smallest of the apple trees and wrap their roots in damp burlap sacking.

"I think your father has discovered how best to get along with his neighbors," Race observed to Margaret, as they stood on the porch of their house, and sadly watched Papa's wagons vanish around the curve of the road leading north.

"How is that?" Margaret asked, and Race gently patted the swell of her belly.

"He gets along with them best if he has no neighbors at all."

Margaret couldn't bring herself to laugh at that observation, as she had begun to suspect that it was all too sadly true.

Chapter 7 – *Clouds on a Distant Horizon*

The baby was born in the fall – to Margaret's intense relief, after the heat of summer had broken. The child was a boy, plump and fair, and sweet-tempered, and she was not terribly discommoded by his birth. In fact, she was pleasantly surprised at how easily the birthing went, and how swift her recovery. "We'll name him Horace Jamison Vining," her husband said, upon admiring the infant for the first time, and Margaret said, "I thought you did not like the name Horace?"

Race looked slightly embarrassed, "No, I still do not – but it is a tradition in my family, for the first son to be named for his father."

Margaret laughed, "I thought it was the Spanish who held to custom so strictly – yet Esteban Menchaca did not name his firstborn after himself!" Race's friend from San Antonio, Esteban Menchaca, had married the year before. His wife had produced a son, in mid-summer. So entranced was Esteban with his child that he had only visited Gonzales once or twice since.

"Esteban named little Porfirio after his grandfather," Race answered, mirthfully "So he still hews to tradition, Daisy-mine."

"I wish that he still came to visit, out of all your friends." Margaret wrapped a fold of blanket more firmly around her child, "I think he is the most like to you, in nature – a brother of the mind, rather than the blood. And I wish that Papa had not seen fit to remove so far that it presents such a difficulty in visiting." She had two letters from Mama, since departing – letters which were cheerful, in the main. Waterloo, so tiny it could barely even be called a settlement but rather a handful of log huts and hunter's camps, was in a most beautiful situation – even more beautiful than Gonzales, wrote Mama. The country around their new home was a land of gentle hills, set about with groves of tall green oak and pecan and cypress trees. Papa had replanted the apple trees almost at once, even before completing the house. The only thing that Mama regretted about their new home was that there was no school, so that the boys were in danger of forgetting everything they had learned in the scant years they had attended.

"I do not think your brothers were cut out for scholarship, Daisy-mine," Race had said in consoling tones, when Margaret had shared that portion of the letter with him. "I was able to teach them just enough of letters and numbers so that if they ever want to learn more, they will be able to read it for themselves. Some lads are just not cut out for a schoolroom."

Winter passed, those days with a chill wind blowing out of the north and the ground grey-hazed with frost in those mornings which had been especially cold. One cold night in the following spring, when it had rained and then frozen hard as the rain continued to fall, Margaret and Race woke in the morning to find a world entirely glazed in ice – each tiny twig and leaf encased in a layer of clear crystal. When a breeze stirred the branches they rattled, and as soon as the sun came up it began to melt, tiny shards of ice dropping from the leaves, with perfect print of the leaf fleetingly preserved – until it melted also. Race looked upon this extraordinary sight and taking in a breath of the frigid air, began to cough.

"Mine own dear Daisy, this is exactly the climate I came to Texas to escape! I'll settle before a warm fire with a good book, until all this melts and the summer birds come back to sing."

That spring, it seemed to Margaret that there was a change in the air. At first, she thought it was to do with being with child again. But no, it was not just her; Sue Dickinson was with child also. Benjamin Fuqua – who had at once tentatively courted her – had married also, a neighbor girl named Nancy King. His brother Silas's son and his wife's younger brother became fast friends: Galba Fuqua and young Will King were boys of thirteen, pupils in Race's classes. Margaret liked the two boys; wistfully, they reminded her of Carl, especially Will who was also reserved and sweet-natured. More and more of the inner town lots were built up, with houses and businesses. Now there was another general store, a tavern, and Almaron Dickinson and his good friend George Kimble had even collaborated in building a hat manufactury. The town seemed burgeoning with families – babies, small children and lively youths alike. Margaret enjoyed the society and company of her friends enormously. How Mama would have enjoyed this, she mused to herself time and again, wondering if Mama bore any resentment for being made to give up a settled life for the wilderness. Margaret also wondered if Mama regretted having such a strong affection for Papa. As Margaret herself grew older, she realized that she would not have been inclined to be so patient with Papa as Mama was.

But troubles loomed and Margaret could not deny them. It was as ominous as storm clouds on a far horizon, rumors and whispers instead of thunder grumbling at a distance. There was trouble in Anahuac, much of which could be blamed on the officious Colonel Bradburn. Not only did he take a martinet's stance when it came to enforcing every prerogative to the letter when it came to levying duties on all imports by ship into Texas, but it began to emerge that the soldiers of his garrison were of an unsavory sort; the sweepings of the nearest jailhouse was how they were usually described. In the early summer of 1832, four of them attempted the vilest kind of attack on the wife of a settler, on a farm near Anahuac. While her husband was at work in his fields, the four soldiers went to the house and barred the door from the inside, but the woman screamed and fought back with such energy that neighbors heard and came to her rescue. Three escaped, but the ringleader was caught – he suffered hot tar poured upon him, and then feathers out of the woman's own household feather bed. The soldier was paraded, riding on a rail back to the customs-house citadel. Colonel Bradburn was told by angry settlers that others of his soldiers would have the same or worse done to them if captured after committing that or any other such crime.

"Alas, the common run of Mexican soldiers are much the same dregs," Diego Menchaca commented with regret when he heard of this, one summer evening when he and Juan Seguin had come to visit. "No, this does not surprise me, although such men can become paladins when bravely led. The noble Lopez de Santa Anna is one such." Diego's face lit in hero-worship, "Now, he is a true patriot! He will be the savior of Mexico. He upholds our Constitution, and the rights of the common man!"

"Why should we put our trust in a single man," Juan Seguin drawled. "One man who may be corrupted by power, as this Coronel Bradburn has been. You put an intolerable burden upon your gallant hero, Diego. I would trust rather the wisdom of a party of good men, even if they sometimes take an intolerably long time to come to an agreement on anything."

"Alas, men like our General Washington are rare," Race acknowledged. "A soldier pure in motive, without excessive ambition . . ."

"Lopez de Santa Anna is such," Diego insisted. "I believe it with all my heart!" He believed it so firmly that shortly afterwards, he went to Mexico and joined a regiment under Lopez de Santa Anna's command. Esteban wrote, in wry acknowledgement that there was no commission available in that regiment for a man of good blood but no money, so Diego served as a common soldier, but his abilities were such that he advanced to a sergeant's rank very rapidly.

It did not surprise Margaret or Race in the least to hear that Lawyer Jack's partner, Buck Travis, was a ringleader in the party moving against Colonel Bradburn – nor did it astound them in the least when Buck Travis was ordered locked up in the citadel's brick kiln for two months.

"I would wager that he hectored his guards unceasingly, and that was why they let him go at last," Race said when they heard of his release. But the troubles continued in Anahuac. Bradburn and a handful of his officers would eventually be driven from his command there. In Mexico, the vicious conflict between factions would end with the man whom Diego Menchaca thought the finest and most noble soldier in all Mexico, Lopez de Santa Anna, turning his back on his former principles and rejecting the Constitution of 1824. Wiser men than Diego had considered Lopez de Santa Anna a true friend of liberty, and being firm in his support of a federation of Mexican states. When he made himself into a dictator over all of Mexico, others beside Margaret saw the skies darkening. From then on, Margaret sensed that every day brought the hovering shadows a little closer. The Gonzales Rangers, the town militia – in which all men of age and fitness, including Race – held membership, performed on their drill days with special attention to the perfection of their exercise and marksmanship

But every day also brought to Margaret such personal happiness and fulfillment: John Henry, her second child was born that summer, as handsome and tranquil as his brother Horace, and with much the same ease. The care of two children, one an infant and the other just beginning to toddle around in his short baby dress, made much work for her, and she no longer had the leisure to sit of an evening and read her husband's books, or pay as much mind to the talk in her parlor.

In the summer of the following year, an epidemic of the dreaded cholera stalked the countryside and the crowded streets of cities and towns. Margaret would have barely known of this – the cholera bypassed Gonzales, so far out in the country, away from the mephitic vapors and crowds of the larger cities and settlements – save for hearing conversation outside in the breezeway one afternoon, as she was setting a baking of bread to rise. She did not worry, for John Henry was asleep in his cradle and Race was watching Horace. But she emerged from the house anyway to see if the person Race was talking to warranted hospitality, to find James Bowie with Horace sitting on his knee gurgling with laughter as he toyed with the hilt of Mr. Bowie's huge brass-backed hunting knife.

"Miz Vining." Mr. Bowie made as if to rise, but Margaret said, "Oh, pray continue as you were, sir. It amuses the little one so much."

"Gladly." Mr. Bowie sank back into his chair and smiled a rather charmingly gentle smile – an expression which sat oddly on his blunt features. "A fine little boy, Miz Vining, Race. You are to be mightily envied."

Race beamed, proudly; Margaret winced, as Horace began chewing with slobbery enjoyment on the metal pommel of that great, deadly knife itself. "I fear that he is cutting teeth," she said, and made as if to take him into the house, but Mr. Bowie stayed her hand, saying, "No, Miz Vining, he ain't doing no harm. Fact is, that may be the most soothing purpose this ol' knife of mine was ever put to . . . inn't it, boy?" He bounced Horace on his knee, smiling at him with such indulgence that the child laughed gleefully and leaned into Mr. Bowie's embrace with the same exuberant affection that he did with his parents.

"I see that you now have gained yet another faithful follower!" Race observed. "The pity of it, he is hardly taller than that knife of yours."

"Yes, be some years afore he'd be of any good riding out into the Llano, huntin' for silver mines an' such." Mr. Bowie leaned back in the rawhide and wickerwork chair, settling Horace onto his chest. It seemed to Margaret that very briefly, his eyes were bright with grief suppressed. "M' wife and I were blessed with chirren, but ours . . . perished with her."

"I am so sorry," Margaret said, and recollected the talk of him – that he, the dangerous rogue with the equally dangerous past, had indeed married the gently-born daughter of the former governor.

"My fren's brought me word. She died of the cholera just six months past, when I was in Louisiana and sick to death myself," he said with such honest simplicity that Margaret thought that very likely he had loved the daughter of Veramendi, at least in a portion for herself, and not entirely for the riches and connections that she brought as part of her marriage. "I'd like to die myself when I heard of it," he added, starkly. She pitied him, at that moment. If one knew exactly how long, if one could meter out the years and the days of perfect happiness allotted, one would not be distracted and spend those days pursuing other errands, thinking carelessly that there would always be enough time.

"I am so sorry," Margaret said again. "Let him settle to sleep upon you, if you do not find that so familiar, but let me bring you a cloth. He has a delicate stomach and sometimes becomes sick without any warning." She cringed at the thought of Horace vomiting onto Mr. Bowie's elegant waistcoat. What a repayment that would be for his indulgence! She rushed inside to fetch a clean rag, and when she had returned, Bowie and Race were back to discussing politics again – the matter of forming a local committees of public safety. Such committees had begun sprouting up all over the American settlements.

"Thank'e kindly, Miz Vining," he said, in an aside, as she tucked the rag into the neck of Horace's baby dress, and he smiled a fond and somewhat bashful smile. "Cute little ticks, ain't they? I reckon that's why they have to be – so we pore fools go soft and let 'em grow out of being sich a bother."

"Thank you for indulging him," Margaret replied. From inside the house as she worked the bread dough into loaves, she occasionally looked out, shaking her head at the very incongruity of that sight – her son, fast asleep in the lap of one so famous as a violent and brawling scoundrel! *We mothers make allowances also*, she mused – *and forgive almost anything of one who is good with our children!* The voices of the men floated inside.

"All I'm sayin' Race . . . just knowin' that certain of us are meetin' an' talking 'bout all this. It won't go over right well." That was Bowie's gravelly Kentucky drawl. Margaret pricked up her ears. "It might turn out to be right dangerous – an' something that a man with a family oughta consider."

"But it is our right to take action with regard to our own governance!" Race answered, heatedly. "Even more so, with a wife and family – for their future and happiness, their security and safety, even – it would be no less my right than yours!"

"You mebbe right but that ain't how the regular Mexes will see it. You an' your Yankee frien's, you'all are thinkin' American . . . have a town meet, a convocation, gather up ever-one who is galled sore, and talk it out . . . an' ever-one goes home happy, an' the *ayuntimayo*, an' the governor, they don' care, thet back in America it's they way we ben' doin' things, ever since we slung the British out. But I ben' sayin' an' sayin' – you best go careful, since the Mexes don't work that way. They have a gov'ment on top, mebbe the head man, he changes out ever oncet in a while . . . an' then, they got the most folks down at th' bottom. I am tellin' you straight-out, when the folk on th' bottom starts holdin' a meetin' of the kind y'all are talking 'bout, then the Mexes look on it askance. They'll be thinking rebellion, an' sedition an' god knows what. They ain't real used to seein' the folk thinkin' they have a right to any say-so . . . even folk like Lorenzo de Zavala an his'n."

"I did not think you were one of the Peace party," Race said, in what sounded like disappointed reproof.

Mr. Bowie sounded impatient, when he answered, "No, and I ain't no *Centralista*, neither. I'm jus' sayin' that when y'all go through with this, the Mexes ain't gonna look too kindly on it. You'd bes' be prepared."

"I don't know how they could read sedition and treason in our concerns," Race insisted. "After all – we were promised that we could keep to our way of doing things, when we first came to settle here. Why is this any different?"

"They hol' to a constitution jes' like the one we lived under before y'all first came here," Mr. Bowie answered. "Truth to tell, didn' seem much difference a'tall in the politics of it at first. But there's a difference in the way mos' Mex big chiefs see the common folk – and I don't think they'll take kindly to y'all's way of doing things now. I'm jist sayin', Race – take it as a warning – if they see it as a fightin' matter an' it's my opinion they will – then you and those of your party might have to finish the fight they start."

"I pray every night it will not come to it through my own actions. I don't wish a fight." To Margaret's ears, her husband sounded as if he feared that very thing.

"It don't matter none," Mr. Bowie answered. "You mayn't want a fight, but the fight may want you, regardless."

By the time Horace was four and nearly old enough to be taught his letters and Baby Johnny a toddler, what Mr. Bowie feared came to pass. The whole of Texas, the American colonies which Margaret had thought of since childhood as a veritable Garden of Eden, had devolved into a welter of unrest and disputation. Mr. Austin, who had ever been the strongest, most authoritative voice in favor of accommodation with the Mexican government, went to Mexico City to plead the cause for Texas to separate from Coahuila and to allow the colonists the same degree of freedom to organize their own affairs as they had enjoyed at the beginning. The sober and responsible citizens in Gonzales and Mina and farther east began to form Committees of Safety, as rumors flew that thousands more Mexican troops would be dispatched to Texas. People feared that such troops might be of the same foul cut of cloth as those who had been sent to garrison Anahuac. Poor Mr. Austin was arrested and imprisoned in Mexico City for more than a year before being allowed to return to Texas. Meanwhile, Colonel DeWitt, who was of the same sympathies, went to the territorial capital of Monclova, bound on the same kind of errand, and perished there most unexpectedly of the cholera. Feelings ran very high against the Centralists, and Margaret understood that in San Felipe the American settlers were open about wishing to separate from Mexico. General Lopez de Santa Anna, who had appeared to be the noble and patriotic soldier, fervently upholding the 1824 Constitution, had cynically reversed himself now that he scaled the pinnacle of national authority.

"A Caesar," Race said bitterly, as they spoke in bed one night. "Or worse – veiling naked ambition in the robes of republican sympathies! All who believed in him as a Constitutionalist – have been deceived, Daisy-mine. He often compared himself to Napoleon. How apt that boast now appears! Napoleon was once a soldier of the Republic, and once he rose to the highest power in France, he cast aside what he represented to be his ideals and became an Emperor, using his skill as a commander and the love of his legions as a means of conquering the civilized world. I fear for us, Daisy-mine

– not just for our little family or our gathering of friends, but all of the settlements."

"We are of a proud and independent getting," Margaret answered, hoping to comfort her husband. "Accustomed to the frontier and those places which we have made our home for how many years? And we have friends and champions – surely that does count for something? Napoleon was a man of old Europe. Our sons, our friends and our brothers are of the new world, brave and true and tried against the hazards of the frontier. And there are those among us, Americans and Mexicans alike, who are reasonable, and do not wish a war which would risk destroying us all."

"I fear that they may be outnumbered by those who carelessly rush ahead without consideration," Race sighed. In the darkness, he turned, and drew her closer to him. "I feel sometimes that we are living in a box of dry tinder, waiting for a spark to fall."

"It has not fallen yet," Margaret reminded him. She settled against his chest, feeling the quiet beat of his heart against her ear. "And it may not – and if it does, we have each other, the boys, and our home. Sleep now, my love."

"I will," he answered, but Margaret thought he lay awake for a long time.

In the end, the spark that Race so feared fell without warning, early in September – and it fell in a place that Margaret would not have expected. On that afternoon, she left Johnny sleeping in the middle of their bed. The voices of Race's pupils reciting the multiplication tables reminded her of the monotonous droning of cicadas. She put on her bonnet and took Horace by the hand.

"I'm going to Zumwalt's," she whispered to Race, as she passed by him standing in front of his class for the day. "The molasses crock is empty, and I need a paper of black thread." He nodded to her, understanding, and Margaret recalled how she and Edwina had whispered together in the back row when she was twelve years old and dreamed of marrying the young schoolmaster. She walked briskly along St. Francis Street, in the direction of the river, running deep and pale green between high banks. Horace skipped along beside her, now slower and now faster. She turned at St. James, walking now towards the civic plazas that described a broad cross across the middle of Gonzales. Interspersed with gardens and trees, outbuildings and corrals, many of the inner town blocks closest to the river had been entirely filled up – houses and businesses like Mr. Zumwalt's and Mr. Eggleston's stores, Sowell's smithy and the Turner Hotel, and the tavern that Benjamin Fuqua had opened. The summer heat had abated somewhat: Margaret was certain that autumn was her favorite time of year, when the oak leaves began to be touched with the color of bronze and copper, and frost crunched on the grass of a morning.

"Mama, there's some sojers," Horace remarked, as they came up to Zumwalt's emporium. Half a dozen Mexican soldiers, in their colorful coats and tall shakos stood at ease in the street or before the door, as if waiting on someone or something. "What're they doing here?"

"Just passing through on their way to Goliad or Copano, I expect." Margaret answered. In spite of rumors, Margaret had never had cause to be nervous of those soldiers from the garrison at Bexar who now and again passed through Gonzales. No one there had ever been given cause to complain of their conduct. Anyway, there were only five or six, and a mule-cart piled high with their gear, waiting patiently. They parted respectfully before her; the one standing closest to the door even smiled at Horace and patted his head. They all looked very young, none of them taller than Margaret and very brown of skin – of that lower class which was mostly Indian blood. Margaret knew of the elaborate gradations of caste and color among the Mexicans; Esteban had gone to much trouble to enlighten her regarding this, which she found appalling and had said so, at which Esteban had pointed out how Americans had done the same with regard to Negro slaves.

Zumwalt's store was dim inside, for lack of windows and for all the crates and barrels of goods piled up inside. The doors were propped open to admit customers and the fresh air. Margaret inhaled – she loved the way the store smelled; redolent with the scent of coffee, of ripening cheeses, of beeswax and lamp oil, flat boxes of dried fruit, and the dusty smell of burlap sacks, all overlaid with the faint odor of the cut lumber that the store had been built from, not all that long ago. There were half a dozen people in the store, all of them of her acquaintance save another Mexican soldier in the same uniform as the soldiers waiting outside. He was looking over the merchandise as if he were deciding what to buy. Margaret wondered if he were also searching for smuggled goods; he certainly looked bad-tempered about something, not like those cheerful boys waiting outside. The soldier was taller, and also fairer of skin – with marks of rank on his sleeves, so he must be in charge of the others. She nodded to Jesse McCoy, the town sheriff, and waited patiently for Adam Zumwalt to finish measuring out a length of homespun wool for Mrs. McCoy. There was a step at the door, and Will Arrington stepped through the doorway, laughing over his shoulder as he exchanged remarks with someone outside.

Jesse McCoy moved towards the doorway, saying, "Will, I've a question for you . . ." and just as he stepped past the Mexican soldier, the soldier turned and brought the butt of his rifle down on Jesse's head, once and twice again, as if he were chopping a tree to the ground. Jesse McCoy crumpled to the floor, blood pouring from his head. Margaret gasped in horror, and Mrs. McCoy shrieked. The violence came as swiftly as a thunderclap from a clear blue sky, so incredible that all within Zumwalt's store stood frozen in place by the very horror and suddenness of it, disbelieving and unable to react as the soldier slung his rifle sling over his shoulder, and stalked out of the store without another word. There was a quick rattle of Spanish from the street outside, as Mrs. McCoy went to her knees beside her husband, begging, "Oh, help him – for he is bleeding so!"

At Margaret's side, Horace began to cry. It was the young alcalde of Gonzales, Andrew Ponton, with whom Will Arrington had been outside laughing in the instant that Jesse McCoy had been struck to the ground.

Will and Andrew rushed inside, Andrew exclaiming in disbelief, "What did he do, to be struck so savagely?"

"Send for a doctor, I beg you!" Mrs. McCoy pleaded, taking her husband's gory head onto her lap, as Adam Zumwalt and Margaret answered at once and together, "There was nothing done – he was attacked for no reason . . . no words, no exchange of words . . . I saw nothing of a provocation!"

"Lives he still?" Will asked, with no little urgency, as Margaret knelt beside Mrs. McCoy.

"He does," Margaret answered, for Mr. McCoy was moving and groaning a little, although the wounds on his head still put forth copious amounts of blood. It seemed he had only been struck insensible for a bare moment. "But ask Dr. Miller to come at once." Will hurried away, while Andrew and Adam Zumwalt and the others within the store, all of whom had seen what had happened, murmured uneasily together.

"What – has it come to this, that our loyalty and respect should be abused so?" Adam Zumwalt asked, with quiet anger. "That one of us should be attacked by one of their minions and beaten bloody for no reason – and in full view of all?"

"It seems," answered Andrew Ponton, with careful judiciousness, his face pale with shock, "that such qualities count for nothing, now that the *Centralistas* have complete control." He might have said more, but at that moment Will returned with Dr. Miller. Mr. McCoy was sitting up by then, groaning as his wife daubed carefully at the blood. Margaret bought her molasses and thread, and walked home carrying Horace for most of the way, for the child was so frightened and distressed by what he had seen at Zumwalts' that he whimpered and dragged at her hand until she finally boosted him up onto her hip.

By suppertime, the news of Mr. McCoy's beating was all over town, and being discussed by grave-faced men and apprehensive women. A few, like Dr. Miller and Race, thought it a momentary aberration, a fit of inexplicable violence on the part of a single man; that a written complaint to Colonel Ugartechea, the commander of the garrison in Bexar, was a perfectly justified response. Others, such as Almaron Dickinson, were outraged to the point of talking rashly about how a military dictatorship was about to be established, that Mr. McCoy's savage beating was just a harbinger. Others whispered ominously about rebellion against Mexican authority in the event of military law being the new law of the land – but without exception, all in Gonzales were distressed and horrified. Andrew Ponton counseled patience, as did Dr. Miller. Within weeks, all were reassured by a letter from Colonel Ugartechea, insisting that he had no orders or intention of sending soldiers to Gonzales, that such tales were merely rumors.

"Colonel Ugartechea is, I fear, a *Centralista* – and not one inclined to look with favor upon American settlers," Andrew Ponton confided to Race, during one of those evenings when Race and his friends sat on the porch, smoking and talking over the news. "He has never had much of a garrison at Bexar – but he at least allowed Seguin's militia to go to Monclova to the aid of the Federalists."

"His arm was twisted mightily," Almaron Dickinson observed with sardonic humor. "But my friend Ramon Musquiz tells me that his garrison has been reinforced over the summer. He now has two hundred cavalry at his command. The Colonel is in a much better position to talk peace out of one side of his mouth to us, and war out of the other to his superiors."

"What would it benefit Mexico, to institute martial law against us?" Dr. Miller asked reasonably, and drew deep on his pipe. "For to Mexico, this is the farthest frontier. They never could get more than a bare handful of their own people to settle on the land. They have made an honest bargain with us and our duty is to abide by the terms."

"They've changed the terms of the agreement, Doctor," Almaron Dickinson answered, glowering. "And changed them so many times I think our misgivings are justified."

"As may very well be," the doctor answered, "but we still benefit from them, is it so? And it strikes me that to act intemperately regarding the matter of Ugartechea's enlarged garrison poses another danger."

"And what might that be?" Almaron asked. Dr. Miller was an early settler in Gonzales and had served fearlessly in the Gonzales Rangers for many years. Of all in Gonzales he was the most outspoken for conciliation. He had the respect of those who did not agree with him, for he was a principled and thoughtful man.

"I am thinking as a tactician, mind you." The doctor pointed the stem of his pipe at Almaron. "It occurs to me that we must avoid giving Ugartechea any reason to declare martial law against us. We must not respond to a deliberate provocation, for then we would appear to be in the wrong. We should delay and delay, hold our tempers – and obey the laws as stated."

"Ah . . . but if he cares nothing for the appearance of wrong or right – what then?" Race asked, and the doctor sighed, deeply.

"I do not know. But we should consider that any action of the Colonel's may be an attempt to stampede us into an unconsidered action and one to our disadvantage. Was it not Napoleon – the real one, not Lopez de Santa Anna – who advised that anger should never go farther up than your chin?"

Margaret, listening with her sewing in her hands, considered this a very fair and thoughtful piece of advice. She thought that Race and the others considered it wisdom also. Alas, within days Almaron Dickinson was proved correct; Colonel Ugartechea was talking peace out of one side of his mouth to them, and war out of the other to his superiors in Mexico.

"I had it from Will Arrington, who had it straight from the messenger from Goliad. Now will you believe me?" In the middle of the day, Almaron Dickinson had come straight from his place of business, tight-lipped with anger. Race had hastily dismissed his pupils for the day, as a meeting of the militia had been called for at once. "General Cos had landed at Matagorda with a force of five hundred men and is marching towards Bexar. They say that he intends to drive all of the American settlers out of Texas and that he carries eight-hundred sets of chains and shackles, intending to drag certain of us back to Mexico for trial and execution. So much for conciliation," Almaron snarled, "Chains, Race. Chains and shackles, as are fit for slaves – how is that for provocation?"

"'Tis not so deep as a well nor so wide as a church-door, but 'tis enough, 'twill serve," Race answered, grimly. "You'll get no argument from me – we were deceived in Colonel Ugartechea, deceived most willingly. But I would still advise that we consider our response with care."

"We'll not have much time to consider that," Almaron said, and he was clenching and unclenching his fists as they talked, "for Andrew has also received a message from Bexar. They want the cannon back. Ugartechea has already dispatched a fatigue party with a wagon to come and take it back to his garrison. They'll be here in a day or two – they will use it against us, I'll be bound – disarm us and make us helpless to resist their rule!"

"The cannon?" Race exclaimed in disbelief. "That useless little thing? By God, Almaron, it's only good for starting a horse race with. They must have a hundred spiked six-pounders rusting away in their armory. Why bother with this one?"

Almaron was shaking his head, "Oh, it could be repaired easily enough. Fill in the old touch-hole and drill a new one. Smithwick, or Sowell and I could do it. Stay a moment." Almaron looked suddenly sober. "Race, is this their manner of provoking us, the way that the doctor warned us of? That we should resist and give them an excuse thereby to impose martial law?"

"With Cos marching towards Bexar, what use have they for a pretense?" Race answered, his face set stern and proud. "The die has been cast, Almaron. The other militia companies in the settlements must come to our aid if we ask for it. They must, or wait for the shackles to be put on their own wrists!"

Chapter 8 – *One Little Cannon*

Margaret took the boys and walked over to the Darsts, after Race shrugged into his coat and hurried away to the militia meeting. She found Sue Dickinson already there, with little Angelina; they let the children play together on the floor of the breezeway. Maggie Darst was baking bread, and Sue had brought her knitting basket. Davy Darst, all of fourteen and nearly grown, had already gone to the militia meeting with his father.

"What do you suppose they will decide?" Sue asked, as Margaret brought out her own mending.

"They will take a vote on what to do," she answered, "return the cannon, as Colonel Ugartechea asked, or not. I think the answer they will decide upon is 'not.' And then, therefore, they will need to talk about what to do next."

"And then?" Sue asked, and Maggie Darst was also looking at her, as if she wished to know. *How curious, to be considered as some kind of oracle, merely because she listened to the men talk, and her husband talked to her.*

"I don't know," Margaret answered. "I expect they will stall while they send for help from the other settlements. My husband thinks that help will come, for even Mr. Austin has come around to agree with the War Party."

"And no wonder," Maggie Darst said, with indignation. "To be arrested and imprisoned for years, for asking no more than was our right to ask for! There he was the most conciliatory of them all, and now agreeing with men he would have thrown out of San Felipe two years ago! The worm will turn, given time enough, I guess."

"Will they truly come to our aid?" Sue whispered; her eyes large with apprehension. "Will they dare?"

"I think they must," Margaret answered, soberly, "for the only alternative will be to graciously accept and bind themselves with the chains that General Cos is bringing with him. And I cannot see men like my husband, or either of yours, or Mr. Bowie – or any of them doing that. They must join together and soon or be defeated separately."

They talked for a while, as afternoon shadows lengthened, gossiping about how Mr. Eggleston – who had lately opened a general store in Gonzales – had married Sarah Ponton, the alcalde's younger sister, who was barely half his age. She and Sue admired each other's children, and Maggie Darst's house. Margaret was reminded vividly how at the building of it that she met Race again, and how they had stood under the redbud tree while the breeze shook down raindrops from the leaves. Presently Davy Darst came running along the street, shouting exuberantly.

Margaret gathered up her sewing basket and Johnny, saying, "I believe they are finished with the meeting. I must haste home and see to supper." She bid a farewell to the others and kissed tiny Angelina, thinking wistfully that she would so love to have her next child be a daughter. When she got home, Race was packing his saddlebags and rolling up one of the coarse wool Mexican blankets. Bucephalus stood saddled and bridled, with the reins tied to a porch post.

"I am sent as a courier to Mina," Race explained over his shoulder. "If you may fix me something to eat quickly, I told them I would be away before sunset."

"So, the men have decided to defy Colonel Ugartechea?" She ventured, and Race nodded. "Three voted to give up the cannon, but the rest said 'no.' We have actually decided to stall for time," he explained, "take the damned thing down from the blockhouse and bury it in George Davis's peach orchard, while Andrew respectfully asks for the request to be clarified by the good Colonel's superior. Those with good horses scatter across the countryside begging for aid, and everyone else pretends to go about their own business."

"When will you return?" Margaret set down her basket, and the baby, swiftly taking up a knife and the end of a knuckle of smoked ham from the kitchen safe. "Maggie Darst was baking bread, and gave me a fresh loaf. I wonder if she expected this?"

"Bless her – fresh-baked bread." Race flashed a quick smile over his shoulder. "I expect to be back before the first demand arrives." He ate what she prepared for him standing up, impatient to be away as she made a few more sandwiches for the journey. "And bless you, my dearest Daisy. I will do my best to return swiftly, but you will be alone with the children tonight and possibly tomorrow. I will take my two pistols, so you should not fear for my safety. Latch the door, if you should fear for yours."

"I will not fear." Margaret tightened his warmest scarf around his neck. He had already put on a heavy hunting coat. She whispered, "But I will latch the door. Stay safe, my dearest."

"I will," he promised – and she was utterly confident that he would. He and Bucephalus were away in a clatter of hoofs; she could hear other hoofbeats drumming on the roads and track-ways leading north, east, and to the south, the tracks that only the men familiar with the countryside could negotiate in twilight and at a fast canter.

The party of soldiers from Bexar arrived at mid-morning, announced by a shot and a shout from across the river, a shout in Spanish-accented English, demanding to know where the boat was. Margaret had taken the boys and gone to thank Maggie Darst for the bread. The truth was, her own house felt empty without her husband in it, and dreadfully quiet without the students at their lessons. Perhaps visiting with Maggie again would pass some of the nervous hours. Johnny played or slept on the rag rug at their feet, while Horace amused himself in the yard, enlarging a den for himself among the roots of the redbud tree where Maggie's son and his friends had played when they were smaller.

"Thank the lord they hid the boats in time," Maggie said, as Jacob Darst cursed and caught up his hat and musket from where they hung from pegs close to the door. He hared down the road towards the ferry landing at a run. Maggie and Margaret sat in the breezeway, as they had the day before. "They're stuck on the 'tother side of the river, poor babies. I doubt there's another boat or a low-water crossing for miles. They could try swimming."

"And ruin those fine uniforms?" Margaret answered. "I'd think not."

The two women waited nervously for what seemed an age, but was only part of an hour, while a splash of sunlight falling through crept across the scrubbed pine floor. Now and again, Maggie or Margaret stood and went to the edge of the porch, looking for anything to be seen at the top of the river landing.

"They cannot force their way across the river if there are only a handful of them," Margaret reasoned out loud. "They will not be expecting a refusal. They will not know what to do, if they are only simple soldiers. They will have to return to Bexar and seek guidance from one of higher rank. How many men of ours stand on the Gonzales side of the river today, Maggie?"

"My husband said besides himself and Captain Martin and Will Arrington, there were fifteen . . . only fifteen!" Maggie's voice cracked, and she wrung her hands together. "They have dispatched a letter from Andrew Ponton to Colonel Ugartechea by messenger – a letter refusing to return the cannon, in most civil terms."

"My husband said that Colonel Ugartechea was only sending a small squad," Margaret reasoned, to comfort herself as much as Maggie Darst. "So I cannot see more than five or six. They are on the other side of the river . . ."

"Oh!" groaned Maggie, "our fellows can't come fast enough! How soon do you think they will come to our aid?"

"Sooner than the Colonel can send more soldiers," Margaret answered. "Our fellows will come on horseback, as fast as they can travel, and most of his soldiers will have to march all the way from Bexar." The two women bent their heads over their sewing until Margaret heard the voices of children, several small boys having joined Horace under the redbud tree.

"Look – here come more visitors for you, Maggie," she said. "It seems Sue and Mary Millsaps cannot endure waiting alone on this day either."

Sue Dickinson, with Angelina in her arms, puffed as she came up the steps, "I can't bear another minute," she said. "My husband came away from the landing for a moment to fetch some food, but he could only stay for a moment." Mary Millsaps followed Sue more slowly, unobtrusively led by her oldest daughter. Mary was entirely blind, although one would ordinarily not have noticed save for the peculiar opacity of her eyes.

"What is happening?" Maggie inquired anxiously. "We cannot see the riverbank from here."

Sue shook her head, "Nothing very much at all: there are four ordinary soldiers and a corporal remaining on the riverbank with the cart, calling back and forth to Captain Martin. Almaron says the soldiers seem baffled. They unharnessed a horse from the cart, and a soldier took it away, but he has not come back yet."

"Gone to ask for instructions from Bexar." Margaret set aside her sewing, and took Angelina onto her lap for a bit until she wriggled to be set down on the rug next to Johnny. "My husband thought they would do this. Their soldiers are men who wait for someone in higher authority to tell them what to do. Good morning, Mary."

"Good morning, Margaret," Mary smiled as if she could actually see Margaret. She was a plain woman but her gentle smile transformed her face into fleeting loveliness. "Show me to a chair, Sarah-child," she added as an aside to her daughter. "And give me my knitting." Although blind, Mary managed in her own house and garden, with the help of her children and everything in the household set in an unvarying place within the house. "I thought as I am not going to get anything done this morning, I may as well come with Sue and not get anything done. Isaac has gone as a messenger, to Beeson's Crossing and beyond," she added, and took up her knitting.

The slow minutes and hours ticked by, as sluggish as a trickle of molasses on a cold winter morning; the four women worked at their knitting and mending, occasionally reproving the children for playing too loudly. Mary Millsaps now and again asked for quiet and listened carefully with her head tilted westwards, but there came no sounds of voices, gunshots, or horses, all that long day. At sundown, Margaret took the boys home. Horace and the Millsaps children had made quite a deep burrow at the foot of the redbud tree.

"We're digging a fort," Horace announced proudly, and Margaret asked, "Why are you doing that?"

"'Cause the Meskin sojers are coming soon," he answered. Margaret's heart sank. She had so hoped to protect the children from the knowledge of what was going on that they would remain safe in the bubble of their own childlike and wondrous world. The following day, she resisted the temptation to go to Maggie's house, in spite of Horace fussing that he and his friends wanted to make their fort bigger.

"We have chores to do at home," she said firmly. All that interminable September day she swept the house and worked in the garden to harvest the last of the gourds and beans, rattling in their sun-dried pods. In the afternoon, she sat Horace on one of the school benches and told him that he would have lessons. The day passed rather faster, aside from being distracted by every distant noise. In the early afternoon, she thought she heard the sound of many horses – not from the ford, where Jesse McCoy and Will Arrington stood guard with two other men of the town – but from the north and east. The sound grew louder, more definite, and she could hear men shouting, but not their words or discern what language.

"Come into the house, Horace," she commanded quietly, and scooped up Johnny into her arms.

Horace lingered, looking towards the direction of the sounds, and saying, "Is that Papa coming home?"

"I don't know. Come into the house until we see who it is." He would not obey and she hesitated in the doorway, for now the horses were very close, and very many of them.

Across the road, she saw young Will King dash out from between Dr. Miller's house and the stable next to it. He shouted, waving his hands in the air, "It's them – it's Capn' Tumlinson, from Mina! They're here!" Margaret sagged against the doorframe in momentary relief, and then snatched at the back of Horace's shirt as he made a dash for the steps. A cavalcade of dusty, tired horsemen spilled through the streets of Gonzales, whooping exuberantly. One of them drew rein in front of the house, snatching off his hat and calling across the yard to her, "Miz Vining!"

"Yes?" She recognized James Tumlinson's brother, knew him well for he was another friend of her husband's.

"Race said to tell you he's coming with Burleson and his company – they're a day behind us."

"Thank you for that word!" she called. "How many are with you?"

John Tumlinson's teeth flashed white as his dusty face split in a wide grin, "Forty-eight and more coming. Rob Coleman an' me, we wanted to hustle ahead, so we wouldn't miss the fandango!"

All that afternoon and evening, all night and into the next morning, bands of horsemen poured into Gonzales; parties from Brazoria, as far away as Columbia on the Brazos, from LaGrange, and Lavaca, from Beeson's Crossing, and gathered from the tiny settlements and distant hamlets along the Colorado and the Brazos; everywhere that men had settled after accepting a grant from Austin, from DeWitt or a lesser impresario. They camped on the plazas and in the old fort, the overflow from there spreading bedrolls on the porches of nearby houses. Winslow Turner's wife and their neighbors set up a camp kitchen by their hotel, for many of the volunteers had come so far and fast they carried very little food – or much besides ammunition – with them. Sometime around late afternoon, a dozen volunteers stealthily crossed the river and captured the Mexican soldiers, still waiting patiently on the opposite bank. One escaped, but the others were quickly locked up in a stoutly-built smokehouse.

Margaret cooked dinner for the children and moved around her house feeling oddly secure and safe, seeing the glow of so many campfires on the plazas, so many lights. She took a tin lantern, and setting a candle in that, hung it on a hook by the front door. When it was dark, she took the children into bed with her and slept well content – until just before sunrise, when Race tapped on the plank door and called her name. She sprang instantly out of bed and unbarred the door.

Her husband stood outside, nearly dropping from weariness, "Oh, god, Daisy-mine, what a ride!" He fell into her arms with an exuberant embrace. "I shall never feel so tired again in all my life, no matter how long I live. Burleson and his company rode through the night from Mina. Oh, 'tis good to be home! I saw Captain Martin, just now. He says we have more than a hundred men encamped within Gonzales, and more to come with daylight." He shed his hunting coat and sat on the edge of the bed to kick off his boots. "I'll tell you all about it, Daisy-mine," he added with a yawn.

"Let me start up the fire," Margaret pulled her shawl around herself and knelt to build up the fire, "and start breakfast," but when she turned around again, Race had lain down at full length on the bed in the place where she had slept with the boys curled against her and fallen asleep in his clothes. So much for breakfast. There was a little room left on the bed, between the wall and the children; Margaret lay down on it, and reached across the sleeping forms of the boys to embrace her husband, who slept as if nearly dead, in complete exhaustion.

He roused at last, at mid-morning, by the slight noise of Margaret baking pan after pan of cornbread, for Will King had come with a message from the Turners asking for such, to feed the men assembled. The boys still slept in their nest of blankets, curled together like a pair of kittens.

"There will be a militia-drill in the afternoon," Will whispered. "Special-called. There has been a message received from Bexar. There's a hundred soldiers dispatched from the old citadel, marching along the road towards us. The messenger says Colonel Ugartechea was in a bad temper about it all."

"I imagine he would be," Margaret answered, "since his own words have been proved a lie."

Will grinned, "All of Gonzales and the settlements are buzzing like someone threw a great many rocks into a hornets' nest. Let's see how those sojers of his like it, when they walk straight into it. And Mrs. DeWitt sent to say she has a question to ask of the schoolmaster. They're staying at the Turners – the ladies there are making a flag, and they can't think of something proper to put on it."

He took himself away, and Margaret busied herself with her baking, until her husband stirred. He sat up with a jaw-cracking yawn, saying, "I did not mean to sleep so long, Daisy-mine, but if ever a man needed a few hours." Margaret brought him coffee, sweetened with molasses, and told him of the militia drill and Mrs. DeWitt's request. Outside, a fresh breeze stirred the tree leaves, and their shadows arrayed on the floor. "A moment of peace," he remarked, "infinitely to be treasured at a time like this. I'll help you carry all this to the Turners. A hundred against our hundred – I am no soldier, but I think those good odds."

Indeed, the town seemed every bit as much of a hornet's nest as Will King had said; a bustling hive of purposeful activity. Never had Margaret seen so many people in Gonzales at one time, or so many horses penned in makeshift corrals. They walked past Sowell's smithy, carrying the baskets of bread that Margaret had baked, and heard the ringing of hammers against metal. A small cotton-cart sat propped on blocks outside the forge, with the customary spoke-wheels replaced by solid rounds of cottonwood trunk, as if reinforced to bear something heavy.

"What is that intended for?" Margaret asked, looking curiously at the sturdy little cart.

"It looks like a cannon-carriage." her husband answered, with a wry twist to his lips. "It seems that having insisted on our possession of the thing, we are intending to use it in earnest. Almaron said it could be quite easily repaired."

They left their baskets of bread in the Turners' summer kitchen, which stood as a separate building behind the main house. Smoke from the cook-fire filled the air, and the scent of roasting meats. Inside the Turners' parlor it was quieter, but almost as crowded. Mrs. DeWitt and her daughters worked around a center table, upon which a length of white fabric had been laid out. Eveline and Naomi industriously hemmed the edges, while Mrs. DeWitt carefully outlined two shapes upon the silk with a slip of dressmaker's chalk.

"We picked out the seams of Naomi's best silk dress and took a panel from the skirt," Mrs. DeWitt explained. "She can wear it, still – but we needed enough for a proper flag. The gentlemen of the committee worked out a design, and I think it very pleasing. What do you think of it – this is our cannon, and a single star for Tejas, all embroidered in black thread outline?"

"You'll need a motto," Race said, and his smile broadened. "What about 'Μολὼν λαβέ', just below the cannon, in big black letters?"

"Heavens above, I don't know what it means!" Mrs. DeWitt exclaimed. "What was that which you just said?"

"I said it in Greek," Race answered, "quoting the words of King Leonides of Sparta to Xerxes of Persia, when Xerxes asked the Spartans to give up their arms. The king answered, 'Come and take them'."

"I like the sentiment," Mrs. DeWitt answered, "and it would make a fine motto, but we would have to put it in English. As it is, you'd likely be the only man in town to understand it."

Through that day, tension mounted, as volunteers continued arriving from the farthest districts. Margaret, unable to endure an afternoon alone in the house, with all that was going on, left the boys with Mary Millsaps at midday and went to offer her assistance with the needle to Mrs. DeWitt, who accepted gratefully. Thus, she was able to follow her husband's report of the militia meeting, and even see and hear some of what transpired during that long day.

John Moore, the captain of a company of men from Columbus on the Colorado River, was elected colonel at the militia meeting, as he was acknowledged by all as a wily and experienced fighter. The other captains of the militia companies would serve under his authority. During the militia meeting, one of the Mexicans escaped from captivity in the smokehouse – although as Race said afterwards to Captain Martin, "I expect that he will take a good account of what he has seen this day to his officers, and with all speed."

"Yes, I expect that he will," Captain Martin allowed cheerfully, and both men exchanged broad grins. Very shortly thereafter, a messenger arrived under a white flag of truce from an officer of the Mexican Army. He stood on the bank opposite the ferry and waved to Jesse McCoy, asking permission to bring over a message. The messenger was one of those who could swim – he paddled across the river, carrying a sealed and waterproof pouch with a message in it from an officer who signed himself with a number of unnecessary and flamboyant flourishes *F. Casteñada, Lieutenant of the military garrison of Bexar in the State of Tejas y Coahuila.* Jesse McCoy immediately brought the message from the riverbank landing, as the militia meeting was finishing.

"Their officer wants to meet with you," he said to Andrew Ponton.

"Alas, I am unavailable, being painfully indisposed," Andrew answered, and Jesse grinned. He was quite recovered from the effects of his beating at the hands of the Mexican soldier in Zumwalts' store. But the bruises on his face were still visible as fading dark yellowish patches.

"You look well enough to me."

"You are not a competent medical man, sir – your eyes grossly deceive you. I am desperately unwell. Have Joe Clements send a reply – he's on the town council."

The mass of soldiers from Bexar arrived very shortly afterwards, Lieutenant Casteñada again demanding to meet with Andrew Ponton, in his office as Alcade and senior civil authority of the town. Their horses drank water at the river's edge, but that was all they could do, for all the boats had been well-hidden and the river was too deep and fast to ford. They withdrew a little to the south, to camp on a low hill, as the sun slid lower and lower in the western sky.

The flag was at last finished, the star and the cannon, and the letters all outlined with embroidery. Race came to Margaret saying, "There is nothing more to be done today, Daisy-mine. Let us go home for a peaceable night. Colonel Moore has ordered that we shall act upon whatever the Mexicans do tomorrow. All is in readiness, and now most of us should rest and await what comes in what peace of mind that we can find for ourselves."

"I would like that very much," Margaret answered, for her nerves jangled like the strings of a broken harp, and perhaps sensing that, Race put his arms around her.

"Dear little wife, if tomorrow brings an irrevocable change to everything in our world, I would prefer to spend the very last night of the time of things-as-they-used to be in tranquility, and domestic content . . . to have a plain supper, and sit and read Vitruvius for a while with you, after the boys are asleep, and then to go to sleep in your arms, thinking that there is nothing better than to spend an eternity there. No talk of soldiering, or the War Party, or Colonel Ugartechea's men camped across the river. Only ourselves, the boys, and supper together. Can we manage that, Daisy-mine?"

"We can," Margaret took his face between her hands and kissed him, heedless of the fact they were standing in the street before Turners'. *How very wise and sensitive he was, the very best of husbands in the world!* No, she would never regret marrying the schoolmaster, taking his name and bearing his children.

"One last word about the matter." Race caught one of her hands in his, "and then no more. When we march out to meet Casteñada's soldiers – and I think that we will, sometime tomorrow or the day after – take the children and sufficient food and blankets, and conceal yourself in the woods of the bottomlands, south of town, until we return. I am breaking my own request to not talk of this – but I cannot put out of my mind the reports of how General Lopez de Santa Anna's men were rewarded for defeating the militia of Zacatecas by being allowed two days of rapine, looting, and murder. I would see you safe, Daisy-mine, as I promised when we exchanged vows – but in the event that our efforts meet with failure, then I would like to be assured that you and the boys remain safe."

"Of course we will be safe," Margaret answered, "for I have every faith in you. But I will take the boys to the woods . . . and then we will come home and I will prepare dinner and we will read, and see the boys to sleep in their bed; then we will go to ours, and all will still seem to be with us as it was before – no matter what happens on the morrow."

"Thank you, Daisy-mine." Race kissed that hand of hers which he held. "Ah, the scripture was more correct in this that most men believe – of the great powers in the world, the greatest of these is love, and that which endures beyond all in this world."

The combined militias of the settlements – all those who had come to Gonzales – marched out of Gonzales late the next afternoon, under a blood-red and purple-clouded sunset; a brave rabble of men, young and old, and with every sort of weapon imaginable, although all carried sheathed knives at their belts. Such was that fashion which Mr. Bowie had started, Margaret thought, with no little appreciation of the irony. Only half were mounted on horseback. The little cannon trundled bravely along, pulled by two yoke of oxen, and the white flag which Mrs. DeWitt and her daughters and Margaret had sewn floated on a staff before all. Around midday, Lieutenant Castañeda had taken his men and dragoons and had gone north, searching for a shallow fording-place by which they could cross over the river and come to Gonzales and arrest Andrew Ponton – and indeed all of those among the town council who had stood in the way of reclaiming that practically useless little cannon. The soldiers from Bexar were stealthy followed for a little way by several scouts. The closest such fording place was by Ezekiel William's outlying farm, some seven miles or so upriver from town.

"We shall follow and meet them on equal terms." Race came home to eat a hasty supper, to saddle Bucephalus, gather up his long hunting rifle, his two pistols, hunting-knife, and put on his rough hunting clothes once again. "Remember what I said, about the woods, Daisy-mine. Rise early in the morning, and take the children to the woods. We have nearly two hundred gathered to us, and the advantage of picking and choosing when to show ourselves . . . but should this venture go against us . . ."

"I do not see how it can, with so many of our folk to outnumber those soldiers!" Margaret answered swiftly, and her husband smiled.

"Ah, but overconfidence has brought down many a general and campaign, as I would know from my studies of history. We may expect and hope for the best outcome, my dearest love – but the wisest of generals also prepare for the worst eventuality. I would like to know that those whom I love best in the world will not be sitting helpless within walls, but as free in the greenwood as a doe with two fawns."

"I shall do as you say," Margaret promised – as did quite a few other women of Gonzales and their families, early the following morning. The night had been quiet, although she had seemed to wake at every small noise. In the morning – a cool morning, pearly with fog and the slight patter of condensation falling off the tree leaves – she dressed the boys and fed them breakfast, telling them that they were going for a picnic in the woods. She took Race's volume of Bunyan, slipping it into her apron pocket, a small basket of bread and cheese, a gourd canteen, and several blankets, including that red one which Mama had woven and walked down into the thick woods, in the river-bottom south of town. Many of the leaves still clung to the trees and shrubs, offering a fair concealment. Having found what she thought a safe enough shelter, she spread out a heavy horse blanket on the sparse grass in the midst of those woods and thickets. With Horace's enthusiastic help, she propped up several slender willow poles against the bank to make a tiny brush arbor, hardly large enough for the three of them. Johnny was content with gathering colorful fallen leaves and interesting pebbles from the riverbank, before falling asleep in her lap. Horace played a while, and then came to eat bread and cheese and listen to her read *Pilgrim's Progress*, and to tell them some of the stories which Mama had told to Margaret and her brothers when

106

they were small. All the while, Margaret kept an ear attuned for any odd noise or sounds of a violent affray. She prided herself that she kept her apprehensions from the boys, that her voice was calm and level always. Above them in the branches of the trees, the birds sang cheerfully and undisturbed, and the river-shallows lapped at the muddy bank. The sun passed through its accustomed arc serenely and without interruption; Margaret even dozed for a while herself. Late in the afternoon, while she was still undecided about whether to remain through the night in their wood refuge or risk returning to the house, she heard Race, calling her name. Joyfully she answered, and within a few moments he came scrambling down the low bluff, leading Bucephalus. He was smiling, so she knew the day must have brought success for the militia-men.

"Oh, it went well, Daisy-mine," he answered her unasked question as they embraced. "Although with considerable elements of farce. Those among us hoping for a bloody battle must have been quite disappointed, but I confess that I am relieved, for the only immediate casualty amongst us was a bloody nose, for one of our horses startled at the sound of a gunshot and threw Dick Andrews head-first to the ground . . . fortunately, it was a plowed field. 'Zekiel William's watermelon field, as a matter of fact."

"A battle, Papa? Were you in a battle?" Horace demanded. "Weren't you frightened?"

"Yes, I was and yes I was – and any man who says he was in a battle and wasn't frightened is a liar, little man; the bravest fighters of all just hide their fears from everyone and do what they must."

"What happened in Mr. William's field?" Margaret asked, gathering up the blankets and basket as her husband fondly lifted first Horace and then Johnny into Bucephalus' saddle, where Horace drummed his feet against the horses' flanks until his father chided him, and then continued with his account.

"The fog . . . did I say there was a dense fog before sunrise this morning? We had marched through the night, and when dawn came the fog lifted. There were the Mexicans, no doubt as surprised to see us as we were to see them, so close. We fired a warning volley at them, and they at us, upon which we fell back to conceal ourselves amid the woods along the riverbank. They sent a messenger, Doctor Smithers – he does some doctoring and a little horse-trading in Bexar. I bought this good fellow from him, as a matter of fact. Dr. Smithers asked for a parley, and so Colonel Moore went to meet their officer, Castañeda . . . poor chap, he is one of us in sympathy, being a Federalist. He demanded to know why his men had been fired upon. Colonel Moore answered that his forces represented those of Lopez de Santa Anna, who had become an enemy of the colonists in Texas and all those who honored the 1824 Constitution . . . and if he truly was a Federalist then he should immediately surrender and join us in defending it."

"Oh, my," Margaret exclaimed. "That was most certainly bold of Colonel Moore! What did the officer say in return?" Race chuckled, and they began walking back towards town and home.

"Oh, he claimed that he could not. As an officer, he must obey the orders given, no matter how he felt personally. He was ordered to fetch the cannon, and so . . . where *was* the cannon? And Colonel Moore turned and pointed towards it, saying 'There it is, on the field – so come and take it.' Then he waved his arm and shouted 'fire!' – And at that, the boys did so. What an almighty crash it made! A great puff of smoke and the whistle of scrap-iron hurtling through the air – and then it was all over, Daisy-mine. The Mexican troops wheeled around and departed the field in good order and at some speed. I think that Lieutenant Castañeda felt honor was satisfied. I expect that he has gone to ask for new orders, since he could not carry out the old ones."

"And that was all?" Margaret asked, in considerable astonishment. "This is passing miraculous! A battle won – just like that!"

"Aye, it did seem somewhat of an anticlimax," Race set his arm around her waist, "And thin material for any bard hoping to make a stirring ode out of heroic battlefield deeds. But what happened in Williams' fields today has great significance, which I think Castañeda and his commander, and General Cos, will not fail to appreciate to the fullest. Lopez de Santa Anna most certainly will see this defiance for what it is – since it has happened in a manner that I wager has not been seen before."

"And that would be?" Margaret tightened her arm around his waist. Her husband was covered in dust. His clothing smelt of black powder and sweat.

"Open and well-armed rebellion, among all degree of settlers here," he answered, "Certainly there have been hotheads and malcontents stirring the pot and preaching independence – but until now they have always been countered by honest and well-meant men such as Mr. Austin, and Dr. Williams, men who were as loyal to their oaths as today was long. No more. Even the Peace Party has been driven to open defiance. When sober and reasonable men of business, long resident here, put down the tools of their trade, take up a musket, and travel to the aid of their friends in answer to a plea . . . that is a matter of note, Daisy-mine. Today has importance out of all proportion to what actually happened with our little affray and our little cannon."

Chapter 9 – *The Bells of Freedom Ringing*

In the chill October dawn, horses and men, afoot and mounted, milled around in Market Square on the edge of town by the timber citadel. A white mist rose from the river below, which flowed with barely a ripple and appeared gunmetal grey in the directionless light. The Army of Texas had gathered at Gonzales, an assembly of men volunteering from the various American settlements. They had enlisted to go to Bexar and lay siege to General Cos's troops – and send them packing back to Mexico. Now they prepared to depart. Stephen Austin had been acclaimed their leader. Although he had no experience as a soldier, he was respected by most and revered by many. Seeing him again, Margaret thought that he looked so much older and wearier than he had appeared when he came around to pay calls on Mama and herself and Carl, after Papa had quarreled with him. Mr. Austin had been imprisoned for a year in Mexico City, despite all the careful and diplomatic pains that he took in representing the interests of those Americans who had settled on his land-grants with the Mexican government. He had been a fair and conciliatory man. His reward had been to be treated as a criminal. Rumor now had it that he and other leading men of the American settlements would be arrested by General Cos. If such as he were now driven towards rebellion, as Race had explained to her, then there was no use treating any more with the *Centralistas*, with Colonel Ugartechea, and Lopez de Santa Anna.

Among the mounted volunteers she saw many familiar faces; faces of neighbors from Gonzales, friends of her husbands'. There was Mr. Bowie, on a horse right next to Mr. Austin. Curious that they might be companions in leadership, when they were such opposites; Mr. Austin the soft-spoken gentleman and diplomat, and Mr. Bowie celebrated for his long hunting-knife and his prowess as a fighter. "He should do very well as a commander," Race had commented to her, upon reading in the *Telegraph & Texas Register* that Mr. Bowie had rallied to the Texian Army, where his reputation had earned him a position as one of Austin's most trusted lieutenants. "He has been raring for a fight all of his life – and now in this rebellion, he has one worthy of him, rather than dribbling away the substance of a warrior soul in petty tavern brawls and duels."

There was hardly anything like a uniform among them, Margaret thought ruefully. In nothing did the Texian Army resemble pictures that she had seen of armies on the march, or the detachments of Mexican soldiers and dragoons, all with their uniform coats and trousers and belts that crossed their chests just so. The volunteers wore hunting coats of buckskin or homespun jeans fabric, or plain round jackets in every color from pale yellow to black, and carried every sort of weapon – long rifle to shotgun, and often no weapon at all. Almaron Dickinson and old John Sowell had sharpened metal files and bound them to sturdy bamboo poles to make lances. Such a rag-tag army – yet, a messenger from Goliad had arrived with the news that other Texian volunteers had taken the presidio at La Bahia, which commanded the road between Copano and San Antonio. General Cos would be cut off from reinforcements and re-supply from the sea, as Race had explained – in turn, he would be surrounded. Perhaps he might be forced to surrender. The cruel treatment meted out by Lopez de Santa Anna's army to the people of Zacatecas would be spared them! Texas was very far away from Mexico City and the vengeful and treacherous Lopez de Santa Anna. Margaret devoutly hoped that Austin's army of Texians could hold fast – Texas was their home, her home! They had settled the land, planted trees, raised fine crops, and built houses – all those things which Lopez de Santa Anna was not inclined to do.

That very night after they had received the news of the taking of La Bahia, a huge blazing star appeared in the sky, a star that trailed a long diffuse tail after it – a comet, Race called it, saying that it was one of those which appeared only rarely. Everyone thought it was an omen; but for good or ill, none could say. Race took the boys from their bed, well-wrapped in quilts, and carried them in his arms to the middle of St. Francis Street, dimly silvered with starlight, to point out the passage of the great comet, saying that it would be seventy-five years before it would appear again. "Look well, and remember, boys – you will both be old men when it returns again!"

Around Margaret, women stood weeping or stoic-faced, their smaller children pressing close to their skirts like chicks to the feathers of a mother-hen, while the older boys looked with envy on those of their older brothers or their fathers who were going with the riders. Race was not one of these; as Captain Martin acknowledged freely, he was too valuable as a courier, between his knowledge of the country and the speed of Bucephalus. Margaret was secretly glad, for she could assure herself that he was keeping warm against the cold, and that the constitutional weakness of his chest would not bring him down untimely. She could not do this if he was gone to Bexar for months, although she knew that he was at least halfway tempted to go with Almaron and his friends. She was glad that Captain Martin had been so blunt – and that Race was away, bearing messages to the convention of colonists meeting at Washington-on-the-Brazos on this day, three days hard ride distant, so he was spared the sight of his friends riding north.

At a command which she barely heard among the clamor in the square, men began mounting up and forming by twos. They would cross the river and follow the road north, the road to Bexar. Suddenly, she saw Sue Dickinson appear among the crowd, a purposeful Sue with a determined expression on her face, Angelina on one arm, a large bundle over her shoulder and a basket in her other hand.

"Sue! What are you doing?" Margaret exclaimed. Sue barely looked at her, her eyes roving amongst the mounted men, just beginning to filter out of the square.

"Looking for my husband . . . oh, there he is. Goodbye, Margaret."

"Sue!" cried Margaret and she followed as Sue plunged into the crowd of men and horses. The two of them came out of the sea of departing troopers, practically under the nose of Almaron's horse. Both horse and the man on it looked down upon them with similar expressions of dismayed surprise.

"Sue!" Almaron shouted, much as Margaret had, only much louder. "What are you doing?"

"Coming with you, me and the baby," Sue announced, resolutely. "You cannot leave me here. I married a man, not his empty boots."

"You cannot!" the young blacksmith cried indignantly, and then thought to lower his voice. "You cannot, Sue – this is the Army of Texas going to Bexar, and to fight Cos – we can't take you along!"

"Yes you can," Sue answered, "Not the Army – but you. I am your wife, and where you go, I will go also even if it is only an army camp." She lowered her voice, so that only Almaron and Margaret could hear in the clamor. Sue's eyes looked huge, and pleading – yet with assurance in them that her husband would yield. "Entreat me not to leave thee, or to return from following after thee: for whither thou goest, I will go; and where thou lodgest, I will lodge: thy people shall be my people and thy God my God . . ." Almaron's shoulders slumped in acquiescence.

"Dear God, Sue – I cannot resist when you quote that at me," he said, and reached down with one arm. "Give me the baby." He took Angelina up onto the front of his saddle, and hung the bundle from his saddle-pommel. He gave Sue a hand up, as she placed her foot on top of his, swung up and settled herself at his back, riding astride behind him with the skirt of her dress indecently rucked up to her knees. Sue looked over her shoulder at Margaret, and Margaret thought she would have waved in careless and triumphant farewell, save that she still clutched the basket in one hand, and around her husband's waist with the other.

I wish I had the nerve to do that, Margaret thought, as she walked away. *Save for that I have two children. I love Race as much as she loves Almaron – but I am assured that he will survive all this.*

On a chill morning in mid-November, she heard a wagon coming up the road from the direction of the ferry. She listened warily as it stopped in the road before their house; there had been many men lately come to town to join the Texian Army. Most of them had gone to Bexar to join the forces besieging General Cos, but the drunken wastrels among them had given much offense to local women, and made it sometimes quite unpleasant. Race was gone to San Antonio, bearing messages; she was alone and would be for the next few days. Margaret had taken very good care to latch the door and all the windows at night. She opened the door to call to Horace, and her heart skipped a beat in her chest, for it was Papa's wagon – a smaller wagon, repaired and cut down to travel easier on the rough Texas roads. It was pulled by two yoke of his oxen, the same familiar and gentle beasts which he had brought from Pennsylvania. There was a saddle horse tied behind the wagon and Papa himself helping Mama down from the seat. Margaret flew down the steps to embrace them both, crying joyfully for her happiness at seeing them again.

"It seems an age, dearest M'grete!" Mama drew her close and Margaret clung to her, relishing the faint scent of dried verbena which always called the presence of Mama to her mind, since Mama was most fond of putting little sachets of it among her clothing and linens when they were laid away in the clothes press. Papa stood, absently playing with the stock of his whip, and beaming down on Margaret and Mama.

"It has been so long, my dearest duckling!" Mama wiped a tear-trickle off her cheek. "I have thought of you every day, you and the children . . . I must see the children, of course, and your dear schoolmaster."

"He is a courier for the Army of Texas," Margaret answered. Mama patted her cheek.

"So you had written in your last letter . . . ach, the way things have come to pass. Your brothers are with the Army surrounding Bexar. I wish Carlchen would have stayed at home, but your father would not countenance Rudi going alone, and Rudi would go whether your Papa gave permission or not."

"Papa, have you joined the Army also?" Margaret turned from her mothers' arms to Papa's briefer embrace. She had been watching volunteers – Races' friends, and the husbands of her friends go towards Bexar for months. Now her heart went cold, knowing that her brothers were among them.

Her father grunted in disparagement. "No, M'grete, I am not such a fool as to cast my lot in with freebooters and sots. I have been asked by our neighbors in Waterloo to represent us at the consultation called to Washington-on-the-Brazos to organize the army and the affairs of an independent state . . . but I brought a wagonload of cornmeal and smoked meats to our encampment at Bexar, for all our communications with the commanders there spoke of a crying need for such. Your mother could not remain alone in Waterloo – so I brought her here to see her grandchildren while I am away."

"Of course, you must stay with us!" Margaret embraced her mother again – how like Papa, impulsively appearing as if he had written a letter about this weeks ago. "You will adore the children – Horace has just begun learning his letters and Johnny to talk sensibly. You should not be alone in Waterloo – and I shall be glad of your company, Mama, for Race is away more often than not. Gonzales is a town of women, bereft of husbands and sons who have gone to join the Army or a ranging company. Indeed, I think we are all very lonely."

"I could not bring my loom," Mama smiled cheerfully, "but I have bought two baskets of yarn, so I will not be a burden."

"Mama, you would never be a burden!" Margaret answered, "and you have many friends here who recall you with affection."

"I shall leave the wagon and oxen here." Papa beamed impartially upon them, "for you and whomever it may please you to lend the use of them. I must make all speed to Washington tomorrow – but we have brought gifts for you. Pecans and a barrel of our apples. Not many, but of a pleasing flavor."

"And a smoked ham," Mama added, a dimple appearing in her cheek, "as our harvest has been most bountiful – we will be pleased to share it with you and with those of our men – each of whom is as dear to us as the boys!" Something of her pleasure faded as Margaret led her parents towards the house; Mama added, "I wish I could be assured that Rudi and Carlchen are having at least a taste of what we have brought . . . I wish . . ."

"Fear not for those young scamps and their hungry bellies," Papa chuckled. "You remember, Maria – when I told the boys that I had enough of them scanting their chores to go play in the woods? I forbade them to come to the table for meals; you do not work, I said – then you do not eat."

Mama clicked her tongue, chiding Papa and saying, "Alois – you spoke before thinking, for it was summer."

"What happened then?" Margaret asked; obviously nothing much, as her parents seemed rather to be fondly amused. She opened the door to the part of the house which served as winter kitchen and sleeping room – the other side being parlor, schoolroom, and library. She relished the swift glance and the

113

look of approval on Mama's face, as she and Papa stepped inside. Margaret had taken considerable pride in the comforts and homeliness within – that the rough plank-walled room was whitewashed clean, the floor was daily sprinkled with river sand and swept, and that all the cooking things were polished or spotlessly clean and neatly arrayed. The kitchen-safe, with its panels of pierced tin, sat in one corner, and the dish-cupboard in the other, displaying a mix of rough pottery and fine English china with a blue toile pattern. Hers and Race's bed was built into another corner, with Horace's pallet and blankets stowed for the day underneath. Johnny had not yet gone from the cradle to sharing the pallet-bed with his older brother. He was sleeping in the cradle which he was near to outgrowing. Horace lay on his stomach in the middle of the room, playing with a toy horse and wagon that Jacob Darst had whittled for him for his third birthday.

"Little man, come and meet your Oma and Opa!" Margaret exclaimed, sweeping him up into her arms, and he looked at her parents with his father's clever hazel eyes grown big in his infant face. "These are my mother and father – and Oma has come to stay with us," she added. Mama cooed in approval, as she took Horace to her arms, for he went to them with an open smile as soon as Mama admired the cart and horse most extravagantly.

"He is beautiful, and so well-grown!" Mama said, "It may be that I have forgotten exactly how tall a young gentleman of four-and-something ought to be!" With a twinge in the region of her heart, Margaret realized that Mama had spoken in German, and her son had not understood a word. Such was the way of the world – the language of her childhood was a thing unknown to her children. None of their neighbors in Gonzales spoke German, certainly none of Horace's playmates. So did the Old Country pass away, save in memories and in certain old stories and customs. The new country claimed them now.

To cover her discomfiture, she asked, "So, what of Rudi and Carlchen, spending all summer in the woods?"

"Not a bite of food at my table," Papa said, still sounding amused, "until they would do their chores and young Rudolph answered to me 'very well then, Papa – a fair bargain.' And so they went off into the woods."

"They hunted," Mama answered, shooting a severe look at Papa, "They snared rabbits, and fished in the river. The Harrells – our closest neighbors – they told us the boys traded with them; venison for cornmeal and salt. And there were of course, pecans and grapes and wild plums in the thickets." Margaret restrained her amusement. Papa must have been simply furious with her brothers, successfully flouting his authority. It appeared he had come to feel pride in Rudi's determination and resource. Mama would have brought him around. Now Mama added, "They did this for an entire summer. Until finally, I tell your Papa, enough. Harvest is coming . . . allow them to come to the table. They are good boys – let them choose the work they do."

"So now they are off," Papa added, with a deep sigh. "When the harvest was brought in – and upon hearing a call for volunteers. I tell you, M'grete, I care nothing for politics. All I wish is to be left alone. This General Cos, he will not let us alone. So." he shrugged. "Our lads, they take a part in making him leave us be. As long as they are home in time for spring planting, yes?"

"I hope so, Papa," Margaret answered, thinking that Papa had spent too much time communing with his apple trees and cornfields – anything which did not talk back. If he did not wish to contemplate some matter, then it was of no import to him. If he did, no one had any peace until Papa was tired of the matter himself.

"And I am off to Washington-on-the-Brazos in the morning," Papa continued. "Someone must speak up for Waterloo, for our neighbors. Might as well be me, eh, M'grete?"

"Mr. Harrell says that your Papa has so many strong opinions," Mama murmured, "he may as well be generous and share them with more than just our neighbors." Margaret again stifled an urge to laugh. Yes, Papa had been outspoken with the neighbors. For Mama's sake she hoped that Papa had mellowed – and would not soon contrive a dreadful quarrel out of an ordinary disagreement with anyone. She did not think Mama could endure another dismembering of her household, or to begin again on another plot of land, farther out in the wilderness.

In the morning, Papa saddled his horse: she and Mama and the children waved to him from the doorway, and he turned in the saddle, waving his wide-brimmed planter's hat in one hand, his fair hair bright against the gray morning. When he had ridden out of sight, Mama sighed and hurriedly passed the corner of her apron across her eyes. She took Margaret's hand in hers, saying, "Your Papa says that he does not know how long he will be. I am so sorry to be a burden to your household, M'grete."

"No, Mama – never a burden." Margaret set down Johnny on the floor and closed the door against the morning chill. "I am cheered, having you stay with us rather than remain all alone, far away up the river in Waterloo. For you to become acquainted with my children – is an unlooked-for gift. You would have known them well if Papa had not quarreled with Colonel DeWitt and Mr. Smith."

"I know, M'grete." Mama kissed her very gently, a kiss like a butterfly brushing her forehead. "Still – I have never faced the prospect of being apart from your Papa for more than a month, since he returned to bring us to Texas. These times are so troubled, M'grete."

"And my husband is often sent to bear messages, at a moment's notice," Margaret answered. "No, Mama, I am glad of your presence for however long Papa is at the convention. Very glad indeed."

So Margaret was and her sons also; her mother's presence kept her mind from dwelling overmuch on what might be happening in Bexar and on what dangers might affect her brothers, the convention in Washington-on-the-Brazos, or the winter cold and damp which might imperil Race's health. It also entered Margaret's mind that the presence of Mama in a household already established – with hers and Race's habits and customs – might also pose the same kind of peril and disruption, but such fears proved groundless. Mama was so gentle and self-effacing when Race was home that she hardly made a ripple in the quiet passage of their precious days together. They made a place for her in the parlor-room of their house, a comfortable bed high-piled with quilts and blankets for those cold nights, to which she withdrew early on those evenings which Race spent at home. During the day, Mama knitted, helped Margaret with the cooking, and played with the baby, while Horace had his lessons from Race or from Margaret. Those weeks passed in a state of unbroken tranquility within her house, and also in Gonzales; as if Mama brought serenity with her, as faint but pervasive as the scent of verbena clinging to her garments. Horace adored her immediately, for she told him wondrous stories of elves and kobolds, and princes' sons on quests, and beautiful princesses under curses. To Margaret, now being a married woman with her own children, it seemed as if Mama was not only her own mother, but also a comfortable friend, richly blessed with the wisdom of years. If Mama worried for the boys, or for Papa, she kept those fears to herself.

Late in November, word arrived – first by messenger, and later confirmed in the *Telegraph & Texas Register* – that there had been a terrific fight, somewhere on the outskirts of Bexar, over a Mexican pack train. Also that General Austin had gone to the convention at Washington-on-the-Brazos, and now the general in charge of the Texian Army was Sam Houston.

Race shook his head when he read that. "He had a reputation as a good soldier, once – in Congress very briefly and governor of Tennessee also for as brief a time, and Andrew Jackson's darling boy – but that was then. He's a friend of Bowie's though. But," Race hesitated and Margaret looked up from her knitting. By the fire, Mama paused, in her telling of a story to the boys.

"What of this Houston?" Margaret asked, curiously.

"Well, that he is one of these men who blows either hot or cold, nothing steadily temperate and in-between – rather like Father Becker, or so I am reminded. He was the hero of Horseshoe Bend and a general of the militia, very much the rising young man. But then he got caught up in some unsavory dealings, abandoned his wife, and went to live in the Cherokee Nation. And when I say nothing temperate, I do mean intemperate. The story is that he didn't draw a sober breath for three years and he came to Texas to escape charges for brawling outside of a Washington boardinghouse. The other man, whom he was accused of beating half to death, was a Congressman." Race paused with a wry chuckle. "Houston settled in Nacogdoches. I don't think there's any way that Mr. Austin would have accepted his references in the early days."

"Your Papa said that Mr. Austin wanted sober men of good character and industry," Mama added, "Of whom nothing but good would be spoken by their fellows."

Race chuckled again, appreciatively. "That would not be Sam Houston. Rumors have it that he dresses like an Indian when it pleases him, and indulges in the overflowing bowl much too often for the comfort of serious men like Mr. Austin, or even Colonel Fannin. Still," Race's countenance sobered. "He was a colonel in the militia. As a matter of practicality that must count for something more than Jim Fannin's time at West Point."

"What of the siege of Bexar?" Margaret asked. "Is Houston in charge there, now?"

"No, I think not – he has gone north to negotiate a peace settlement with the Cherokee. Very wisely, since he is the best of friends with the tribes."

"A pity," Margaret returned her attention to her knitting. "It seems that we need a strong leader there."

Her husband shook his head, smiling. "No, dearest Daisy – we have a sufficiency of strong leaders. Getting them to agree on a single course of action – I believe *that* is what we truly need,"

Miraculously, within days of reading of the skirmish over the pack train, word arrived that General Cos had surrendered, after four days of bitter fighting in the stone and adobe houses surrounding his garrison and troop positions. He and his men were paroled, promising to leave Texas at once and never returning to bear arms against anyone living peacefully there.

"So much for arresting our leading men and taking them to Mexico in chains!" Margaret exclaimed. "Does this mean that we are free, free to have our own state?"

"Our own country!" Race chuckled, "if we can keep it . . . remember, Daisy-mine," his face sobered. "In the spring, Lopez de Santa Anna's armies will march on us, as they marched on Zacatecas and the other federalist states which utterly rejected his autocratic rule. He cannot, I think, come by sea from Copano or some other landing, since our men command the road from La Bahia. But as soon as there is fair weather again, and pasture for his horses and the oxen that haul his cannon batteries, he will come overland from Mexico. Cheer up, Daisy-mine – that is a very long and arduous journey for an army, and we will be well-prepared by then!" He gave her an exuberant embrace, and went to set his foot in Bucephalus' stirrup. He was off again, leaving Margaret still with the feeling of his arms around her, and his parting kiss on her lips; she to be alone in the bed which they shared, the essence of him lingering on the sheets and pillows.

With the victory at Bexar, volunteers came streaming home in mid-December, their enlistments having expired. Jacob Darst came home for a time, to spend with Maggie and Davy. Some of the other men of the town returned to their homes, although Dick Andrews, a lieutenant of volunteers from Fort Bend, was not among them. It was he who had been thrown by his own horse and gotten a bloody nose when the men of Gonzales and those who had come to their aid in September were fired upon by Lieutenant Casteñada. He died, grievously wounded in the first assault upon Cos' troops in Bexar. It was whispered among the men who had been his comrades that he had suffered for many hours – lying on the bare ground, tearing at his wounds that they might bleed faster and so bring a merciful surcease to his agony.

"Where there no doctors among you? Or provision for those who might be wounded?" she asked of Jacob Darst when she heard of this, and Maggie's husband looked at the ground with a shamed face. They had met by chance, in the street outside of Adam Zumwalt's store.

"No, I think whatever provision there was for us was what we could think of and perform on our own, for our friends."

"I am sorry then, for Mr. Andrews, and for others who may fall on the field," Margaret replied. "Truly, I fear we are not fully prepared for the exigencies that war brings upon us." She walked home from thinking and hoping that a proper provision might be made with regards to this, and to other matters, before spring, when they would face the fury of Lopez de Santa

Anna. Dr. Miller, who despaired of seeing the American settlements achieve that accommodation he had so often urged upon them, had departed with his family from Gonzales. *'I am too old for this,'* he had said to Race, in farewell. *'And I have too many friends here, to watch war come upon them all. Forgive me – I will not be driven to take part in it and I cannot bear to watch.'*

She was cheered as she walked back along St. Francis Street and saw that Bucephalus was already pastured behind the house, munching peacefully at a quantity of corn in his manger. There were two more horses there as well, horses which she did not recognize. Race had brought friends with him, she thought, with a slight sinking of her heart at the thought of demands for additional hospitality – but then, Mama was there. She and Mama would cope together.

She opened the door, hearing Mama's happy exclamation, "M'grete, your brothers have come for a visit. They may spend Christmas here!"

"H'lo, M'grete! Merry Christmas!" Before she could say a word, a tall, fair-haired young man swooped her into a vigorous embrace, lifting her feet clear from the floor.

"Rudi!" she gasped. "Put me down! I cannot believe it is you – you are as tall as Papa!"

"Taller," Rudi grinned wickedly and let her go. "We are on leave for a bit, M'grete, home for Christmastime. Our company is going to garrison La Bahia, now that Bexar is in our hands. Fine times, isn't it? Better than looking at the arse-end of an ox team and a plow, eh, little brother?" Margaret looked at her brothers, not quite believing her own eyes. She had thought of them as still little more than children. It had been nearly five years since she had seen them, since Papa had taken Mama and her brothers north to the Upper Colorado. In that time Rudi had grown into manhood; lively and vital, filling the small room with his exuberant presence. Next to him, Carl was gawky and quiet, a tall gangly boy with sky-colored eyes. He smiled at Margaret almost shyly – still self-contained, as if he watched from the edge of a crowd for something or someone. His hair and Rudi's had grown long and fair, apparently untouched by scissors the whole time they had been off soldiering. Both of her brothers wore rough homespun clothes – Margaret recognized Mama's weaving, and their loose hunting coats bulged with all sorts of odd pockets. Two long flintlock muskets leaned against the wall by the door amid a pile of strapped blankets and haversacks, cartridge boxes, and powder-horns.

Race slapped Rudi on the shoulder, saying, "Sirrah, unhand my wife if you please. The boys have been telling us all of what's been happening in Bexar."

"Just the bits that we can talk about in front of Mama, o'course," Rudi added with a still-broader grin. "Don't look at me that way M'grete – I am a man grown and Carlchen is nearly so! Little brother was all moon-faced this year after Harrell's fourteen-year old daughter. He couldn't put two words together . . . ."

"Shut up, Rudi," Carl mumbled, flushing as red as one of Mama's pickled beets. Heedless, Rudi continued. "Well, little brother can't say more than two words anyway, it's a wonder that she could tell the difference . . . ne'er mind." Rudi draped his arm affectionately across Carl's shoulders. "He may not talk much, but he proved himself as a sharp-shot. The Mex riflemen were up in the trees, sniping at our fellows at the Veramendi house all during the worst of it. They got poor Ben Miliam, who led us into Bexar. Dropped the poor man like a stone between one word and the next. Our little brother helped put an end to that, M'grete! Didn't you, Carlchen?"

Carl looked at the planks of the floor between his feet and mumbled something inaudible to Margaret's ears, while Mama set Johnny down from her lap and said, "Then, your sister and I will prepare supper while you tell us all of what happened in Bexar."

"I will tell of the biggest jape that ever was," Rudi answered, with enormous relish. "I only wish that I could have thought of it. Our camp got word of a train of mules, under escort by a company of Cos's men." Margaret swiftly dropped a brief kiss on Race's lips and bundled Johnny into his lap. The child smiled at her, and at his father – and Margaret marveled anew at how alike they looked; Race's sensitive and intelligent features translated to an infant face but animated by the same look of interest. Mama had already put wheat bread on the rise and punched it down into loaves ready for the iron bake-oven. There was the end of ham which she and Papa had brought, potatoes to bake in the coals, pickles of Margarets' own preserving, and two pies, one of pumpkin and one of dried-apple – but that last with a piece already cut out of it. Margaret looked towards her brothers with exasperation.

"That was meant for supper; who has already helped themselves?"

"I did," Carl answered. "I was that hungry, M'grete. We had come from all the way from Bexar and I do like apple pies!" he added with a look of pleading so like that on the face of her sons when they begged for a sweet or some such other treat that Margaret's heart was entirely melted. However, she found it within her to answer with a most severe expression, "Then you have already had your share of it, Carlchen. For a sweet, you must have pumpkin only and I will have my eye on you!"

"Yes, M'grete," he answered, and Margaret felt as if her heart had turned entirely over in her breast. How – why had Papa allowed him, he who was her dearest little brother – go away with Rudi? He was a child still, her baby brother, although it seemed from Rudi's telling that he had done good yeoman's service in the siege of Bexar. Mama had already taken the ham from the food-cupboard, shaking her head.

"There is not enough for us all from this," she said. "I know very well how the boys will eat. A stew of beans, with the ham, M'grete. I had put some to soak in the coals for later – providential, was it not?"

"Indeed," Margaret agreed. She began to chop up onions to flavor the beans and ham while listening to Rudi tell how a rumor swept the Texian camp that a heavy-laden mule train approaching Bexar carried a burden of silver and gold to buy supplies and pay wages for the Mexican garrison.

"So the general sends Colonel Bowie and a company of mounted skirmishers out to intercept the mule-train and the soldiers guarding it. Then Gen'ral Burleson sends out another hundred after them – but the whole army has heard about the gold and silver and wants in on it by now. Cos sends reinforcements from Bexar, all that and a six-pounder as well." Rudi waved his hands. "Back and forth, infantry and cavalry and that cannon all mixed up together in a tangle of ravines and creeks. Finally, we beat them into retreating, leaving the mule-train in our hands. Oh, you should have seen the fellows' faces, when they opened those packs!" He laughed heartily, and Race asked, "So was there silver and gold in them?"

"No – nothing but grass!" Rudi answered. "Fresh-cut grass – fodder for their horses! All that ruckus over bags of grass! We fought a whole battle over nothing but grass! It was enough to make a cat laugh."

"What for?" Margaret couldn't contain her curiosity. "Why would anyone take the trouble – was it some kind of joke for them?"

"Not a joke," Carl explained, softly. "Fodder for the cavalry horses inside Bexar."

"Ah," Comprehension dawned on Race's countenance. "So they were desperate. That was how your commanders knew the siege was having an effect."

"Well, there were some men of the town given parole to leave," Rudi acknowledged. "They said conditions were getting bad for Cos' men . . . but I shall remember to the end of my days those faces when they opened those packs!" He leaned back against the wall at his back and laughed again, laughing until they all felt drawn to laugh with him, even the baby Johnny, who could not understand why but only laughed because they did so.

Chapter 10 – *The Sound of Thunder in the North*

Margaret's brothers remained through Christmas and into the New Year. Papa was detained in Washington-on-the-Brazos during that time, for which Margaret at first felt some regret, but not on further consideration. If he had come to Gonzales, she feared first that he might make some sort of quarrel with his old neighbors, most of whom were now good friends of hers and her husband's – and that second, he might find some loudly-expressed fault with Carl. In the midst of war and uncertainty, a peaceful respite between last year's turmoil and the new year's darkening future was too precious to cloud with Papa's unconsidered venting of his disappointments or to hear him once again compare Carl to Rudi. She said as much to Race one night when they were in bed. The dying coals of the fire shed a final and dim orange light within the tiny room.

"Not the most comfortable of fathers," Race agreed. "And he is not deliberately cruel or unkind, save in that one respect. One cannot deny that he has provided well for you all." He tightened his arm around Margaret where they lay curled trustfully into each other. "I can see the day coming closer when Carl will leave: It will come all the sooner for his having been a soldier, and accepted by his comrades as a man of worth. He will not long endure Father Becker's slights. A boy might, but a man will have no stomach for it."

"You are certain of this? Where would he go?" The very thought distressed Margaret, and her husband answered,

"I am. He will shake off those bonds of affection for home and family and do what he would like. Fear not, Daisy-mine. He is a likeable lad. I think of him as my own brother. He will have a place of refuge as long as I have a roof to call my own."

Margaret took comfort from those words. Like other matters which gave her concern but about which she could do little, she set them aside in favor of those which she could. Christmas proved to be merry and for now all seemed secure. Her children and her husband were in good health, and many friends – those men of Gonzales who had served in the militia – were home, either on leave or because their company had disbanded after the retreat of General Cos and his garrison in Texas. The turn of the year passed: Rudi and Carl rode away south, to Goliad and the old Presidio La Bahia, which guarded the road from Copano, leaving Margaret with the unaccountable feeling that hers and Races' house was suddenly empty and quiet. Her husband began teaching his class of students again, but in mid-January disquieting news arrived; there were rumors of a large Mexican force gathering on the Rio Grande. Although the confident opinion put about all fall and winter that Lopez de Santa Anna could not advance until winter had passed, it seemed to Margaret that the assurance which had filled them all after General Cos' retreat had been replaced with a sense of nervous unease. Late that month a large party of mounted volunteers stopped over in Gonzales on their way from Goliad with orders from General Houston. James Bowie came at midday to pay his respects to Race.

"The Gen'ral has given orders that Bexar is not to be held at a cost of lives," he explained to Race, as he warmed his hands at the fire. Race was bringing in another armload of wood for the fire. The cabin door banged closed behind him as he came in and added those logs to the pile by to the fireplace. Mr. Bowie declined Margaret's offer to take his coat, that she might hang it next to the fire so that it might dry faster. "No thank'ye, Miz Vining. Don't want to put you to the trouble. I've got a bit o'chill in m'bones, rather keep it on. Gen'ral Sam, he wants me to finish demolishin' the old presidio out east of town, bring all the men and cannon in it here, an' to Goliad. He sez it's too far west, plumb too isolated to fight proper for. He thinks we otta fight where we hold our own ground, not at a fur-away outpost like Bexar."

"But that would leave Gonzales as the western-most . . ." Margaret spoke at once, before her husband. Mama looked up sharply, from where she sat in the rocking-chair with Johnny and Horace in her lap. Margaret thought Mr. Bowie was taken back a trifle, but then he nodded, as if he might be used to considering womanly advice.

"That'll be the nub of it, Miz Vining. Will Santy-Anna and his army come by land, from Saltillo an' the Rio Grande? In sich case, then Bexar is our first line of defense. Should he come by sea from Copano, then La Baheer is our stronghold."

"My brothers are sent with Colonel Fannin to defend La Bahia," Margaret exclaimed in some distress, and Mr. Bowie reassured her immediately and with an expression of great cheer,

"They are in a good position, Miz Vining, a better position than Bexar. La Baheer is a stout-built fortress, purpose-made for that end! That ol' Alamo mission – that place is right ruinous, too large for any but a good force to hold! Don't you worrit about me, an', don't you fret none about your brothers!" He smiled at her, and Margaret felt something of that dangerous charm which led men to follow him and women to think that they held his heart. "They are in a commandin' place, and led by good stout fellows. There are companies and men arrivin' almos' every day from the East, just rarin' for a good ol 'ruckus with Santy-Anna's army. We'll be right ready for 'em soon enough. Hope I may throw off this ague I ben feelin' of late afore they do," he added. Margaret thought he looked very tired, tired and ill. "Feelin' porely like I do, ma'am, I don't rightly relish the thought of a ruckus."

"I shall fix you some sage and ginger tea, then," Mama offered, first in German and when Mr. Bowie looked blank, she repeated herself in English. "That is good for fevers," she promised. When he thanked her, Mama beamed happily and busied herself about the fire, pouring hot water from the kettle into a tall pottery cup over a spoonful of crushed and dried sage leaves and gingerroot. Mr. Bowie talked with Race; matters to do with carrying messages, and where he would be found in Bexar during the weeks that he would be there. He also admired young Horace, saying,

"Won't be long now, 'fore this young fellow 'ull be rarin' t'ride along with my fellows."

"So he will," Race answered, "But it would be my wish that he go to Bos – go back East to school, first."

"Too much book-larning will take all the spirit out of a lad," Mr. Bowie grumbled, and Race laughed. They passed a companionable half-hour or so, with Mr. Bowie refusing an invitation to stay for supper and perhaps break his journey with them.

"No, thank-ye," he said, rising from the chair. He swayed a little as he did so, and Margaret thought that his face suddenly looked paler, more lined. "Long ride, getting' to me," he passed off the moment with a laugh. "I tol' the Gen'ral we'd be in Bexar tonight."

"Take care, then," Margaret said, in sudden concern. "Do you have friends who will offer better hospitality than a cold barracks or an army camp?"

"M' wife's cousins, Miss Juana an' Miss Gertrude," Mr. Bowie answered. "They'll see to me ifn' I don't get better. Miss Juana, she married Doc Alsbury last year so I c'n always call on him if he's back in town." He took his leave, still looking pale and somehow hollowed out; a man who was indifferent to death, she thought – and so death might seek him out easily enough. Margaret was uncomfortably reminded of a certain tree on the bank of the river near town, which appeared large and healthy from one side, but when seen from another side, was all crumbling wood-rot within.

The cold month of February dragged on. It rained more often than Margaret could ever remember. At mid-month, Race made a trip to Bexar and thence to Washington-on-the-Brazos, carrying messages to the Convention. He returned home carrying his dripping-wet coat and saddlebags, and shaking his head. The end of his nose and his cheeks were flushed deep pink in a face otherwise pale from the chill, and he was shivering. Margaret took his wet things, wrapping him in a blanket hastily warmed before the fire; he stretched out his feet towards the fire as soon as he had shed his boots.

"The Convention and the governor cannot agree on anything. It's like a sack full of tomcats. No wonder General Houston is sick of it. He's off negotiating with the Indians again. They intend to reinforce the walls of the Bexar presidio after all – now there are many more men in the garrison. Some regulars – do you know who their commander is? That young hothead from Anahuac, Buck Travis, while Colonel Neill's off on leave! I have a comic tableau in my minds' eye, of him standing up the garrison and lecturing them with one of his harangues, while all the men look sideways at each other and wonder where it will lead and how much longer it will last! Bowie's in charge of the volunteers, so I can't imagine too much going wrong. He's gotten everything turned around, as they were all in a sour mood until he got to work. Almaron Dickinson and Esteban Menchaca are having a fine time. They're like boys building sandcastles on the shore, with all those cannon to play with."

"What of Sue and the baby?" Margaret asked, recalling how Sue had blithely gone with Almaron on the back of his horse that October day that the Army marched out of Gonzales.

"Staying with Ramon Musquiz and his family in their house on the town square." Race smiled, gratefully pulling the warmed blanket closer around his shoulders. "Do you know, I cannot recollect my father or his friends telling me that our founding fathers and the Continental Congress were this deeply sunk in acrimony? Father Becker is in his element; among the other delegates he hardly stands out for hot temper and hasty judgment." Margaret knelt to peel off Race's socks. He had left wet footprints across the floor; they were sodden and his feet underneath them felt icy to the touch of her hands.

"You are soaked to the bone," she chided her husband. "Mama should fix you one of her teas, and I will bring you warmed socks and another blanket. It will not be my fault if you risk your health in this awful weather!"

"Dear little Daisy-mine, other men are risking more than their health," he answered, in a light tone. Margaret clicked her tongue and went to fetch the second blanket.

Within a week, a pair of messengers arrived on lathered horses from Bexar with shattering news. Both of them were well-known in Gonzales, for they had lived in Texas for a long time, as time was counted by settlers. Dr. Sutherland, limping on a badly bruised leg, had a grant from Stephen Austin.

John-Will Smith, a skilled carpenter and woodworker by trade, had lived long in Bexar and married a Mexican lady from one of the old established families. The news they brought galvanized and horrified all of Gonzales, and doubtless all of Texas, American and Mexican alike. Lopez de Santa Anna had brought an immense army across mountain, desert, and rivers all in winter, and now they had invested that broken-down citadel in Bexar. Dr. Sutherland and John-Will had seen this army with their own eyes – thousands of soldiers and dragoons, with team after team of oxen pulling cannon and bombards after them. They and other couriers had been sent by Colonel Travis with messages to Gonzales, to Goliad and to the Convention meeting in Washington-on-the-Brazos, begging for help and reinforcements. The old south road climbed a series of low heights; from the highest, John-Will and Dr. Sutherland claimed to have looked back on Bexar and seen a blood-red banner flying from the tower of the old grey church of San Fernando – a banner meaning 'no quarter,' once the battle had begun.

There had been a goodly crowd at Andrew Ponton's house asking questions of an exhausted Dr. Sutherland and John-Will. Margaret had pressed through it to speak to Dr. Sutherland, saying, "Doctor, can you tell me of Colonel Bowie? He is a friend of ours, of my husband's. When he visited us before going on to Bexar some weeks ago, he confessed that he felt in poor health . . . indeed, I thought he looked very ill."

Dr. Sutherland wearily rubbed his hand against his eyes if he was trying to put back something of a memory of what else that he had seen. "He has not made a full recovery, I fear – in fact, very much the opposite. His illness was of a peculiar nature, not to be cured by any course of treatment. At least, not any that I could prescribe under the circumstances."

Margaret could hardly bear to bring this last news to her husband. As she had feared he developed a severe chill accompanied by a high temperature and a rasping cough. He had lain for days tossing in their bed, sometimes speaking in a delirium. He was so ill that she had taken to sleeping on a pallet on the floor, that she might snatch whatever scraps of uninterrupted sleep that she could. When he would be in his right mind again, she could scarce bring herself to find the words to tell him of this latest news. So many of his friends and comrades trapped within the sprawling walls of that stone and adobe-brick compound: Esteban and Almaron, Juan Seguin, Mr. Bowie, and Lawyer Travis – that fiery and trouble-making young man from Anahuac who was now a colonel of Regulars, as ill-considered as that might have seemed. The Mexican Army had come upon them with all their preparations to defend the ill-built fortress half-done, or perhaps even not properly begun.

Race was deep in sleep when she returned. She was cheered, for his sleep had been fitful. Mama had already begun quietly preparing supper. She looked up from the fireside, and seeing Margaret's face, seemed to know instantly that something was the matter.

"What is it, M'grete-my-dearest?" she whispered.

"The garrison in Bexar is surrounded." Margaret answered. Saying so brought the reality of it crashing in, "By Lopez de Santa Anna's army. They say that it is huge, that all of the Tejano settlers and townsfolk who are Federalists have left their homes, fearing the worst."

"Oh, my dear child," Mama's face paled. "What are they doing now? What plans do they have, for this? What of your Papa? Has he sent word?"

"The news has only just come, Mama," Margaret answered in a whisper, "Colonel Travis and Colonel Bowie have sent messengers pleading for reinforcements, for they only have a hundred and forty some men and barely any supplies. George Kimball is calling out the company of mounted rangers, so I expect they will go as soon as they may be assembled."

"Who may be assembled?" Race's voice was cracked and hoarse from coughing, unnaturally loud after Mama's whispers. Margaret was horrified. She was so sure he had been asleep, but no, he was sitting up in the bed, pushing the blankets aside. "What has happened, Daisy-mine? Has Santa Anna, come at last?"

"Yes," Margaret's lips felt stiff, ice-cold. "He brought an army overland from Mexico. Our men have withdrawn to the Alamo fortress and are begging for help."

"I'd be begging, too," Race swung his feet to the floor. "The place is a tumble-down wreck, for all that Bowie's volunteers can reinforce it. I heard you say that George is calling up the ranging company. Bring me my trousers, Daisy-mine, and my boots."

"You cannot go from your bed," Margaret exclaimed, "You are sick and it is bitter cold outside!"

"Daisy-mine." Race attempted to stand. "I will do no more than going to tell George that I will go with the others. We can do nothing less. They came to our aid last fall when we asked for it. We must now go to theirs." He swayed and sat down abruptly on the edge of the bed, face in hands.

Margaret went to his side, pleading, "You are sick, my dearest. I will go and tell Mr. Kimball that you will ride with the company as long as they do not intend departing tonight. Please – lie down. You will recover in good time." She was torn between worry for him and relief that he obviously could no depart at this very hour; Race gave way without protest and she drew the blankets over him.

He caught and held her hand, as she did so. "Tell them that I will ride, without fail," he whispered. "Honor demands nothing less."

"I will," she promised, "Rest now, so that you will be strong enough."

But Race was not strong enough. He lay in a restless delirium for nearly a week. To soothe him, Margaret made a show of packing his saddlebags and haversack, and rolling up some supplies in a blanket to strap behind Bucephalus' saddle. She brushed his warmest coat and hung it all over the foot of the bed, so that he could see that all was in readiness. But when the Gonzales Ranging Company assembled in the city square three afternoons later, he was no fitter to rise from the bed than he had been on the day that such a desperate plea had been received from Bexar. Margaret took Horace by the hand and walked toward the town's central square, thinking it was only fitting for her to see them away; so many husbands of her women friends, so many fathers of Race's pupils. But she had a chill in her heart that she did so, a chill to match the cold of the day, standing with Maggie Darst and her son, and Prudence Kimball with her toddler son Charlie in her arms and the bulge of another child below her apron. So many responsible men of town were headed away with the company – Jesse McCoy, the sheriff and Mary Millsaps' husband, Isaac. How could Mary cope, without her husband and only her children to aid her? *There were too many fathers of children*, Margaret thought. How could John King bear to take himself from his children, all nine and the eldest, Will, just a boy of fifteen? And too many of them were still boys, not a few having just departed from school. There was Will's friend, Gal Fuqua. It was surely only weeks ago that they were sitting on benches in Race's classroom with Johnnie Gaston; three lively lads who should still have been at their books. Instead Johnnie and Gal stood by their restless horses, haversacks and saddlebags packed and bulging with supplies and ammunition. It tore her heart; they seemed little older than Horace and Davy Darst, who stood with his father's arms around his shoulders. Their heads were bent close together, their faces grave. Jacob was clearly giving last instructions and advice to his son.

Prudence Kimball hugged her son to her breast, saying softly, "He came to me and said that he must go. He must answer the call, but that he might not return." Tears trembled on her eyelashes, and Maggie Darst answered firmly, "Men always say that. They hope that you will be 'specially sweet to them, before they go." She murmured a ribald suggestion.

Prudence laughed painfully between her tears, and answered, "Of course we did. But oh, Maggie – what will I do without him? I shall miss him terribly."

"We will manage." Maggie sounded brisk and matter-of-fact. "We always do. And we will have our friends about, all to help each other."

Now it appeared they were ready: Jacob finished speaking to his son, and embraced him and then Maggie, one and another. He set his hat straight on his head, and put a foot to stirrup. He leaned down from horseback to kiss Maggie one last time. "We'll be back, as soon as we get them Mexes straightened out," he said, and Maggie answered, "You do that and you see that you come straight back to me safe, you hear, Jacob Calloway Darst!"

Jacob touched his hat-brim with his fingers and smiled down at her, before wheeling his horse towards Pru's husband, and Albert Martin. They were already forming up, two and two. John-Will Smith rode at George Kimball's elbow; having carried the message from the Alamo fortress and knowing the countryside nearby very well, he would guide them back by the best way, under the cover of dark.

Suddenly, Will King appeared in the square, solemn-faced and dressed for the trail. He darted into the press of horseman until he came to George Kimball and caught the reins of his horse.

"Cap'n, let me go," he cried, "Let me go in Pa's place! I'm old enough, and Ma and the little ones, they still need Pa at home."

"Will!" John King, Will's father, followed after his son. "Don't fret after me, boy – it'll be all right." But his face was ashen, and Will's next words seemed to groove deep lines in his face.

"No, Pa! The little ones is sick, an' Ma is run ragged with trying to nurse them and see to the farm. Please, Pa – Cap'n Kimball. Let me go in your place. Gal an' Johnnie aren't much older'n me, and they're riding with you! I can do a man's work in the ranging company, but I can't do the work that needs doin' at home. Please, Pa – stay with Ma an' the chirren, let me go with the company. I'll do you proud, Pa, I'll promise."

George Kimball looked between the faces of father and son, with anguish clear in his eyes. Finally he said, "John, your boy's well-growed. I'd take him into the company. But two from one family, when one's needed at home? I can't do that. There's no dishonor implied to the one who stays behind. One or the other goes with us today to Bexar and joins them in the Alamo; you or young Will – your choice, and don't linger over it. We're ready to ride."

"Please, Pa," Will's face was alight with pleading and youthful determination. "Let me go. Ma can better spare me than she can spare you."

"All right, lad," John King's shoulders slumped in resignation. "I'll stay. But you take care, now. Your Ma and I, we'll be waiting to see you come home safe. You take care, boy – keep yourself as safe as you can and return to us. Your Ma may not forgive me, otherwise." He dismounted, and held his mount's head long enough for his son to take his place in the saddle. He handed the reins to Will, saying, "Let me shorten those stirrups for you. Remember – this ol' boy, he don't like loud noises. He skitters to the left when startled. There's a big packet of coffee in the right saddlebag. George – that is, Cap'n Kimball, signed for a shipment of 52 pounds of it to use on our way and for our boys in the Alamo." Will gathered up the reins into his hands; his own face reflected excitement and exuberance, even as his father continued. "Remember, Will – do as Cap'n Kimball orders, and above him, Colonel Bowie. This ain't be no boy's game." John King's face seemed to break with emotion, as a dam breaks, holding back a flood that could not be held. "This is a serious matter, Will – no game for you lads."

"I know, Pa," Will answered, but his face was wholly and boyishly excited. His father slapped the horses' wither and turned away, perhaps to hide the tragic expression on his own face. Will joined the tail of the company with Gal and Johnnie. A ragged cheer rose from the watching crowd in the square as George Kimball and John-Will Smith led the company down towards the ferry landing. Pru turned away, as soon as the leaders were out of sight, tears streaming down her face. Gal, Johnnie, and Will were laughing and jubilant, larking about at the tail of the column as if they were off on the greatest adventure in the world. Margaret considered them and Carl – just their age and already a soldier – *so young, so young!* Her heart seemed to freeze within her. Maggie Darst put her arm comfortingly around Pru's shoulders from one side and Margaret from the other, and they walked a little way towards the Darsts' house together, reassuring Pru, who shook with the force of her weeping.

"No bright banners, no brass band," Margaret remarked. "I don't think we do what is supposed to be the spectacle of a proper army very well. But then our men aren't really soldiers, are they? Farmers, storekeepers, carpenters, and blacksmiths. Only fighters when they need to be."

"I don't want George to be a soldier," Pru sobbed. "I want him here, and safe by the time the baby is born, to hold his child and play with Charlie!"

"Don't cry, Pru. You want him to think of his last sight of you as being brave," Maggie said, her own cheeks wet. "A stalwart Spartan woman."

"I don't feel brave or stalwart," Pru sniffled. "I've lost one husband before I wed George, I cannot bear loosing another."

"They will return," Maggie answered firmly. "They will. And George will hold the new baby in his arms and think you have done marvelous well, and then he will tell you all about how he and our ranging company fought like raging wildcats and defeated all of Santa Anna's soldiers and sent them packing back across the Nueces. It is an honorable thing they do, Pru – although I like it as little as you do."

"*I could not love thee, Dear, so much, Loved I not honour more.*" Margaret quoted a line of poetry that she knew from Race's books. "A Cavalier soldier to his lady, explaining why he was going to fight for his king."

"It sounds like something written by a man," Pru said, on a sob. "Making an excuse to do what he wanted to do anyway."

"Dearest Pru, I don't think he wished to go from your arms," Margaret answered. "No more than mine own husband will want to go from mine. But Lopez de Santa Anna has sent an army upon us. If we have safety for ourselves and a bright future for the children, then our men think it a worthy cause. Race will go as soon as he can rise from his sickbed and climb into the saddle, or so he assures me. "

"All what you say may be true," Pru blinked away the tears from her eyes, as they seemed to well up again, "but – oh, that it would be so hard to see them ride away, and go home and spend the nights alone . . . thinking only of them and hoping they are safe, and yet not knowing."

"How does Mr. Vining fare?" Maggie asked with sudden, but very real concern. "Is he improved any?"

"A little," Margaret sighed. "He tries to rise from his bed, assuring me that he is recovered, then he faints upon the edge of it, or in the middle of the breezeway."

Maggie Darst shook her head, in commiserating fashion. "Your man always puts me in mind of a high-bred racing horse. Fine and elegant and as swift as the wind, none better at winning a race, but in such need of careful tending. Now Pru, your George; he's a good sturdy cob. Slow, steady and trustworthy when hitched to a carriage; not elegant, but serviceable enough, the salt of the earth." Her affectionate words made Pru laugh in the midst of her tears.

"And so what manner of animal is your own husband, Maggie?" she asked, in tease, and Maggie laughed.

"In all but the getting of children, my husband is a big, stubborn Kentucky mule, broke for the plough and pulling heavy burdens without complaint. Tireless and strong as the day is long; gentle for those he feels affection for, but a swift kick and a bite for those he does not. Here is my house, Pru, so I must be to it but if you do not wish to be alone tonight, come and sup with me and Davy. Stay with us, if you have a mind to – in your state, you should best not be alone. There is no shame in looking to your friends for comfort."

"Thank you, Maggie, I believe that I will." Pru smiled, a watery smile in a face streaked with tear-tracks. Margaret took her leave of them, with Horace quiet at her side, feeling some satisfaction that Maggie and Pru would find comfort in sharing their worries and a meal together. In her way, Maggie was like her husband, given to carrying heavy burdens cheerfully and without complaint; her stoicism would be good for Pru.

Left to herself, as she walked towards St. Francis Street, Margaret swung Horace up into her arms, relishing the feel of his little arms around her neck and the weight of him on her hip. Children – that dearest of blessings; too soon grown and gone about their own concerns, but none the less dear for all of that.

At her house, Mama had taken the baby into the other portion of the house. Race lay sleeping quietly, for which she was grateful. If his illness allowed, he would have been among the men she and Pru and Maggie had bid farewell to that day. She thought again of the boys – Johnnie, Gal and Will King, laughing as they followed the rest of the company down the road to the ferry-landing. Schoolboys – and how their schoolmaster had wanted to go with them!

Her husband recovered slowly from this illness – the first serious one he had suffered from in all the time of their marriage. The racking cough that afflicted him seemed to hang on and on. He was able to get out of bed and move around the house, with careful deliberation within a week, but Margaret thought the very effort left him drained and exhausted. Outside it remained bitter cold, the sky a clear and rain-washed blue. Spring seemed suspended, the usual new leaves and wildflower buds hesitant to show themselves. The news arriving in whispers and on the tight-packed pages of the *Telegraph & Texas Register* from San Felipe was not reassuring. Race sat before the fire with the latest issue, reading the tiny print with difficulty by the light of the oil-lamp.

"*Written from the Commandancy of the Alamo, Bexar – February 24th, 1836,*" he read out loud, to Mama, Margaret, and Maggie Darst, who had come to pay a visit and bring a loaf of her bread as a gift to Race, who liked her bread-baking enormously. "*To the people of Texas and all Americans in the world . . . Fellow citizens and compatriots, I am besieged by a thousand or more of the Mexicans under Santa Anna. I have sustained a continual bombardment and cannonade for twenty-four hours and have not lost a man."*

"Thank the lord for that!" Maggie exclaimed, in cheerful relief, at which Race smiled. "That's good, is it not?"

"Yes, very good. Most fortunate, actually." Race continued reading from the *Telegraph*, *"The enemy has demanded a surrender at discretion; otherwise, the garrison are to be put to the sword, if the fort is taken."*

"Oh, dear," Mama said, and Margaret silently took Maggie's hand, for she had gone quite pale, at those words. They had already known of the blood-red no-quarter flag, seen at a distance from the tallest tower in Bexar, but it was another matter to have it acknowledged in Colonel Travis' dispatch.

"I have answered the demand with a cannon shot, and our flag still waves proudly from the walls. I shall never surrender or retreat. Then I call on you in the name of liberty, of patriotism, and everything dear to the American character, to come to our aid with all dispatch. The enemy is receiving reinforcements daily, and will no doubt increase to three or four thousand in four or five days. If this call is neglected, I am determined to sustain myself as long as possible and die like a soldier who never forgets what is due to his own honor, and that of his country. Victory or death – signed, William Barrett Travis, Lieutenant Colonel, Commandant. Post Scriptum; the Lord is on our side. When the enemy appeared in sight we had not three bushels of corn. We have since found in deserted houses eighty or ninety bushels, and got into the walls twenty or thirty head of beeves."

Race folded the paper and set it aside. "I can only hope that such stirring and desperate words have had the desired effect, and that our Army and volunteers are on the way."

"I pray every hour that our volunteers were the first of many," Maggie Darst said proudly, although her face was ashen, and she had gripped Margaret's hand very tightly, so tightly that her fingers were numb. "I have heard that Colonel Fannin has already set out from La Bahia, and General Houston is coming to Gonzales to rally the Army here for a march on Bexar."

"What better place to meet Santa Anna's army head-on, before they are farther into our settlements?" Margaret answered to reassure Maggie; she looked carefully at her husband's face. He looked haggard and more ill than he had in days. With her acute sense of his thoughts, she did not ask until later that evening, when Mama had gone to her bed, and the boys were asleep. She saw that he was reading the *Telegraph* again, the page with Colonel Travis' message on it.

"It was fortunate that they found corn enough and beeves to supply the garrison." she commented, tentatively.

He answered, with a strained smile. "Most fortunate, Daisy-mine." There was a long pause, while he folded the paper again and leaned his head back against the tall back of his armchair. "Daisy-mine . . . you have never seen the old mission, the Alamo, have you?"

"No. I have never even been to Bexar, although so many talk of the town with affection that I almost feel that I have. What does it look like, this fortress that Colonel Travis is determined to hold?"

"It's not really a fortress," her husband answered, sounding as if he was wearied down to his very bones. "It's a mission built by Spanish monks to minister to the Indians a hundred and more years ago – on low rising land, across the river from Bexar proper. There are cottonwood trees nearby, lining the riverbanks. The convent is two stories tall, well-built. That was what the Mexicans made into the barracks when the place became a garrison. That and the church next to it are built of stone – although the roof caved in over the main part of the church. The rest of it . . . well, it's of mud-brick mostly – a long rectangular compound, a tall wall lined with single-room houses. A good few of them are ruinous, too. The rubble has been used to reinforce the outer wall. Jim Bowie had his men fill in others to make cannon-mounts at the corners and in the end of the church. Almaron and Esteban were very proud of their battery when I was there last. Given enough time, I suppose it could be strengthened even more."

"Colonel Travis sounded very confident," Margaret ventured, "but you do not, my love. Why?"

"Because it is a huge place," her husband answered, in bleak tones. "There are barely two hundred men to hold the whole of it against twenty times and more their number. Unless General Houston may rally a large relief force to break the siege and come to their aid . . . I fear so deeply for my dearest friends, Daisy-love, but I would not say so to any but you."

"What do you think they will do?" Margaret asked, horrified by the implications. He answered a sentence or two in a strange language, and laughed a mirthless laugh. "From Herodotus, my dear Daisy, writing of the Spartans in their battle against the Persians at the place called the Hot Gates: It is said that on the eve of battle, the bravest Spartan warrior, Dienekes, was told there were so many Persian archers that their arrows would block out the sun. Dienekes replied laughing, 'Good. Then we will fight in the shade.'" And Race looked into the fire, with such an expression, that Margaret thought that if he had been a woman, he would have wept openly.

Chapter 11 – *A Message from Bexar*

The hours and days of March dragged past at a snail's pace; a week and a half since the Gonzales Ranging Company had ridden down towards the ferry and the road to Bexar. Surely they had achieved a safe passage into that crumbling and shabby fortress and other reinforcements were on the way? Now and again, Margaret fancied that when it was very still – at dawn, or just after sunset, and the light breeze came from the north that she could hear a faint continuous rumble, like distant thunder – the sound of cannon-fire. Toward the end of that time, rumors swept Gonzales, each more dreadful than the last. The worst of them had the Alamo fallen and all the defenders put to the sword, but that tale had been brought by a pair of Mexican cattle-drovers, who – as it turned out, had not seen anything of the sort, but had heard the dreadful tale from another drover.

Within days of reading Colonel Travis' declaration and plea in the *Telegraph,* soldiers, militiamen, and rangers began arriving in Gonzales, singly or in organized companies. Colonel Neill, who had taken leave from his duties at Bexar, thinking that all would be in order and there would be time enough to finish reinforcing the Alamo, began gathering those new recruits to a new army, an army commanded by General Houston. Race, with his face seeming to be pale skin stretched over the bones of his face, at last recovered enough strength to resume his duties as a courier and dispatch rider.

Margaret went with him to the sprawling encampment on the Military Plaza, on the pretense of extending the use of part of their house to the General, or whoever of his staff might have need of lodgings. The gathering volunteers had set up there, at some distance from the back of those houses along St. John's Street. The morning sun sent spreading shadows all across the grass and the tents; grass and canvas alike were sodden with morning dew. A line of small campfires sent narrow columns of smoke up into the air. Under the shelter of a spreading oak tree, a handful of rough-dressed men riding winter-shaggy horses were just dismounting and tying their reins to stakes and picket-posts, as if they were awaiting momentary orders sending them on some errand. Race greeted one of them, a rangy man with a long and slightly crooked nose. Thinning hair straggled over a high forehead, and his ears stood out from the sides of his head like the lugs on a sugar bowl.

"Erastus," Race said, and then repeated himself, slightly louder. "Erastus, is General Houston within?"

"He is, that," the man thus greeted answered, in a slightly flat voice, which at once sounded as if he spoke a little too loud. "He's in his tent, but he's mighty busy at the moment with Colonel Neill. I can bear him a message, though. How you been keepin', Race? You don't look so good."

"I've been better," Race answered. "Erastus, I don't believe you have met my wife, Margaret – her father is Alois Becker, that big outspoken Dutchman with a tract at Waterloo on the upper Colorado, and her brothers are with Fannin's company. Daisy-mine, this is Erastus Smith – a gentleman of Bexar, a scout and tracker of truly legendary skills. To hear the stories, he is an equal to Natty Bumppo, but in truth, all the better for he is real, and Natty merely an engaging fiction. No scout knows Bexar and the area around as well as he, not even the wild Comanche."

"I am very pleased to meet you," Margaret answered, and Erastus Smith bowed over her hand, looking slightly puzzled.

"You will have to speak louder," Race said, in an aside. "I fear that he is very hard of hearing." Margaret repeated herself, feeling slightly foolish – surely she ought to have noticed – and Mr. Smith answered, "And I you, Mrs. Vining."

Searching her mind for a polite and social topic of conversation, for such seemed to be expected, she said, "We are waiting on such tenterhooks for news from Bexar, news of our friends – as I have no doubt that you are also. Did your family remain there? Do you have assurance of their safety?"

"So we all wait." Mr. Smith looked grim and rather tired. "Though the General will not be content to wait patiently much longer. As for my own family, Mrs. Vining, I had my wife and kin removed back east to Fort Bend. Such stories as came to me through my wife's relations over the winter about Santa Anna's armies made me fair uneasy. I thought to take them out of harm's way, although my wife was most reluctant to leave her kin, thereabouts." Mr. Smith scratched his jaw, reflectively, "I could not make others perceive the dangers which I did, to my own sorrow. I spoke as plain as I could."

"There are those who perhaps cannot hear," Race observed, to a wry and almost boyish grin from Mr. Smith. "Which is a social inconvenience. Then there are those who *will* not hear – which can often lead to tragedy; or at the least, a degree of embarrassment."

"And what of your particular friends in Bexar, Mrs. Vining?" Mr. Smith asked. "Were they not urged to leave the city?"

"No." Margaret thought of Sue Dickinson, with her arm around Almaron's waist. "The friend for whom I am most worried went eagerly to Bexar with her husband last fall. Susanna Dickinson and her little daughter; her husband is the commander of artillery within the Alamo. She would not be parted from him, under any circumstance. They were staying with the Musquiz family, and I pray that she remained under their protection rather than go into the fortress."

"We all pray for their safety," Mr. Smith answered, the tones of his voice bleak, instead of hopeful. "Their safety and safe return, although hope for that dies a little, every hour. Henry Karnes and I go out today to scout along the Bexar road in hopes of putting the worst rumors to rest."

"Thank you," Margaret answered softly, and her husband added, "Erastus, if you would be so kind, convey my compliments to Colonel Neill and General Houston. I am more or less fit to return to service. And my wife and I can make part of our house available to any of his staff who need lodgings, as well as any friends among those arrived."

"I thank ye," Mr. Smith replied, "and I will pass that on with your compliments. We may not stay long enough to have need of lodgings, though – I fear we will be living in the saddle for a mite. Report to my second tomorrow, with your horse and all your gear. You may as well have one more night under a good roof."

Silently, Margaret and her husband returned to their home; that General Houston and the army would not remain long in Gonzales was disquieting to Margaret. What did that mean? If the Alamo fortress had fallen then there was no use in going forward. Would the General and his men wait for Lopez de Santa Anna to move against them?

"I do not know," Race confessed when Margaret put the question to him. "We do not have cavalry to match his. To fight on the open plains against such horsemen? Such an attempt will not turn out well." In the morning, Race added a few things to his saddlebags, embraced the boys, and smiled patiently at Margaret as she tied a thick knitted scarf around his neck.

"Keep yourself as safe as you may," she said, with a catch in her voice and a pain in her throat, "and as warm and dry as you can."

"Daisy-mine, I am likely going only as far as General Houston's camp," he answered, with deep amusement. "If there is no need of me by tonight, I might very well come back and sleep at home."

And so she thought it was Race, early that evening, as the setting sun painted ruddy light against the western-facing window, for that was a man's booted footsteps walking across the porch. She wondered briefly why he did not open the door and come in, but when he tapped instead on the door she knew it was not her husband but a stranger. She opened the door, to a heavy-set young man in a buckskin hunting coat. He took off his cap immediately; he had bright red hair and a pale face splattered with freckles.

"Ma'am," he ventured awkwardly, "Are you Miz Vining? I'm Harry Karnes. Deef sent me ahead with a message, on account of you bein' a friend of Miz Dickinsons'. That is you an' not this other lady, ma'am?"

"Deef?" Margaret was taken back. Mama, rolling out pie-crust dough on the table, looked as if she was keeping herself from smiling. The young man reddened with embarrassment.

"Deef Smith. They call him that on account o' him being deef as a post. That is, he don't hear too well. You are Miz Vining, ain't you?"

"I am," Margaret was still puzzled, but young Mr. Karnes freckled countenance looked momentarily brighter, and then went somber again.

"Deef said you should come at once. He said it would be best to have another woman there; a friend, if you can. We found Miz Dickinson and two darkies today, twenty miles out from here on the Bexar road. She was mighty wearied, so Deef stayed with her an' sent me on ahead. They came with a message to Gen'ral Sam from ol' Santy-Anna." At his words, Margaret felt a sinking in her heart, and Mama let the rolling-pin fall. It fell against the pie-dish with a clatter.

"Let me get my shawl," she said. "Where are we going?"

"To the Gen'ral, at the inn. That's where Deef said he'd bring her."

"Mama?" she said, over her shoulder, "I'll be at the Turner's. I don't know for how long. Don't wait on me for supper, the boys will be hungry soon."

In silence, she walked with Harry Karnes, he having offered her his elbow with something of a tentative air as if he had been told that was the proper courtesy for a lady, but never having had much experience with actually performing it.

Presently, she asked, "What of the Alamo? What did Susanna tell Mr. Smith of events there? Has it truly fallen to the Mexican army?"

"It has," Harry Karnes' lips tightened to a pale line. "I can say no more, Miz Vining. Deef said that the Gen'ral must hear of it from her first."

"What of the garrison?" Margaret demanded, in some shock, although such tidings had not come entirely as a surprise. Rumors had been flying for almost a week. "Mr. Karnes, I only ask as many were men of Gonzales, men of worth and substance, our friends and neighbors. Surely you can tell me of their fate, and if any survived!" Young Karnes looked bleakly ahead, his plain blunt features working with emotion.

"None did, ma'am," he answered, and Margaret felt as if she had suddenly fallen with great force, and had the breath knocked out of her. "A bare handful who survived the final assault were cut down in cold blood by order of Santy-Anna hisself an' in his presence."

"All?" Margaret repeated, more to herself, trying to get her mind to adapt to those few words.

"Yes, ma'am." Harry Karnes looked straight ahead, as if he was trying to do the same, save that he had had more hours in which to force his mind to accept the enormity of such news. They walked on in silence, out towards the Turner's hotel, and the canvas sprawl of tents and brush-arbors, away out in back of it. It seemed as if the camp had grown just in the few hours since the day before.

As they approached the steps of the hotel, a little party on horseback came upon them: three men and a woman, with a Negro man, striding along on foot beside and looking almost cheerful. Margaret knew Erastus Smith at once but at first she did not recognize the woman with a Mexican blanket pulled shawl-like over her head, slumping with exhaustion in the saddle of her horse, with a child in her arms. The Negro man was leading her horse by the reins; a second Negro man rode behind. Only when the horseback party came closer did Margaret know for sure that the woman was Susanna. All the mischievous gaiety and liveliness in her had been quenched, her face as ashen as the grey-powdered coals of a fire long dead. Her hair hung lank and uncombed, straggling around her face. She stared straight ahead, as if she had no energy or mind to do anything else.

"Ma'am, the Gen'ral's waiting for ye inside," Harry Karnes went from Margaret's side to Susanna's, and reached up his arms towards her. "Hand me down the little 'un. We sent for yer friend, Miz Vining. She came to be with you when you talk to Gen'ral Sam. Don't you fret, Miz Dickinson. He's a kindly man . . . it's just that you are sent with a message, and the first trusty party to come out of the Alamo, so he must speak to you."

"Give him the baby, Sue," Margaret commanded, gently. "I will carry her for you, she knows me." For a long moment, Sue's eyes went between Margaret and Harry Karnes, and then to Erastus Smith, who had also dismounted and hovered close by.

"He won't take Angelina?" Sue answered, in a distant voice. "General Santa Anna was taken with her. He said he would adopt her and send her to Mexico City. But I said no, once and again, and finally he stopped saying that he would. "

"Gen'ral Sam, he won't do any such thing," Harry Karnes answered. "He ain't that kind of general – and I ain't that kind of sojer would go 'long with that. If you like, give the little 'un to Miz Vining."

"Let me hold her, Sue," Margaret urged her again. "She knows me, she will not be frightened." And she reached up towards Sue, who reluctantly yielded up Angelina to her; a fearfully silent and filthy child who smelt of dirty diapers and hid her face in Margaret's shoulder. "Come with us into the house, Sue. You are safe now."

"No," Sue shook her head, even as Harry Karnes and Mr. Smith, each took her arms and lifted her carefully down from the saddle of her wearied horse. Her knees buckled momentarily, and then she stood straight, the skirts of her dress just brushing the toes of her shoes. Margaret noticed that the hem of it was dabbled and edged almost all the way around with rust-colored mud, as if Sue had waded through a puddle and allowed her skirt to drag. The stains were the color of dried blood. Then she realized, with horror – they were indeed bloodstains. "I am not safe, and neither are any of you. Santa Anna has sworn to hang our leaders as rebels and chase the rest of us out of Texas."

"He shall not do any such thing," Margaret rejoined, swiftly, "for our homes are here, homes which we built and lands that we settled ourselves – not him or any of his soldiers. We have our rights and General Houston has gathered hundreds of our own here, ready to defend those rights."

"So they said," and Sue laughed, a mirthless laugh. "Our rights and our lands . . . but for all of Colonel Travis' fine words? They are dead, Margaret – all of them and my husband among them. They came to our aid – but not so many as could hold it. Now they are all dead, and Almaron is dead and Colonel Travis, too, and my child is an orphan. They burned their bodies, there were so many of them fallen! There were two great pyres on the road leading to Powder House Hill. They sent me with the message."

"Sue, Sue . . ." Margaret tucked Angelina into one arm, and embraced her friend with the other, "Oh, Sue my dear! I am so sorry to hear of this! But you are the first come to come from Bexar, who has seen what happened there. These men need to hear what you have seen."

"That letter from General Lopez de Santa Anna," Sue replied, "may tell all that these great men need to know!"

"Dear Sue," Margaret said in answer, "a letter for the General; that may be one thing. But of what you have seen, and may yet tell of it is another. We must know of what befell our friends."

"I don't know what I can tell!" Sue cried, "I was with the other women, in a little stone room in the church. My husband came to me shouting that the Mexicans were within our walls. He kissed me and begged that if I were spared to save his child. I did not even see him die, so I don't know what I can tell of others!"

Behind Margaret, someone cleared their throat – it was Erastus Smith, who said, in somewhat louder tones, but with exceeding tenderness, "Ma'am, tell us as little or as much you can. Come with us into the house, and I will give Santy-Anna's letter to General Sam, and when you have answered such questions as I cannot, then you may rest." He took her arm, with careful and fatherly tenderness. Margaret walked on her other side, the heavy weight of Angelina in her arms. At a gesture from Harry Karnes the two Negro men followed after them. The big parlor of the Turner hotel now seemed cramped, the air in it thick with tension and crowded with men. Men stood in the corners or along the rough-plastered walls, gathering wherever there was room. It was hot and airless with so many within, especially after the evening chill outside. Three chairs and a small table sat in the middle of the room; as they entered, a tall man sprang up quickly from the largest.

To him, Erastus Smith handed a much-folded oblong of heavy paper, sealed with a blood-colored ribbon and a wax lozenge, saying quietly, "This is Miz Dickinson an' her little girl, Sam. Her man was Colonel Travis' commander of artillery, an' she was in the fortress up to the very last. This is the message that Santy-Anna sent with them. Miz Vining was good enough to come, also . . . thought it best, meself, having another woman present. These two boys here – Ben was a servant of Colonel Almonte and sent to escort them. This other is Joe. He b'longed to Colonel Travis, but he did not see much until after it was over."

So this is General Sam, Margaret thought; curiosity momentarily distracting her from her concern for Sue and her distress over the tragic news that she brought. He was ruggedly built and dark of hair and eye, with a cleft in his chin and strong features which just missed being handsome. He seemed to crackle with energy barely reined in, and the same intense vitality which drew people to her brother Rudi, like iron-filings to a magnet. But Rudi was young, hardly more than a boy. General Sam was at least twice his age. He reminded her of a panther, or some other large cat, prowling restlessly because he must move, having too much energy to merely sit still.

Now he took both of Sue's hands in his, saying with curious gentleness, "Mrs. Dickinson, we grieve with you for your sorrowful loss and the loss of so many brave and loyal sons of Texas. Would that we could allow you seclusion, and a proper time of mourning, but there is no time. Pray forgive us our intrusion on your grief, but I and my officers, and your friends of Gonzales seek answers, and you are the one person who may reliably provide them. We will take no longer of your time then we need. I will look at this letter first, and leave you time to compose yourself. Mrs. Turner will bring you some small refreshment . . . no?"

Upon Sue's refusal of food or drink, he settled Sue in the chair in which he had been sitting, and turned to Margaret. "I thank you for your assistance and your time, Mrs. Vining." His hands were warm, and very strong. "You are of this settlement, then? Pray assure me that your husband was not among the Gonzales company which answered Colonel Travis' plea."

"He would have been," Margaret answered, "but he was ill on the day set for departure, although he has since recovered. He came to the camp today, to take up service again."

"Ah," Houston's eyes lightened; he immediately appeared more cheered. "He was pointed out to me. The schoolteacher with the splendid black horse! I taught school once, but I did not have as fine a horse as that, for all the pains that I took! Be assured, Mrs. Vining, Houston will have better use from him and that noble steed than to be mewed up in a fortress. He has already been dispatched to Mina, with instructions for the militia there! Do sit, Mrs. Vining – close, that you may attend on Mrs. Dickinson. Pray pardon me for a moment. I have a communication from the Napoleon of the West which must take my attention." Margaret sat, arranging the half-asleep Angelina in her lap, while Houston broke the seal of the letter and opened it.

"Gentleman," he said after a moment spent scanning the lines written on a sheet of fine heavy paper, "the General-in-Chief of the Army of Operations of the Mexican Republic writes to us as the inhabitants of Texas, doing the courtesy of addressing us as citizens and also calling us a parcel of audacious adventurers . . . dividing amongst themselves the fertile lands contained . . . Oh, here is contained an especially good portion," and Houston read from the letter, his voice fairly dripping with sarcasm and mockery. "*It became necessary to check and chastise such enormous daring; and in consequence, some exemplary punishments have already taken place . . . Your city and the fortress of the Alamo are already in possession of the Mexican Army, composed of your own fellow citizens; and rest assured that no mass of foreigners will ever interrupt your repose, and much less, attack your lives and plunder your property. The Supreme Government has taken you under its protection and will seek for your good.*" Houston crumpled the letter, half contemptuously, and tossed it down on the table. "Gentlemen, I care little for a supreme government taking me under protection and seeking for my good. I'll not waste the ink in reply but make our response in black powder and shot. Now, Mrs. Dickinson," and Houston's voice softened. He sat himself down at Sue's other side and took her hand in his once again. "Tell me – tell us all, of what befell in the Alamo since Colonel Travis's final messages. Tell me also of his fate, and the fate of my friends, Colonel Bowie and Colonel Crockett. I presume they made a brave end?"

"Colonel Bowie . . . he was dreadful sick," Sue whispered. "Some said he was dying already. He was not able to leave his bed for many days, or take any part in the defenses. Joe said . . ." she looked across the room, to where the two Negro men stood. "A Mexican officer took him around afterwards, to tell them the names of the dead officers. Colonel Bowie was bayoneted by many soldiers where he lay in his sickbed, in a little room apart from the other wounded. Colonel Travis, he died at the beginning of the last assault of the walls."

"On the north wall bat'ry," the younger of the two Negro men said. "Shot clear in the haid, fell down stone dead. I doan' know what happened then."

"What of my good friend Colonel Crockett?" Houston pressed her hands, and Sue's voice grew stronger,

"He wasn't a colonel, not really. He told them all to call him a high private. He was so good and kindly . . . and so funny, with his stories. He and Mr. McGregor from Nacogdoches – they had musical contests sometimes, to see who might make the most noise; Mr. McGregor with a set of bagpipes and Mr. Crockett with an ol' fiddle he found someplace. I know nothing of how he fell, but I saw him dead in a heap with many of his Tennessee folk, not far from the church doors, when we were brought away from that place in the church where we had taken refuge. I knew him at once from his fur cap. That was the place that his Tennessee company were to hold, for it was the place of weakness, with just a timber wall. The church was to be the last defense."

"Go on, Mrs. Dickinson," General Houston encouraged her. "What of the last day? What can you remember?" Margaret re-settled the sleeping Angelina in her lap, thinking how well she had grown since she had seen her last. The child slept still with a thumb in her mouth and something clutched tight in her other hand, something small hanging from a string around her neck. Margaret gently prized the object from her fingers – a heavy gold ring with a dark stone, a man's ring. It did not look like a keepsake from her father.

"That was Colonel Travis' ring," Sue said. "He gave it to her just before the very last day. He asked her to keep it safe for him, and tied it around her neck. That was the last time we saw him."

"The families of the Gonzales troop – they will want to know of what befell them," Margaret tucked the ring back into Angelina's hand. "Did you see anything of those friends of ours which might give comfort to their families? Did any other have time to send a letter or a memento with you?" and Sue shook her head, as tears began to pour down her cheeks.

"Nothing which would give comfort," she answered, brokenly. "I saw only Gal Fuqua. He ran into the little room where we were and he tried to tell me something, but I do not know what, for he was shot through the jaw and could not speak so that I could understand, even though he tried to hold his face together."

Margaret closed her eyes – oh, what a horror. She thought of the three boys – Gal, Johnnie, and Will, larking together at the back of the column on the day that the Gonzales Company departed. They had been so excited to have been allowed to join the older men, to take their place in the company and play the part of a brave soldier. That would truly be a stab in the heart for Race, knowing that his cherished students had gone ahead, gone into that fire- and blood-streaked darkness, in the shade of the arrows. Sue went on speaking, although Margaret could not take in all of what she was saying. The room had gone silent, although she was aware of more people gathering outside the door and the windows, of whispered confabulations among them, as those who were near enough to hear passed along what was said. She opened her eyes, at last. Someone had lit a lamp, which only made the parlor seem hotter. General Houston sat, still holding Sue's hand, and weeping unashamedly.

After a time, which seemed like hours, General Houston thanked Sue, and gave her over to the care of Mrs. Turner, who took the sleeping Angelina into her own arms. When Sue had left the room, so pale and drained that she looked like rag wrung entirely dry, General Houston dismissed all but Margaret, Harry Karnes and Erastus Smith.

"Mrs. Vining," the General said at last, dragging the sleeve of his coat across his face, "may I impose upon your time for a little while longer? I have a sad obligation to undertake for the citizens of Gonzales, in which you may best assist, before I give orders for yet another such. We have been assailed all this day and the day before with queries from the kin of those who were called to the greatest honor. Now that we know of their sad fate, I take it as my duty and obligation to inform them of what has befallen husbands and sons. You are well-acquainted with the families of those who sent their most beloved to the aid of our forces within the Alamo? Good. Then if you would, tell me the names of their wives and parents who live within the town. This is a duty which no commander relishes," and to Margaret's ears, he sounded as if he choked on those very words, "but which I am obligated to undertake. Their loved ones are owed the honor and courtesy of hearing such news from me. Of those which are best known to you . . . where may their kin be found at this hour? They will be sent for at once."

144

"There is Maggie Darst," Margaret began, feeling at first that she might also choke on her words. "She lives in a house just down the street at the corner of St. Lawrence and not a block from here. She and Jacob Darst had a son, David, but everyone calls him Davy. And Prudence Kimball may be staying with the Darsts as she is with child. Her husband commanded the company. John King – his oldest son Will took his place in the company on the day they departed from Gonzales, so that he and his wife will want to know. The Fuquas live halfway between the Darsts, at the corner of St. Lawrence Street. And the Kelloggs – they sent two of their kin in the company." She went through the list of the Gonzales Mounted Rangers, each of their faces and the web and weft of their friendship and connection within the town clear in her own memory, as she called them up, one and another for the General. She felt as if she sang a dirge for them, and for their town, naming each, and their trade, their family and friendship connections. And at the end of it, the General sat with her hands in his, just as he had sat with Sue, and she had the feeling that he looked out into a dark future as well as a bleak present. The Turner's house echoed with the sound of many heavy feet, as the General's staff and officers came and went. Outside the parlor window, there was a great bustle in the camp, campfires burning with a red-gold blaze and torches flaring and moving against the darkening sky.

"I thank you, Mrs. Vining. Nomads such as I have been for too many years without counting – do not know so much of the close friendships and connections of an established town such as this; but I assure you that I have taken careful note. All of those that you spoke of shall be sent for within the hour."

"It speaks well of you, sir, that you will take on this task, yourself," Margaret said, and General Houston laughed, a very short and bitter laugh.

"It is perhaps only slightly less pleasant to me than the other task that I will undertake tonight, Mrs. Vining – and that will be a matter which, in ordinary times, would be seen as a tragedy of the magnitude which has befallen Gonzales."

"And what might that task be?" Margaret asked. "I cannot think of anything which would add more to our grief this day." She did not think that he would answer in any other than an oblique fashion, and added hastily, "I do not really look for an answer, sir; you need not give me one if it is not something which affects us directly. I know little of military matters, other than what which my husband has shared with me from his books."

"Alas, my dear Mrs. Vining, my other task today will affect you and your neighbors substantially." All animation had drained from General Houston's features as he spoke the next words. "I have already issued orders to abandon Gonzales. Our forces will withdraw from here, falling back to the east bank of the Colorado. Fannin has been ordered to forsake La Bahia and meet with us at Victoria. We must also evacuate those settlements and holdings west of the Colorado without delay – destroying all foodstuffs, animal stock, and shelters as we go. Santa Anna's armies must find a barren wasteland. Your husband is a schoolteacher? Is he acquainted with the deeds and strategies of Quintus Fabius Maximus in the Second Punic War?"

"I believe so," Margaret answered, thinking that when she returned home she would have to refresh her memory with Races' copy of *Plutarch's Lives*. "But I cannot call the specifics to mind. My younger brothers are with Colonel Fannin, sir. Have you heard anything of their situation? Are they likely to be besieged and risk the same fate as those in the Alamo?"

"No matter – the strategies of Fabius are more agreeable to the mind of a soldier than a soldier's wife." General Houston answered, with a quick and reassuring smile. "With regard to your brothers, Mrs. Vining, I have not received word yet of such an undertaking by the Mexican Army, although the garrison at La Bahia may yet be at such a risk until my orders pry Colonel Fannin and his troops out of their little stone shell." General Houston shook his head. "I fear that massing our few companies in such strong points is a trap of sorts. Mobility is our best defense, and the key to victory will be choosing the right field for battle and at the right time. Fear not for your brothers, Mrs. Vining – or at least, not over any others in our army." The General's face went somber again. "The heart of the matter pertaining to Gonzales is that we must present a scorched earth to the Mexican Army. By that, in plain terms is that the families of our soldiers must evacuate with us tonight. As soon as you are safely gone, Gonzales will be put to the torch, along with everything that might be of use that we cannot take with us."

"I see," Margaret answered, battered by what had happened in the Turner's parlor over the last hour into an odd and accepting calm. With a tiny portion of her mind, she thought – that if they had not just listened to Sue's account, and the few words of the Negro servant Joe, than this would be a blow beyond withstanding; that her home, and all those of her friends, the Zumwalt's store, and George Kimball's hat factory – all would be no more in a few hours. "This soon, sir?"

"This very night," General Sam answered. "I regret that I have kept you so long, Mrs. Vining. And I regret most of all the necessity of what must be done now."

146

"I understand," Margaret said, although it was the juiceless and polite response, rather than reflecting her true emotions. She rose from the chair, and the General rose also. "Good night, sir."

"Good night, Mrs. Vining," he bowed over her hand, and then hesitated – just for a moment he looked boyishly uncomfortable. "May I know if we can be of further service to you and your family? We are abandoning much of our baggage so that our wagons may carry those women and children who have no conveyance of their own at hand."

"I thank you – but we have a wagon and two yoke of my father's oxen at our disposal," Margaret answered. The General's face lightened, just a little.

"Good. Follow us as best you can, Mrs. Vining. By departing tonight, we will have gained some time – time that will be the saving of us all. Karnes!" he suddenly shouted, and Harry Karnes put his head around the door of the parlor. He was gnawing on a hasty meal of bread and cured ham slapped together. He put it into his other hand, and saluted casually.

"Sir?"

"See that Mrs. Vining is safely home – either yourself, if your duties allow, or task another trusty man."

"Aye, Gen'ral," Harry Karnes took a gulp and a swallow. "Sure enough, Miz Vining. I'll see ye to home . . . although I swear, the boys are too busy tonight to give offense to any woman."

Margaret took his proffered arm; he was still somewhat uncertain about how to manage it, but seemed to have gained some confidence by his most recent essay in chivalry. She walked with him, back along St. John Street. But looking back at the camp, she saw now that the soldiers and volunteers were striking their canvas tents and burning them in the campfires.

"Aye," Harry Karnes said, when he saw that she had noted this. "It's the Gen'rals' orders now that we move fast, and without our trash an' traps. I'm sorry for this, ma'am, for it will cost your home an' all. Special sorry, as I am one of the rearguard detailed to stay behind and see to the burning of it; better us, than Santy-Anna's sojers, picking over all, ma'am. I'll try an' burn your place respectful an' all. Do not delay – at once, take what you can of what is precious to you or wrap it in oilcloth and bury it in a place that you may find again easily. That's my advice, ma'am, and sorry I am to be giving it to you tonight."

Chapter 12 – *The Runaway Scrape*

In silence Harry Karnes walked with Margaret until they reached the front of their house. Now Margaret looked upon it with silent heartbreak; she had loved their little house, homey and weathered to a comfortable gray. This very moment was the last time that she would look upon it as home, this place where she had been a good housewife, lain with her husband, borne him children, celebrated their daily happiness and contentment. Lamplight glowed comfortingly behind the two tiny, oiled-paper windows: Mama doubtless had kept supper warm for her.

At her side, Harry Karnes ventured awkwardly, "Ma'am, you should not waste any time in packing your traps. The Army moves tonight with all speed, towards the McClure place, on Peach Creek, ten mile east, as the crow flies."

"I understand," Margaret answered. "Good night then, Mr. Karnes."

"Ma'am," Harry Karnes took off his hat. "Be away before midnight." Then, jamming it on his head again, he hurried away.

There was already an unaccustomed clamor of voices, men shouting and the occasional whinny of a horse, the scrape of wood against wood filling the night from the direction of the gathering of soldiers camped on the military plaza. From a distance, she could hear the sound of a woman wailing in demented grief. What was it General Sam had mentioned, almost in passing – that Race was sent to carry orders to Mina? She and Mama would have to manage alone, although she supposed that if it came down to it, she might appeal to any of their neighbors or one of Mr. Karnes' men.

On the porch, Margaret paused, taking one last look at the dearly familiar aspect; the trees standing in the town-lot opposite, their leaves faintly silvered with starlight, the shapes of the roofs of other houses along St. Francis Street, the young oak tree in front, where her children were accustomed to play and where her husband taught school. Jacob Darst had come with his ox team and ploughed up the garden plot for them when Race was so ill. That was his last act of friendship before he rode away with the Gonzales Ranging Company. Margaret had meant to begin raking over the tumbled earth, breaking up the hard, heavy clods for her spring garden. It was too early to plant seeds – now she might never have the chance to coax another season's growing out of the rich dark earth of her garden. On the other side of the house, Papa had left his wagon, with the ox yokes propped against the porch, and the harness chains neatly coiled in the storage box under the wagon seat. The bleached canvas wagon cover shone pale against the dark sky and the trees beyond. Out to the west, beyond the line of trees along the river, she saw pale lightning flicker on the horizon. A fateful harbinger, for there was more than one kind of storm coming.

Margaret squared her shoulders and took a deep breath. It was time. She put her hand on the latch, and the door swung open. Mama looked up from the fireside, a bit of mending in her hands. The boys lay in their truckle bed, next to the big bed. Johnny was asleep and Horace lay as if he was nearly so, but she saw the gleam of a reflection from the fire in his eyes.

"Mama," she said, "the General has told us that Lopez de Santa Anna's army is coming. Our army is abandoning Gonzales and retreating east. We must pack the wagon and go within the hour if we can, for he intends to fire the town and all in it, to deny supplies and shelter to the enemy."

"Tonight?" Mama dropped her mending. "Surely, my heart – not tonight!"

"Tonight, Mama," Margaret answered with grim implacability. "Pack the boys, our clothing and bedding, all the food that we can carry in Papa's wagon. We must follow the Army close, or be left without any protection at all. Let us hasten, Mama – we have only a short time."

"But to where?" Mama pressed her hands to her heart, still unbelieving. "Where are we going, M'grete? And by what road?"

"To the Colorado." Margaret replied. "I don't know the road, Mama, I think we are just meant to follow the Army eastwards." She tied her shawl around her waist – she needed to work with her arms free, and there was so much to be done that she did not think she would feel the cold. "Roll up the bedding, Mama. Tie the blankets and our clothes into bundles with the sheets. Once we have loaded up the wagon, put the biggest straw tick on top of all so that we may have a place to sleep." She began taking dishes down from the dish cupboard, the prized china dishes which she had used for their best and most honored guests, blue toile patterned china, all the way from England.

"Mama!" she explained in exasperation. Mama was just standing there, uncertainly looking from the dish cupboard to the tin-covered trunk which sat in the far corner.

"But your supper," Mama ventured. "You have not eaten supper, and I kept it warm for you, M'grete."

"There is no time for that, Mama." Margaret held on to her patience by a mere thread. "Put it aside for me, perhaps I can eat it later. Now I must bury the dishes in a corner of the garden plot, and no, I will not use that trunk for our clothing. Empty out what is within and set it aside. I shall need that for my husband's books. Our clothes, Mama – then what foodstuffs that we have!" She took the jug of molasses which sat on a lower shelf, nearly full, and thrust it into Mama's hands. "Put that in the wagon, Mama. Start with that, and then the box of wheat flour. And the cornmeal, the coffee, and the coffee grinder. Mama, we have only an hour or so! Please, I beg you – we must pack the wagon and be gone, for they will burn this house and the whole town. I cannot bear to watch that. Let us be away before then!"

Mama obeyed, although she seemed still to be struggling to comprehend what was happening. Silently, she opened Margaret's bride's chest, and taking out a clean pillow cover, began to fill it with clothing. Horace sat up in his bed, with eyes so huge in apprehension that he looked like a baby owl.

"Mama?" he asked, "Are the Meskin sojers coming?"

"Yes, they are," Margaret snapped; there was no time to equivocate, to soften the facts of the matter. "Get dressed, Horace. Wake and dress Johnny."

"Is Papa and them going to fight the sojers, when they come?" Horace's eyes rounded, even more.

"Dear God, no, Horace – we're going to run. General Houston and your papa are going to go to a better place to stand and fight, and we must go with them. Get dressed, child – we have no time." Margaret bundled the last of the china dishes into her apron, careless of the risk of chipping or cracking them – *By the Almighty,* she thought fiercely, *when we return, we won't have a house, but we shall have good plates to eat off of when we do*! There was barely enough light to see at the corner of the garden nearest the house, and closest to St. Francis Street, where the soil had been turned up and softened by Jacob Darst's plow. She knelt, heedless of the mud and set the dishes on the ground. Taking up the shovel leaning against the side of the house, she parted the soil to make a shallow hole, feeling for a moment as if she were digging a hasty grave for her dishes. No time, no time – already she could hear more voices as the town roused. She tumbled the earth back with her hands, gently so as to spare the fragile cups, and measured with her eye the distance to the oak tree. Yes, she could find this place again.

Mama had begun piling their foodstuffs on the porch; she came out of the door gasping breathlessly with the weight of a full sack of cornmeal in her arms. Inside, Horace was dressed, but Johnny was not. He whimpered miserably, his thumb in his mouth.

"Leave him alone for now," Margaret commanded. "I have a task for you, Horace." She held a paper spill to the hottest of the coals in the fireplace and lit the two pierced tin lanterns; they relieved the darkness outside just a little, but she groaned to herself, thinking of how difficult it would be to harness the four oxen in the dark. At least, they were good and gentle beasts; Papa would not have tolerated any else. Thanks to Papa she had a wagon and teams to pull it. Other women would not; she remembered how General Houston had spoken of using the Army wagons to carry them. Maggie and her son, Pru and her baby – they would be in such need!

"Horace," she called her son to her, as she knelt at the hearth, so that her eyes would be on a level with his. Oh, to find the words to impress upon the boy without frightening him, words that would inspire him to be older than he was, to be a help, rather than a hindrance. "Horace, your Papa has gone to take a message for the Army, so we must manage ourselves. Can you take this lantern and run to the Darst's house, where Davy lives, just down St. John Street by the Market Square? You are a big boy now, you aren't afraid of the dark, are you?" When he shook his head, in a resolute no, she continued, "I want you to run to her house, and if she is still there, I want you to tell her that Oma and I will come presently with a wagon. She is to pack up what she can, just as Oma and I are doing. Tell her there will be space enough in our wagon for her and Davy. And if Mrs. Kimball is there with her, she ought to do the same. As soon as you have given her this message, come straight back to me and tell me what Mrs. Darst said. Can you do that for me?" She held her sons' eyes with hers, trying to fill him with a calm and a reassurance – a calm and certainty which she barely felt equal to herself. But she could not let her sons be frightened; most of all she could not let them see her own fear. She must be an example for them, and not be wilting from fear in adversity. She thought of General Sam, a rock of assurance and determination, and young Horace answered, very firmly, "Yes, Mama. Only silly babies are afraid of the dark."

"Then," she kissed him lightly on the forehead, "take the lantern, and run as fast as you may."

She heard his light footsteps thumping on the porch as he ran; the quick patter diminished almost at once – yes, he was running, obedient and fearless, in spite of all the terrors and uncertainty of this awful day and dreadful night. Mama had left the tin-covered trunk empty of the clothes and blankets which it had contained: Margaret could drag it easily herself, with the lantern in her hand, across the breezeway and into the other half of the house. She kicked the door wider open and lifted the lantern, regarding the shelves of Race's precious collection of books. Her heart contracted – too many, too many, even if most of them were duodecimo volumes, which fit comfortably in her own two hands. There were some most especially treasured – heavy and thick quartos and folio-sized volumes. They could not take books. There was no room in the wagon, if they were to carry Maggie and Pru, their children, and their hasty-gathered belongings. Food, bedding, clothing, the shelter of the wagon; these were the necessary priorities in this dire emergency; not frivolous things such as books and china dishes. She considered burying the trunk of books in the vegetable garden, and rejected that notion at once. She could not dig a hole sufficiently deep and wide enough for concealment, not by herself and not in a few minutes. Then she recollected the deep den which Horace and his friends had dug at the roots of the redbud tree at the Darsts. Yes, that was deep and wide, enough for the trunk of books and whatever Maggie wanted to place in it. She piled certain of the heaviest books across the bottom of the trunk. When those had made it nearly too heavy for her to lift, she carried the trunk to the wagon tail, and took down the gate. She hoisted the part-filled trunk to the level of the wagon bed and hurried back for another armful of books.

Mama had carried out all of the stores of food that Margaret had in the house. Margaret cast a glance over the random pile, reassured by the size of it but mourning in her heart what they would have had from the garden, and what would be left to burn in Zumwalt's and Eggleston's stores and warehouse. From her armful of books, some little duodecimo volumes slipped sideways from the stack in her arms; one, two of them fell at her feet. She took the time to stack them loosely in the trunk by feel, and returned to the house for another stack. Finally, she jumbled them in her apron, as she had with the dishes.

"Mama, just begin packing the wagon," she gasped. "Don't bother with being tidy, we don't have time." At last, the bookshelves were empty, the last books fitting neatly in the top of the trunk. Nothing more which could be taken from the parlor save the quilts and bedding from the bed where Mama had slept. Margaret snapped the catches of the tin trunk closed, and hung the still-lit lantern from the first wagon-bow.

Mama called from the house, "M'grete, can you help me with the chest!"

"Yes, Mama – is the baby dressed?"

"No," Mama gasped, for Johnny still sat in the middle of the truckle bed, with his thumb in his mouth and an uncharted depth of bewilderment in his eyes. There was no time to comfort him. She and Mama carried the wooden bride's chest to the wagon and pushed it past the tin trunk. The bride's chest contained her most precious belongings; her hand-pieced quilts, lengths of lace that Race had bought for her, the tiny memento portrait of him, painted on a slip of ivory and framed in gold, her children's baby clothes.

"Throw everything else in over the sides," Margaret ordered. The pillow covers filled with clothing, the blankets and quilts rolled into bundles – all went into the bottom of the wagon bed. She caught up Johnny in her arms, wrapping him in the bedclothes as he began to whimper. "Johnny-love," she gasped. "Don't cry. We're just following after the Army so that we will be

152

safe, and soon we shall see your Papa again!" As she hurried out of the house, with the sniffling child in her arms, she saw a faint light bobbing along St. John Street, flickering as it appeared between the houses. The shadows of two figures moved along with the lantern, one small, one tall: Horace, with Davy Darst following after.

"Mama," said Horace in tones of the utmost gravity, "Miz Darst, she said she would come with us, and Miz Kimball, too. Miz Kimball, she was crying so, she couldn't rightly say nothin'."

"Anything," Margaret automatically corrected her son, "Anything – not 'nothin'."

"Yes, Mama." Oddly, Horace seemed rather relieved at this little touch of absolute normality. "What should I do now, Mama?"

"Sit with your brother in the wagon and comfort him," Margaret said, as Davy Darst said, in a boy's gruff voice which cracked painfully between a child's and an adult's, "Ma said I should come and help with the oxen."

"Oh, Davy – that would be good," Margaret exclaimed, as she put Johnny over the side of the wagon box into a nest of piled-up bedding. Horace scrambled up the wheel and over the wagon seat to curl up next to his brother. "Do not worry, they are gentle enough." Under the speckled lantern light, which swayed from the wagon bow, she could see that Davy's face was pale and set, as if he did not wish to disgrace himself with a display of grief; there was nothing to say at this moment, but she gently cupped his cheek in her hand, and said softly, "He was a fine man, was Jacob Darst, a brave one, and a dreadful loss to us all."

"Yes, ma'am," Davy gulped, but remained dry-eyed. *Perhaps there would be a time for grief later*, Margaret thought, *but not now.*

"You should be as proud of him, as he was of you," she said, and went to bring out another armful of precious bedding from the house. Mama had found a box for the pots and ordinary tin plates, the cooking utensils they used every day. Margaret picked up the box which rattled in her arms as she looked around at the inside of her house. No room, no time for those pieces of furniture, not if they were to have space for Maggie and Pru and prevent the wagon from bogging down in every creek-crossing. She was as dry-eyed as Davy Darst. She did not even bother closing the door or putting out the oil-lamp. What was the use – it would all burn soon. The last thing she took was the shovel, putting it into the wooden toolbox strapped to the side of the wagon-box.

Now for harnessing the oxen; Margaret thanked hers and Mama's good fortune they had brought them in every night from where they had been pastured at the edge of town, and stalled them safely in the stable at the back of their town lot. She and Mama led the gentle oxen clumping slowly after them in pairs, while Davy Darst held up the wooden ox yoke and snapped the bows closed, settling the heavy yoke on their shoulders. It was difficult to work at this in the dark; finally Margaret resorted to holding the lantern as high as she could, above the oxen's backs, so that Mama and Davy Darst could hitch the harness chains from yoke to the wagon tongue and whiffletrees. As they finished this, Margaret could hear men's voices, as if they were shouting, but at some distance, and the faint rumble of thunder from the storm. Lightning flickered again, closer.

"We are ready," she said, evenly, calmly. "Mama, get into the wagon with the children. Davy, you can drive an ox team, can't you?"

"Not so much," he answered. "I've helped my father with plowing, though."

"And I have watched my father drive his," Margaret answered, consolingly. She handed him her father's bull whip, neatly coiled. "My father hardly ever used this, save for making a noise. I shall walk along with you beside the team, and we shall all help each other. Gee-up," she added, tremulously to the lead team, and to her gratification, they stepped forward obediently. Out into St. Francis Street, the wagon rolled easily after the oxen. "Gee!" Margaret said with more confidence and the team pulled left, and then left again at her command. Down the two dusty blocks of St. John Street, to the house on the rise with the redbud tree standing sentinel in front of it. "Whoa!" Margaret commanded the oxen; again, she was pleased and mildly gratified at their instant obedience. Two shadowy figures sat on the steps of the Darst house, a pair of women wrapped in shawls. Margaret petted the near ox's shoulder; Papa had trained them very well. By leaving them with Mama in Gonzales he had provided for more than just Mama and Margaret's family.

"Help me with the tin trunk," she told Davy. "It's full of books and too heavy to take with us. I thought to bury it in the hole the children dug by the redbud tree, if your mother has not already filled it with her things."

"She has not." Davy shook his head. "Ma does not put much of a value on worldly things. She says that we lived without much when first we came here, we can do so again." In the darkness, one of the figures on the steps stood and moved towards the wagon, a ghostly shadow in the deeper shadows.

"Margaret?" Maggie Darst asked, softly, "We have gathered that which we are taking. You must help me with Pru. I cannot reason with her as she is nearly insensible with grief and wishes to remain here."

"They told you of Sue's message? General Houston wished to tell you himself."

"No need of that," Maggie answered, in a steady voice. "We have known for hours. Davy was listening at Turner's this afternoon. We should make haste, Margaret. There is a storm coming in."

It took little time to half drag and half carry the tin trunk to the deep hollow beneath the redbud tree with three of them helping and Mama holding up the lantern. It sat well deep in the hole, and Margaret said, "Maggie, there is room for anything of yours to add before I fill it in."

"No, my dear Margaret – all that I value in the world comes with us." Maggie answered, gasping with exertion. Margaret began scraping the shovel across the ground, pushing enough soil into the hole to hide the trunk and make the ground seem more or less level. It seemed to take an age, her nerves afire with impatience. They must be away soon, the oncoming storm had blotted out the stars, and the candle in her lantern was close to flickering out. She was aware of Mama's voice in soft remonstrance with Pru. The night was eerily alive, with noise, distant voices, the bawling of oxen, and the rattle of harness. The tree above her seemed alive too, the bare branches, new-trimmed with pink ruffles of flowers, twisting and swaying over her head. A gust of wind swept St. John Street, sending all the trees along the way writhing like ghosts. Done. She picked up the shovel and the lantern, and followed the other three women towards the wagon. Pru and Maggie's few bundles had already gone into it, followed by the weeping Pru; Davy had fastened up the wagon tail.

"Where are we going, then? East?" he asked.

"Towards the McClure's on Peach Creek," Margaret answered. "That is the way that Harry Karnes said the army was going."

They continued all the way down towards St. Louis Street, passing Market Square which overlooked the river bank. St. Louis Street began the road to the east, across Kerr Creek, close to where Papa's house had been when he and Mama and the boys lived in Gonzales. They skirted the camp on Military Square – a sea of half-struck canvas tents and flaring torches, of fractious animals and half-packed wagons. Margaret's wagon joined a ragged train of wagons, carts, and single lonely figures pushing barrows ahead of them.

"Not a moment too soon," Margaret said: across the square, at the far end of town, more than torches lit up the far sky. The ox teams leaned into their harness. Now that she was walking with Davy and keeping pace with the patient, plodding oxen and not laboring with packing the wagon, she felt the cold most keenly. She wrapped her shawl over her shoulders. The afternoon, when Harry Karnes came to get her and she had first snatched it up to draw around her against the spring chill felt as if it were an age ago. Embracing Race in farewell, felt like something that had happened in another lifetime altogether. That morning, she had expected to have supper with Mama and the children and sleep in a warm bed under the shelter of a roof – but at midnight of this chaotic day, she and Mama had become poor and homeless vagabonds! Margaret sensed that all now looked to her for guidance, for a plan, for knowing what to do next, but she had no plan, only to walk east next to the oxen, and follow the army, for Lopez de Santa Anna's army was coming, bearing a vengeful blood-red banner of no quarter. He had given his soldiers free rein after the defeat of the militia of Zacatecas – what battlefield liberties would he allow them after the citizens of Texas had defied him on so many contested fields? And where was Race, on this stormy, fire-streaked night?

They walked in darkness, she and Davy and the oxen, Gonzales and the army camp were left behind. They were out in the country; there were wagons ahead, their covers shaking as their wheels rolled over another set of small rain-washed gullies in the road. Thunder grumbled at their backs, and a streak of lightning momentarily lit all with a queer, white-green glow. There was a quiet swish of long skirts in the tall grass. Maggie Darst appeared at Margaret's elbow.

"Davy-lad," she commanded quietly, "go and ride in the wagon for a while. I wish to walk for a while, and you must be tired and ready to drop. Rest a while, laddie-buck – Mrs. Vining and I will see to the ox-team."

"Yes, Ma," he answered with reluctance, but he obediently handed her the coiled driver's whip. He stopped and let the wagon catch up to him, climbing deftly over the turning wheel. Maggie walked on with Margaret, who was trying to think of some words of condolence which wouldn't distress Maggie.

Maggie saved her the trouble. "I wanted to walk awhile," she said, abruptly, "and think of him, and weep a little if I felt like it. Mostly I wanted to recall him in company with someone who would not be covertly watching and waiting for me to turn to glass and shatter into a thousand pieces. I even wanted to laugh a little, if a tender memory came to us – but there are too many who would think it unseemly and silently accuse me of having a hard and unwomanly heart."

"He was your husband," Margaret answered. "No one ought to think ill of you if you should be weeping and wailing – or not, as your temperament urges."

Maggie laughed, laughed with a catch in her throat. "So you say, but I believe others would not be so generous! I have been grieving all this week; I

156

knew in my heart that he was gone, without any doubt at all. I woke in the early morning before the sun rose, five days ago it was. It was still dark outside, but I thought – or I dreamed that he opened the door and walked into the room where I lay sleeping. I was that joyful, M'grete, I thought it was himself come home. I said, 'Where are the other lads?' He said nothing in reply, but he smiled. I thought it strange that he seemed to glow with an odd, shining light to him. In that moment he turned to one side a little and then vanished entirely. By that I knew, although I could not say how I knew it so certainly, that Jacob was dead, most like at that very hour. I have heard of visitations, at the instant of passing from one world into the next – but I did not want to be thought mad, or to distress poor Pru, in my own certainty – or give cause for others to think I had special reason for believing that Santa Anna had taken our fortress . . . so I kept silent."

She fell quiet, and Margaret said, "You have borne up bravely, Maggie. I would say in answer to any criticism of you for lack of grief that your bearing is like to that of the noblest of Roman women."

"With a hard heart, not to have dissolved into floods of tears?" Maggie answered. "My dear girl – we grieve differently, but most would have us bear ourselves alike in our sorrow. I would prefer not to make a show of myself. He was a good man, we loved each other very well, and how he is gone. What comforts me is the thought that he was with brave companions, defending us all from the rule of vile, backstabbing toads like Santa Anna and his cronies. It was the cause that Jacob chose, and he stood up for his friends. I'd have rather that we both lived until we were old and grey and walked each on two canes, but that was not his way. We differed about many things, M'grete – but not on what mattered between a man and wife. I had him as a husband for sixteen years; those are the years that I shall think on as a gift generously given to me, and remember every day of them with affection for all of my life. He is gone, but I have been richly blessed."

"Then you should have no need of my defense of you," Margaret said, putting her arm around Maggie, who laughed a little.

"Dear M'grete, shall I tell you a secret? I can be sentimental. On every parting from my husband, no matter for how short a space of time, the last words that we would say to each other would be, 'I love you.' It was a habit begun when we were courting. Should something dire happen whilst we were parted, than the other would be able to take comfort in knowing that the last words exchanged were loving and affectionate. I can think of nothing more ill than the memory of having said harsh words to one's beloved and those words fated to be the last words ever said. No matter how vexed that I was, that

Jacob was going off to fight the Indians or to take an afternoon to plow a neighbor's garden patch," at that, she returned Margaret's embrace, with an affectionate brief squeeze, "or even just to go to a militia meeting on the plaza, we were in the habit of saying those words. I am glad of this – it is a habit which I recommend."

"I think it very loving thing to do," Margaret answered, "I marvel that I did not think of it before this. I am quite sure my last words to my husband this morning were also loving. How horribly fast this has happened, Maggie!"

"Aye, dear M'grete – so it did." Maggie sighed, and they walked onward, through the dark, following the dimly seen wagon ahead of them. Two or three times over the following hours they were passed along the side of the road by riders, men who appeared to be either guarding the ragged train of wagons, or chivvying them along, like dogs guiding a herd of sheep, urging them by their presence to keep moving. Once the horseman proved to be the son of an old neighbor of Papa's, David Kent, who reined in and asked breathlessly, "Mrs. Vining, Mrs. Darst – have you seen Mary Millsaps and the children? Are they with you?"

"No," Margaret answered, while Maggie shook her head. "We have not seen Mary in a day or so. Do you fear that something has happened to them?"

David had already dug his heels into his horses' flanks, and answered over his shoulder. "I thought it odd they were not among the others – I fear they have been forgotten in the mad rush this evening. Fear not, if I cannot find them, I will demand of General Sam that he send a party to seek them out if they have been left behind."

Margaret thought that she had gone beyond exhaustion, when Mama called to her from the wagon seat. She had been walking mechanically, moving one foot regularly in front of the other, she and Maggie and the ox teams.

"M'grete! Have we somehow turned around on the road?"

"Why, Mama . . . whoa!" she added to the oxen, who halted, and stood, heads drooping. The wagon in front of them had halted also, a little distance ahead. The driver of it was pointing at something in the direction from which they had come – a dull orange glow, illuminating half the horizon and painting the edge of the storm cloud which hung just above it with bands of sullen gold.

"Oh, my dear lord," Maggie Darst breathed as Mama came down from the wagon-seat, and hurried towards them, gasping, "It looks as if the sun is rising," she said, uncertainly, "Below the storm clouds – but it is too early."

"It is the wrong direction," Margaret answered her. "It is the west, Mama. We are going east."

"Gonzales burns," Maggie Darst commented softly. "It makes a fine welcoming bonfire for Santa Anna and his soldiers, don't you think? Let them loot the stones, the ashes, the coals, and the thorns, if those are the riches they expected to take from us!"

"I did not think it would make such a show." Margaret blinked away the tears that suddenly welled up in her eyes. She could almost see the line of high-leaping flames, hear the greedy crackle and roar of a fire well alight, a fire that burned up and up, leaping from roof to roof, from house to stable and store, from tree-top to chimney-top. All would be gone by morning; ten years of work and happiness, of building houses such as they had done for the Darsts, on the day that Race Vining came to the roof-raising – all would be reduced to so much burnt kindling. All they had not been able to take with them – gone forever. With a niggle of worry, Margaret wondered how she would find her china plates and Race's precious books, in a town where every familiar landmark would have been burnt. Perhaps the trees would escape . . . then she recollected that Maggie Darst's house had been set on stone pilings, above the ground. Those, at least, would mark where it had been. Of her own house, the stone step would endure, certainly. As they watched, a dull booming sound came to their ears, as if a single artillery-piece were firing. Margaret wondered if that were the sound of cannon – but whose?

"We should move on," she said, at last, hearing that the wagon ahead of them had begun moving.

"I shall drive the wagon, a while," Mama offered, and in the darkness she touched Margaret's cheek. "You should rest in the wagon with the children, M'grete. Go now, the oxen will obey me." Margaret at first thought to insist that no, she was not tired. Soon it would be dawn – the real dawn, breaking clear in the sky ahead of them. But then she felt unutterably weary, and her feet hurt. She obeyed her mother, climbing up into the wagon on limbs which trembled from exhaustion. Pru and her son, Horace and Johnny slept soundly on the largest mattress tick, Davy sitting slumped on the wagon seat, his head resting on a pillow on his lap. Margaret lay herself down next to her children, wrapping her shawl over her head, and at once fell into deepest slumber, even as the wagon wheels continued jolting and creaking along, east towards safety on the far bank of the Colorado.

Chapter 13 – *Following the Army*

Margaret slept long in the wagon. When she woke, the wagon was not moving, and speckles of sunlight danced over the outside of the wagon cover, for it was broad daylight: midmorning by the look of it slanting through the trees overhead and the openings at the back and front of the wagon where the cover had been loosened. Johnny and little Charlie Kimball slept curled next to her, as kittens sleep with their bodies pressed close to the mother cat, seeking comfort and reassurance. It was the noise which had awoken her; the noise of a man's raised voice, and the irregular tramp of many footsteps attempting a regular rhythm and failing utterly – to the loud and profane exasperation of that voice shouting the cadence at them. The tail of the wagon was taken down, as she could see clearly, when she sat up – carefully, so as not to waken the children. She slid carefully across the tick where they had all lain, groaning faintly to herself at the aches in her legs, arms, and shoulders, stepping carefully across the jumbled cargo in the wagon towards where she could clamber down from the wagon tail and look around.

They were at the edge of a wide meadow dotted with majestic oak trees. Beyond the largest of them was the McClure house, one of those large and well-built houses, surrounded by the outbuildings of a prosperous and well-established plantation – as well-established as one could have been out on the far edge of the frontier. The meadow was full of rough campsites, pieces of canvas or blankets mounted on sticks, or wagons and horse-pickets and hasty campfires. Everywhere were men, men in hunting clothes, in rags of uniforms, patched coats or blankets around their shoulders. Twenty or thirty of them were at conscientious drill, marching back and forth across an open space and going through the motions of loading and firing their muskets under the tutelage of a drillmaster who sounded ever more exasperated by the moment. Many more men slept in apparent utter exhaustion, sprawled out on the ground with their heads resting on packs and haversacks. The sky was thick-spotted with fair-sized clouds, heavy with rain, by the appearance of gray at their centers, but fair and sparkling white as cleaned cotton drifts around their edges. There were other wagons and carts scattered in rough campsites around the periphery of the main camp, other exhausted women moving listlessly around campfires preparing food, or fetching buckets of water from Peach Creek.

Close to the tail of Papa's wagon, a small fire sent a sullen thread of smoke into the air; Mama and Pru huddled over it on the bench taken from the wagon, and a seat made from a small half-empty cask of molasses. Horace was curled up in Mama's comfortable lap, but Maggie Darst and her son were arguing in tense, low voices.

". . . the Gen'ral is calling for volunteers!" Davy insisted. His face was pale, his voice resolute. His mother looked no less resolute.

"I forbid it!" she answered, her voice on the thin edge between reason and hysteria. "Davy, you are only fourteen! What did your father tell you before he rode away with the company? You were to obey me, see to our property and lands . . . what are you thinking of, Davy?"

"What is Davy thinking of?" Margaret asked, in her calmest and most reasonable tone of voice, as she climbed down from the wagon tail and settled her skirts around her.

"He wants to volunteer for General Houston's army!" Cried Maggie – after her resolute calm of the night before, the agony plain in the tone of her voice and expression on her face took Margaret aback. "The General has called for all to join with him, to train and prepare to fight – and Davy will go, whether I permit or not, and I cannot bear it, M'grete – to loose a husband and a child is more than anyone should be called to endure! How dare you ask me to bear this, any of you – not least the General! Aren't there enough fools in Texas already, must my only child be taken?"

"Ma, I'm not a child," Davy answered, so stung with embarrassment that his face was primrose pink. "Gal and Will King – they weren't all that older than me, and they went with the company!"

"Gal and Will are dead!" Maggie's voice rose. "Foolish boy, they are dead, and their bodies burnt with all the others by Santa Anna's order. Do you think that you would be exempt from such a fate by the excuse of being young! Men die in battle, Davy – they die, no matter how old or how young, how well-favored or no, loved or no! They die, by shot or grape or bayonet – they die by chance and mischance, they die suddenly or after hours of agony, alone or among friends – they die!" Maggie's near-hysterical voice carried – not a few heads of the volunteers at drill turned towards her in sudden distraction. Davy turned a deeper shade of crimson and Pru began weeping silently.

"Ma! Everyone can hear you!"

"I do not care if they can hear me or not, as long as you are listening to me, David Darst!"

"Ma, I will go to the General this minute and enlist," Davy answered. His soft young boy-face suddenly gone hard with completely adult determination, and at that, Maggie began sobbing anew. Davy picked up his coat and put his hat on his head.

"Where are you going?" Maggie demanded through her tears. Davy answered,

"To tell General Sam that I will do as my father would have allowed me!" and he set off, threading his way across the crowded meadow towards the McClure house, where a small group of men held purposeful counsel, standing or squatting on the ground under the shelter of that towering oak tree. Margaret recognized General Sam and Erastus Smith among them; so the General was holding conversation with his staff. The expressions on the faces they could see were grim and exhausted. The very manner in which they held themselves spoke of weariness and despair, but also of resolution. Margaret cast a frantic eye around. Mama was simultaneously comforting the weeping Pru and the bewildered Horace, for whom raised voices among adults was an unusual and distressing thing.

"You will do no such thing!" Maggie shrieked, following after her son, and Margaret caught her arm.

"Maggie," she counseled, even as she felt her heart sink, "Let me come with you. Perhaps he will listen to me, or at any roads, we can talk to the General, explain the matter to him . . . he is a reasonable and kindly man." Maggie made no answer, save for picking up her skirts so that she could walk a little faster. Davy had nearly reached the General and his consort of officers. *Oh, dear – he was going to interrupt them*, Margaret thought, and inwardly cringed, just as Maggie called her son's name. General Sam turned, taking off his hat – a dark felt hat which Margaret noticed had a brim quaintly turned up in three places, styled after the old-fashioned tricorn. As soon as he saw Margaret and Maggie hastening towards them, his face brightened in recognition of her, which Margaret found most pleasing. Davy had already blurted out his reason for approaching the General, and from the expressions on the faces of those around General Sam, they seemed either exasperated or amused. *Oh, poor Davy*, Margaret thought; *he would be so humiliated – again, to be treated like a child*. General Sam, though – and bless him for that, seemed inclined to consider it as a serious matter and Davy worthy of being treated as an adult.

"I am sorry for troubling you, sir!" Maggie gasped, entirely out of breath.

"It is no trouble," General Sam answered, most courteously. "This young man has come in answer to an appeal to serve in my army – which is most appreciated, even though we usually prefer our soldiers to have a little more . . . er, seasoning to them. In our current straits, however, we aren't inclined to be that particular. Mrs. Vining." he nodded towards Margaret. "And Mrs. Darst, is it? Of Gonzales – I thought as much. Your grief is shared, Mrs.

Darst, of that you have my assurance. Mrs. Vining was kind enough to tell me a little of the temper of those men who gave their lives in this noble cause. So now, this young man wishes to take up where his father set down his burden."

"He is only fourteen!" Maggie cried. "I forbid it on that account!" and the General nodded, sympathetically.

"So I can see, ma'am. I can also see that he would not be the only one in my army . . . unseasoned to that degree."

"He is an only child of a widowed mother," Margaret pointed out, in a quiet voice. "His mother and I and another of our friends – Mrs. Kimball, also widowed at the Alamo – have only him of an age to be a help with our wagon and the oxen who pull it."

"I see." General Sam's eyes narrowed, thoughtfully. "A moment, gentleman," he added, in slight reproof of those of his officers who were shifting impatiently at this interruption. "This is a matter worthy of at least a moment of my attention. Every recruit gathering to our cause is a gain to us." He seemed lost in thought for a moment, regarding Davy and the two women, before he snapped his fingers. "See here, young Darst. You wish to join our army, serve under my command and the orders of those officers of your company, and to do so freely, upon careful consideration? You may swear openly and honestly to me that no one has made you do this?'

"I do," Davy answered firmly. "Nothing has influenced me but the example of my father and his friends!"

"But you are indeed only fourteen years of age?" General Sam asked, and when Davy nodded, Maggie said, "He will be fifteen in five months, on August the third – and who would know better than his mother?"

"Well then," General Sam answered, "I shall accept your enlistment, Private David Darst, but on one condition; you shall serve on a special detached service under the command of Captain Smith, until such time as we cross the Colorado River, or to some other point when Captain Smith shall convey other orders to you."

"Thank you, General Houston, sir!" Davy's face was alive with worship and gratitude, but Maggie cried out, a sharp keening wail of unbearable distress, and Margaret held her as she seemed about to crumple to the ground.

"Not so fast, Private Darst," General Sam continued. "Until you hear my orders and conditions. You are also very young – and my army is not yet in such deep need as to recruit children from their mothers' arms and throw them before the enemies' cannon – indeed, not even well-grown and eager lads of fourteen and fifteen or so. I make an exception for you, in honor of your father, so hear me out," and General Sam's voice turned gentle and grave.

"The safety and security of all the citizens of Texas is a matter of deep concern to me. Why do you think that we burned our tents, dumped our cannons and such of our supplies which we could not carry into the river, so that we might safely evacuate the women and children of Gonzales? We took as many as we could in those wagons as we had . . . aye, and there will be more, many more, as the word of our retreat to the Colorado is passed. Darst – you will serve me well in this respect – stay with Mrs. Vining's wagon as we retreat to the east bank of the Colorado, and make yourself of use to other civilian refugees. I know there will be other civilians fleeing their homes. We must assist them as we may. You must reassure them, bring to bear your best efforts and render aid. Your efforts would bring honor upon the Army of Texas, and my name as commander. Can you do that for me, for the good of Texas?"

"That I can, sir," Davy replied, somewhat crestfallen, as he realized the full import of Houston's words.

"Good," General Sam answered, and as Davy hesitated, he added, "Now, as your duties with the refugee train permit, and assuming that our camp and yours are co-located, you are tasked with attending regular drill with Captain Smith's company or whoever else may be practicing the *Manual of Arms* in my camp. We will be departing from here within the hour, and our next camp will be on the Lavaca River, tonight. You will make your way there, with Mrs. Vining and your mother and any such others as require your assistance. You will take any further orders from Captain Smith. If you do not have a musket or a rifle and the proper gear, you will be issued such, as soon as we refresh our armory. You are dismissed, Private Darst."

"Sir." Davy sketched a hesitant and wavering salute, at which General Sam nodded, with an amused expression on his craggy face. "Thank you, sir."

"Be fair to him," Margaret whispered to Maggie, whose face was wet with tears, as they walked away from the tiny huddle of the general and his officers, below the veranda of the McClure house. "General Sam has done a very wise and proper judgment of Solomon. He has accepted Davy into his army and salved his feelings, but kept him with you, as safe as any might be!"

"He is a child!" Maggie whispered. "The veriest child!"

"No," Margaret shook her head, suddenly feeling terribly wise, "In these times, not a child. My own little brother is only a year or so older, and he is with Colonel Fannin's company at La Bahia. Our boy-children are not torn from our arms, Maggie. They go willingly, wishing to be counted as men. And to be a man, a gentle perfect knight – Maggie, that is a commendable thing to be, and that is what our sons long to become! How can they not, when there are so many splendid examples around them, to emulate and follow! Allow Davy to drill with the company, let him think that he has had his way in this . . . and think on a way to thank the General." She put her arm around Maggie then, for comfort. "We must be as good friends as we can, to each other, Maggie. In this present emergency, the comfort of loyalty of friends is all that we have . . . oh, see – look at that, my dear, they have managed to find Mary and the children!"

There was an ancient one-horse Mexican cart, with solid wheels, creaking slowly into the camp, under the escort of a handful of horsemen lead by David Kent, whose face was beaming with triumph and exhaustion. Mary Millsaps and her children sat in the cart, on the top of a pile of straw and bedding. Margaret and Maggie ran towards them, Margaret exclaiming, "Oh, my dear! Where were you all this time – Mr. Kent came looking among the wagons for you last night, but we truly did not believe you had been forgotten!"

"Margaret?" Mary's face lit with her lovely smile. "I am afraid that we were, but it was no one's fault but our own. We thought that we should leave the house and hide in the thickets, and everyone thought we were with someone else. Where are we, now?"

"At the McClures' on Peach Creek." Maggie reached up and embraced Mary, as her older children helped her down to the ground. "Thank the Lord that Mr. Kent began to wonder, upon seeing that you were nowhere to be found."

"We hid in the woods, taking nothing but a few blankets for the children," Mary answered. "These men were kind enough to find this cart, and round up a horse to pull it. I think the horse is one of Kent's. We are so many and the cart so heavy that we must walk as much as possible to spare the poor thing. Is it true that Santa Anna's army is just behind us? Last night we thought we heard cannon firing again and again, but Mr. Kent says that it was only barrels of whiskey and gunpowder exploding as they set fire to the stores."

"Perhaps not just behind," Margaret reassured her. "We may have a little respite, before we move on. Come share a little of our breakfast with us. My father had left us his wagon, and so we were able to bring away a little more. But the Army is to march within the hour so we may not linger over it."

"Thank you," Mary said, with gratitude, and her sightless eyes seemed to look out across the camp with tears welling up in them. "Oh, dear! I wonder where we shall sleep tonight, or next week. How rapidly our lives have changed, between one hour and the next. My husband gone from us, and never even being allowed a proper grave by that hateful man! All of our towns and farms emptied out, falling back to the Colorado, or so said Mr. Kent. Whatever will happen next, I wonder?"

"I shall think no farther on than the next day," Margaret answered, resolutely lifting her chin and taking Mary's hand to guide her. "And follow the Army as closely as we can."

Even as she and Mama hastily cooked more mush for the Millsaps children, the soldiers were forming into companies, kicking their friends awake, and lining up in ragged ranks. Seeing this, a worried and uneasy murmur arose from the women and their children. Unbidden, Davy and the eldest of the Millsaps boys began hitching up the oxen to Margaret's wagon.

"We dare not fall behind." Maggie began sorting out those few things they had brought from the wagon. There were deep worry lines scored around her eyes. "We have no protection, otherwise, from Indians or Santa Anna. Is there such a thing as a pistol or a musket among us? Or did all of these things go with our men, leaving us truly defenseless?"

"I believe so," Margaret answered, with grim honesty. Maggie was strong, brave, and practical. Mama seemed stunned by the suddenness of it all, adrift in a frightening world without the strong anchor of Papa and the boys. "There is a hatchet in Papa's box of tools. And several knives in the kitchen things."

"Jacob left his old hunting knife when he went with the Company," Maggie said, with an air of something just remembered. "I thought Davy should have it, but I will ask for it back again. It never kept a sharpened edge for long, though – which is why my husband did not favor it so much."

"Better than nothing at all," Margaret said, as Davy brought up the second ox team. She nodded at him, adding to Maggie, "You should compliment him on being so brisk and prompt with the oxen. General Sam has done very well, reposing such trust in him."

"Aye, so I should," Maggie answered, but she still looked terribly worried. So far to go today, after the journey of the night before – and they only had been able to rest three hours or so! But every foot set one before the other took them farther away from Santa Anna's vengeful army and closer to safety, over the Colorado. Margaret looked at the clouds beginning to lower overhead, as if it was considering a good heavy rain. Where, she wondered, was Race? He had been sent to Mina two days before. Surely he must be on his way back by now. He must know that the army was falling back, that General Sam had decided to abandon Gonzales and all west of the Colorado. How worried he must be, at this juncture. Margaret considered this, as she and Mama finished repacking the wagon. Race would have known that the army was going to retreat to the Colorado, so he must also know that the civilians would be going with them. He would be looking for her and the boys wherever the army was. Another good reason to follow the army close, Margaret told herself. Oh, she was tired and aching still from last night's journey – but Race would come looking for them within a day or so, and she would tell him triumphantly that she had saved his precious library, burying it in a tin trunk under Maggie Darst's redbud tree. Of course, they would have to return to Gonzales somehow. Again, Margaret put that thought aside. She could do nothing now, save follow the army doggedly, taking Mama, Maggie, Pru, and Mary and all their children with her. A return to home – or to the place where home had been, was as far away now as the far side of the moon.

It was a ragged and desperate little train of wagons and carts following the army's baggage wagons and ammunition limbers out of their stopping place at the McClures'. A straggle of women and children walked bravely among them, as everyone wished to spare the team animals as much as possible. Hers was nearly the first wagon ready among the civilians, Davy Darst striding out manfully next to the lead ox team. The cart that carried Mary and the Millsaps children followed after, although the horse drawing it was in such poor condition that Mary also walked, led by her oldest daughter. Margaret took the younger children into her wagon with Mama and Pru. At the last minute, place in the cart was given to Sarah Eggleston, the much younger sister of Andrew Ponton. She was hugely pregnant with her first child, although barely older than Davy Darst, and grimaced painfully every time the solid wheels went over another bump in the road. Margaret set her face towards the east, inwardly pleading with God not to allow Pru and Sarah to have their children by the side of the road. They must win this war somehow, Margaret told herself – they must find a way to win it, rather than be homeless vagabonds, without homes or a safe place to lay their heads. Maggie found a piece of a canvas tent, abandoned in the trash left by the Army; she and Margaret walked on either side of the cart, holding it over Sarah so that she might have a little shade. Even as they walked down the road east, the McClures were packing their own wagon to leave.

And so they marched, falling behind the marching column of Sam Houston's army, yet stubbornly following as fast as they could force their own faltering feet and those of their tired and poor-conditioned team animals. Margaret and Maggie walked together, all that long and wearying day. They dared not take time to rest, for then they might fall behind. Now and again, they saw columns of grey and black smoke rising on the horizon – the clear signs of other homes and farmsteads put to the torch – and another straggle of women and children came to join them, with carts and wagons haphazardly packed and hitched to winter-thin and scraggly animals. Panic was in the air, the smell of it stronger than that of the trampled grass, or the scent of rain borne on the light wind, a rain that soon pelted down upon them, in ice-cold drops. Their feet sank to the ankles in the churned mud. Yet they must plod onward, ducking their faces against the driving rain. *Think no farther than the next camp*, Margaret told herself, *think of no other effort than to put one foot in front of the other, for ahead lay safety and behind only peril.*

With some difficulty, the civilians' carts and wagons were brought across Rocky Creek, and then through the ford on the Navidad River, although because of the recent rain, the water ran high in both of them. Margaret and Maggie were soaked to the waist, walking after the wagon and holding onto the tail to steady themselves against the icy river current as they followed after. The sole of one of Maggie's shoes began to tear loose, through constant soaking and abrasion against the rocks. With Isaac's second-best hunting knife, Maggie cut a length of fabric from the top of a half-empty grain sack and bound it tightly around her foot. As the march continued, it did not seem to help all that much.

"If it weren't for the cold, and the roughness of the road, I would be better served by going barefoot!" Maggie lamented to Margaret, who added up that one small thing to her store of matters to worry herself about. The Millsaps children were without shoes, having tied pieces of blanket around their feet to spare them from the cold. Mama had no proper shoes, only a pair of Indian rawhide moccasins, and Margaret feared that her own shoes might not last very much longer than Maggie's under the hard wearing of this trek.

The first elements of that straggling train of refugees reached the camp on the Navidad around sunset. Margaret and her party were among them. Margaret felt as tired as she ever had after giving birth – yet, in this present emergency she could not just rest, exhausted in the bed and triumphantly admiring the new child, before going to sleep. Now she must see to finding a campsite for her wagon and the clumsy cart which carried Sarah Eggleston, sort out forage for Papa's oxen and the spavined horse which drew the cart, see to comforting Maggie, Sarah, and Mama, mop up Pru's exhausted tears, assure Davy of his manly competence, sooth the Millsaps children and reassure their mother. It was all too much – and when would it ever end? And why had it all fallen to her? Margaret raged briefly and inwardly at that unfairness, and then took up her work. Who else would take up the burden which had fallen to her? The progress of a pilgrim, for sure – to do what seemed to be needful, take up the responsibility. In the end, she would be judged, and by more than just her friends. Rebellion against fate would not water the horse, pasture the oxen, feed the children and comfort those of her friends who labored under their own burden of grief and fear.

They could not rest here for more than one night. In the morning they would be gone again, in the trail of the army, wading through the mud. But for now, as soon as she came from the river-edge with the older children, bearing a few buckets of water, there was a good fire burning, a fire that had burned down to incandescent coals, which could be cooked over – and a pair of ragged young soldiers bashfully adding to a pile of wood stacked nearby. Margaret set down the buckets – there was the wagon bench taken from the wagon, with Mama holding Johnny in her lap.

"We thought we should perform this kindness for you, ma'am," said the tallest, who spoke with the clipped accent of New England. "Seeing that you ladies are in such need."

"Our sergeant said," added the other, in a soft Carolina burr, "that some of you were widowed by the action at the Alamo. This is the mos' kindness that we can do, ma'am an' ma'am an' ma'am," he nodded politely at Maggie, at Pru and Mary. "It is no' so much as we wish to do but as much as we can do."

"And we are grateful," Maggie Darst replied gruffly, as if she feared that her voice would break with emotion. "For any consideration, no matter how small – it is substantial to us, in our present reduced circumstances."

"Aw, no ma'am," replied the southern soldier, in some distress, "It weren't no trouble at all. As soon as we reach the Coloradda, we shall turn and fight! You'll see, ma'am . . . an' ma'am . . . an' ma'am! We'll throw Santy Anna an' all of his lot clean out, you jist wait an' see. We'll have a right good revenge on 'em for what they have done, you trust Burleson's boys for that!"

"So we all hope, very much," Margaret answered, as the two soldiers dropped the last armload of wood and bid the women goodnight. Darkness was falling. She was reminded of that first night in Texas, the evening of her twelfth birthday watching the sparks fly up into the sky while she held her little brother in her lap and Mama busied herself cooking supper over a fire.

"They brought us some fresh beef," Maggie Darst said, "For they have slaughtered some beeves to feed the army and say that we shall not go hungry, ourselves. Oh, what I would have given that we thought to bring along some of our own hogs . . . wandering in the woods they were, and not enough time to round them up."

"They'll be there for you when we return," Margaret answered, "and all the fatter for eating acorns and things in the woods. Tonight, leave a pot of beans to soak in the coals, as the fire burns down."

"Ah, I remember well that old trick," Maggie laughed a little, lamenting. "Molasses on pone for the children. Oh, all the things that we would have brought, had we the time!"

"We will be home, in a while," Margaret insisted, firmly. The other women had been reassured; their hopes revived a little, by the consideration of those two soldiers, the gift of a warm fire and some meat for their supper. She must put on the brave face for them now, Margaret realized. She must never show doubt or fear, even if she felt such, she must not share them. How very lonely, to be always seeming brave and able. How had it come about that she seemed to be their leader, to feel the responsibility for them all – for Mama, and Maggie, for Pru and Sarah and their children? How very lonely, but a burden once taken up could not be put down! She wondered briefly if General Sam felt that kind of loneliness. She raised her eyes and looking beyond their campfire, saw a party of men on horseback, with three men a little in the lead, riding towards them and towards the army's main camp, which was a little beyond theirs. It was almost too dark to see them clear, but one of the leaders' horses looked like Bucephalus . . . and if so . . . Margaret's heart lifted, almost painfully. She ran towards him, crying out his name – for it was indeed he, and the other two with him were also familiar – Erastus Smith, and Juan Seguin. All three men looked tired to death and very weary, but somehow exultant, in spite of it all.

Race slid down from Bucephalus' saddle and caught her in his arms, a fierce and hard embrace, saying, "Thank the gods, you are safe! I carried the orders to Mina, and the message that General Sam was evacuating Gonzales, but I did not know what the message was until I had arrived. I prayed every moment that you and Mother Becker and the boys were safely away, Daisy-mine. I was in torment until this very moment!"

"We are safe enough, my dear love," Margaret whispered in answer, seeing that Erastus Smith was looking away from them with somewhat of an embarrassed expression, while Juan observed with frank approval. "With Papa's wagon, and Mama and Maggie and Davy to help, we had enough time to bring the barest of what we needed, and to offer assistance to Sarah and Pru. I could not bring your books, dearest . . . but they are safely buried," she added, seeing a fleeting look of anguish in his face, as she said those words, an emotion quenched as quickly as it had arisen. "I put them in the tin trunk, and Davy helped me bury it under the redbud tree at Maggie's house. You know, where the boys had hollowed out a den to hide, and play soldiers?"

"Providential, indeed," said Race, with a catch in his voice, and embraced her again. "Daisy-mine, you are a woman whose price is above rubies. My books are dear, but you and the boys are a treasure above any price. Still – I am scholar enough to appreciate that you have taken care with them all."

"You know about the Alamo and the fate of our friends?" Margaret ventured, a catch in her throat, and Race nodded. Grief darkened his voice.

"Aye. Erastus told me. I wish I could say that it came as a surprise, Daisy-mine, but it did not. Esteban and Jim Bowie, Isaac and Almaron, the boys . . . 'tis a pagan thing to say, but the smoke of their burning upon a pyre has lit a fire for all to see, a signal rising up to heaven, the sign of a worthy sacrifice."

Juan Seguin snorted in disgust. He dismounted, lightly as a bird swooping from branch to ground. Still holding the reins of his horse in one hand, he took Margaret's hand with the other and gallantly kissed it. "Lopez de Santa Anna – he is a hypocrite and a fraud, as I have said many times to my poor deluded cousin, more times than there are leaves on that tree! Esteban, Señor Jaime and the others will have honor and a proper resting place. I have taken a vow, Señora Vining, a vow on my own blood and honor as a gentleman to see that this is so – but first, we shall cram the mouth of Lopez de Santa Anna with the ashes of those he has cruelly slain and denied burial. And then," he concluded jauntily, but his smile was edged with sharp bitterness, "we shall make a tall mound – a mound built of his head and the heads of those *Centralistas* he has brought with him. My dear friends, you have no idea of how to begin being a pagan! Me, and my men, we shall show you, eh?"

"And this is the man who insists that he is a proper Catholic," Race laughed, as Erastus Smith also dismounted, rather less gracefully than Juan.

Erastus also took her hand briefly and asking, "Miz Vining – you are also prepared and fitten' to move on tomorrow? Speed is of the essence in our current circumstance. The Army as it is must find safety behind one river or another. Colonel Fannin's garrison would double the amount of soldiers at General Sam's disposal, as soon as he and they present themselves. Until then, we are not . . ." he looked earnestly, deep into her eyes, "entirely safe and secure from Santy-Anna's army. Sorry I am to say this to you, Miz Vining – but we are not. I will not tell you comforting lies to imply that such is not the case."

"I see," Margaret straightened her shoulders. She was thought worthy of confidences by these men. She must now bear herself as a woman of courage and consequence. "I had no other plan in mind than to follow the Army to east of the Colorado. If there is any other to be considered, then tell me now – and I shall tell the other women accordingly."

"That will do, excellently, ma'am," Erastus Smith answered, and Margaret thought that he did so with a certain amount of relief.

"So," she answered, "may you now tell me of what matters you have been about? I cannot tell lies, or make up some cheerful story for the other women. How stands our current situation, husband – Mr. Smith, Señor Seguin? I must know, so that I may answer honestly to the other women. You cannot know how desperate they are, how fearful! We are turned out of our homes. Now many of my friends are widowed, without any place in the world, shoeless and dependent upon the charity of our fellow refugees and the Army! I must give them some kind of hope to cling to – how close is the menace of Santa Anna's army? That is almost our worst fear!"

"We are doing the bestes' that we can." Erastus turned the brim of his hat over and over in his hands, while Juan Seguin replied gallantly, "You should have little fear, Señora Vining. My company of vaqueros and *Bejarenos* has been set in place as a rear guard to follow behind and see that none straggles. There is no sign yet of close pursuit from that devil Lopez de Santa Anna, but he has sworn openly to drive all the Americanos from Tejas. So," Juan Seguin shrugged, lifting his hands in a typical Mexican gesture. "We expect that he will soon bestir himself from contemplating his great victory. You are safe tonight, señora, and perhaps safe for a little tomorrow and the day after, but until we reach the Colorado," he finished with one of those eloquent shrugs, and Erastus Smith concluded, "and meet up with Fannin's company, and gather to us more volunteers . . . stay with the army, Miz Vining."

"Thank you, gentlemen," Margaret recovered her composure. Under cover of their farewells, Race whispered into her ear, "I am detailed to serve with the scouts, Daisy-mine, but I am certain that I will be permitted to spend a few hours with my family! I will return in a little while."

"*'And with a stronger faith embrace a sword, a horse, a shield.'*" Margaret quoted, and he smiled, the quick wry smile that she so loved to see.

"Devious Daisy, quoting poetry at me. I shall treasure every hour of your company, and especially relish it at such times."

Margaret, thinking of Maggie and Isaac and what Maggie had said, of loving words, answered, "Never forget that I love you always."

"Nor I," he said, and wheeling Bucephalus, was gone into the twilight after the others.

Chapter 14 – *A River of Tears*

Sometime past sunset, when the moon had just begun to rise, swinging up in the star-sprinkled sky and edging the clouds with ghostly pallor, Race came to their campsite with a roll of canvas over his shoulder.

"I have procured this from a friend who has a friend – you need a tent, for there is no room in the wagon for all of you, and it looks as if it is going to rain tomorrow, or even sooner."

"Bless you, indeed," Maggie Darst said, in swift comprehension. "We were too tired last night to do any more than sleep where we dropped."

"I must be away at the crack of dawn," Race added. "I am riding out with Erastus to serve as his messenger so these few hours with my family is all that I am allotted. Nonetheless, it is more than most of the fellows have. Some have even taken unauthorized leave so that they might go assist their families. Every settler between the Guadalupe and the Colorado has been told to flee. General Sam is furious, saying that he would hang deserters . . . but at heart, I don't think he can blame them. Many of his volunteers not lately come from the States all have families here."

"We shall be safe, once over the Colorado," Margaret said, firmly. She was reassured and comforted by Race's presence, even for those few hours – and later by the inexpressible delight she took in the sound of his breathing next to her and the security of his sleeping embrace. With tactful and unspoken delicacy, Mama and the other women left the tent to her and Race and their sons – a tiny shred of privacy. They slept on two blankets, hastily laid over a pile of wiry scrub cut from nearby, with the boys curled at their feet. In the dark of early morning, Margaret stirred from sleep to see in the dim moonlight sifting through the canvas over their heads that Race was also awake, his eyes open and staring at the canvas above their heads.

"I must be away soon," he ventured at last. "It's likely to be a long scout, two or three days. Stay with the army, Daisy-mine, as you have been doing. With luck, when I return, it will be to find you safely over the river."

"Be careful," she whispered, and he turned to prop himself upon an elbow and drop a kiss on her lips, a kiss that lingered as she drew him to her. With sudden fierce energy, he rolled silently onto her body and took her. Fumbling her shift and drawers out of his way in the darkness under the blankets, he thrust that male part of himself into her body with an urgency that left her breathless, doing so until he was himself spent and gasping for breath.

"I thought you must be away, soon," Margaret whispered, when she could speak again, for the shivering of delight that most always attended these encounters.

"Daisy-mine," and she knew that he was amused from the sound of his voice, "I hope that I would always have time for leisurely congress with you, dearest wife . . . no matter what other matters I would need attend to. A husband's duty, you know."

"And I ask for a bit of time, when we are abed together," Margaret answered, demurely, "for is that not a wife's duty also, to consider her husband's pleasure? Or so has been my reading of such things."

"Dearest little wife," Race embraced her again, laughing softly. "You are the most beloved of all my pupils. Of all, I believe you are the one who has absorbed the best part of all that I have to teach. If I have a master-work in me as a teacher, then that master-working is you." He seemed to grow somber, for when next he spoke, his voices sounded grave, serious. "Learning, knowledge – those all are an armor and protection against the vagaries of fate; a light in a dark place, a fair weapon against a tide of ignorance and superstition, a comfort in adversity . . . even a way to earn a living, especially if one is cast up amongst those who have none and desire to acquire it. We are living in perilous times, Daisy-mine – although I am convinced through my readings in history that all times are seen as perilous by those who must live through them! If I am fortunate enough to survive our current troubles – even as so many of our friends have fallen, and may yet still fall . . . my conviction remains that I will not make old bones, regardless of what may happen when we meet the Mexican Army in battle. I am not a rich man. Most likely all that I would leave you with is a town-plot in Gonzales, a fine horse and my library. Care of the boys, our most precious children will doubtless fall to you. Life is uncertain, Daisy-mine, and I must be honest with you. Often I doubt my own survival of the duties I am called to perform, and what may yet befall us. The fates toy with us as they will. I will face whatever they have in store for me, certain in my faith that I have conveyed to you every resource that you might need, to survive and thrive."

"You have done so marvelously well, my dearest," Margaret answered, and put her arms around him, keep him with her for a few moments more. "I am content – and happy that you are my husband. Stay a little longer."

"My beloved Daisy – that is not the nightingale, but a lark. I must away . . . otherwise I am certain that Erastus will come and roust me out, no matter what the embarrassment it may cause to our family life." He slid out from under the quilt that covered them and fumbled for his outer garments and boots in the darkness. "Stay with the Army as best you can," he said again, a darker shadow against the pale tent canvas, "In a few days you and the other families should be safer still as other companies come to join Houston's men, and we fall back to beyond the Colorado."

"And will there be a battle then?" she asked, quietly. "Will you be in it? Do you think we will win against a power of three or four times as many?"

"Ah, Daisy." He sat on the rough branch pallet next to her to pull on his boots, and leaned over to brush her cheek with his lips. "Truly, in answer – I do not know, but my best estimation as regards your three questions is: very likely, very possibly, and . . . we must win, regardless. Never underestimate the power of knowing that you must succeed when there is no good alternative. There was a cousin of my fathers' – he was a much older cousin, when I knew him – but as a very young man he fell out with his militia company upon the green at Lexington on that storied day when the British troops came a-calling. He said, he never felt so frightened in all of his life as he did looking across the green at all of those fine-uniformed soldiers but he would not have been anywhere else for all the world. And afterwards they chased the British soldiers all the way back to Boston, laying an ambush for them at every turn of the road and place where there was a stout fence or hedge. Cousin Peter told me years later – that he and his comrades knew then they would have to win, that they *must* win, even though they couldn't quite see how they might bring that miracle to pass. He knew that, with so deep and certain a faith. He knew that as surely as I am assured of our mutual love. Just so am I convinced, Daisy – as dark as the hour might appear – we shall prevail. When I was a boy," and Race laughed, somewhat self-consciously, "and even as late as a year or so ago, when I first confided to you of this matter, I wondered how my cousin could be so very certain of eventual victory. But now I feel something of the same assurance. I do not claim to know how, or by what means we will prevail, but prevail we shall, even if the going between now and then may prove hard, as hard as it did for my cousin. He lost three toes to frostbite at Valley Forge. I shall have to send him a letter soon, dearest wife. It would amuse him, I think, to know how I have come to comprehend his assurance in these matters." He kissed her lightly upon the lips and then on the forehead – just as the boys began to rouse from sleep, asking querulously what was happening and why their sleep would be so disturbed. Race kissed them very briefly. "Be good boys and a help to your mother," he commanded them, with a very good essay at fatherly sternness.

"When will you return, Papa?" Horace asked, and their father smiled at them so cheerfully, none but Margaret could have guessed at the effort which it cost him to make it.

"In a few days, little man," he answered. "Be a help to your mother and your grandmother. Reassure Johnny, and be a brave soldier for me . . . that's my good boy." A swift embrace of them both, Johnny still querulous with sleep and confusion, and then Race put back the flap of the tent and was gone into the darkness. Margaret thought about lying back in the warmth of the little space they had made, holding the memory of her husband's fleeting presence to her. No – the boys were awake; it was nearly dawn and time to shoulder the burden of leadership again. Time to see the boys were dressed in the clothes they had brought with them, time to see the cook-fire was refreshed and burning again, and that neither Pru nor Sarah had been overtaken by the pangs of childbirth during the night. Another consideration to add to Margaret's considerable list of cares – a midwife, should that need arise. And it would, soon enough, for both of them were heavy with child and Sarah near term. She sighed and rose from the nest of blankets and springy branches where they had all slept, pulling on her own dress and petticoat, over the shift she had slept in. She fumbled for her shoes, feeling not very much more rested than she had when she lay down.

Beyond the opened tent-flap, the sky to the east was lightening to an ominous russet color, streaked with dark violet clouds. The air was heavy with damp, that grass which had not been trampled flat was already heavy with moisture and bowing to the ground. Someone had already lit a lantern, hung from the wagon-bow, and by its dim yellow glow Maggie Darst labored to induce the campfire to burn. She looked up at Margaret's soft step, and said, "I thought it looked as if it would rain last night, so I put some wood under the wagon . . . but that didn't help much, since it is so green."

"If it weren't for the children being hungry, "Margaret answered, "and the want of a little coffee for myself, I would forget about lighting a fire at all. It sounds as if the Army is ready to move, already."

"So it is," Maggie tilted her head, listening to the sounds from the Army's camp, the sounds of men's voices and footsteps, the whinny of horses and the rattle of wagon chains floating on the darkness. "How many more days of travel until we reach the Colorado, M'grete?"

"If the Army follows the San Felipe road, then we should be at Beeson's Crossing in a day or so, I think. But if it rains, and the wagons are bogged down . . . ." Maggie's shoulders slumped, and she lamented, "Oh, if this wretched wood would only burn faster!"

"We have so very few comforts," Margaret said, as she crouched close to Maggie and added her own breath to blowing on the few sullen coals, "that I confess, I do not like to be deprived of that little quantity within our powers to enjoy . . . such as a hot breakfast and a cup of coffee."

"Small things, but treasured," Maggie laughed, between puffs of breath at the fire, which eventually reached out a few laggard flames and consented to burn with slightly more energy. "So, what did your husband tell you – regarding where we are going, and what is supposed to be our fate?"

"Little enough," Margaret replied. "He is sent to scout – and Mr. Smith and our friend, Juan Seguin – you mind him, Maggie? The son of the magistrate in Bexar – he has ever been a strong Federalist and has a company of his friends, his fellows from Bexar and thereabouts. They are tasked with guarding the column as we withdraw. So we are not entirely without shelter and friends. Recall how the men of Burleson's company brought us wood and meat last night? And it is expected that Colonel Fannin and his company will join forces with General Houston, once across the Colorado. Be of good cheer, Maggie – we shall endure and prevail!"

With the fire well alight, she took a bucket and went on a search for water. The campfires of the Army were already burning brightly, crackling with an energy which she wished that she could draw upon – or at least, their own small fire could match. It appeared General Houston was adamant about beginning the day's march by sunrise. Knowing that they would eventually be pursued, Margaret heartily approved. And that would mean a reunion with her brothers, as well. Mama would be cheered to have the boys with her, for even just a little. To Margaret, it seemed as if all that happened was almost too much for Mama to bear. She was lost without Papa, without the comfort of her loom, a safe home and the security of four walls. As she carried the bucket of water towards Papa's wagon and the circle of wagons and carts which carried the refugee women of Gonzales, Margaret concluded that it would be a good thing for Colonel Fannin to abandon La Bahia – both General Sam and her own husband did not seem to think highly of waiting in a fort for Santa Anna to come and lay a siege; the fate of the Alamo garrison well-argued their point. What had General Sam said about Quintius Fabius, when he talked about withdrawing to the east? Margaret cast her mind back. Oh, yes – something about the Punic War, and that she had meant to look it up. But she had never the chance, and now Race's books were safe-buried in the ground at the foot of Maggie Darst's redbud tree. She had best ask Race when he returned from his scout.

The ragged army marched at sunrise, and to Margaret and the other women's dismay, seemed to be forsaking the well-traveled and familiar San Felipe Road. They stood watching the straggling column going more in a northerly fashion, followed by first one baggage wagon and then another.

"The general has decided that the open road is too dangerous," explained a young man. He was one of those from the General's staff who had been present when Davy Darst had been readily enlisted and promptly detached on special duty. "So we are heading towards Burnham's, to cross over there. It's fifteen miles or so, as straight as the crow flies."

"We are not yet being pursued?" Maggie asked, suddenly as tense as a mother hen when the hawk flies overhead, and the young man shook his head, "Not so far," he answered, and squinted at the lowering clouds overhead. "The General, he's convinced that if it rains good and heavy, it might hide our back-trail, somewhat."

"Hide the tracks of five hundred men and a few dozen wagons?" Maggie snorted. "He's not been on another spree again, has he?"

"No," the young man shook his head and looked slightly offended. "The General would not indulge at such a time as this."

"He'd better not," Maggie said, under her breath, so that none but Margaret could hear.

That day of their march proved a miserable one, since the rain poured down steadily. Without the beaten path of the established road they could move the wagons but slowly. One day and part of another brought them finally to Burnham's Landing on the Colorado, where they were urged to cross over quickly and to continue moving east.

"Cap'n Smith says we should go all the way east, towards San Felipe, or even to Harrisburg," Davy Darst reported with solemn urgency on the afternoon of their arrival. "He and several others scouted back towards the Navidad and met up with an advance party of their scouts. He thought there was a small company following close upon them, so he did not dare do any more than capture one of them."

"Your Papa remains yet in Washington-on-the Brazos," Mama appeared almost cheerful, speaking to Margaret. "If he would come to meet us, part-way! And if the boys were here! Is there no word yet from Colonel Fannin?"

"No, ma'am," Davy shook his head. "There is not any message from him, so far." He looked somewhat apprehensively towards the cluster of women – his mother, Margaret, Pru, Maggie, and Sarah Eggleston – and hitched the old Brown Bess musket that he had been issued a little higher on his shoulder. Maggie had been incensed that the armory had given such thing to her son.

Margaret, left during the next days march with enough time for one of her 'thinks', was still uncertain if Maggie was angrier at General Sam or at her son. But having the musket among their party was something of a comfort to them all, as an assurance of their security. "Cap'n Smith says that the orders from the General are that women and children should remove to the east as soon as possible. The Army remains on the western bank to cover the evacuation of families. Then they will hold the line of the Colorado." He hitched up the musket again, for the very weight of it was sliding off his narrow shoulder. "But Cap'n Smith and the other scouts are worried. There has been no word from Colonel Fannin. There are more companies coming, more men every day, and word of two new cannon arriving from Velasco, but Colonel Fannin had the greater part of the Army and volunteers with him."

"Perhaps he is delayed by the rain," Margaret said, by way of an explanation. The constant rain plagued them. If the misery of walking in sodden garments and shoes were not enough, the smallest creeks had been filled to the brim, the currents running swift and mined with mud and tree debris washed in from farther upstream. The wind stabbed like a blade of ice to those in wet clothes and wetter blankets. "We may take comfort in that Santa Anna's troops must be feeling every bit of the cold and rain as we are. We will soon be in San Felipe and seeking shelter from our friends there."

Her friends and Mama seemed cheered by Margaret's words, but over the next days there was little else to take cheer from. A violent thunderstorm with hail the size of birds' eggs overtook the ragged train of refugees, pelting the wagon-covers and the shoulders of the women on foot as if someone were throwing stones at them. They struggled on; at times it seemed like everyone in the American settlements had taken to the road, abandoning all – home, goods, and stock – behind them. The refugees soon became spread out along the road, not in an organized train as they had been at first, since leaving the protection of the Army. They drew together at night, though, for it was whispered among some of the other families that there were renegades and robbers hiding in the thickets. Something of their panic abated, once the Army was encamped on the east bank of the Colorado at Beeson's crossing. As far as anyone knew the Mexican army was still on the west side and prevented from crossing over themselves for the height of the river and a lack of boats. But the wagons moved slowly in the mud and bogged down at the creek crossings, and Margaret and the others began to see abandoned goods, pots, and pieces of furniture left by the wayside. On one terrible, rainy morning, they came upon another over-laden wagon, with two pair of mules standing in harness by the side of the churned mud that had become the San Felipe Road. It was pouring rain, and the wagon was blocking part of the track.

"Why cannot they move?" Maggie fretted when they halted the oxen just behind the obstacle of that other wagon. They thought at first it was broken down, but upon closer look there did not seem to be anything the matter with it. "They are blocking the road. We risk bogging down if we go around." Margaret held the piece of tattered canvas over her head; a meager effort when it came to staying dry. All that it did was ensure that she was rather less wet than she would have been without it. She thought there might be people with the wagon, for there was a handful of women and children – white and Negro both – standing a little apart and beyond it, veiled in gray by the falling rain, and near hidden by the dripping trees beyond.

"I'll go and ask them to move the wagon aside," she said to Maggie, and picked her way around the halted wagon, her feet sinking deep with every step. Behind her, Papa's oxen stood patiently, with the rain running in rivulets down their backs, and the Millsaps children looking out curiously from the shelter of the wagon cover.

Approaching the settlers whose wagon part-blocked their path, she saw that three of the white women must be related – an older woman who looked enough like the two younger to be their mother, and two very young Negro women, hardly older than children themselves. There was but one man among them, a Negro slave – an older man, and hatless. The rain ran from the curly grey hair, and his rough clothes, just as it did the patient oxen, but he was not standing still. He was laboring with a shovel, digging a hole into the soft ground while the rain poured down . . . a hole – which Margaret saw, as she approached – already half-filled with water. The slave lifted up shovel after shovel-full of mud. Margaret thought of how she had buried her good china plates in her garden on the night they abandoned Gonzales, and wondered briefly what of their goods they could be burying here, so close to the road. It wasn't as if they might find the place again. She opened her mouth, as she came close enough to speak softly, as of the children saw her – a boy of Horace's age, holding a handful of field-flowers, already drooping in his small fist from the wet. With his other hand, the child pulled on the skirt of the woman he stood next to; a woman with a bundle in her arms and an expression of indescribable grief on her face. Horrified, Margaret realized the bundle was the size of a child, a small child. That it must be in fact, a child, and the hole that the Negro man was digging was a grave.

She closed her eyes, briefly; to put a beloved child into such a grave, half-full of water, to fill it in and hurry on, leaving only the smallest of markers!

What tragedies, large and small were suddenly made to cascade upon them all! The oldest woman, standing next to one who held the body in her arms – the children's mother? – met Margaret's eyes.

"Hurst," she said, and her very voice was cracking with grief, "I b'lieve this is deep enough. Go move the wagon, for I think this party must go past."

"I am sorry," Margaret began to say, as the man set aside his shovel. "Is there anything we can do for you?"

"No, nothing," the older woman put her arm around the younger, in a gesture meant to comfort.

Nothing could be done, to assuage the grief of a mother who must lay her child in such a grave with little ceremony; Margaret turned away, unable to watch any more. The Negro man, Hurst, walked with her towards the wagons and Papa's oxen waiting patiently, with Maggie standing by the lead ox.

"Are your people in need of any help?" Margaret ventured. "We have no medicines, if there is sickness among them, but we can spare a little food."

"No, ma'am," Hurst answered, firmly. "Miz Elizabeth's Jeffy, he weren't nebber in good fettle. He had de fits, now an' again. Dis col' an' de wet done for him, ma'am, not de cholera or somet'ing."

"If you would . . ." Margaret hesitated. "Convey to your people . . . our sympathies. This has all become a very great trial for all of us."

"Sho' nuff," Hurst agreed, with a brief and flinty flash of humor. "But ol' Massa Burnett, before he went to jine Gen'ral Sam, he done tol' me to do the bes' I can – an' my bes' be pretty good, Miz – " He looked questioningly at her, and Margaret answered, "Mrs. Vining. Hurst, you should tell the ladies that we were told to go east, as far as Harrisburg to be safe. We are traveling slowly, with oxen . . . should they care to travel with us."

"I doan reckon what Miz Burnett may say," Hurst answered. He swung up into the driving seat of the Burnett's wagon, capably gathering the reins into his strong brown hands. Within a few moments, he had moved it clear of the road. Margaret's party moved on, although she looked over her shoulder every now and again until the driving rain and the turn of the road around a clump of oak trees took the Burnetts' wagon out of sight.

"They were burying a child," she explained softly to Maggie, who did not seem much surprised. "A sickly child, so their slave man told me. The cold and the rain just made his condition worse."

"We should hope for better weather," Maggie ventured after some moments of thought, and her eyes in her face were shadowed with worry. "I fear such cold and constant damp will affect all – even those who are in good health. We risk the agues and lung-fever, or worse, every day this continues."

"The burden of a pilgrim, Maggie," Margaret answered, knowing in her heart that Maggie was right.

A handful of days, and painfully slow travel brought them within a short distance of San Felipe. Margaret and her party were hopeful of reaching shelter and refuge – hopes dashed when they met with a small party of men from San Felipe itself who warned them to turn away from that town and go towards Groce's Plantation on the Brazos. The men, who were returning to the Army after sending their own families east, bore appalling news. San Felipe had been burned at General Houston's orders. Worse yet, General Houston had also given orders to fall back yet again, to a defensive position along the Brazos, abandoning all to the west.

"Why is this being done?" Margaret demanded of them in agitation, "What of Colonel Fannin and his men? I thought they were all to join and hold fast along the Colorado and that was to be the line of our defense."

"Ma'am," the leader of the San Felipe men turned his hat in his hands, "They say Colonel Fannin was defeated in a fight on Coleto Creek days ago. He surrendered all of his men. I wouldn't credit such a thing, myself, but Gen'ral Sam must believe it, or he wouldn't be retreating east so fast."

Margaret felt as if she had fallen from a great height and knocked breathless. Colonel Fannin defeated, surrendered – what of her brothers! What of Rudi and Carl? She wanted to cry out, thinking of how all had assured her – first that Fannin's company held a strong position, and then that he would withdraw and join with General Houston's army. Now it seemed that everyone had lied to her. What would Mama say, once she heard of this? She was in the wagon with the children, as she and Maggie and Mary Millsaps talked to the men. There was small means of keeping such awful news from her. Perhaps it was only a rumor; that thought gave momentary rise to her hopes, but a few more questions put to the men from San Felipe only cut that hope to the ground again. It must be true – she acknowledged to herself.

"Say nothing to my mother of Fannin's surrender," she said to the other women, "until we know it to be absolutely true or not." Maggie nodded in somber agreement.

They continued on their slow way towards Groce's crossing on the Brazos, plagued by rain and cold, the labor of caring for the children and urging the oxen over just one more creek, swollen with ice-cold water. Margaret pondered how to tell Mama that Colonel Fannin had been defeated and her brothers most likely in captivity, but before she could come to any decision on the matter, Papa appeared miraculously – and to her immediate and overwhelming joy, in company with Race and a small handful of scouts who overtook them one morning as they were breaking camp. She did not recognize any of them at first, for they were travel-worn, dirty and unshaven; it was Bucephalus who looked more nearly familiar than her husband, who had always been clean-shaven.

"Alois!" cried Mama, joyfully. She ran to Papa's embrace, which lifted her feet clear of the ground. Margaret blinked away tears from her own eyes; Mama seemed to revive like a cut and wilting flower placed in a vase of water. Papa was holding her close, murmuring fond endearments – for which Margaret herself had little time to notice. Her husbands' arms were around her, warm and solid, their bodies fitting together as they always had. Horace and Johnny flung themselves at his legs, incoherent with excitement.

"I have missed you, Daisy-mine," he kissed her cheeks, her lips, "Every morning and every evening and every moment between. Dear love, you look like one of the mer-people, as if you have been swimming in the ocean."

"I have been," she laughed, and then choked on her own laugher. "I think I have been swimming since our last meeting – as if Texas has become an ocean. Dear love, where have you been all this time?"

"On long scout," he answered. "A matter of military import, Daisy-mine. And now we are going again. The Army is camped on the Brazos and we are sent to spy out the enemy, west of San Felipe."

"So they are not far behind us?" Margaret gasped, and Race answered,

"No, our reports are of small parties of scouts only. Smith has waited behind to hear the latest dispatch, and will catch up with us presently. Oh, Daisy," he seemed most overcome, "I am cheered beyond all measure to find you and the boys safe and well. We are fortunate indeed." Margaret embraced him again – yes, they were indeed fortunate, but only for themselves. She thought of her brothers, of what the men from San Felipe had told them.

"Race, love," she took his face between her hands. "There is something I must know. We talked a few days ago with some men coming out of San Felipe – they said that San Felipe was burned at General Houston's order."

"Well, it burned," Race interjected, "whether by order from General Sam, or by accident hardly matters."

"They also told us that Colonel Fannin had been defeated, and all his men taken prisoner. That was why General Houston abandoned the Colorado. Can that be true? We haven't told Mama, for fear of her worrying about my brothers, but is it true?" Her husband nodded, somberly.

"It is true, Daisy. Lopez de Santa Anna split his forces, and sent an army – dragoons and cavalry, with light cannon to sweep along the lowland settlements. Their commander is a General Urrea. He's said to be a decent man, a professional soldier, not a careless butcher like Lopez de Santa Anna."

"What will happen to the prisoners among them," Margaret whispered. "What will they do?"

Her husband smiled, seeming almost to reassure her. "I don't suppose they will want to tie themselves down with guarding the lot, or taking them all back to Mexico in chains, while the fighting is still on! In the end, I think they will parole the lot – just as we did with Cos' men in Bexar last year, or with those we took at La Bahia. Take away their arms, extract a promise never to return, and send them packing – to New Orleans, perhaps."

"You are certain?" Margaret was no little relieved by this assurance. "I shall tell Mama so, saying that my brothers will be paroled. She will not worry so, then."

"I am certain," Race embraced her once more. "They may be an enemy for now, but they are civilized men and as such they surely crave the good opinion of other civilized men!"

"How long can you remain with us?" Margaret recovered a little of her composure. "Might you stay for a little while – we have made the fire to burn hot enough for coffee."

"The drink of the gods," Race smiled. "Mayhap a few minutes, with the excuse of waiting for Erastus to catch up. There was a courier arrived with a dispatch for General Sam just as we were departing. Erastus remained in order to hear the latest reports. He told us to go – that he would be able to track us."

"Well, is he not the veriest Leatherstocking, the prince of trackers?" Margaret asked, and her husband laughed outright.

"For the space of half an hour," he allowed, and the other scouts also dismounted and tied their horses. For a wonder, it had not rained for hours. Maggie had been able to coax the fire to burn well that morning. The oldest Millsaps daughter ground a few more beans from Margaret's precious stock for a fresh brewing of coffee, while the other scouts – three weathered horsemen whom Margaret did not recognize at all – reassured the children and gently chaffed Davy for being, as they claimed, a garrison soldier, used to a soft life. Margaret reveled in seeing her husband, seeing their sons gathered to his lap as he drank the coffee that Maggie brought him. Papa and Mama sat together, a little apart. Margaret was certain that Papa must be telling Mama about the boys, and the surrender of Fannin's company. Papa was the best person to break the news to Mama, she felt certain. Mary and Maggie were treated by the scouts with special respect, once Race explained that they were neighbors from Gonzales, and what had happened to Isaac and Jacob.

"Race," she suddenly remembered to ask, "General Sam spoke to me of General Fabius Maximus . . . of his tactics being more pleasing to a soldier than a soldiers' wife. I meant to look it up, but that very night we had to leave your books behind. Can you explain anything of his words to me?"

"Most certainly" Race answered. "He was a Roman commander during the Punic Wars and fought with Hannibal by avoiding a fight. He went dancing up and down the countryside with Hannibal's army, staging a skirmish here and an ambush there, cutting off Hannibal's supply trains and laying waste to the countryside around . . . and when he was good and ready, and had the right ground, and Hannibal's men were tired and hungry and worn out . . . then Fabius turned and fought. And won a smashing victory."

"I see," Margaret considered his words. "Is that what General Houston is doing? Always just a day ahead of Lopez de Santa Anna, and letting him get worn out?"

"Yes it is," Race looked pleased. "And what General Washington did before him. Retreat as we may, as long as we have an army we are winning. And the Army grows every day – though too many of those new-come to it are over-eager to engage in battle. They rail against General Houston's rule, call him a coward." His face turned somber, "But there is a small difference between Fabius and General Sam, Daisy-mine. I think General Sam hesitates to engage in a battle . . . because our army has only got one good battle in them, and General Sam desires to hold off fighting it until all is in his favor."

"When will that be?" Margaret asked, and Race sighed and shrugged.

"I do not know. And I do not think General Sam will know until the moment is right. But the farther east we go, and Lopez de Santa Anna and Urrea follow close . . . then we are deep into the lands which we have settled among the piney woods and the lagoons, and the farther they are from theirs – the open plains and shallow rivers. I fear it will take time, Daisy-mine. Hold fast to faith in us – we will prevail. Besides," he added with a wry twist of his lips, "I cannot endure winters in Boston, you know. I should rather stay here and fight against the Mexicans for the home that we have chosen."

"I know," Margaret leaned against him; oh, the joy of being close to him, even if only for a few moments more. He told them a little more about the Army, about how the citizens of Cincinnati, away up the Mississippi River, had raised the money to have a pair of cannon made and sent all the way to Texas. He reassured them all, saying that companies of volunteers were joining every day, how he had made a friend of a restless young poet named Bo Lamar, who had just come rushing back to Texas from settling his affairs in Georgia. He even recited one of Bo Lamar's poems, and made them laugh

185

by saying they were not as good as Mr. Keats, but far more vigorous. And the marvelous steamship *Yellowstone* was tied up at Groce's Landing, ready to transport the Army wherever General Houston desired it to go.

Papa sat with Mama at his side on the bench brought out for the wagon. Mama's face was streaked with tears, but apparently Papa had been able to reassure her about the boys – or maybe, Margaret thought with a twinge of unease – he had not been able to bring himself to break the news to her. Another unhappy duty for her, then. She finally thought to say, "It was fortunate that you left the wagon and the team with us, Papa. I don't know how we could have managed otherwise."

"Good fortune, hey?" Papa answered. "At least, you are taking care of my property! Maria, I cannot say what will be the fortunes of our home, while we are away. The woods are full of thieves and banditti looking for loot wherever they might find it. My only hope is that Waterloo is so very far to the north that most of them will be too fearful of the Comanche, eh?" Suddenly, he shaded his eyes, looking past the group around the campfire. "Is that Smith, at last? About time – he would take twice as long to listen to a dispatch."

For it was Erastus Smith, lean and leathery, with his ears sticking out under a plain billed cap and a single blanket rolled up behind his saddle.

Race put the boys out of his lap, sighing, "Duty calls, Daisy-mine. Or it will, as soon as he is within range. I do not know when we shall be able to contrive another meeting. You must go as fast as you may to Harrisburg. So everyone says – even cross over at Lynch's Ferry, if you can. There should be some security for you there and at least a respite from travel." He kissed Margaret briefly and embraced the boys, as Erastus slid down from the saddle of his shaggy paint-pony, a little outside the circle of men and women around Margaret's campfire.

"Race – a word w'you now," Erastus called, in his slightly over-loud voice, beckoning with a crooked finger. "Just yourself alone." Race's eyebrows rose.

"The schoolmaster reproved," he murmured slightly under his breath, and joined Erastus just a little out of earshot. Margaret wondered if Erastus were annoyed that Race and Papa had taken a few minutes to be with their families; surely he could not grudge them that! Duty must on some occasions give way to tender feelings for loved ones. Looking at Erastus Smith's countenance, though – she could not see that he appeared to be particularly vexed. No, he looked . . . and Margaret's heart began to hammer with apprehension. He looked as he had that day when he brought Susanna and the two Negro men to see General Houston, to tell them of what had happened in Bexar; the face of a kindly man bearing bad news, worse news, resolute yet dreading to tell it. Margaret pressed her lips together; she would know the news that Erastus Smith brought, and know it now.

"Go to Oma," she whispered to the boys. She swiftly stepped from the company around the fire, although the other scouts were already readying themselves for a long ride, and Papa was chuckling as Mama chided him about keeping water out of his boots. Now Race had the same expression that Erastus Smith did, of horror, grief and shock mixed all together.

"What news did your dispatch rider bring, Captain Smith?" she asked clearly, proud that her voice did not quaver. "Was it of some matter that particularly affects my own family?"

"Yes, ma'am," Erastus Smith answered, "it does. I 'collect you and your Pa both telling of your brothers – his boys – being at La Baheer. They were still there, to the best of your knowing, a week, two weeks gone? They had not deserted away to help you, or to go with Doc Alsbury?"

"No," Margaret answered. "They went back to La Bahia after Christmas. Mama had a letter from Rudi in February, saying they were in Captain Pettus' company. I know there was a battle with General Urrea's forces and all were taken prisoner when Colonel Fannin surrendered." At those words Erastus looked even sadder. *Oh*, thought Margaret – *this is disaster. He must know that Rudi and Carl fell in the battle, and he is afraid to tell me, and even more afraid of telling Papa, for this will certainly kill him.* Aloud, she said, "My brothers are dead, then."

"I'm afeared so, ma'am." Erastus Smith replied, with infinite gentle sympathy. "All the lads with Fannin . . . they wus held in La Baheer for a time, after surrendering. An' then they were taken out of that place, an' shot down like dogs in a ditch. All o' them, every man-jack, executed by order o' Santy-Anna – even the wounded. Last o'all, Jim Fannin hisself. They piled up the bodies and burnt them, or jest let them lie."

"There were almost five hundred in Fannin's command," Race sounded as if he had been dealt a hard blow to his body, and he shook his head in disbelief. "All of them, executed – for what crime? This is inhuman. What monster could give such an order and what criminal would obey?"

"Santy-Anna hisself," Erastus Smith answered. "An' his orders were carried out. I'm pow'ful sorry, Miz Vining, to bear this news to ye. When I left, the Army was in a heap o'fury, hearing of this. The boys, they're all swearing vengeance an' damnation, an' promisin' t' give Santy-Anna his own quarter, the same quarter he gave t' ours." Margaret could think only of Carl; how he had pulled at her hand as a toddler, playing in the river or scratching

187

out letters in the dust, the weight of him as a child in her arms, the solemn face and the quick shy smile when he was amused. And Rudi – all that spirit and vitality quenched, forever. *'Do you think that it hurts to die, M'grete?'* he had asked once, as a child. Oh, please god, that it had been quick – and that it had not been painful, as she had promised him them. The agony of grief and remembering went beyond human feeling; she was scarcely aware of Race's arm around her, of Erastus Smith's awkward sympathy.

"This might be all our fates," Race looked as if he would curse; being pale with a fury that Margaret had never seen. "We must win this contest, Erastus, or we will be dead men."

"Fer a schoolmaster, you do catch on quick 'nough," Erastus Smith answered with grim humor. *So that was what the conjure-woman saw,* Margaret thought – *that day on the riverbank when I was twelve. She said only that she saw black smoke around Rudi, when she looked at his future – this, then, was what she saw.*

"We must tell Papa and Mama," she said at last, obscurely relieved because her voice sounded so steady; a Spartan woman to the bone, strong in the face of the unbearable. Because – after all, there was no alternative.

Chapter 15 – *A Muddy Field Near Harrisburg*

Erastus Smith took the burden of telling Mama and Papa about the boys, and the butchery of Fannin's command. He told them plain and simple, in kindly words, taking them a little aside, as he had taken Race and Margaret, while Maggie and Pru watched intently, shushing the smaller children into silence. Of course, they recognized the harbingers of bad news – it was as if they could plainly see scavenger birds circling. Mama reached out in blind grief, reached toward Papa, whose face went pale and then red. He spurned Mama's hands and glared at Erastus, at Race and Margaret.

"It cannot be," he answered, "Lies . . . all lies." Margaret could barely endure to look at Papa, at the bottomless depths of grief and fury in his eyes.

"Not so," Erastus Smith answered with calm certainty, "this news came by trusty messenger, wi' reports from my spies and all in agreement."

"Damn your spies!" raged Papa, "Damn them all!" He turned on his heel, blindly shoving past Race and Margaret. Margaret had no idea of what Papa intended, but Erastus Smith's long arm shot out and gripped Papa's elbow.

"Becker, I'll ask you not speak slightingly of my folk," he answered, peaceably. Without any visible effort, he spun Papa around to face him – Papa breathing heavily like an angry bull, Erastus Smith seemingly calm and easy as always. "I'd 'low you to go back to camp, or stay here an' comfort your womenfolk. Or you might come 'long and do the necessary 'bout those who kilt your boys. Yore choice, Becker, but if it is to come 'long, then I'd ask you to keep yore temper no higher n' your chin. You want to git yourself kilt doin' revenge, that's your affair, don't drag me an' mine into it. Save it for when we meet Santy Anna face to face. For' now, I got work to do. You in, or you out? All th' same to me, Becker; foller my orders, an' don't kill th' first Mex you see. There'll be a Santy Anna quarter taken, but it's the Gen'ral's choice to make as to when, not mine nor yours."

"As you say," Papa breathed, but his eyes were like cold pebbles of granite. He was already gone beyond them in humanity, in a way that Margaret could sense – and have some sympathy and understanding with – but also to fear. Erastus Smith gathered Race and the other scouts to him with a brief gesture, a look and a word. It was time for them to ride towards San Felipe, the women and children to continue their hopeless trek east, seeking a place to rest and wait upon what resolution General Houston's army could bring.

"Daisy-mine . . ." was all that Race could say, and all that he needed to say, for his final embrace and hasty kiss said all that words could not. Papa walked to his horse as if all were invisible to him, even Mama, his face set and terrible. In a moment, Erastus Smith and his party were gone out of sight, the sounds of their horses at a fast gallop fading into the morning. Margaret went to Mama, still sitting on the wagon bench, crouched with her arms wrapped around herself, rocking back and forth. She was silent, although unceasing tears poured down her face. Maggie and Pru, the latter heavy with the unborn weight of her child, hovered and regarded Margaret with hesitant sympathy.

"Mama . . ." Margaret put her arms around her mother. It was still something too huge to grasp; that Rudi and Carlchen were gone from this world, gone so cruelly and abruptly. They had packed their saddlebags and gathered up their weapons with the air of boys going on an adventure in the woods, on that day in January when they had ridden away from Gonzales. Margaret could only hope that they had been together at the last. "Mama," she said again, and Mama looked at her straight, her eyes swimming.

"Oh, M'grete," she whispered brokenly, ". . . the boys, both of them . . . the grief of this will destroy your Papa! I would have made Carlchen to stay with me, but he would go with Rudi, and your Papa would have it so. Oh, my boys!" and she dropped her head onto Margaret's shoulder. She made little other noise as she wept; merely a soft strangled moaning which sounded to Margaret like an exhausted woman in the agonies of the most painful childbirth imaginable. She held Mama to her, while Maggie and Pru hovered close in wordless sympathy, patting Mama's and her shoulders. Margaret found herself moved somewhere beyond grief, and yet queerly dry-eyed.

Lopez de Santa Anna had done this vile and cold-blooded murder – if not him personally, those of his minions who readily obeyed his orders. How had they done it, she wondered, taken them out several at a time before a firing squad? Or many at a time, for the Mexican soldiers to aim into, shooting and bayoneting until all were dispatched? Would the others of Fannin's company have been made to watch and listen, as they waited their turn? *'Do you think that it hurts to die, M'grete?'* In that moment, a hard knot of hatred congealed in her breast, a knot of hatred as hard as stone, for Lopez de Santa Anna, all who wore the various uniforms of his army, and did his murderous bidding. Race's friends, Juan Seguin and the Menchaca brothers, they had once talked of him as an honorable man, a committed federalist, a man who might have been the George Washington of Mexico – and yet he stood ingloriously revealed as a turncoat, tyrant, and murderer! He had driven her and her friends from their homes, vowed to take back those lands which had been settled by Americans at such cost and care, and willfully murdered sons, husbands and brothers. *O God, that I were a man! I would eat his heart in the marketplace,* Margaret raged silently, *and I would cut it out with my own hand. I shall never be able to read those lines without thinking of this! But I would, I truly would. I would take a knife such as poor Mr. Bowie was famed for . . . I would take it in my own hands and cut out Lopez de Santa Anna's living heart, and I would feast upon it, before his own dying eyes. He and his have cruelly killed mine own, and for that I will hate him to the end of my own life. Blood for blood, until they withdraw from our lands, go to their own homes, and leave us to ours!*

When Mama's first grief was spent – at least for a little – they hitched up the wagons, put Mama, Sarah, Pru, and the youngest children into them, and went on. Davy shouldered his old musket with renewed determination.

"I ain't afraid of ol' Santy-Anna," he declared to Margaret resolutely as they walked together by Papa's lead team. "Gen'ral Sam will see him off, he an' Cap'n Smith and all. We won't have anything to fear once the Army turns and fights, yes ma'am!" She would have thought it boyish bravado, save for the stern and very adult expression on his face. He was a man grown now, or near enough to it, and a soldier. This put him as much at risk as any other boy and man in the American colonies – and he knew it well, from the example of Will King, Gal Fuqua . . . and Carl, her brother.

"When do you s'pose Gen'ral Sam will fight, Miz Vining?"

"When the time is right, Davy," Margaret answered.

"When might that be, Miz Vining?" he asked, with earnest intent, and Margaret considered her answer for just a moment or two.

"When he sees that the time and place are right," she answered. "But I do not know when that might be. Did you ever hear of Fabius Maximus, Davy?"

"No, ma'am," he answered, "I don't believe Mr. Vining had mentioned him, least, not as far as I can remember,"

"Than I shall tell you about him – as much as I can myself recollect," Margaret answered.

They reached Groce's Crossing on the Brazos early in the afternoon. The Army had already arrived some days before, and set up a vast encampment on the western side of the river, opposite the Groce Plantation. The Brazos flowed wide and deep, deeper and swifter than usual because of the rain, that rain that had plagued them ever since abandoning Gonzales.

"There are ever so many more soldiers," Maggie observed with no small satisfaction. "It looks like they have been arriving for days . . . and they have a few more proper tents."

"And cannon," Davy interjected, "Aren't they fine? Six-pounders, I reckon."

"Quite the expert cannoneer, you are now," his mother affectionately ruffled his hair, and Davy flushed beet-red.

"I expect that we shall be told to cross over," Margaret observed, for she could see no women or children among the encampment, only men, intent and purposeful. A large number of them were at arms drill, marching and counter-marching, then halting in ranks. The first rank knelt and made as if to fire, all the barrels of their muskets and rifles in a ragged line, while the second rank aimed over their heads at an invisible enemy, and the drillmaster shouted commands. Davy looked longingly after them, as they passed by towards the landing, where several flatboats and a tall steamboat flying an American flag with her decks stacked with cotton-bales were tied up.

"Oh, my," Margaret said, "I believe that is the *Yellowstone*. My husband said that McKinney and Williams – the merchants – they have contracted with the owners to transport cotton and goods up and down the Brazos, seeing that there was great profit to be made once we were independent of Mexico."

"A fine sight," Maggie answered, "Just think of it – a mechanical ship plying the rivers of Texas. Now, that is a marvel!"

There were a number of men standing around the pair of cannon, obviously admiring them; Margaret recognized General Houston by his hat, still with the brim turned up to make an old-fashioned tricorn shape. They were to pass very close by the cannons and the horse teams hitched to the heavy carriages, and as they did so, the general turned to look towards them.

"Mrs. Vining!" he exclaimed, his craggy face lit with vitality and seeming pleasure at the sight, as he doffed his hat. It looked to Margaret that the general was having the time of his life. "And Mrs. Darst! I see that the soldier I detached to your service has followed my express orders . . . and not before time, Private Darst!"

"Sir!" Davy saluted awkwardly, converting the gesture to a quick snatch at the sling of his musket, as it threatened to slide off his shoulder. "Captain Smith ordered that we should cross over at once or as soon as we could, that the Mexicans were closing in on San Felipe. Are there any further orders?"

"No, Private Darst – no additional instructions. I have sent my papers to Harrisburg," the general answered, "and I am ordering all civilians there as well. I fear, ladies, your journeying is not quite at an end." The good cheer in his expression faded. "You know what has befallen at La Bahia."

"Captain Smith and my husband told us," Margaret replied, "when we met by chance this morning."

"And you had once told me that your brothers were among them," General Houston took her hand, just as he had Susannah's. Margaret felt tears stinging her eyelids and sternly blinked them back. "Allow me to express my condolences. Upon my own honor, Mrs. Vining, their sacrifice shall be remembered long, and their cruel murders shall be avenged. Houston makes that his personal assurance, Mrs. Vining – do not doubt that for an instant."

"I am surprised that you remembered about my brothers," she answered, and the general shook his head.

"Houston does not forget anything – neither a name of a man nor a service done," he answered, replacing his hat at a jaunty angle, and nodding to Mama and Pru on the wagon seat. "Or least of all – the face of an admirable woman. And now, ma'am – if you would be so kind as to excuse me." He added to Davy, "You should move your party across the Brazos and well on the way east before nightfall, Private Darst."

"Yes, sir!" Davy answered, with his face alight in pure worship.

Once across the Brazos, Margaret's party rejoined the stream of civilian wagons and carts moving east. The rumors passed among the various camps became wilder in the telling. Margaret did not honestly know whom or what to believe; she thought no farther ahead than getting to Harrisburg, the little town on the crossroads among a tangle of bayous. One of the rumors was that the government of independent Texas had taken refuge there; another rumor, relayed by a rider from Fort Bend lower on the river, had it that a large Mexican Army was already riding north. This caused Margaret and Maggie several sleepless nights for worry that they might be heading towards danger rather than refuge. Still another rumor claimed that General Houston meant to head east to Louisiana, luring the Mexican army after, so that a large American force might slip across the border and ambush them. This Margaret doubted, although she did not say so.

Such a long slow way, a struggle along a rutted and bumpy road! Margaret's shoes began to disintegrate, just as Maggie's already had. At the campfire that evening, Maggie cobbled together a pair of rough moccasins for them both from a piece of cured buffalo leather and some lengths of sinew that Jacob Darst had set aside for some purpose and which Maggie had brought, among her own stores. Many folk that they had met along the way were kind and generous, if they had sufficient of their own.

"Sooner you ladies have it than the Mexes," a storekeeper east of Groce's had told them, as he readily handed out from his stocks of cured meat, flour, and cornmeal, upon hearing they had come all the way from Gonzales.

Their march halted a little short of Harrisburg, halfway through April, in a muddy pasture surrounded by thickets of oaks and cypress trees, where several other parties with wagons had cast up. Margaret did not like the looks of it, for the smell of overflowing privy-trenches almost overwhelmed the odor of wood-smoke, but she had no choice. Mama was complaining of feeling ill – Mama who never complained – and Sarah Eggleston was in labor with her child, in labor too far advanced to travel any farther. At mid-morning her water came away all in a rush, as if a pin had pricked and burst that within her which contained the child. She bit her lip, and looked at Margaret with eyes gone huge with fear, although with a brave expression on her countenance.

"Oh, Margaret," she whispered, "It hurts, even now! How much more can I endure, when it feels as if all my insides are ready to be squeezed outside?"

"You won't feel all that much as the baby comes close to being born," Margaret stroked the girl's forehead. "You should make yourself walk a little, Sarah dear – walk and when you feel a pain begin, take three breaths and let them out, and count to ten between each breath . . . we will camp here where there are other people. I have had children, and so has Maggie – and Mary has had many more than either of us."

"It goes easier each time," Mary Millsaps said comfortingly, "After a time, it's as easily as a cat birthing kittens. Certainly the cat doesn't feel so much pain, for they purr with contentment the whole time." She felt for Sarah's hand. "Try to purr, dear little Sarah. We are with you, all of us."

"Can you set up the tent?" Sarah whispered. "I can't bear to know that everyone is looking at us."

"Of course," Margaret answered soothingly. Maggie and her son were already efficiently making up the camp, turning out the oxen and the single spindly horse which drew the cart to find their browse where they could, and fetching out those panels of canvas which made their tent. Pru sat on a scrap of Mexican blanket, spread out on the ground, with the children around her. Mama was nowhere to be seen – oh, there she was, walking back towards their camp from a clump of brush.

"Mama," Margaret called, "where is clean water, here – from the river? We should see that it is settled in the bucket before we drink, for the rain has made it all muddy."

"Yes, my M'grete," Mama smiled, a forced smile, and Margaret saw with sudden unease that Mama looked very pale. Her eyes seemed to sink into their sockets and her face looked as if she had suddenly lost flesh.

"Mama." Margaret looked between her mother and Sarah, smiling whitely between birth-pangs, as Mary Millsaps held her hand. "Mama – are you still unwell?"

"I am afraid so, M'grete," Mama answered, as pale as a deaths' mask. "I have not . . ." She swayed and then crumpled suddenly to the ground, even as Horace shrieked, "Oma!" and Johnny and Charlie Kimball began to cry.

Maggie reached Mama first, followed by Margaret and the children. Pru followed, moving slowly from the weight of her own pregnancy. Mama's skirts and single petticoat were stained, splattered with blotches of dark reddish brown fluid that stank of blood and bodily matter.

Maggie met Margaret's horrified gaze. "It's the bloody flux, Margaret. We must make her drink water, as much as can be. And we should tend and keep Sarah apart from her, for the flux is a filthy disease, near enough to cholera. Keep Pru and the children away, too, lest it afflicts any of them, for it's like enough to kill them, too."

"Then let you and Mary attend to Sarah, lest I bear the contagion to her on my person," Margaret whispered. Maggie's eyes darkened with concern.

"It's a hard job, that kind of nursing," she answered, "And you have two little boys – mine is all but grown."

"Mary and I will see to Sarah," Pru announced firmly. Maggie and Margaret looked up, startled. Seeing that, Pru added, "I'm bearing a child, but not tonight, leastways. We'll see to Sarah and the wean, and you to your Ma."

And so it was done; Mama to lay within the tent, growing weaker by the hour in spite of all that Margaret and Maggie did for her, coaxing her to drink water, with molasses mixed in for sweetness. Davy cut some long poles from saplings at the edge of the river and draped more blankets over them to shelter Sarah. Unbidden, he went to the other refugees huddled among their own wagons and the wreckage of their lives, to see if there might be a doctor among them; there wasn't, of course, although one kindly-inclined woman went to her own scant possessions and offered up a quantity of medicinal salts in a pottery bottle sealed with a cork.

"She says it never fails," Davy reported, "and whatever is not used for Miz Becker, could you send the remainder back, for there are others here, sickened with the ague, and the lung-fever as well. She promised she would look around for some baby linen – but she herself is not a midwife."

"That's very kind of her," Margaret answered. "When you can, point her out to me so that I might thank her for this kindness."

The sun set, flaming briefly in the west, but Margaret's awareness went no farther than the pallet where her mother lay within the tent that Race had brought to them . . . how many weeks ago? Mama's face was ghastly, in the light of the tiny pierced-tin lantern which afforded the only light inside the tent, after twilight had faded from the sky. Outside, their campfire sent golden sparks mounting up towards the sky and the silver sparks of the stars. Margaret was reminded again, most painfully, of how she and her parents and the boys had come from Pennsylvania – of how they had camped along the road, of Mama holding her skirts back as she cooked supper over the fire, her younger face gilded by the firelight as she smiled at Papa and Rudi.

With Maggie's assistance, she made a sickroom for Mama within the tent, taken away the soiled clothing – putting it all aside to be soaked in the river and washed clean. They found Mama's clean nightgown – but alas, that was soon soiled. They had little in the way of clothes and bed linen. The smell of the blood and matter caught at Margaret's throat, no less than Mama's own embarrassment and horror during those intervals when Mama was sensible. Margaret tended her mother into the late evening, feeling herself to be so driven beyond exhaustion and worry as to feel as if she were floating, floating in a pool of things not quite real. She thought that perhaps Pru and Davy, assisted by the children, had prepared some supper. She heard the voices of strangers outside – perhaps the kindly woman with the medicinal salts had brought over some cooked food from her campfire. She was aware of the quiet murmuring from the tent by the cart, where Sarah lay; Pru and Mary's voices, and the half-stifled noises that Sarah made. The baby was coming on fast, by the sound of it. Margaret was barely aware of the children, put to bed in the wagon but whispering among themselves. She lay down and slept, rolled in a single blanket, when Mama seemed to be quieter. In the early hours of the morning, she was roused again by voices, the voices of strangers outside the tent. She could not hear what was being said, but they sounded frightened. She sat up with a groan, quickly stifled, so not to disturb Mama.

The moon had set, and it was dark between the trees, a darkness faintly spotted with the lights from campfires dying down to coals, and the moving flicker of a lantern. Margaret recognized Pru by her pregnancy-distorted shadow-shape in the darkness and Maggie by her voice. They stood a little aside from the wagons, looking at the sky towards the south and east, with several other women whom Margaret did not recognize. Above the darkly jagged outline of the treeline, a narrow band of the sky glowed orange, a strong and insistent glow which seemed to pulse, but not to grow and lighten as the sunrise would.

"It's in the wrong place for the sunrise." That was one of the strange women, although her voice sounded oddly familiar. "We have been camped here for three days, and the sun rises more . . . more easterly. And this is too early. There is no clock among us, but Hurst can tell by the stars."

"It is a town burning," Margaret's own voice startled herself, with her own certainty. "Too big for a single house . . . remember how we looked back and saw the same as we left Gonzales?" She sensed that the other women looked at her, and would have denied what she had said but for the certainty in her voice and the unmistakable evidence before them. Something substantial burned, at a distance; Margaret thought she could almost smell it. Perhaps she might, for their campfires had all burned down to a scattering of grey-ash coals, and the light breeze came from the east. "What town lies in that direction? Does anyone know?"

"This is the road towards Harrisburg and Lynch's Ferry, and I thought we were not very far from either," Maggie answered.

"About two miles," the woman with the familiar voice answered. With a jolt of recognition, Margaret remembered – the woman with her two daughters, on the road towards San Felipe, burying a child in a grave half-filled with water. Mrs. Burnett, who had a slave man named Hurst.

"Who has burned Harrisburg, General Houston or the Mexicans?" Maggie asked, bitterly. "I don't suppose that makes much difference! And where should that leave us, when the sun rises and Sarah's baby is born?"

"Right here, I expect." Margaret drew in a breath. "We cannot go back, we cannot go forward. We cannot move my mother to a safer place, for there is no safety anywhere, if the Mexican Army is now in front of us."

"We've been here for days," Mrs. Burnett answered. "The wheel of our wagon broke beyond our Negro man's ability to fix it. He took one of the mules and went to find a wheelwright or a blacksmith two days ago, but returned saying that all about had fled, or were waiting their turn to cross over at Lynch's."

"Then we shall remain also," Margaret said, firmly. "Until someone comes to tell us we might go home. Look – now, there is the true dawn, right where you said it might be."

She had been too long away from the tent, and Mama's side. She left the other women still looking apprehensively towards the east. The wick in the lantern had burned down very low; after the lighter darkness inside, she could barely see, inside. She raised the wick a little, seeing the gleam of Mama's eyes in the faint light it cast.

"M'grete?" Mama spoke, her voice faint, and weak. "Are you there, M'grete?"

"Yes, Mama," Margaret took her mother's slack hand, alarmed that her hand felt so cold in hers. She would have tucked it under the quilts covering her mother, but that Mama's hand tightened upon hers.

"M'grete, where is your Papa?" she asked querulously, and Margaret answered, "He is with the Army, still – with Captain Smith."

"I wish he would come home," Mama said. "How long since I have seen him . . ." her voice died away, and Margaret thought she had drifted off into slumber again. She was about to settle the quilts over her and lie down, but Mama spoke once again.

"M'grete, can you find my brooch? The little one, my best one, with pearls."

"It's in your trunk, in the wagon," Margaret answered. "Do you want it now, Mama?"

"No, no," Mama shook her head, restlessly. "No . . . just find it for yourself. It was my brooch, from Oma Katerina. She gave it to me when I married your Papa. I meant it for Carlchen, for the girl that he would marry." Slow tears leaked out from Mama's eyes, and Margaret tenderly wiped them away. "But Carlchen and Rudi, they are gone. Take the brooch, M'grete. Give it to Horace or Johnny. For the girl that they marry. Promise me this, M'grete. The brooch . . . for their gift . . . to their wife."

"Yes, Mama – I will promise," Margaret answered, thinking with a twinge of unease, that Mama was worn to a thread with exhaustion. She had barely the strength to speak, and her face appeared ghastly in the dim lantern light.

"And M'grete . . . promise me this also . . . that you will look after your Papa. He will need always . . . someone to look after him . . . Alois . . . he is a good man, M'grete. He speaks . . . hastily. But he means well."

"I promise, Mama," Margaret said again, and Mama smiled, a very faint smile. Her eyes closed, and she seemed to fall back into slumber. Margaret lay down, with her own hand still holding her mothers' for that contact seemed to comfort and reassure them both.

She did not sleep long, though – for then it was Mary Millsaps calling for her, and Pru, too. She slid her hand from Mama's, smoothing the quilts over her. Mama was sleeping sound, her breathing slight but regular. Her eyes were sunken in her face, Margaret thought, but the shadows under them not as dark-appearing as they had seemed to be the night before. Margaret felt lightened by relief – Mama would recover, certainly. She would sleep sound, so Margaret had best go to Pru and Mary before their voices wakened Mama. It was broad daylight now, and Pru stood before the fragile shelter of blankets and willow-poles, her face beaming with triumph, holding up a baby, tidily wrapped in their last clean cloths, a baby who looked around the morning with milky blue eyes rounded with vague astonishment.

"'Tis born safely, and a little girl! Is she not beautiful? Sarah is resting, but I told her you should want to see her daughter first."

"She is beautiful," Margaret said, while a heavy-eyed Maggie nodded agreement. Horace and Johnny, with Charlie Kimball and the Millsaps children gathered around, agog with excitement. "I so envy Sarah that she has a daughter! I would love a daughter – think of the fun of dressing them in pretty clothes, and talking to them of woman-things. Talking to Mama, and our Oma – oh, it is not the same as talking to boys."

"Sons do have much to recommend them, though," Maggie added. "Mine has gone down to stand guard. He is building himself a guard-post in the thicket of trees nearest the road."

"General Sam's youngest and most dedicated soldier," Margaret exchanged a fond smile with Maggie, who continued, in a lower voice, "How is your mother?"

"Sleeping sound," Margaret answered, but that did not seem to reassure Maggie, who said only, "It's not as killing as cholera, but the flux does kill."

"Mama is sleeping peacefully," Margaret insisted. "She ceased voiding the pestilent bloody matter hours ago. I think the medicinal salts and making her drink water have had some effect."

"We pray, Margaret . . ." and Maggie would have said more, but for her son, who came whooping from his self-assigned guard-post.

"Ma! Miz Vining!" Davy called. "It's the Army! They're coming, just along the road there. General Sam and all! The Army is coming!"

"Oh, my God – a prayer answered," Margaret breathed, but Maggie's expression remained bleak. Others of the families encamped in that muddy meadow began to gather as they heard the sounds of marching feet and men's voices raised in the notes of a ribald song, borne on the morning air.

There was a party of mounted men, first – with General Houston among them, on a brave white horse. His face was set with determination, and he looked neither right nor left. The men following were at first hidden by trees around the turn in the road, but the sound of their voices and brisk but uneven marching filled the morning. The song – which truly was rather rude – died abruptly away as the first marchers saw the women and children watching by the roadside. A slight rustle of consternation rippled through the ranks. Margaret searched for her husband among the horsemen, looked for the elegant black shape of Bucephalus, but did not see either of them.

"There are so many more!" Maggie exclaimed, standing beside her. Roused by the noise of the marching men, and by Davy's calls, other refugees were joining them at the side of the road, women looking frantically at each face among the marching ranks, searching for a dear face, familiar garments among the motley throng, or holding up their smaller children. There wasn't a uniform among them that Margaret could see, other than a small cluster of men in grey and others in blue coats – coats with darker patches upon them where shapes picked out in gold braid had been torn off. Most wore plain coats, or round jackets; the men whom she recognized mostly had fringed hunting coats. Every man bore a rifle or a musket, on a sling over their shoulders, though – and all at very nearly the same angle. The general's drillmasters must have been at it night and day, for weeks.

"Dragon's teeth," Margaret said, teased by a faint memory of a tale that Opa Heinrich had told her once, long ago. Maggie looked at her in surprise. "Dragon's teeth. When the dragon's teeth were sown, as we sow corn – the teeth become fully armed fighters, springing up from the furrows. Such were sown, all across our lands, and now here they are!"

The children were cheering, crying excitedly when they saw a familiar face, the face of brothers, uncles and fathers; Mrs. Burnett, with her gray hair straggling down her shoulders, came running from her wagon, hastily rolling it into a bun as she ran.

"William!" she called, "William Burnett – where are you!"

"I'm here, Liddy!" an older man called to her from middle of the ranks of marching men, men who were so much younger it wrung Margaret's heart. "Stay with the girls, Liddy!" Mrs. Barnett darted into the crush and threw her arms around him, snatching a kiss and a brief embrace, before his company marched on. Many faces were familiar to Margaret – neighbors and friends of her husbands', faces which she recognized from last fall when the militia volunteers had come to Gonzales in defense of their little cannon – men from Mina, from Bexar, from Beeson's Crossing, the two soldier-volunteers who had brought them meat and firewood on that first day of this long march east, the flaming red hair and pale freckled face of Harry Karnes, but they were a mere scattering among the larger number of strangers. One by one, with their limbers following, came the two cannon that Margaret had seen in the camp at Groce's Crossing, drawn each by several teams of horses straining at their harnesses to draw the heavy gun-carriages through the mud and ruts of the Harrisburg Road.

"Where have they all come from?" Pru marveled, holding up Sarah's baby, "Darlin' little girl, now you can say you saw the Army of Texas on the march!"

"Where are you going?" Margaret called to them, hardly expecting an answer, but several passing close by answered in chorus, amid jovial laughter.

"To fight Santy-Anna, ma-am! Word is that he has gone up the river looking for us!" "We ain't but a days march away from him, ma'am!" "Oh, but we aim to surprise him, for sure!" "Aim is right, ma'am, aim is right!"

Out of the corner of her eye she saw Davy Darst shrugging into his jacket, running at a purposeful jog, his musket and haversack and a rolled blanket slung over his shoulders.

Maggie saw him too, and cried, "David Darst – where do you think you're going?"

"With the Army, Ma!" he answered, hastily embracing her. "'Bye, Ma!"

"You come right back here, David Darst!" Maggie shouted after him, but he had already run into the mass of men and boys, falling into a place in the march. He waved at them once, cheerfully. Then he was gone, lost in the ranks and leaving Maggie distraught and furious, and Margaret feeling as if she had seen this many times and would see it again. "Come with me," Maggie commanded. "We must fetch him back, at once!"

"I think not," Margaret answered slowly. "I believe he will be in a better and safer place with his fellows than he will be with us. If the Mexican Army comes upon us, with our tents and wagons, and Mama and Sarah's babe – then all they will find will be women and little children. He is a boy of near to fighting age. With that musket – they will assuredly execute him as a rebel."

"But you heard what they said – they are going to turn and fight now!" Maggie was still distraught. Margaret looked after the last of the Army, a handful of horsemen ranging this way and that. None of them were Race, and she sighed a little in disappointment.

"So they are," she answered, with an assurance that she did not in truth feel. "But I have a better feeling in trusting General Houston with the lives of our own. He will not fail us, Maggie – or our men. I am confident of it."

Chapter 16 – *San Jacinto*

Rather than putting the camp of refugees under a cloud of fear and anxiety, the sight of General Houston's army passing by on the way to meet Lopez de Santa Anna had rather the opposite effect. The very size of the army gathered to confront the bloody-handed dictator, the resolution in their stride and the cheer in their faces heartened the women, even Maggie. She was distraught over Davy, often looking down the Harrisburg Road in the next few hours as if she were tempted to take the cart and the single horse and go after him. Margaret wondered if Liddy Burnett might also do the same, having seen her own husband among them. But Maggie did not – and neither did Liddy Burnett, who had her daughters and their children, the family slaves and the remnants of her household to look after.

"I expect Race was out on scout," Maggie finally said, as they walked back towards their meager encampment, Pru carrying Sarah's infant in her arms. "And your father, also. The general would have put out the scouts a little removed from the column, or so I recollect from what Jacob would tell me of the proper military practice of things. Why do men talk to us of their matters, I have always wondered – do they think we should be interested, or are we to sit and admire them for their genius?"

"My own husband wishes me to learn of things, so I expect that is why he talked to me. Still, I should like to have been able to tell Mama that I had seen Papa," Margaret answered, and the thought of Mama erased all else. "Papa is everything to her. I fear that if something happened to him, Mama would not be able to endure living."

"Romantic clap-trap," Maggie snorted, robustly. "One always lives. There is a home to make fair, and children to see to – and if one is left without support, there is a living to make . . . and when one has aged beyond that, there are neighbors and friends. There is always something to live for; a man of one's heart is just a part of that, and unless you are a romantic fool, not the largest part either. Your dear mother has you and your boys to fix upon, should the light of her life flicker out." Margaret smiled, heartened – Maggie, with her robust good sense. Maggie was an unquenchable fire, a sturdy oak tree, or a dependable rock in the midst of the flood. "You said she was sleeping peacefully this morning, Margaret? I heard your voices in the night."

"Her color looked better," Margaret answered. "If she is wakeful, I will see if she will drink some more of the salt-water potion – it seemed to help."

"Good," Maggie answered, but although her voice was cheerful, her eyes seemed shadowed. Margaret thought it was worry over Davy.

"Mama?" she whispered, as she stooped to enter the tent. She had not been away for more than three-quarters of an hour, and in the meantime, Mama still lay peacefully, her eyes half-open and the fold of quilt over her chest still rising and falling, with the faint regular sound of her breathing. Thinking Mama had wakened again; Margaret knelt and sought out her hand. "Mama, we've just seen the army march by. I didn't see Papa or Race. They are probably out scouting. Davy has gone to join the column, for they said they are going to fight Lopez de Santa Anna at last." Her mother's hand was slack in hers, and the focus of her gaze did not change. Margaret knew instinctively that this was not good. No, this could not be – *Mama had seemed to recover, she looked well and had slept peacefully!* "Maggie!" Margaret called. Perhaps she had not been able to keep the panicky note from her voice, or Maggie had been lingering close by, for her head appeared around the edge of the tent almost at once. Pru was there, and Liddy Burnett, all of their faces tender with concern and affection. Maggie stooped low, and came to the other side of Mama's pallet-bed, taking her other hand and testing the thready pulse in her wrist, the blue veins in it seeming so clear under the translucent skin. Margaret saw that the tips of Mama's fingers were tinged with a faint blue tint, as if they were bruised. Liddy Burnett took a place at Margaret's side, kneeling awkwardly; for age had rendered her unlimber.

"What has happened?" Margaret whispered. "She was recovering, I know she was. She talked sensibly this morning, and then she slept. I thought . . ."

"No, dear girl, she is failing. I know the signs well," Liddy Burnett answered, her voice almost calm enough to mask the deep sympathy lying beneath her stoicism. Maggie's countenance was tragic, so Margaret knew at once that it must be so and also that there was nothing to be done, even as Mama still breathed. She dared to hope that if Mama still breathed – she could not be dying, but just as Margaret's thoughts ran frantically to that last refuge, Mama seemed to take one final shuddering breath, then not another. Her hand in Margaret's grasp seemed oddly lax, and her half-open eyes stared at the canvas over their heads without blinking.

"She's gone," Maggie said softly. "I am sorry, M'grete, she is gone now." While Margaret sat, dazed with disbelief, holding Mama's slack hand in hers, Liddy Burnett got to her feet, with painful slowness, for a moment bracing herself with a heavy hand on Margaret's shoulder.

"We must see to the needful now," she said. "I'll send Hurst to you – he will know what to do. There is not a man of God in this camp, but I have a prayer book with the proper service of burial in it. We must do what we must, dear Mrs. Vining, and without delay." She patted Margaret's shoulder consolingly, and Margaret stared at Mama's face – Mama, already gone into eternity, leaving them all behind? No, Margaret reminded herself; the boys would be waiting there for her. And that would be a comfort to hold to now, believing that that Mama and Carl and Rudi would be reunited.

"Mrs. Burnett is right," Maggie said. "Give up her hand, M'grete. You should tell the children now. Don't worry about the laying-out. I can see to it." She took Mama's hand from Margaret's; laying it crossed with the other on Mama's breast, and gently drew up the quilt to cover her face." Margaret sat back on her heels, stunned with the rapidity of what had happened.

"I can't believe it," she said aloud. "It doesn't seem real."

"It never does," Maggie answered. "One just becomes accustomed to it."

The air of unreality persisted, as if a kind of invisible fog surrounded her for all that day. Johnny wept in her arms a little, for Mama had played much with him and told him stories, but Horace looked at her with quizzical concern, as if he did not himself believe it. While she sat there, on the wagon bench with the children, the Burnett's black slave Hurst came from their wagon, carrying a box of tools in one hand and a collection of sawn planks and a long shovel over his other shoulder.

"Miz Burnett an' some o' de odder ladies, they done have me take boards from their wagons," he said, "to build de coffin with."

"That is very kind of them," Margaret answered, "and of you." Hurst looked at her with something of the same kindliness and sorrow on his seamed, dark-brown face that everyone else had looked at her with. The word had flown on wings. Margaret supposed that Liddy Burnett had told them. "You have all been so kind."

"Yass, ma'am," Hurst answered, and at Margaret's elbow, Maggie added softly, "M'grete, we should find a place . . . a good place, nearby. A place for the grave that we might mark well and find again, mayhap even a place that Miz Becker would have liked."

"Yass, ma'am," Hurst nodded, "dat's a good thought, ma'am. You fin' dat place, an' fin' nearby. I won't complain none if de' groun' be nice an' soft," he added, with a glint of humor. Maggie snorted – she sounded as if she disapproved of Hurst's levity – or his over-familiarity in speaking out of turn. As they walked with the children across the road, where the shadows of the oak trees lay dark, Maggie muttered, "Shiftless, no-count nigra layabout!" Margaret hoped neither Hurst nor her sons had heard, and answered, "He is just doing what he was told by his owner to do – I don't blame him for hoping that the ground would be soft enough to make digging easier."

"He didn't show proper respect," Maggie answered. Margaret wondered if her ire was really because of distress over Mama dying and Davy joining the marching column of General Houston's army almost within the same hour.

Beyond the track towards Harrisburg, there was a band of sturdy oaks and then a wide meadow. There were no fences, or sign of habitation within sight. The meadow was green with rich new grass standing upright under the sun, and starred with those tiny white lilies which around Gonzales only sprouted up after a rain. Margaret stopped at the edge of the meadow, underneath the branches of a spreading oak tree, a tree with four branches curving up like a candelabra from a central trunk so large she doubted that she and Maggie and her sons could link hands and comfortably encircle it.

"Here," she said, and for the first time, tears trembled in her eyes, tears that she resolutely willed not to fall. "Mama would like this – to look out upon the flowers. And I will know it again, that is certain."

Hurst had nearly finished a simple coffin by the time she and Maggie returned, built out of the various wagon planks, neatly fastening together the various lengths and thicknesses to make a plain box. He was helped by two small Negro children, a boy and a girl, who appeared to be his kin – there was a resemblance in the shape of their small faces and the similar spark of lively intelligence in their eyes. Margaret could not bear to watch him building the coffin, knowing that it was intended for Mama, although she noted that the children were holding the planks steady to be pegged together or fetching the various tools that he needed.

"My chirren," he said, proudly, when Margaret asked, and complimented him on his skill. "An' I can do mos' things, well enough, Miz Vining. De master allus say, I be a jack of all trades, an' master o' none. Das' what he tole me. Not ezakly sure what he meant by that, Miz Vining, but I t'ink he meant it comp'mentry."

"He did, indeed," Margaret answered. "It means that you can do many things, well enough – but none of them well enough to be a master . . ." Hurst chuckled, with rich enjoyment, and a flash of wry amusement at the discomfiture in Margaret's expression.

"Hoo-wee, dis ol' nigra be a massa? Ol' Miz, she have a fit o' conniptions at dat thought! Ol' Miz, she a lady," he added hastily, "an' kindly nuf. But Marse Burnett, he an' I, we got an' unnerstandin'. He say what he t'ink, I say what I t'ink – long as we say so where no odder can hyere, den we be fine."

"I wish that you were not made to do this," Margaret said, after a brief silence. "Although it will mean so much – and we are grateful. More grateful than we can say." She could not help herself, for speaking. Mama had not approved of holding slaves – she had never – as nearly as Margaret could recall – spoken with open disapproval of the peculiar institution to anyone outside the family in all of their years in Texas. But Margaret was very sure of herself on this; Mama would not have wanted her coffin built by slave labor, nor her grave dug by the same, for all that it was accepted by most of their friends and neighbors. She would never have approved of Papa buying a human being, as he bought an ox or a horse. Paying wages to a laboring man, that was one thing. Buying a man and taking the labor as an afterthought – that was another. Hurst set down his hammer, and looked at her quizzically.

"Miz Vining, Ol' Miz she done tole me to do dis."

"She told you," Margaret answered, "and it was kindly meant towards me, but you are a slave, so you must do as your mistress says. My mother . . . did not approve of slavery. She thought it was wrong and cruel, an offense against God. I can't help thinking that she would not thought well of being laid to rest in a coffin built by a slave, in a grave dug by one . . . it's not to reflect on you." Margaret stopped, not sure of what she meant, and suddenly and miserably aware that she might have spoken hurtfully. But Hurst only weighed the hammer in his hand and regarded her with thoughtful sympathy.

"Miz Vining . . . Ol' Miz, she might have tol' me to gwine here, an' do this. But I do it, 'cause it's de right thang to do, befo' de eyes o' de Lord. 'Fo' de Lord is righteous, he love de righteous deeds an' those upright shall see his face,' so he say in de Psalm Eleven of de Good Book. Ol' Miz, she be up dere, but de Lord, he be higher still."

"Still, I wish that you had a choice in the matter of obedience," Margaret answered, and Hurst chuckled, again in wry amusement. "I wish you did have such – you ought to choose what sort of labor you do and for whom." A sudden thought occurred to her, a way to be fair to Hurst and to appease Mama's shade. "Hurst – would you accept payment to honor my mother and to reward you for your care? I know slaves are allowed by their masters to work for others, and earn wages for themselves. It would please me to know that you have been rewarded in this world, and it would please my mother."

Hurst scratched his jaw, thoughtfully. "I woodn' say no, Miz Vining – an' dat's de cold fact – I cain't say no. Ise long been wantin' to save up, buy the chirren free."

"Then it would be an honor," Margaret answered, swiftly and having made the decision, she acted instantly and without hesitation. She dove into the tent, where Mama lay silent, still, with the quilt pulled over her face. Margaret lifted it back; Mama's eyes still unseeingly looking above. Maggie had not begun the work of laying out and Mama's hands were still slack and limp.

"For you, Mama," Margaret whispered, taking Mama's left hand in hers, thinking with a pang that her fingers were so knobby and callused, worn with work, at the loom, at the fireside and in the garden. Her gold wedding ring was loose upon her finger, her hand seemingly cold, like clay with the warmth of life already fled; Margaret slid it free with hardly any effort, holding it in her own hand for just an instant. No, Papa would never know, whether he returned from battle or not. Maggie would see that the ring was gone, in washing and dressing Mama's body for the grave, but Margaret would tell her what she had done. Of all they had, this was the only thing of value that could be spared. The more Margaret thought, the more fitting it seemed to be, even if Hurst looked at her with shocked horror on his face, although those first and honest feelings were swiftly veiled.

"Take it," Margaret urged him, "and use it to buy freedom for your son and daughter. "It is gold, and of value – and my mother would be grateful in knowing that. Please take it, Hurst . . . for your children's sake."

"Ol' Miz, she might think I stole it," Hurst stubbornly shook his head. "I dassen't, Miz Vining."

"I will speak to her," Margaret answered firmly, "and tell her that I choose to reward you freely with my mother's ring. And if you are so fearful of being thought a thief, then I shall hold it for you, but consider it yours." Eventually, she persuaded him to accept Mama's ring, although he still seemed reluctant, even after Margaret had spoken to Liddy Burnett. Liddy looked even more disapproving than Hurst.

"Pay him for work, Mrs. Vining? You'll give him notions, treating him like a white man, paying him wages."

"I think Hurst already has notions," Margaret answered, and Liddy Burnett snorted, scornfully, "I've told my husband again and again that nigra is too uppity to be of any good to us, but William won't hear of selling any of the folk that he brought from the family place in Carolina, and he won't hear any ill said of Hurst, since they were boys together. Tell Hurst he may keep all of what you give him . . . we Burnetts are not so ill-off that we need hire out the nigras and live on their wages."

"I'm sure that everyone will find that most fair," Margaret said, after considering and rejecting several less tactful responses. Such a wretched and cruel matter, slavery – and yet so many otherwise reasonable people seemed to find it perfectly natural! Margaret sometimes did not know quite what to say, or even if she should say anything at all.

Mama was buried in the afternoon, two days later, for it took Hurst nearly all of one day to dig the grave properly deep in the heavy, rain-sodden soil. Margaret stood at the graveside with Johnny's hand in hers and Horace pressing close beside her, bewilderment plain on their faces. She could not make Johnny understand that Oma was gone, for he insisted that she was not gone, she was in the box, and why – as Hurst and some of the older boys labored with ropes to lower the coffin – were they putting Oma in the ground? A handful of other women from the camp stood with Maggie, while Liddy Burnett read the service of burial from her *Book of Common Prayer*. Margaret closed her eyes, and let the words flow past her, as water in the river flowed past the rocks, until there was an expectant silence, and she opened them to find everyone looking at her, and Maggie with a clump of damp soil in her hands.

". . . suffer us not, at our last hour," Liddy Burnett read, "for any pains of death to fall from thee." She nodded at Maggie, who pressed half a handful of the soil into Margaret's own hand, and knelt so that Johnny and Horace might each take a small clod.

"Now throw it in," Maggie whispered. The boys obeyed, and Margaret flinched at the hollow sound that it made, while Liddy Barnett continued reading. *Mama would have wanted this in German,* Margaret thought. *German was for churchly things like this. Mama didn't really believe that God spoke English.*

"Forasmuch as it has pleased Almighty God of his great mercy to take unto himself the soul of dear sister, Maria Elizabeth Becker, we commit her body to the ground, earth to earth, ashes to ashes, dust to dust in the sure and certain hope of the Resurrection to eternal life." Margaret opened her hand and let the earth fall, and the other women solemnly followed suit, while Margaret tried to stop up her ears against the sound. There was not very much more until it was over, Liddy Burnett closing her prayer book, while the other women and their children scattered away.

Hurst took up his shovel, saying, "Ise made a cross marker, Miz Vining, to mark it proper."

"Thank you, Hurst," Margaret answered, and there was nothing more to be done or said. Just then, it seemed as if there was a rumble of thunder somewhere to the east.

"How very odd," Liddy Burnett remarked. "I don't see any clouds, but it sounds like a storm coming in."

"Doan' sound like no thunder, Miz Burnett." Hurst listened attentively, as the distant thunder pealed again. "De soun' of it too short. Soun' to me mos' lak cannon."

"A battle?" Margaret went cold, thinking of the ragged but eager army that had marched past them, two days before, of Liddy Burnett embracing her husband, and Davy Darst running to join them.

"Ridiculous," Liddy Burnett snorted. "How ever would you know what cannon-fire sounds like, Hurst?"

"I 'member when de British came up-river to Nawleans," Hurst answered. "Massa Burnett, him an' me, we wuz dere." He tilted his head, listening carefully. "Soun' fo all de worl' jes like that."

"Dear God," Liddy Burnett was as pale as a linen sheet, and Margaret met her eyes, and knew that she had the same picture in her mind, of General Sam on his white horse, of the two little cannon trundling past on their rough wooden carriages while willing shoulders pushed hard from behind whenever the horses drawing it faltered at a particularly deep or muddy rut. They stood listening carefully, but the sound of thunder – or perhaps the cannons firing – faded away within minutes, although Margaret thought that she could hear a faint yet irregular rattle and popping sound for some time after that, when the breeze did not stir the leaves overhead and the birds were silenced.

"It must have been summer thunder," Liddy Burnett said, at last, when whatever had made those peculiar sounds had ceased, and they had walked back to their camp, leaving Hurst to finish filling in Mama's grave, "for I thought a battle would have lasted longer."

Around the middle of the day following, though – they found out that it had been a battle, a battle fought at that very hour that they were burying Mama. A man on a lathered horse came galloping from the direction of Harrisburg, waving his hat over his head, and shouting,

"Victory – Gen'ral Houston has a victory, the field is ours!" The rider slid off his horse, in a flurry of upthrown clots of dirt and mud at the edge of their camp; almost immediately, he and his horse were at the center of a crowd of women and children, laughing, crying, calling questions at him, a wiry Irishman whose joyful grin seemed to stretch from ear to ear, a flash of white across a dirty face hazed with a scruff of dark-red beard, "And Santy Anna, the old de'il himself is captured, and made to surrender!"

"'Tis Seamus O'Doyle," cried one of the women, "who went with the army as soon as we heard of the Alamo! Seamus, what are you doing – can this be true!" Gasps of delight and cries of joy greeted the young man's words, amid some disbelief, and the young Irishman put his hat on his head again, exclaiming, "By Mother Mary, Joseph and the Lord, 'tis true and as near to a miracle as I swear I have iver seen – and Seamus O'Doyle has niver been branded a liar! For our fellows have barely a scratch upon them, an' only a handful killed entire, and Santy Anna's men, they fell in rows, like stands of barley reaped at harvest time!"

"It must be true!" the woman who knew him exclaimed, her face alight with hope and rejoicing. "Seamus is a trusty man!"

"When?" Margaret raised her voice over the clamor, "And where?"

"Not ten miles from here, as the crow flies," Seamus O'Doyle answered. "But a wee longer by road, you'll be understanding – and at about half past four of the clock yesterday. There we were gathering, in our ranks – those dear sweet twin ladies in the middle . . . bless the folk that send them to us, an' bless the ones who brought them all this way, for there we were on one side of a meadow where the San Jacinto River flows into Buffalo Bayou, and Santy Anna – oh, that black-hearted scoundrel, why the de'il does not come to drag him down to hell I cannot say for the life of me!"

"The battle," Liddy Barnett demanded, with no little urgency. "Of those who fell, of our men, do you know any names?"

"Aye," Seamus O'Doyle scratched his cheek, thoughtfully, "Nooo, I do not and sorry I am to say. But it was not many and no lads or old men among them, so I do swear. Most fell at the first charge, before our own overwhelmed the barricades." His eyes were alight again with enthusiasm, and he continued, "And the Gen'ral himself rode before us, on his white horse, he was – waving his hat, an' ordering us to dress right and left, all proper-loike, aim and volley . . . but I swear to you the fiery spirit of Cuchculainn took us all, an' Colonel Rusk, he cried, 'If we stop, we are cut to pieces – go ahead, give them all perdition!' an' so we did – we were over their lines an' into their camp, not even stopping to reload. Oh, we gave a proper Mexican quarter, so we did . . . they ran like hares! It would have done your hearts good to see it." Seamus O'Doyle hesitated, a little abashed, "Or maybe not, for some died very ill, begging for a mercy we felt no inclination to grant. And Santy Anna, he was captured this morning – like a coward he was, skulking in the grass where Vince's bridge was burnt. Not so much of a foine figure did he cut," Seamus O'Doyle laughed with huge enjoyment, "for he is a right little man, w'out his braided coat an' gimcrackery hung all o'wer it . . . an' mind you ladies, he was wearing slippers and an ordinary soldier's coat. They brought him to the Gen'ral, lying on a blanket under an oak tree, having his ankle seen to, for he was wounded sorely in the charge – the boys say he had two horses killed under him in the course of that fight – which between myself an' mine, that should put paid to rumors of how he was a rank coward an' afraid to fight."

"About Santa Anna," Margaret raised her voice so as to be heard, and at her elbow, Maggie asked, "So then, is it finished with the Mexican Army, and may we go home at last?"

"Aye!" Seamus O'Doyle laughed heartily again. "For it is indade over – for bein' beaten as sound as a bodhran at a village dance, the de'il Santy Anna must sign over Texas to us, an' order his other armies – for there are other armies about, not just the one we beat between the chime o' the quarter-hour! They must pick up their packs an' traps and march, quick-step loike, back to where they came from – an' to offer no offense or hurt to any they come across, as long as they are gone!"

The women around Maggie and Margaret cried aloud with joy at this, and some began to weep, while Liddy Burnett had her daughter's hands in hers, her face raised towards the sky as she exclaimed,

"Rejoice in the Lord always, again I say rejoice!"

"Can it be true?" Pru Kimball whispered. "Can our deliverance have been this easy, after all that we have suffered and lost?" She hugged little Charlie to her and began crying herself, although they were tears of joy and relief, mixed with the sorrow. Maggie embraced her and Charlie both, and whispered over their heads to Margaret, "Alas, we have no homes to go to, ours being burnt to the ground and our men left unburied in the field where they fell!"

"I do not know what we should do next," Margaret answered, squaring her shoulders, "but I am sure we will rebuild. Gonzales will be built fair and fine." Her own heart sank as she said those brave words, thinking of the labor of building again, without George Kimball, Jesse McCoy, and Isaac Darst – without the aid of all those who had fallen. Her brothers. Mama.

Beginning again. Texas was beautiful, heartbreakingly beautiful; she could hardly think of the meadows of wildflowers, of the stately oak trees, of the forests of pine and cypress, of deep green rivers, and the sky overhead, speckled with white clouds, as pure and fine as wads of unspun cotton, without a pang of fierce affection. Margaret could hardly contemplate living anywhere else – but oh, what a work that would be! Of course, Papa began building a home after every setback – thrice by Margaret's reckoning – but each previous time, Papa had been younger, and with Mama and the boys at his side. And Race? Her husband was a refined, scholarly schoolteacher; with his fine broadcloth coat, his library, and his un-callused hands. He had given a good account of himself in the last year, but Margaret knew he was not one of those naturally given to hewing a home and a livelihood out of the raw wilderness. He was one of those who came along afterwards, when a place had been settled long by enough families with children of teachable age to afford him a living at what he did best. No, Race would be hard-pressed to build a home and living again. It would be like putting Bucephalus to work as a plow-horse; a cruel and ultimately fruitless work. Margaret did not fear for his survival of this battle; she had been promised eleven years with him – and had not this dramatic courier insisted that of those who had perished, none were lads or old men? Davy must be safe, and also William Burnett, and even General Sam Houston, that frank and handsome adventurer with the cleft in his chin and an unfortunate taste for drink – he only had a shot through his ankle. Margaret thought to worry about that for a moment. There were all sorts of poisonings, some of them fatal, which came from an injury of that sort . . . but no. It was in her heart that General Sam was one who would live long, surviving all that fate, Mexican rifleman, or his ill-wishers would ever throw at him.

"Ladies, I must away, to bear the good news farther still." Seamus O'Doyle swept off his hat again, and bowed to them, very gallantly. "I am following the road east, and telling all that I meet of the glorious victory at San Jacinto."

"And grateful we are," Liddy Burnett exclaimed, "for we have been in such misery, never knowing."

"'Tis been a pleasure," And Seamus O'Doyle made as if to kiss her hand, saying, "A pleasure more than I may say, for 'tis often that a man must carry bad news – but for the honor o' bearing such news as this, y'r ladyship – 'tis such a privilege that I would ride twice as fast and twice as far." He swung up onto his horse again, and was gone in an uprush of thrown mud as fast as he had arrived, and leaving the women stunned with the suddenness of it all.

"I suppose it is true," Maggie ventured. "We heard the noise of it – and he is known as a truthful man. Still, I wonder how long it will be before we may all go home. As soon as the army is done with our men, I suppose. You'd think that since there are to be no more battles, then it will be soon."

"I hope so," Margaret answered, and her heart lifted at the thought of Race, of her arms about him, and his around her. "Will you return to Gonzales, Maggie?"

"Most likely," Maggie sighed, "for the sake of Davy and his father's property. Perhaps I will go to Galveston for a time, and stay with my sister there. What about you and Race?"

"I haven't thought of what we might do," Margaret finally answered. "Perhaps we may have Papa remain with us for a time . . . he may need us. I dread telling him about Mama."

"You'll find the right words, when the time comes." Maggie said, comfortingly.

She needed those words sooner than she had thought to need them. Within two days of Seamus O'Doyle's message, parties of returning soldiers began appearing on the Harrisburg Road, ragged men, exuberant with victory, celebrating their return home, and wagons with families, returning from their refuge in the East.

On the afternoon of the third day, Horace turned from helping Margaret hang up wet laundry on a line strung between the wagon and a nearby tree, and shouted, "Papa! It's Papa, and Opa and Davy, too!" Margaret hastily dropped the half-full basket of wet washing and took up her skirts. Who could mistake Bucephalus' gleaming black hide, or the way he fairly danced along the roadway? Race grinned at her, from behind a horrible bush of untrimmed beard, and swept her up into his arms, with an embrace so hearty she felt as if her ribs might crack. Over his shoulder she saw that Maggie was hugging Davy to her, in between upbraiding him for being so tardy in his return.

"Ah, Daisy-mine – the triumphant return. And it is triumphant, for I presume you have heard the news?"

"Two days ago!" she gasped, as she kissed him. "Oh, that dreadful beard will have to go, it's like kissing you with two balls of yarn stuck to your face. We had a messenger, who came and told us. Oh, we were so worried – that one day we heard the cannons but we thought it might be thunder . . . hush, boys." Johnny was throwing himself at his father's knees, crowing in excitement, while Papa, laughing, had lifted Horace up to set him on his shoulders. Margaret was piercingly reminded of how Papa had lifted Rudi just so. Upon that recollection all joy suddenly went out of the day.

"Daisy-mine," her husband whispered, in sudden concern, "what has happened. Why do you look so melancholy?" At just that moment, Papa swung Horace down to the ground, and looked around expectantly.

"Where is your Mama," he asked. "Maria – where is she? I see your wagon, your friends, M'grete, but I do not see your mother." Margaret wet her lips with her tongue and answered, valiantly attempting to keep her voice steady.

"Mama died of the flux, Papa. Four – no, five days ago." It was horrible, to see how Papa's face changed; as if all the animation drained from it, leaving him instantly grey and old, even more lifeless than Mama's face had been. He shook his head in disbelief. Margaret continued. "We buried her over there. By the biggest of the oak trees. It was the flux. I was with her at the end."

"No," Papa insisted, shaking his head. Margaret reached for his hand.

"It's true, Papa – five days ago. Mrs. Burnett's Hurst built the coffin."

"No," Her father swept her hand aside with brutal force, and Margaret couldn't think of anything more. Maggie had an arm around Davy's shoulders, and a somber look upon her own face.

"She is buried by the tree, yonder," Maggie said, gently. "The Burnett's man, he marked it proper. Do you wish us to show it to you?"

"No!" Papa sounded as if he were choking. "No . . . just . . . leave me." He turned his back upon them all, and stumbled towards the trees. When Margaret and Race made as if to follow him, he looked over his shoulder and snarled, "Leave me be, all of you!"

"Best let him go," Race held Margaret back, from following her father. "Daisy-mine, if he wishes to comfort himself by being alone at your mother's grave, then let him." He suddenly coughed, and added, "Confound it, all this sleeping on the ground in the wet . . . no, do not assume the worst, Daisy-mine. I am as well as ever. Tell me of all that had happened, since we were last together." Now that Margaret could weep, she found that she could not. She slid her arm around her husband's waist, and answered, as they walked from the road to their camp.

"Nothing of import, save Mama. Oh, my dearest, I have missed you so dreadfully!"

"And I you, Daisy-mine . . . and I am hungry and thirsty. It will be good to have a home again!" Margaret looked over her shoulder. Papa was on his knees, beside the dark mound of earth, piled up on the grave under the oak tree. She could not tell anything of his expression, for his back was turned upon them all.

Chapter 17 – *Going Home*

The next day, Margaret's family began their return home, departing from the miserable camp with feelings of mixed sorrow and relief – sorrow for leaving Mama's grave behind, as well as Rudi and Carl to whatever accommodation was to be made, relief at returning home, to homes and holdings which – everyone was assured – they would not ever be driven away from again. Davy and Race had brought a bit of camp gossip from General Houston's oak-tree headquarters. Colonel Rusk was to take a detachment to Goliad, to the grounds where Fannin's men had been murdered, and see to the proper burial of what remained after more than a month of exposure to sun, rain, and wild animals. Margaret put that thought aside, as she was becoming accustomed to doing of late. It had been a stab in the heart for to think of her brothers' bodies being left unburied. Best to think of them as they were when she saw them last, Rudi laughing and confident and Carlchen's shy smile.

Papa was heartbroken over Mama, she could tell. He remained by her grave all that night. After sundown, Race approached him, at Margaret's urging. He returned shaking his head, "He has spread out his blanket for the night, saying he intends to sleep beside your mother one last time. I had never suspected Father Becker of harboring feelings of excessive romanticism, but my own father used to say there was a first time for everything."

The once-forlorn camp of refugees emptied, as volunteers returned from the San Jacinto field, or from the army camp just outside Harrisburg to rejoin their families and take them home, or if not home, to a more comfortable refuge. Mary Millsaps and her children were invited to accompany Liddy Burnett, who offered them hospitality at their home on the Brazos. William Burnett averred that as a representative to the Texas government he would join with other patriotic citizens in pressing for some kind of pension or settlement upon her and the other widows of the Gonzales Ranging Company. Sarah's husband Horace Eggleston came for her, overjoyed with relief that the child had been safely born. They were planning to return to Gonzales too, but Horace Eggleston was first taking his family to Galveston, where he might purchase enough goods at the port to return to his ruined store and have merchandise to sell. The road became well-traveled in both directions, much as it had been in years before.

On the very morning that Margaret and Maggie were packing the wagon, a long column of Mexican soldiers marched by, watched in silence by those still in camp – a handful of officers on horseback, dressed in splendidly gold-braided red coats with blue facings, coats whose ornaments and epaulettes glittered dazzlingly in the sunshine. The officers were followed by rank after rank of ordinary soldiers in plainer uniforms, marching in silence and averting their eyes from those who watched from the wayside. Three boys threw mud and horse dung at the marching soldiers, taunting them with shrill shouts of "Go home, cowards!" until their alarmed mothers came and hustled them away. The soldiers did not react, nor did their officers, but they still had their arms. And there were so many of them, still. Race looked on with a grave expression, at the marching ranks, at the several heavy cannon, their ammunition limbers and the baggage wagons following after.

"To think we beat them!" he exclaimed, in quiet awe to Margaret, who also looked on with feelings roiling in her mind, of triumph and dull hatred all mixed together. How very formidable they appeared, compared to Sam Houston's army who had marched in the other direction not a week ago! And that ragged army had beaten this one, beaten them so soundly that now they were marching away. To where, Margaret did not know or care, as long as she would never see the like ever again. But the damage that had been done, the deaths of their friends, the destruction of homes, the loss of her brothers and Mama; that would not soon be forgotten or ever forgiven. Even as she and her husband watched in silence, one of the soldiers – a taller man with slightly more ornate braiding on his coat sleeves detached himself from the column. He approached, a smile of happy relief on his face, and Margaret recognized him as he removed his tall shako from his head. It was Diego Menchaca, Races' old friend from Bexar, who with his brother and Juan Seguin had spent many happy hours in visiting their old home.

"Horace – my dear friend!" he exclaimed, "And Señora Vining – I cannot tell how happy I am, to see you safe and well after all this . . . this . . . this . . . what do you call it . . . this unseemly brangling."

"I'd have called it a war, myself," Race answered, with a tight expression around his lips, but he took the hand that Diego extended and accepted the fond buffet on the shoulder. "You look well," he added, "better than most of Santa Anna's men that we left on the field."

"Ah, that," Diego shrugged, with a wry expression on his sun-burnt face. "It was my good fortune to be under the command of General Gaona these last few weeks, and thereby avoid a sound drubbing. Race, my friend – I begin to doubt that Lopez de Santa Anna is indeed the military genius that I once thought he was. Do not say so to Juan, for he will never cease jesting with me over it."

"The evidence for Lopez de Santa Anna's military genius is strewn the length and breadth of Texas," Race answered in tones as dry and bitter as alkali dust, and Diego had the grace to flush slightly.

"I am relieved that you have lived to make a jest of it, none the less. May I hope that Juan is also alive and well?"

"He lives – he and his company of *Bexarenos*," Race answered, "and they did good service with us, remembering their true loyalty as Federalists and to the Constitution."

"Fortunate," Diego's face went somber, "Fortunate for all of us, but not for Esteban. You must know that he is dead?"

"In the Alamo – yes," Race answered. "Among the piles of corpses burned by order of your hero, Diego!"

"Ah, my old friend – your words sting like a willow switch. My brother had a decent burial. I saw to that, once I found his body below the gun bastion in the chapel ruins. They made of him the only exception because I asked it of General Cos. Do not reproach me for forgetting my loyalties. I hold to those which matter, those between family and old friends. These political matters are as nothing, surely!"

"My brothers are also dead," Margaret spoke for the first time. "Because of these political matters. You remember the two boys who used to visit our house in Gonzales, who loved to look at your horses? They were murdered at La Bahia. Where were you then, Señor Menchaca?" Diego's face paled, and then reddened. He looked at the ground at his feet, seemingly shamed at her words, and finally answered, "I regret most heartily that I was not there. I might have contrived a way to spare them both. But I was not. And whether I will reproach myself for the rest of my life is a matter between God and myself. Goodbye, old friend, Señora Margaret. I do not think that we will meet again." He replaced his shako on his head, turned on his heel, and at a half-trot, followed after the column of marching men, vanishing among them before they were lost around the bend, beyond the trees.

Race looked after him for a moment, with a look of quiet and unspoken grief upon his face. Finally, he murmured, "I believe there is a danger in following after a man on a white horse, Daisy-mine, especially if you believe against all evidence that he is a paragon among men. Fortunately, no one believes of General Houston that he is anything more than human." He seemed to shake off the melancholy, adding then, "Let us go home – to whatever home we have."

They hitched the oxen – she and Maggie and Davy, as they had done on so many days before, although Papa felt moved to readjust some of the chains.

217

They left a handful of wildflowers on Mama's grave and turned their faces west, never looking back as they followed the road towards home.

Near Beeson's Landing, Papa met a neighbor from Waterloo, who told him in passing that the handful of houses and dwellings there still stood. It was such a tiny settlement and so far removed from the known and established settlements that it had been bypassed by the Mexican column which had burned Mina – although the neighbor confessed that some of the houses had been broken into and looted – by brigands or Indians, he did not know which.

"At least your father still has a roof," Maggie observed in consoling Margaret who agreed, saying, "That does make Papa most fortunate. I have not seen anything but ruins all this long day."

For there was scarcely a structure standing, all along the old King's Road which had run from Nacogdoches to Bexar; wherever there had been a house, an inn, a growing town, there was now nothing but a pile of ash and charcoal, or half-burnt logs tumbled together like monstrous jackstraws, surrounded by fields of young corn and wheat trampled and ravaged by armies and wild beasts. The road itself was as busy as it had been, full of refugees returning joyfully to their homes. Most of them were eager to begin building again, exuberant at having beaten back the hated Mexican *Centralistas* and kept them from ever throwing around their weight in Texas again. Now they could truly manage their own affairs without having to travel to Monclova or to Mexico City and scrape for the attention of a lordly official in a gold-trimmed coat, meanwhile fearing all the while to be accused of disloyalty and flung into prison.

It was a relief to know that Papa's holding had remained unscathed, for Margaret had begun to worry as their journey progressed about him and Race alike. Papa seemed unusually dour and distant. He appeared to have little care of his person or his clothing; and no appetite for food or any interest in the companionship of his fellows. He stumped along beside his lead ox team, saying little but commands to them for hours at a time. He barked at his grandsons, Horace and Johnny – and they in turn avoided his company. This grieved Margaret, who had hoped at first that their childish affection and interest might in some way comfort her father. But it was a vain hope, for here was Papa, treating Horace and Johnny as he had Carl. But this was of smaller concern, next to that of her worry about Race's health. He became sick again, as they journeyed – not so sick that he could not remain upright in Bucephalus' saddle, but his face was pale save for unnaturally pink fever spots, and he was increasingly afflicted by a racking cough. Her husband was not well, certainly not fit to live out under the stars all summer long and take an active part in the labor of rebuilding Gonzales.

"I think we must go with my father to Waterloo," she confessed quietly one morning to Maggie, as they prepared breakfast at a campsite on the bank of the Colorado River. The mist rose up from the river, the morning sun was a half-seen pink pearl among the morning fog that had spangled all the tree leaves and bending grass stems with moisture. "I do not like to leave what was left of a happy home and many friends, but the home is gone, and our friends are scattered to the four winds. I fear that Race may become desperately ill soon if we do not find shelter for ourselves. And my father – I fear what will happen to him, left to himself. He will wear himself out with grieving after my mother and brothers."

"You need not justify yourself to me," Maggie answered readily. "I see how it is with your husband and your father. You must think of your boys as well. Perhaps it would be best for you and your husband to go with your father, help him make an accommodation with his griefs for a year or so, and when Gonzales is re-built, return and set up the school. Waterloo is a lovely place," she added, "So they all say, and your mother could not say enough about it. A fair Garden of Eden it sounded to me. I think your mother grieved for leaving that place, and if it is any comfort to you, M'grete, I believe she was very happy there. Perhaps you shall be happy also."

"I may hope," Margaret answered, but in truth to her it seemed more of a laborious duty. Papa would be difficult – that she knew as surely as she knew that the sun would burn through the fog at midday, and that she would long for the days of her husband teaching school on the porch of the little house on St. Francis Street when she was the queen of her own household.

On a fine late spring day, they passed the McClure house on Peach Creek, and knew they were only ten miles or so removed. The McClure house still stood, with an intact roof, although all about had been ravaged and burnt, and the well filled up with bricks and broken debris, but the tall oak tree which General Houston had taken as his headquarters still stood tall and proud in the meadow before it.

"Almost home," Maggie said, cheerfully. Margaret envied her good spirits. Her own journey would be at least a week longer, once they had returned Maggie to Gonzales and retrieved their own property; Margaret's good dishes and the tin trunk with her husband's library. Race's coughing was almost incessant. When she had broached the issue to Papa that they would accompany him back to Waterloo, Papa had been dour but agreeable to her suggestion that they take refuge under his roof, as the only one left standing.

Having passed by and seen the burnt ruins of San Felipe, Beeson's Crossing, and at a scattering of farms and hamlets along the road, they were at least prepared for the ruin of Gonzales.

"It does not look as bad as I had expected." Race stood in the stirrups, looking ahead, as the wagon lumbered heavily up the road from Plum Creek. "At least, all the rain did well in washing away the soot and nourishing those gardens not eaten down to the ground by deer and wild hogs."

"I think there are even some houses left unburnt." Maggie was also standing, on the wagon-bench, bracing herself against the jolt of the wagon by clutching the bow. "No, it looks like someone's smokehouse, and Zumwalt's summer kitchen. Imagine that – everything else burnt to a cinder. But there are folk already returned – I can see the smoke from cookfires."

"I hope the ferry is working again." Race sat back in the saddle, and looked up at the women, "Otherwise we will have to go north a good ways to cross over, after we unearth my books. What did they do with the ferry boat, do you think?"

"Knocked a hole in the bottom and sunk in shallow water," Maggie answered. "It's what Jacob would have advised. Easy enough to refloat, if they remember where they left it and the river current didn't move it."

Between the Zumwalt's kitchen, the regular and right-angled pattern of roads – where the soil had been packed hard by the passage of wagons, horses, cattle, and men, and new-grown grass had not been able to gain purchase, and the look of certain large trees, they were able to deduce where the Darst's house had stood. A pile of charred logs and the eight stone pilings upon which it had stood were just visible above the heads of high grass, bowing gently to the light breeze. Beyond it stood the remnants of Maggie's vegetable garden – corn and beans, potato plants and pumpkin-vines, all straggling up between the grasping weeds, grass, and wildflowers. The redbud tree still stood, although the branches closest to the house had been touched by fire. The dark pink flowers had been replaced by leaves but otherwise it was unchanged even to the gentle declivity between its roots where Davy and then the Millsaps boys and their friends had dug a cave to play in.

"It shouldn't be very far down," Margaret said, and Papa grunted and took up the shovel. The oxen waited patiently, switching at flies with their tails. Within a few moments the shovel scraped the top of the tin trunk; by the time it was fully unearthed, Maggie and Davy had taken their few things from the wagon and set up the tent.

"You should come with us," Margaret begged, seeing how the tent looked so small, so forlorn. "It might be dangerous – just yourself and Davy."

"No," Maggie answered firmly. "We have Davy's musket to protect ourselves with. There are enough folk returned already. In time, more will join us. This was Jacob's land, M'grete, and his livestock are wandering on it somewhere, if the Mexicans and the Comanche let them be. If I do not remain and reclaim it all, what will Davy inherit then?"

"How will you live?" Margaret asked; it tore at her heart to think of Maggie and Davy, scratching out an existence in the ruins. Maggie only smiled.

"As we did before, M'grete. There is our garden. We had pigs and chickens – even Jacob's cows and horses were in their winter pasture all this spring. We will have enough."

"If you are certain." Margaret began, and Maggie embraced her, saying again not for her to worry. Margaret looked over her shoulder, as Papa's wagon rolled away. Maggie was already at work, kirtling up her skirts and inspecting what remained of her garden.

Of her own garden there was nothing, for nothing had been planted before they came away. There was less of their house than there was of Maggie's, since theirs had been built of sawn planks, which fire had swiftly consumed.

"Let me use the ramrod from your rifle, Papa," she asked.

"What for?" Papa grumbled, but he brought out his old rifle from beneath the wagon-bench. He had brought a rather battered British musket away from San Jacinto, that and a very fine pair of ivory-ornamented dragoon pistols – found in the Mexican lines, Race had explained, with a wry twist to his lips.

"I left my good dishes buried in the garden, but only a little way beneath," Margaret answered. She took the slender metal ramrod in her hands, and walking carefully away from the tumbled stones where their chimney had been, began probing into the ground with it. Within a few minutes, she felt the tip of the ramrod strike something hard, a second probe, something hard again. She pulled the earth aside with her fingers, not wishing to chance breaking any of the blue-painted dishes. Cups, plates, saucers – all there, where she had tumbled them into a hastily-scratched grave on the night that Gonzales burned; she stacked them carefully as she unearthed them, and carried them triumphantly towards the wagon.

"Don't forget the ramrod, M'grete," Papa grumbled. "For china dishes, you might have ruined a good ramrod."

"They are a treasure of mine, Papa," Margaret answered. "For I set a fine table for my friends – and these dishes are a promise that I shall again."

She did not look back, upon the second time of leaving Gonzales in Papa's wagon. There was too much to be done, and no time for mourning that which was gone. Not her house, not the town, not the friends encompassed within those timber and sawn-plank walls – but Margaret grieved for the years of sublime happiness spent there. The river did not pass the same riverbank, ever again.

The Colorado River ran wide and smooth at Waterloo, clear as green glass with small ripples in it, cradled between steep banks and immense feathery-leafed cypress trees all tangled with grapevines. Wildflowers spread carpets of pale pink, blue, and yellow in the glades between the trees. The hills around loomed taller, clothed in summer green, a green that seemed deeper and even richer than in the lowlands. In the morning, the mist from the river rose up, masking the low-lying meadows in barely translucent layers, from which the hills rose like islands, islands which floated on the fog, the farthest of them being shades of blue and violet which varied with increasing distance. As the sun rose on such mornings, fingers of light pierced the fog in perfect columns, falling through the tree branches in shafts of palest gold. Deer grazed in the meadows between, lifting their heads to look incuriously at the passing wagon before returning to their browsing again. Papa, stumping along beside the team, displayed a similar incuriosity.

"It is so beautiful," Margaret exclaimed to her husband as they traveled slowly up the winding track which followed the river. Race had reined in Bucephalus next to the wagon and carried Johnny on his saddle-bow. The child was owl-eyed with excitement, and Horace was begging for his turn. "I might almost believe it the fairest garden in Texas. And I had thought the land around Gonzales to be beautiful, but this is fairer still. I thought Papa had acted hastily in forsaking a grant in San Felipe, and then in departing from Gonzales . . . but this, I might grow to love."

"Father Becker told me there are buffalo about," Race smiled, and then paused for a fit of coughing. "They wander down from the high tablelands, beyond the hills. He says the boys once wasted four or five shots trying to kill one, to no avail."

"Are you all right?" Margaret asked anxiously. She feared above all else that her husband would sicken as he had after being caught in that spring

222

rainstorm – how could he ever regain his health, riding about in all hours and weathers when what he needed was a sheltering roof and a cozy fire?

"Nothing to worry about, Daisy," he answered, with a smile. "Your father says we shall be at his holdings today – and if what Mr. Harrell told him was correct, he still has a house." Race laughed heartily until he began coughing again. "The possession of which will put him in rare and princely company."

That afternoon, as the sun began to drop in the sky, burnishing the river with reaches of silver and shadow, the track that Papa and his oxen followed crested a range of hills. From to top of the hill, Margaret and her children could look out from the wagon, seeing where the double line of wheel-tracks crossed a single vast meadow dotted with a scattering of immense trees. A few scattered threads of smoke rose from unseen chimneys, here and there.

"We're almost there, children," Margaret said to her boys, for Papa had snapped his whip in the air over the oxen's backs, and given them a command. A fainter line of wheel-tracks veered from the main, tracing a pale scribble up the hillside, where the rain had begun to wear gullies into the ground left bare by the passage of men and beasts. Presently, Margaret could discern old wheat stubble with new green shoots thrusting upwards; much of it trampled by hoofed feet, and a row of trees beyond, and spaced at intervals too regularly to have been established by nature. With a lift in her heart, she saw that they were apple trees, and that many lifted branches laden with tiny, pale-green apples towards the sky above. The apple trees surrounded the crest of a hill. Beyond them were a pair of chimneys and a ramble of zig-zagging rail fences surrounding a tall log house and a scattering of smaller buildings, all roofed with cedar shingles weathered to pale gray. The whole of it – house, outbuildings, and the fence connecting them – all had a definite air of neglect about them. Part of the fence had fallen down, and it appeared as if someone had climbed up and stripped off many of the roof-shingles. With a pang in her heart, Margaret saw that someone – probably Mama – had planted three rosebushes in the dooryard; their lanky stems held up pink flowers as bravely as the apple trees did. The cabin was built as squarely as a fortress, without the usual breezeway, set on a tall foundation of stone, with stoutly shuttered small windows high up in the towering walls. There was a deep porch across the front and around all sides, as they could see. The windows were shuttered, but the door stood halfway open, as if someone had kicked it in.

The stable, built of green timbers so widely spaced that it looked like a corn-crib, stood a little beyond. Papa halted the oxen in front of it, saying gruffly, "Well, here we are then, M'grete. Not as fine as some of those houses in Washington or San Felipe. Best get to work, then. There's a springhouse round the side, if you're looking for water." He jerked his chin in the direction of Race, who had already unsaddled Bucephalus. "Best keep that horse of yours locked in the stable. The Comanche do come round of an autumn night." And with that, Papa bent to un-harnessing the oxen, while Margaret and her husband exchanged looks. This was a cool welcome. If it weren't for Race's health, Margaret almost wished they had remained in Gonzales with Maggie. Only – Margaret squared her shoulders – there was nothing there for them. And at least Papa had a house with a roof over most of it, and a spring, and apple trees. *No*, Margaret told herself – *I will make the best of this. We will make the best of this.*

Inside, it was not as bad as she had feared. Leaves had blown into the largest room, through the opened door and the hole in the roof, and the rain had come in as well. Parts of broken chairs lay on the floor, some of them within the cavernous limestone fireplace, and many of the small things which Mama had cherished were nowhere to be seen. She explored the other two rooms; the first must have been the parlor and Mama and Papa's bedroom; the other was a kind of shed built out onto part of the back porch, a room built of sawn planks with a slanting roof and a single and larger window, built on at the back of the house and barely large enough for Mama's loom and some narrow shelves set on pegs driven into the log wall for her baskets full of wool and hanks of spun thread and yarn. It was closed off from the rest of the house by a sturdy door with a heavy latch: Papa had evidently intended the two rooms of the main house to be a fortress, and the shed to be a place to be closed off, in case of danger. Whoever had looted the house had smashed the fragile parts of the loom batten and taken whatever weaving Mama had left on it, leaving nothing but a forlorn tangle of broken warp and heddle strings. A small ladder in the parlor led to a loft above; Margaret climbed up a little way. There were two straw pallets in the loft; her brothers must have slept there. She and Race would take the small room where Mama's loom had been for theirs. Once the loom was taken apart, there would be enough for a bed for themselves, and space on the shelves for her husband's books.

Piece by piece, Margaret oversaw the reassembling of their lives. Papa and Race took the wagon cover and draped it over the hole in the roof, until Papa could cut new shingles to repair it. She swept out the house, and arranged the few things she had saved from their house in the smallest room. Papa had concealed a pair of trunks and some pieces of furniture which Mama had particularly cherished, by burying them at the back of the stable in a pile of last summer's hay, so it was not as if everything had been stolen or broken apart. Papa rebuilt the broken chairs, and a new table, and then set them in the porch for them to take their meals. He built a narrow cot for himself in the corner of the kitchen, preferring to sleep there at night.

It was too late to plant a garden, but Margaret attempted to do so anyway. Mama had saved away seeds in one of the concealed trunks. It was too early for gathering wild grapes, persimmons, or pecans from the multitude of trees, almost too late for mushrooms and greens, although Margaret and the boys explored the woods around Papa's house and the riverbank where the cypress trees dropped their knobby roots into the water. A little way from the riverbank stood a huge, pale-barked sycamore, a great castle of a tree with a sheltered hollow between two enormous roots, a hollow cushioned by a layer of last year's fallen leaves and just large enough to comfortably cradle her and the boys together. It looked at first as if a deer had often lain there, sheltered between the roots – but when she looked closely at the smooth grey bark, she could see that someone with a knife had scored letters and lines into the surface within an arm's reach. Her brothers must have come here often – perhaps this was one of their refuges during last summer when Papa forbade them to eat at his table if they would not work.

At the end of a week, Margaret thought they had made a good beginning, although Papa was gruff to the point of incivility, and Race's cough had settled into his chest, not to be dislodged by any simple remedy of her contriving. Horace complained of missing his particular friends, the Millsaps boys, but he was happy enough with the presence of his father that such a loss was almost made up for. Margaret missed Maggie, Mary, and Pru. She had cherished so many comfortable friendships in Gonzales, and taken strength and comfort from their presence in the hard times. This isolation on a tiny farm proved to be difficult at first – even though the surrounding country was of such beauty that she gradually felt soothed. Papa had built his house with such pleasant views of the river, the woods and the great meadow below from the various small windows, and from the porch. Someday, Margaret thought, when the danger from Indians lessened, Papa might be able to have larger windows in his house, with glass in them perhaps. In time Margaret began to treasure those views from the windows and the porches, in their changing beauty from dawn to dusk. It was reassuring to know there were solid walls around them, shelter against storms, or the malice of raiding Comanche war parties. Over the days following their return, they settled into a pattern: Papa worked to repair the house, outbuildings, fences, and furniture, Race assisting as much as his strength and general unhandiness with tools allowed. He gave lessons to the boys when he become exhausted and white-faced from laboring at whatever task which Papa had dictated was necessary for the day.

"I hate it when Papa glares and grumbles at you," she whispered to Race, when they had withdrawn to their little room, leaving Papa to sit by the limestone fireplace in the largest room staring into the fire. Horace had climbed happily up the ladder to the loft; nothing could have better pleased him than to be treated as a grown boy and not a baby. Her husband coughed again, holding his hand before his lips.

"His words do not encourage me to look upon him with unalloyed affection either, Daisy-mine," he answered, when he could speak again, "but I am grateful for his hospitality. Father Becker is just a demon for work. There is not much use for a book-learned man out here." He sounded more wretched than he ever had, and Margaret put her arms about him.

"Yes, there is," she answered, firmly. "Maggie said you were like a high-bred race horse; made to run and win races, not to drag a heavy plow."

"Each to their own talents, Daisy-mine?" At least he was smiling again, and she answered, "Even so – and you have more than just your skills as a teacher to recommend you as a husband."

"I do?" he asked humorously, and Margaret kissed him very firmly on his lips. "And what might that be, then?"

"Begetting children," she answered, secretly amused at his befuddlement. "The boys will have a little brother or sister around Christmastime, I think."

"Devious Daisy." He embraced her first with vigor and then hastily loosening his arms, as if she had suddenly turned to fragile glass. "You always recall me to what is important in life in the here and the now – not what might be, or should have been."

On the very next evening, just as Race had finished reading to the boys while Papa dozed in his chair next to the fireplace, something scratched tentatively at the door. The windows were closed, their shutters bolted fast for the night, and at first Margaret thought she was hearing things, perhaps the wind sending a branch moving against the roof. But no – it had come from the door, not the roof.

"Papa, there's something at the door. Did you have a dog? It sounds like an animal."

"Huhh . . . umm?" her father started awake. "A dog? No. Filthy, useless things." The scratching sound came again, loud enough that it could not be mistaken for anything but deliberately made. Margaret unbolted the door and opened it a bare crack. She could not see at first, in the darkness outside, after the mellow glow of the fire and the tallow candles that lent her husband barely enough light to read. There was a person outside, a gaunt and dirty boy, all skin and bone and ragged hunting coat, who squinted against the sudden light, a boy whose fair hair straggled uncombed to his shoulders.

"Carl!" Margaret exclaimed, first in disbelief, then in a moment of transcendent joy. He was not dead, he lived – by a miracle he had escaped and come home. She threw her arms around him. Oh, he was thin, all but bones – and cried "Papa, its Carl, come and see, he's alive!" Behind her in the room, she heard Race's chair scrape back against the floor,

"What? My God, Daisy, is it really . . . dear lad, where have you been all of this time!" At her side it was Papa, looking past Carl, into the darkness beyond. Margaret drew her brother into the doorway with an arm around his shoulders, silently begging her father to embrace his living son, acknowledge that he had been granted a blessing and a miracle. But Papa only said irritably, "But where is Rudi, then? Carl, why did you leave your brother?"

Her arm still about him, Margaret felt him flinch – and she was appalled. She saw just a flash of agony in her brother's staring eyes, as if he regarded a scene of unbearable horror. Without a word Carl pulled away from her and ran. His footsteps made a noise on the porch, she heard him on the ground below, but he vanished. She called his name into the darkness but the only answer was the distant and mocking hoot of an owl.

"Papa!" Margaret was so angry she could barely speak. "Papa, how could you – what would Mama have said at this!" With shaking hands, she lit another candle, and placed it in a pierced-tin lantern.

"Another for me, Daisy-mine," her husband said softly, "I'll go with you." Her father answered, "That young blockhead – he'll be back when he's hungry enough. Leave him sulk, Margaret." Margaret could not think of anything more heartless. If Will King had escaped by some miracle from that last awful battle at the Alamo, Margaret was certain he would have been welcomed home with unstinting joy and affection.

"Stay with Opa," she told the boys; she and Race went out into the darkness. They called Carl's name, searching the stable, and the springhouse, without result.

"Where might he have gone, if not home?" Race lifted his lantern. It cast a small constellation of bright dots against the ground and the stable door.

"To the Harrells, perhaps," Margaret answered, "They are the closest farmstead . . . and the boys traded game for food last summer, when Papa tried to make them work harder instead of playing in the woods all the time."

"Right, then," her husband sighed. "I'll walk over to the Harrells, and see if he is there."

"There is another place he might be," Margaret ventured; the sycamore tree, down by the riverbank. The more she thought on it, the more certain she was. As the light from Race's lantern dwindled along the path towards their nearest neighbors, she turned the other direction. And she was right. Carl had taken refuge in the hollow at the foot of the sycamore tree, curled into a tight ball, knees to forehead, arms wrapped around his knees, not making a sound, a deeper shadow within the shadow.

"Come back to the house, Carl," Margaret set down the lantern. "You know Papa doesn't mean anything. Rudi was his favorite, that's all."

"Rudi is dead." Carl's reply was muffled; he was speaking to his knees. "They killed us all. Rudi told me to run away. I think some others ran. There was a pretty woman and an officer. They tried to make me leave Rudi, but I wouldn't go. I hid in the bushes across the river and watched their women washing the clothes they took from them afterwards until the water ran red."

"We know about that," Margaret answered soothingly. "We were told. We thought you both were dead, Carlchen. Papa was just . . . startled. You know Papa, Carlchen. Whatever Papa thinks – that is what he says an instant later. Come back to the house, now. Haven't you eaten anything in a month and a half? You look hungry, Carlchen." To her quiet relief, he unfolded a little. In the dim light of the lantern he smiled, that shy quick smile. Perhaps Papa's thoughtless words and cold welcome had not utterly destroyed him.

"Rabbits," he answered. "Mostly rabbits. Caught in a snare. Fish. I made a wooden fishhook. Pecans. Once I ate green plums. They made me awful sick." He sounded as if speech were something he made little use of, as if he had avoided all human contact for weeks. Margaret considered the distance between La Bahia, and Waterloo, of how they had burned their farms and holdings, and the Mexicans had marched after them, across an empty land.

"You didn't see anyone – try and find the Army?" Margaret asked, and Carl shrugged.

"I didn't want to be seen. Thought they were all dead. 'Fraid there were Mexes all around."

"Come back to the house," Margaret urged him once again. "I'll fix you a good supper. The Mexicans are gone. General Houston beat them all, weeks ago, and threw them out of Texas for once and for all. You don't need to hide."

"That's good." He sounded rather cheerful; he stood up, obediently following after. "M'grete? Where's Mama?"

Chapter 18 – *The Prodigal*

Margaret took a deep breath, and answered Carl's question about Mama. In the light of the lantern, she saw no reaction to the news in her brother's features. It was as if he had been battered beyond feeling anything; pain, sorrow, loss. He had been Mama's favorite, as much as Rudi had been Papa's. He said only and after some moments, "Oh. I wondered why you were here."

"Our house is burned, and there will be no children in Gonzales for a school for some time. We thought it better to come to Waterloo for a time."

Race had returned from the Harrell's by the time Margaret came up the hill with Carl. From across the door yard she could hear him arguing with Papa; Race's voice low and intense, Papa's raised in anger. She didn't know what they were arguing about, only that as she opened the door, Papa was snarling, "You see to the conduct of your own sons, leave me to speak as I see fit to mine!" Both men stopped speaking at once, as she came into the room with her brother. A heavy silence fell; Horace and Johnny were looking apprehensively from their grandfather to their father.

"Bedtime, boys," Margaret said at once. "Wash your faces and say your prayers, your father and I will be along in a few minutes." Horace and Johnny went from the kitchen with alacrity; by which Margaret knew that they had been frightened by whatever exchange they witnessed between Race and Papa. "You," she added to her brother, "Follow them and wash up yourself." The heavy silence fell again, broken only by the sounds that Margaret herself made, cutting bread for her brother and ladling a plate of the stewed beef from the pot hanging at the edge of the fire.

Abruptly, Papa said, "I'm going to bed. We're starting work early in the morning." Without another word, he pulled off his boots, padded across the room to the rough bedstead in the corner of the kitchen and laid down. He turned his back upon them, pulling the quilt over his head. Margaret's heart sank. It was not going to be comfortable, living here with Papa, especially if Papa was going to have words with Race. She carried the plate and the bread into the parlor, where Carl had unlatched the shutter and stood at the window, looking out at the sky and the stars, as silent as they were, and revealing nothing at all of what he might be thinking. Margaret sighed. It was going to be a very long summer.

On the surface, all appeared well for weeks. Margaret wrote to Maggie in Gonzales, and to Pru and Mary at the Burnetts' plantation, telling them of Carl's miraculous survival. Maggie would be glad to know of this, Margaret thought – so would those of their remaining neighbors who had known the Beckers. The days grew hotter as they approached midsummer. Mercifully for Margaret, feeling the first pangs of pregnancy, Waterloo did not suffer the same brooding, oppressive heat of the lowlands. Papa ordered Carl to begin plowing the largest of his fields, saying that he would try to put in a late crop, as it was better than no crop at all. Carl went obediently to any task Papa set him over the next few weeks, without question or complaint. He was silent at meals and in the evenings, when Race read to the boys. He did talk with Horace, for Margaret heard their voices in the loft above, early in the morning or late at night. Quite often Carl took his blanket and went elsewhere to sleep, especially when the heat of the day lingered in the loft. Margaret tasked him with this, the first time it occurred.

"It's closed in," he answered. "I don't like that, M'grete."

He even was silent at a gathering of their neighbors in Waterloo to celebrate the 4th of July, lingering on the edge of the merry gathering as if he did not really wish to be there at all. The Harrells and several other families had built a sturdy stockade near Shoal Creek, with rooms and a small stable lining the inner walls, and a stout gate which they took every care to fasten at night, especially when there was a full moon. On the 4th of July, the gate stood open, and Mary Harrell and the other women had spread out a bounty of good things to eat, on tables set under the trees. The men who owned horses raced them – Bucephalus won the first heat, of course, but after that, Race laughingly refused to run him again. Since he was so far and away the swiftest among them, it was hardly fair to the others.

Margaret rejoiced in a gathering such as this, a respite after months of hard work, and the brutally difficult journey to Harrisburg and back. But Carl would not answer questions about what had happened at Coleto, at La Bahia, or during his journey home, meeting all such with single word or a blank look and a shrug – and if the questioner persisted, Carl would vanish as quietly as a ghost. After a while, everyone stopped asking.

"The boy's always been an idiot," Papa said to Mr. Harrell with what sounded like grim satisfaction. Mr. Harrell looked quite skeptical at that, but maintained his own tactful silence. It was one of his daughters whom Carl had been taken with last year – that time which now seemed to have been another lifetime entirely.

High summer merged into autumn, and the sycamores turned golden. Papa had cut enough shingles to repair the roof before the winter rains began. He and Carl and Race finished with the roof before midday, and upon climbing down Papa said abruptly, "I saw from the roof that the grass in the lower pasture is dry enough to cut for hay. Take the scythe and cut hay this afternoon, and when you have cut enough I'll bring the wagon down." In assent, Carl shrugged, which response seemed to irritate Papa immensely.

"Remember, boy – no running off to the woods this time. No work, no meals under my roof." That reproof brought no reaction at all from her brother, earning him another black look from Papa. Margaret wondered if Papa was trying to goad him into some kind of rebellion, to give Papa an excuse to unleash his own bad temper. Carl's very passivity seemed to grate upon her father. *How Mama had ever endured this?* Margaret wondered. Perhaps Papa's ill-temper had not been so marked when Rudi was alive. Margaret thought of how Race had once speculated that Carl would not remain at home for long, once having been a soldier.

After the midday meal, Carl went to the hayfield, carrying a whetstone and the scythe over his shoulder, while Margaret busied herself in the kitchen, sweeping up the dust and wood chips that had been shaken down by the repair of the roof, and Race gave lessons to the boys. Papa was at the top of the ladder, ensuring that all had been fitted tightly together and made weather and waterproof, especially around the chimney. The sound of Papa's hammer, pounding in small slips of wood masked the sound of a horseman, riding up the track from the valley below, until Margaret heard the rider calling.

"Hello! Hello, the house. Is anyone at home?" She went out to the porch with the broom still in her hands. The boys came from the parlor. It had been so long since any visitor had come to Papa's house that they were mad with curiosity. The noise of Papa's hammer continued over their heads; he was on the opposite side of the roof, where he could not see the visitor. The rider doffed his hat – a tall black beaver – immediately as Margaret appeared. He was a well-dressed man, an Easterner, Margaret thought, but he sat his horse well and had an air of capability about him. "Good day, ma'am – can you tell me if this is the house of Alois Becker?"

"It is," Margaret answered. "I am Mrs. Vining – his daughter. Do you wish to speak with my father?"

"Not so much him as his son," the visitor answered. "If that is possible. My name is Nathaniel Vanderpole, western correspondent for the *New York Evening Post* newspaper . . . have you heard of it?"

"I have not," Margaret answered truthfully, but behind her, Race answered, with no small interest, "I have, but I cannot imagine what would bring you to Waterloo, and what here would be of earthly interest to your readers. Come in, Mr. Vanderpole. I confess to being eaten up with curiosity."

"Thank you." Mr. Vanderpole wiped his sweating face with a very white handkerchief, and dismounting, tied the reins of his horse to the porch-railing. Margaret set aside the broom, and fetched him a jug of cool spring water and several tin cups, while Race introduced himself. "I am grateful to you, Mrs. Vining, most grateful. No, indeed – our readers are most interested in this Texas matter; I confess, I was personally disappointed that your war was wrapped up with such masterly dispatch. I had only just gotten as far as New Orleans and poof! – it was all over."

"We might have dragged it out a bit longer for you," Race said, dryly, "but we had nearly run out of country, by then."

"Oh, no need to have troubled on my account," Mr. Vanderpole answered, with a flash of ironical wit. "Bless my soul, the accounts that I have transcribed of extraordinary events – such accounts of heroism, of noble sacrifice, I find it more satisfactory to have them recollected in tranquility. I confess, I shall probably write a history of General Houston's campaigns, relying upon the testimony of eyewitnesses. Such a volume would do the subject better justice than what brief details will fit the constraints of a newspaper account. Nonetheless, readers everywhere are fascinated, since more of the true story may only be told now."

"A quest for knowledge," Race ventured. He and Margaret exchanged an amused glance. Margaret could only imagine what had been said to Mr. Vanderpole about General Houston, especially by those who had accused him of cowardice, all along the retreat across Texas.

"Exactly," Mr. Vanderpole nodded. "I was entertained two weeks ago at the home of William Burnett, where I mentioned my desire to speak to as many direct participants in the events of this war as was possible. One of his houseguests – a Mrs. Kimball – told me of a miraculous survival, that of a young man who escaped from the massacre of his fellows at Goliad, the youngest son of Alois Becker of the town of Waterloo."

"That would be my brother-in-law," Race shook his head. "But he has not been forthcoming about his experiences, and we have not pressed him."

"Still, I would like to speak with him," Mr. Vanderpole clasped his hands and gazed very earnestly at them both, "There were but a bare handful who survived the Goliad. It is my conviction that such have a duty to history, to their fellows, to their country, even – to bear witness to events."

There was a heavy footstep upon the porch, and Papa appeared, hammer still in his hand. He was sweaty and disheveled from working upon the roof in the heat of the day.

"Who's this?" he growled, as he poured water for himself, swiftly draining several cups. Mr. Vanderpole rose and began to introduce himself again, but Papa interrupted him.

"So, what d'ye want with us?"

"He wants to speak to Carl," Margaret answered, "about what happened at La Bahia."

"What are you waiting for, girl?" Papa growled again. "Go and fetch him."

Margaret obeyed with reluctance, instinctively feeling no good would come of it. She put on her bonnet, refilled the pottery pitcher at the springhouse, and walked down towards the hay meadow, where she could see her brother at a distance industriously swinging the scythe through hip-high grass. He had already left swaths of new-cut hay behind him, advancing slowly across the field, the scythe moving in a precise rhythm, while a scattering of sparrows flocked behind him, pouncing upon the insects that sprang up from the felled grass. Carl had left the whetstone and a gourd-canteen of water in the shade of an oak tree at the edge of the field. Margaret waited by it. Carl was coming towards it with the slow and unhurried pace of a reaper. He would have to sharpen the scythe at the end of this pass across the hayfield, so she waited patiently with the jug full of fresh and cool water.

When he had come near enough that she could speak without raising her voice, she said, "Papa sent me – there's a man at the house who came 'specially to speak to you; a man who writes for a newspaper, back East."

"Oh?" Carl answered, without any particular interest. "What does he want to speak to me about?"

"Goliad, and what happened there," Margaret answered. "He is writing a history of it all, he says."

Her brother shrugged as if it were of no moment. He took the jug from her hands and drank deep from the edge of it, looking at her with guileless eyes as clear and blue as the sky beyond his head, saying earnestly, "I don't want to talk about it at all, M'grete. I really don't. It's a bad memory."

"Papa sent me for you," Margaret repeated. "He wants you to talk to him and answer his questions. The newspaper correspondent, I mean. He – that is, Mr. Vanderpole – he has spoken to Race and I. He seems like a good person, Carlchen. One of the things he said is that there is a duty in bearing witness to events . . . especially when there were so few who escaped. They cannot tell of it themselves. You would be speaking for them."

"Do you think I should talk to him?" Her brother asked, and Margaret nodded her head.

"You would bring honor to your comrades and to Rudi, if you did."

She listened from the kitchen, while Race was continuing with the boy's lessons for the day outside on the porch. Pa and Mr. Vanderpole had gone into the room which served as their parlor, but their voices were very clear; Mr. Vanderpole's deft questioning, Papa's occasional gruff interjections, but mostly her brother's light, uninflected tones. The whole dreadful story unfolded in his words as if it were something that had happened to someone else; of long weeks of boredom within the walls of La Bahia, of Colonel Fannin's indecision upon receiving increasingly urgent messages from all quarters – from the Alamo, from General Houston, and news of the Mexican army advancing, of muddle and delay, and finally a desperate bloody battle in the open at Coleto, just short of woods that would have sheltered them.

"They brought up cannon during the early hours and raked our square with it. Colonel Fannin went out to parley. There was no water, and the wounded men were crying out something awful. It wasn't any use to fight any more, so the officers said. The Mex soldiers took away our muskets, and knives too – I put mine in my shoe-top when I saw what they were doing. They had us march back to La Bahia under guard, and kept us all locked in the chapel for a week, although they let us into the courtyard during the daytime. It was dark in there – the Mexes boarded up all the windows and all. The officers told us likely we'd be paroled, sent back to the States in a week or so.

"Colonel Fannin, they kept him apart in another room. They took him to Copano, to see about a ship, I think. They made Captain Shackleford and the other doctors attend on their wounded. On the morning of Palm Sunday, they roused us out and made three groups. We thought we were being marched to Victoria, or Copano, under guard. The Mexes had their best parade uniforms on, a line on either side of us. We went out the gate, and there was a pretty lady standing there with an older lady and an officer. He had gold braid all over him. The gold-braid officer came up to us with a sergeant, and took Ben Hughes out of the line – he was Captain Horton's orderly. The officer said to Ben and me, 'You are just boys, too young for this. Señora Alavez would have you stay with her,' but I said 'no, I will stay with my brother,' and the officer let us go, and we marched out the gate."

Carl's voice faltered, and Mr. Vanderpole gently encouraged him. "So, you were out of the citadel, and on the road towards . . . Victoria, was it?"

"Yessir . . . there was this brush fence along the road, where this field led down to the river. Right then, the Mexes on our left, they faced about and went through us to the other side, and they lifted their muskets . . . and they commenced to firing at us. But Rudi, he was between them and me, and there was this gap in the brush fence. Rudi, he pushed me towards it, shouted at me to run, make for the river . . . but then he fell dead in the road and the smoke hid me and I ran." His tone was dispassionate, and yet Margaret sensed he could not have told the story otherwise.

"You concealed yourself along the riverbank?" Mr. Vanderpole asked. "How long?"

"Until dark," Carl answered. "In a stand of reeds on the far side. Their dragoons were hunting all day, sticking their lances through the bushes. I waited, and waited. When I came out, I thought I would just strike north and come home. I wasn't really thinking sensible, sir. I was done with officers in fancy uniforms and soldiering. I didn't want to be caught by the Mexes, or be locked up ever again. I had my knife, and a piece of string to make a snare with, and a flint and steel to make a fire. I'd find a place to hole up during the daytime, and walk at night, following the stars and the river."

"Astonishing," Mr. Vanderpole murmured. "I am truly in awe of your enterprise and determination, young man. A journey such as this – with only what you had in your pockets on that fatal day – why, that rivals the best of the *Leatherstocking Tales* . . . an odyssey for the ages!" Margaret couldn't clearly hear Carl's response to that; it came out as an embarrassed mumble.

"Well, then – got what you came for?" Papa asked, and Margaret winced at the brusque tone of his voice. Mr. Vanderpole seemed unaffected, and was thanking Carl and Papa for having agreed to speak with him. She thought she might remedy Papa's discourtesy by asking if Mr. Vanderpole would stay and share supper with them, but as she stepped into the open doorway, he was shaking Papa's hand, and Papa said, "Oh, but you should have known Rudolph, my oldest son. He was such a promising boy, worth three of this one any day of the week."

"A great tragedy and a loss to you – and a matter of regret to me," Mr. Vanderpole replied smoothly, "at not having another witness to this atrocious event," but Margaret thought he was considerably taken back by Papa's unfeeling words. She herself was horrified. She could barely bring herself to look at Carl standing in the middle of the parlor. His face was absolutely blank of expression, as if he had been struck so hard that he couldn't feel any pain at all. He walked out of the parlor without a word or a look at any of them, not even to Race, who upon hearing Papa's words had gotten up from his chair, out on the porch.

"Carl, your father . . ." but Carl merely shouldered past him as if he were invisible. He picked up the scythe from where he had left it leaning against the wall and went back to the hayfield.

"There's work to be done today," Papa said with an air of finality. "We have ours, and I presume you have yours. Good day to you, Vanderpole." He stumped out of the parlor, leaving Mr. Vanderpole with his hat in his hand, shaking his head slightly.

"Your father-in-law is an interesting man," he observed to Race, as he took his leave. "I've been thrown out of a rich man's place of business with more ceremony. No, you needn't apologize to me. All in my own day's work."

At supper the next day, Carl was nowhere to be found, which made Papa irate. He had not appeared at breakfast, which no one had thought odd at first, for Carl had very often taken some cold pone and gone straight to whatever task Papa had directed him to perform the night before.

"He was supposed to finish the hayfield today," Papa grumbled, "instead of loitering around in the woods all morning – which is where he is, I'll be bound. He's taken that old musket I had from San Jacinto without asking. He may find out that he's not too old for a good thrashing!"

"When did we see him last?" Race asked, while Margaret thought back to the previous night; the boys had gone to bed at the usual hour. She didn't think that it was one of the nights that Carl had stolen down from the loft – but the blanket from his pallet was gone, and so was his jacket – curious, because the nights were still mild. He would not have needed a jacket.

"Horace," she asked of her son, "did you see Carl this morning?"

Horace, with his mouth full of cornmeal mush, nodded in the affirmative. Swallowing the mouthful, he answered, "Yes, Mama; he was awake when it was still dark. He was rolling up his blanket, and I asked why he was doing that. He didn't say – just that he was going to the Harrells, and I should go back to sleep."

"Did he say anything else, son?" Race asked, and Horace screwed up his serious little face, in obvious thought.

"No . . . only that he said goodbye."

Race got up from the table immediately, saying over his shoulder, "I'll go to Harrell, and see what has been going on."

He returned barely an hour later, grim-faced. Papa had gone to finish the haying, grumbling under his breath. Margaret was searching out any of the early-ripened apples from Papa's trees and wondering if there were enough to make a pie for the evening meal.

"He borrowed a horse from Harrell and was away at sunrise. Harrell said he looked as if he meant to make a journey of it, but he didn't ask to where and your brother didn't say . . . not in so many words. No, Daisy-mine – he's been gone too long for me to catch up, even if I knew what road he took, or had enough woodcraft in me to track him. Yesterday with Vanderpole and your father was the last straw."

"I was afraid no good would come of it," Margaret answered. "Where do you think he has gone?"

"To Columbia-on-the-Brazos. Harrell had heard gossip that Erastus Smith was recruiting a company of Rangers, to be paid by the state in land certificates and ammunition. I recall, at the 4th of July festivities he asked me about it, since I know Erastus so well. Your brother was listening and most particularly interested. I am almost sure that is where he has gone." Race sighed, "I foresaw this day, Daisy-mine. But I thought it would have happened sooner, rather than later."

"To leave without saying goodbye – that is hurtful." Margaret felt as if she would weep, but she also had sensed her brothers' deep unhappiness. Upon further questioning, Horace had confessed that Carl's sleep in the loft had not been restful and often broken by nightmares. "Papa will be furious – but it will have been his fault!"

"Alas, the greatest and better portion of your father," Race embraced her, lovingly, "was your mother. Without her, I am afraid he is lost to all tender feelings. Were my own father anything like him, I'd have left without saying goodbye myself and gone farther than Columbia." He laughed, and Margaret rejoiced in the feel of his amusement, and was comforted as well by it. *Yes, she had made a fine marriage.* "I do confess, Daisy-mine, I shall count the weeks and months until we can return to Gonzales and re-open my school. Your father is at best as prickly as an acre of those Mexican cactus-plants."

Papa took the news of Carl's departure with a sour face, but made little comment. Race's supposition was true; Mr. Harrell's horse was returned to him several weeks later, by a wagoneer from Columbia-on-the-Brazos who had been paid a small sum by a very young, fair-haired man to bring it thus far.

"I shall write a letter to Erastus," Race said, upon hearing of this, "Merely to assure ourselves of where he has gone, and in what company. I am sure that he will answer, as a friend of mine and a comrade of Father Becker's."

He wrote a letter, receiving a reply late in November. Yes, Carl had joined Erastus Smith's new national ranger company, and been very welcome at that; Erastus wrote that he was a fine shot, a good rider, and a very fair tracker, well-respected by his comrades in spite of his relative youth. His company

237

was tasked with protecting Texas against a new invasion from Mexico. By the time Race received the letter, Carl was gone south with them, into the harsh desert wilderness of the border country. Early the next year, there was news of Smith's company skirmishing with a large body of Mexican soldiers, which raised great excitement for it was the first time since Santa Anna's surrender at San Jacinto that Texians and Mexicans had fought. Then for all intents and purposes, Carl truly vanished; Margaret did not see him again for nearly three years, and in all that time, Papa never mentioned his name.

Margaret's third child was born on a cold winter day, soon after Christmas – another son, which briefly saddened Margaret. She had hoped for a daughter, to be named Maria, after Mama. She had so been convinced that the baby would be a girl that she had thought of – and even spoken to the unborn child, calling her Maria. But no – perhaps next time. She and Race would have more children, certainly. They named the baby James Bowie Vining, recalling how Race's friend had admired their oldest son and let him play with his knife. Perhaps a bit of James Bowie's roughneck spirit attached itself to baby Jamie, or he grew into the name, for he was larger than either of his brothers had been at birth, and possessed of a fearless and adventurous spirit. He resembled Margaret's brothers more than their father. That likeness to Carl and Rudi pleased Margaret very much. It made up, in a small way, for Race falling ill again. The raw cold of winter affected him deeply, and he had never managed to throw off that persistent cough which had afflicted him since their return. Margaret silently resigned herself to remaining another year with Papa in Waterloo. A letter from Maggie to them both revealed that the rebuilding was going very slowly, that although many of the landholders were returning, their families were not. Horace Eggleston was one of them with Sarah and the baby; for them he had built a two-room cabin to the usual pattern, but it was many months before more families returned.

Race recovered by spring, but to Papa's infinite disgust, he would not assist with the heavy work of the farm. Instead he taught a tiny class of students; Horace and Johnny, Jacob Harrell's youngest son and one or two other children, in exchange for a sack of wheat or corn, a side of venison or a cured ham. Margaret carried as much of the household work as she could; the garden, preparing meals, and doing the washing, simmering with resentment whenever her father spoke slightingly of her husband, decrying his lack of skills and strength. She thought often and longingly of Gonzales – but there were no children for a school, and to rebuild their home themselves was beyond Race's abilities and resources.

In midsummer, a party of visitors came to Waterloo and stayed with the Harrells. To her husband's infinite joy, one of them was friend, a comrade from those turbulent weeks and months of the year before – the cavalryman poet, Bo Lamar. He rode up from the Harrells to visit them, regarding with frank approval Race's tiny school, the handful of children with their slates and earnest expressions, all lined up on the porch.

"I see that you have reverted to your former useful profession," he remarked, smiling widely, upon Race welcoming him to the house. Margaret was in the middle of baking bread, and feeling at a disadvantage with her hair falling out of it's braid and her hands and apron sprinkled generously with coarse wheat flour.

"He is notorious," Race said impishly upon introducing him to Margaret, when the children had been dismissed for the day. "For his horsemanship, his poetry, and for being promoted with all speed – he hardly had any choice, for his parents christened him Mirabeau Bonaparte."

"Ma'am," Race's friend bowed over her hand, a wiry man in his late thirties, with dark hair falling over a high forehead and a courtly manner about him. He had clever eyes, and an educated Georgia drawl as sweet and mellow as dark molasses dripping from the jar. "Your husband, although the most cultured and well-educated man I have ever met in Texas, is also prone to greatly exaggerate – about everything, save in one aspect, where I vow that he does not exaggerate sufficiently. Or perhaps I should not say 'exaggerate' – but speak the unvarnished truth."

"And that would be?" Margaret asked, thinking *Race? Exaggerate?*

"He does not exaggerate the qualities of Mrs. Vining sufficiently, to my way of thinking. Is not a good woman above the price of rubies; should not her husband praise her unceasingly? *'Her children arise up, and call her blessed; her husband also, and he praiseth her. Many daughters have done virtuously, but thou excellest them all!'*"

"He would not be the only gentleman I know, given to exaggeration," Margaret answered, demurely. "Some of them are within this room."

Race laughed. "Daisy-mine, it comes naturally to him, for he is a politician as well. In the space of a day, Bo went from ordinary private soldier-volunteer to commander of General Sam's cavalry. Now he is the vice-president. I won't ask what he did to gain that significant honor. I assume it was something spectacular, based on my witness of his battlefield promotion – and given that, I presume that his second elevation involved something heroic and before the eyes of all."

"Not a salute from the Mexican lines," Bo Lamar drawled, but then he took on a serious expression. "Not this time. Merely hard work and a concern for the well-being of us all; is it not every man's right and duty to engage in politics and the guidance of our nation? Why did our people fight two revolutions, if not that!" his expression turned slightly less amiable. "I support General Sam's policies – but I still maintain my own independency of thought on various matters as the Indian question and the education for our children."

"Is that what you are doing, all the way out here, Bo? Fighting Indians, or serving as the inspector of schools?" Race asked, with mock-solemnity, and Mr. Lamar laughed heartily.

"Neither," he answered, as he and Race settled onto chairs. Margaret had made them comfortable, with patchwork cushions, and as always, the view of the shallow valley down below, and the broad reaches of the Colorado was incomparable, with the afternoon sun turning certain reaches to silver. "I had heard of this place as being of unsurpassed beauty. I wished to see it for myself and to ascertain whether it would serve a certain purpose – and also for a little hunting. Do you know, I shot a buffalo this morning – extraordinary creature!"

"There's a trick to that," Race began, and Bo Lamar laughed again.

"I know – from the side, and aim into the ribs just behind the forelegs . . . Joseph Harrell took care to enlighten me. Ah!" he stretched out his booted feet, with a sigh of pure enjoyment. "A paradise indeed, but if certain of my own plans come to fruition, you might very well have to share it with more than just Joseph and his neighbors."

"What do you mean by that?" Race asked curiously, as Margaret gave the last turn to her bread dough and slapped the whole mass into the trough for another rising. She dusted flour from her hands and came to join her husband and his friend. Visitors were so very rare in Waterloo that she could not bear to deprive herself of the pleasure of company and the sound of other voices besides that of Papa, Race, and the children.

"We're giving thought to establishing a proper capitol city," Bo Lamar answered, "and looking over likely situations. Oh, I know that folk think of Washington-on-the-Brazos, or perhaps Harrisburg or San Felipe as a place to house the proper government of Texas . . . but all were destroyed in the fighting, in part or entire. As far as rebuilding goes, everyone is beginning from the same place, with none having any advantage over the other. And starting a new capitol city from the ground up is a way of compromising between those already established. Finally," he looked earnestly at Margaret and her husband, "I have been convinced that our leading city should rightly

240

be in the center of our territory – not clinging to the present boundaries or the seacoast like a frightened child, unprepared to let go of a mother's hand . . . although," he added with a quick and charming smile to Margaret, "these convictions should not by any means, be construed as a slight against a loving mother and her concern for a child. It is merely an acknowledgement of realities," he continued, with his expression returning to its former gravity, "and the reality is that our boundaries after Velasco encompass a country – our own beloved and independent country – of not inconsiderable size. Our chief city should be an ornament to our state, both in location and in those necessary offices constructed for that purpose of government."

"But Waterloo occupies the farthest frontier," Margaret answered swiftly. *Oh, how could she be so forward*, she wondered, *to break in upon her husband's conversation with his friend.*

To her gratification, Bo Lamar answered with interest and courtesy, "So it is, Mrs. Vining. But I believe to the bottom of my soul that we must think ahead, just as I am considering those requirements of education and higher learning. This is our land, and we must therefore possess the whole of it. And what better way to make it clear to all then by establishing our capitol city here?"

"Oh, Bo," Race shook his head, a rueful expression upon his face. "Waterloo is, as my dear Daisy says – the farthest frontier, on the very edge of civilization. Convincing anyone in the legislature, or in office that they should establish a city here . . . Bo, the legislature is a sack full of tomcats. That you are seriously considering such a course of action – they will think you have gone mad!"

"Oh, I believe I shall be able to convince them." Bo Lamar smiled, an expression of utmost charm and confidence. "Just watch."

241

Chapter 19: *A Shining City On a Hill*

Race was cheered by the visit of his friend, Mr. Lamar – a cheer which increased when he discussed the vice-president's intentions with Margaret. They had gone on talking until nearly supper-time; so much had happened in that momentous year of 1836! The expectations of Texas immediately joining the United States had been dashed most abruptly. As Margaret understood it, influential senators from the Northern states who were opposed to slavery spoke vehemently against the annexation of Texas as a new state. Mr. Austin had died suddenly in December, worn out with many years of labor on behalf of his settlers and his imprisonment in Mexico, to say nothing of the hardships and terrors of that dreadful year just past. Margaret remembered again how he had come to visit Mama during their stay in San Felipe – more tears dropped into that river of sorrow! Margaret had to excuse herself to begin preparing the evening meal, lest Papa vent some of his bad humor upon them all. It offended Papa to see anyone not laboring with their hands, in field or garden; Margaret feared what he might think of Race spending a few hours of daylight speaking with the vice-president of Texas.

"We might well remain in Waterloo, rather than return to Gonzales." Race was in good spirits for the first time in months, as he and Margaret talked after dinner that night, while Papa slumped in his chair and snored faintly. "There would be more scope for establishing a school here, if Bo's hopes for establishing the seat of government come to pass and we have the patience to wait until it does. Besides," he added thoughtfully, "he has tasked me with traveling to the United States as part of a group of emissaries for a year or so, to speak to influential people, to encourage the establishment of stronger trade ties, now that outright annexation is entirely removed from the table. The death of Mr. Austin left us without a strong and guiding presence. He was a statesman and a pioneer, a gentleman without peer and above reproach."

"Would you want to leave us for that long?" Margaret's heart sank at the thought of another separation from Race. She had not minded those months when he had returned to Boston to settle his father's affairs, for that had been when they were just new-married. "And what of your health, in the cold of northern winters – you were sickened enough just this winter past; how badly would the ice and snow treat your lungs?"

"As tenderly as ever," her husband answered, with a wry twist of his lips, "But on the other hand, I would be able to consult with the finest doctors regarding my old malady and to see my brothers and sister and . . . my family again. No, Daisy-mine, our time together is as precious to me as ever, but once more I have been asked to serve a larger cause."

"Then you should join this delegation," Margaret answered bravely, for as much as she doted upon his companionship, she knew also that he did not feel altogether useful in Waterloo, where Papa's constant denigration of him wore very much upon them both. "If Mr. Lamar convinces the government to establish a city here, you must buy a town lot or two; one to build our own home upon and another adjoining for your school."

"Practical Daisy," he said. "Have I said so often enough? No, then I will say it again – practical Daisy, a domestic general at the head of a household. I will bring back some proper adornments for it, at the very least."

"More books," Margaret said, "for your school, and for us."

"Your wish is my command, fair general Daisy." Race laughed, and so it was settled. He rode away on Bucephalus on a bright midsummer morning several weeks later, whistling cheerfully, until Margaret caught up baby Jamie and ran after him.

"Wait!" she called. "Wait – there was one more thing to tell you!"

"What can that be?" he asked. "Is there something I had forgotten?"

"No," Margaret answered, remembering what Maggie Darst had said, her words about the last words exchanged between husband and wife. "Always remember that I love you."

"And so I do, and never to forget," he answered. Then he rode away, as he had so often in previous times, but she was comforted, knowing that he was not going onto the field of battle, or on a dangerous mission as a courier.

His letters proved also to be a comfort, for he wrote to them often as he and his fellow emissaries traveled – from Galveston and New Orleans, and up the Mississippi by steamboat. In each letter he told where their next destination would be. Margaret would try and send a letter, and to coax Horace into writing also, without wasting a sheet of their precious letter-paper. Chief of her concerns all that summer and autumn was that any of their neighbors might be journeying to Columbia or Harrisburg, wherever they might meet someone journeying even farther, who would bear a letter – or perhaps even bring one in return. Race wrote of receiving those letters of hers, but often they had been months on their way to him, and therefore all the more precious. He penned lively accounts of what he had seen, of lectures and exhibitions, of concerts and consultations with great men, of artists and theatrical performances. In New York, he visited Barnum's American Museum to look at the many educational exhibits there, although he was particularly scathing in describing the preserved body of a mermaid; nothing but a half a dried monkey sewn to half of a large dried fish. He visited Boston, purchasing more books for his library. He did not write very much of his family, his half-brothers and sister. Margaret recalled that Race once said they were very much older than he was, and so had not been particularly close.

He spent many weeks in Washington, lamenting that he had been unfortunate enough to discover another place besides Texas, in which the summer heat was equally sticky and unrelenting. But what was planned for Washington City entranced him no end, although he lamented that many of the fairest buildings and monuments were unfinished, and the presidential mansion was not nearly as fine on the inside as it appeared. His letters provided a window to another, larger world, of some refinement and varied amusements. He must always have felt so isolated, in tiny frontier towns like San Felipe, in Gonzales, and most especially in Waterloo. No wonder that he had so many friends, maintained such a large circle of correspondents – and when all that was not enough for a gregarious soul, no wonder that he would return to the East with such alacrity. Sometimes Margaret envied her husband for his experience of that larger world. Yet at other times she did not, especially those mornings when the sun rose like an enormous gleaming pearl half-veiled in rising mist, a mist which twined around the towering oak and cypress trees. On those mornings, she thought of her sons; someday and very soon, Mr. Lamar would have his city, and as it grew, they might have all the advantages and opportunities that their father had from Boston.

The year and months passed, as slowly as the river slipping past, marked by the turn of the seasons, as Papa's apple trees were robed in white blossoms, and then in green leaves turning to russet as the apples themselves ripened and blushed pink and ruddy red. Horace turned seven, the image of his father. Jamie, a tall and sturdy toddler, nearly the size of Johnny although Johnny was two years older, began walking and beginning to talk. They did not have much to do with Papa, who paid them little enough mind, save when it came to doing chores. Margaret insisted on regular lessons; Race would have wanted that, no matter that Papa felt strongly otherwise.

That December, Mr. Lamar was elected to the presidency of Texas, and most importantly to Margaret and the boys, Race returned from the East, escaping once again, so he claimed, just ahead of the icy jaws of a pestilential winter. A week before his expected return, a wagon-dray sent from Galveston arrived at the house, containing several packing-cases of books, a few pieces of furniture and ornaments, and an oil lamp with a delicate glass shade trimmed with a fringe of tiny beads, a brass-trimmed portable writing-desk, and a mechanical tin windup toy for each of the boys. There were also a dozen bolts of fabric – mattress-ticking, fine muslin, figured calico, and stout machine-woven flannel, for Race had not forgotten how expensive it was, before independence, to import fine-woven fabric. Papa grumbled at such a lavish display and expense, but he took the boards that the packing-cases had been made from and went to work pulling out the nails and making a pair of bookshelves from them. Margaret was touched; it was nearly the first kindly-considered thing he had done for either of them since returning to Waterloo. The little log-walled parlor looked so very fine now, the finest in all of Waterloo, with the golden light from the oil lamp playing across the gilded lettering and edges of her husband's precious library. Even Papa said so, looking around it on a dark winter evening from the doorway to the kitchen, shortly before her husband's return.

"It looks very fine," he said abruptly, the evening that Margaret had finally shelved all of the books. There had been so many added to their library that she had no time or leisure to examine them. Outside the wind went through the branches of the trees with a roaring sound, like the surf of the sea, and it was chilly outside, but the parlor was an oasis of warmth. Papa had sealed up all the cracks between the logs that autumn, once the harvest was gathered, and Margaret had hung blankets over the windows. Even though the shutters were tightly-closed, drafts leaked through the cracks and around the edges. She was reading to the boys, with Jamie on her lap, half asleep with his thumb in his mouth. "Your mother would have liked it so," Papa continued. "Young James, there. He minds me of your brother, at that age."

"He's very like Carlchen," Margaret answered fondly and without thought, for in the next moment Papa's expression went dark and thunderous.

"No, girl – he's the image of Rudolph. Do you not see it?"

"Of course, Papa," she answered quickly, but to an empty doorway. From where she sat, she could hear his heavy tread on the split-log floor, and the creak as he sat on the edge of his cot to take off his boots. *Poor Papa*, she thought. *In all this time, that was the first that he had talked of Mama. And then he went away again, like a snail pulling back into the shell.*

Race arrived a week after the dray; Margaret first saw a rider on a black horse, far away on the river road. As they approached, she recognized Bucephalus and called her sons in from where Papa had Johnny and Horace helping to gather up a basket of twigs and chips from where he had been splitting logs for firewood all the morning.

"Boys, wash your faces and hands, your father is coming home!"

She smoothed her hair, quickly took off her apron; her every-day homespun dress was at least clean, the house was spotless. The gifts from the East had been arranged in their parlor, and Papa had even finished a third and smaller bookcase. She took Jamie up in her arms. He looked up into her eyes – his own so very blue, the color of the sky, the same as hers and her brothers had been. Jamie indeed had the appearance of Carl at that age, and her heart contracted again. In the year and more that Race had been in the East, she had never heard a word from or about her brother. But she resolutely set that thought aside – this was a homecoming, and Jamie's brothers had already run down the hill, running to meet the horseman.

"Such a good big boy," she cooed, breathlessly. "Your papa will be amazed at how you have grown!" She followed her sons more slowly, drinking in the sight of him as he reined in Bucephalus and swung down from the saddle. The boys flung themselves at his legs, shrieking happily in welcome. He was thinner, she realized with a pang, but oh, how finely and fashionably dressed, as a gentleman from the East. He would have had to dress well and she was reminded of how he had appeared to her on the day she first laid eyes on him – the schoolteacher and dandy, with his elegant brocade waistcoat. Now he looked over the boy's heads, always with that smile and look of frank affection, just for her and only her.

"Oh, Daisy-mine, it seems an age!"

She sank into his embrace, rejoicing in the crush of his arms around her, burying her face into his shirt-front and neck-cloth, barely aware of having set Jamie down. How could she have endured a year and more without his company and affection? All those days without, and the nights as well! She resolved in that moment that she would not endure another such again. She cupped his face in her hands and kissed him, once and again.

"It was an age without you," she answered, and he laughed and gathered up Jamie. He leaned to one side, seeming to mock the weight and growth of his youngest child.

"Who is this big boy, then?" he asked, and Jamie gurgled and laughed happily. Margaret gathered that happiness and joy around herself – her husband was home again, set as a precious gem in the adoration of his sons. Nothing could or should spoil that, not even the bad temper of Papa. But something did mar the joyous homecoming, for her and in a small way. They walked up the track towards Papa's house together, Race having put Horace and Johnny in the saddle, while he led Bucephalus by the reins and put Jamie on his shoulders. She saw the momentary flicker of disgust in his expression when he regarded the house – plain and made of rough-hewn logs. On the portion of the porch nearest the stable, Papa had piled two ox yokes, with the tangle of chains and leathers that made up the harness. There was a scythe and a hay rake leaning against the wall above them, and a litter of small tools, buckets, and baskets made it appear as if Papa had just dropped them all where he had no more use of them for the day. Papa's ax was sunk in the large stump close to the house that he used to split logs upon – where the boys had been gathering up chips and twigs – and a tall stack of split firewood was piled up against the side of the house, sheltered from the wet under the overhanging roof. The vegetable garden presented a tumble of earth, having been ploughed under for next spring's planting; nothing about Papa's house appeared prosperous, but rather mean, rough, and squalid, now that Margaret considered it through her husband's eyes. Prosperous farmsteads in the East did not present so poor an appearance. He had become accustomed to the appearance of things there. But the expression of distaste was only momentary and replaced with a look of pride as Horace took Bucephalus' reins, insisting that he would see to unsaddling him and turning him out to pasture.

"He's grown so tall," Race marveled, "and so very responsible, Daisy-mine. I confess that a good may have come from Father Becker, not molly-coddling the boys." As they went into the house, his face lightened again – and Margaret thought with relief that his happiness at returning to her and the boys remained unalloyed.

Over the first months following his return from the East, all still seemed well. It was Papa who gave Margaret cause for unease, for he seemed to have little appetite for the work of the farm. At first she wondered if he were beginning to feel his age, and then word arrived that Mr. Lamar had prevailed upon the legislature to approve building a new capitol at Waterloo. Papa and Joseph Harrell, and the scattering of families and single men settled around the creeks and springs near Waterloo, all received offers to purchase their tracts of land. To Margaret's vague surprise, Papa accepted at once, without demanding a better price. The only portion he held back from selling was a portion of fifteen acres or so immediately around the house.

"I thought Papa would drive a harder bargain," she said, when she and Race discussed this matter in bed that night. "He does not readily give up anything that was his – but when he did he immediately moved to another situation."

"Is he planning to purchase another tract elsewhere?" Race asked, thoughtfully, and Margaret shook her head.

"No. I did ask him if that was what he intended. I said that we would purchase a town-lot for a school, but he just beetled his brows and grumbled at me under his breath. Then he said that the house would be mine to do with as I pleased, that I would order the household as much as Mama ever did, for as long as it suits me to do so. He might stay in Waterloo or he might not, as he was still thinking of what to do with the money from the land."

"Was he serious?" Race asked, "or just too stingy to hire a housekeeper – much less one who would go with him out to the wilderness again?"

"Oh, he was entirely serious – I am his daughter, and in Papa's way of thinking that is what the womenfolk do."

"With a husband and children of their own, they must attend on their father?" Race answered dryly. "I can imagine what my sister Minnie would say to that."

"Even so," Margaret agreed. "Still, it saddens me that Papa does not have any plans. He always did before."

"The mainspring of his life was your brother Rudi and your mother," Race mused, after a moment or two. "Having lost them, earthly ambition has abandoned him entirely. Perhaps Lamar's new city might restore to him more interest in life than chopping wood and pottering around in the garden or the corn-patch – anything at all to keep him from scowling at me over the breakfast table!" That made Margaret giggle, but the more she considered his words, the more she agreed with them. Having the prospect of a proper town – that would please Race and Papa both; and she herself was pleased because within months of his return she was again with child.

The new city was to be called Austin, after Mr. Austin; this was a matter upon which all agreed, even General Houston who described him as the Father of Texas; he had first obtained the largest grant in Texas, and negotiated favorable terms with first the Spanish and then the Mexican government. In all that he had ever done for the American settlers, no one – even those who disagreed with his policies – ever doubted that he had done as he thought best for the benefit of all. The prospect of the new city of Austin unfolded marvelously over that summer, first the surveyors with their theodolites and compasses, their poles and chains, measuring and marking out the land with blazes cut in the trunks of trees, or stone cairns. When that was completed, the streets of the city were marked out. In August, when the heat of summer became so unbearable that Papa moved his cot out onto the porch to sleep where it was slightly cooler at night, the town-lots were auctioned off and the new owners began to build upon them almost at once. Was there not room for optimism, for Austin was to be their queen of cities and showplace to the world? To Race's disappointment, his bid for several likely lots was topped again and again, and he returned from the auctions in disappointment.

He also returned with a renewed cough, which grew worse within days. Margaret was beside herself. He had never been ill in summer before. He lay tangled in sweat-dampened sheets, coughing as he had never done before, in a delirium that surpassed the illness which had prevented him from riding with the Gonzales Company. Margaret tried every remedy at her disposal, from camphor drops in a bowl of steaming-hot water, to birch bark infusions and sage tea, to no avail.

A week after Race fell ill, he coughed so hard that he vomited blood. Margaret was terrified, more frightened than she had ever been. The specter of consumption, which had stalked her husband for all his life, had finally caught up to him. She feared his lungs would dissolve into bloody clots, and finally he would not be able to breathe. He would die, leaving the boys fatherless and herself alone; she could not bear that thought. She settled his head back onto the pillow, feeling as if she could not breathe herself, faintly nauseated from the new child growing within her. The boys were shucking corn on the porch as Papa brought baskets and baskets of it to them. She ran past them to the cornfield, seeing Papa's ragged wide-brimmed planter's hat among the standing cornstalks.

"Papa, I think we must send for a doctor for Race – he has begun to cough blood." She tried to keep her voice calm and low. Papa looked briefly at her, and continued pacing along the rows, deftly stripping ears of ripe corn from the stalks and throwing them into the deep basket slung on his back.

"Aye?" he said. "And what's the doctor supposed to do for him then?"

"His condition is beyond my ability, Papa – and I fear for him, very deeply. I cannot stand by and let him fall to consumption."

"Why not, girl?" Papa answered. "If it's consumption, he'll die of it anyway, and the sooner the better. If not, he'll get better with or without the doctor. He's a useless weakling." He paused to swipe the back of one hand across his forehead, and continued, "It's been a miracle that you got children from him in the first place. Who'll pay for a doctor's visit? I'm telling you now, girl, it won't be me."

"Papa, you can't mean that," Margaret stared at him in horror. "What would Mama say to that!"

"What would she say! There was no doctor for her when she died of the flux, why should there be one to help your fancy-man die of consumption!"

"Papa, that's not fair – we did everything we could for Mama!" Margaret cried, stung by her fathers' unfeeling words, but her father only scowled.

"You didn't do enough, else why would she die, then?" He turned away, with an air of finality, as immovable as a rock, or the river in its bed. Margaret walked slowly back towards the house, feeling suddenly and appallingly alone. The happy voices of her sons came to her, as they tore shucks from the golden ears of corn . . . no. Their father was desperately ill. She – she was the only one, the only one who could do anything. She was walking between the apple trees and the weight of that responsibility suddenly felt like a physical burden dropped across her shoulders. She sank to her knees in the shade of the nearest apple tree. The sparse grass underneath was carpeted with last years' fallen leaves, from which a faint odor of cider and dried windfalls arose.

She was entirely alone, Margaret realized slowly. The boys were children; they were not capable of bearing this, nor was it right to even think of laying it upon them. Carl was far away with a Ranger company, if he still lived. No, her brother would not bear any of the burdens of her family. He was gone, fleeing his own burden of hurts and seeking salvation and refuge in the wilderness. Papa had just adamantly refused – no, there was no one to depend upon but herself. It was, she realized slowly, akin to that day when General Sam and Harry Karnes had told her that Gonzales would be burned. She had packed the wagon, with Mama's help. With Maggie Darst's assistance she had carried Mama, Sarah, and Pru along with her by sheer force of will. Others had been of help along the way – Hurst, the Burnett's Negro slave, young Davy Darst, but most of the burden was hers. She had been equal to it then, she must be equal to this different burden now. And with responsibility came the duty to act, without seeking permission or approval. She stood up, brushing off her skirts where dead leaves clung to them, and walked back to the house, considering and mulling over what she might now do, and what advantages she possessed besides a strong will, the education which her husband had conveyed to her, and the stubborn determination which was Papa's gift of inheritance . . . inheritance. Oh, that was it, she realized in a blaze of enlightenment – the house. Papa had said she could do with it as she wished and order it as Mama had, if she willed it so. She was filled as she had been on the night of leaving Gonzales with adamantine resolve, calmly reviewing what she must do. The only different thing was that she had not to empty a house today – but to fill it.

The first that she said of this plan was to the boys:

"Save all the fine corn-husks very carefully – when you are finished with the corn, spread out the husks to dry in the sun."

"What are you going to do with them, Mama?" Horace asked, his clever grey eyes – so like his father! – alight with mischief and curiosity.

"I am going to make several more mattresses," she answered, "As we will take in boarders." Horace looked puzzled,

"Why are we doing that, Mama?"

"Your papa is very sick and cannot teach school," she answered. "We need money. Taking in boarders is the only respectable way there is to earn it." She sat herself briefly on the edge of the porch, smiling to reassure Johnny, whose eyes were welling up with tears. "So, you may all be a help to me, and to your papa. You may have more chores – not so much for your Opa, but for me. Now, I must walk down to where they are starting the new town, and see if I may find a doctor . . . and if anyone would like to board with us."

"Yes, Mama," the boys chorused, and she took some small pleasure from that. Inside the little room off the parlor, Race lay semi-awake, flushed with the fever, but breathing strongly without coughing. *For you*, she vowed silently, *and for the boys, I will open Papa's house to strangers, work over a hot fire twice daily to fix meals for them, boil wash-water and labor over a scrubbing board. All that I do in keeping house for Papa and for you, I will do for strangers, but I swear I will put no small value on it!*

She untied the apron from around her waist and took out her best straw bonnet. Margaret had made it herself of golden wheat straw from Papa's fields, soaked in water for an age until softened, then braided, soaked again, then sewn and shaped with her needle to frame her face in the fashionable mode shown in the papers which Race had sent her from the East. She had trimmed this confection with ribbon rosettes and a length of cobweb-fine ivory net lace which Mama – her heart contracted again – had saved among those things left in the trunk that she could not take to Gonzales in the fall that war came upon them all. *Oh, Mama – might the memory of your tireless work and patience give me strength for what I am about to do! Let me appear as a lady, a person of consequence, to whom respect and consideration is due, as Esteban and Diego Menchaca addressed me, as Señor Jaime Bowie always did, although once or twice he looked at me as if he were imagining me in my shift. Let me be seen to have pride and circumstance – but not so much that it will put them off renting space on the back porch and settling down to two cooked meals a day, on a rough table.*

She marched down the hillside, towards the sprawl of mud and half-built offices, of shanties roofed with tent-canvas, as busy as an ant-hill, with carpenters hard at work, of wagons laden with sawn lumber, brought all the way from the lower Colorado. Ill-smelling smoke rose from kilns, where they were burning limestone to make plaster and cement. A few trees still stood, but the most and largest of them had been chopped down. As she approached, her heart sank almost to her shoes, for wagon wheels had churned the mud to the consistency of mush. The sight of the litter and disorganization of building assaulted her eyes, just as the noise of it struck her ears – and the distasteful smells of cook-fires, lime kilns, and overflowing privies offended her nostrils. Still, she mused – who would remain here, when Papa's house offered peace and quiet, even at a price? She picked her way towards where the press of work and the new timber frames of building were the thickest, wondering how long it would be before this offered as pleasing an aspect as the meadows and woods that it had replaced. Were it not for the promise of being a fair and cultured city, offering her sons and herself a future of sorts, she would not thought of it as a favorable exchange.

That torturous journey to Harrisburg, following after General Houston's army, had made her confident among men and their concerns. There had been no place for womanly reserve in the wake of an army, and there was not now. She walked up to the first Anglo man that she saw, a young man with a scruffy reddish beard who appeared vaguely familiar. He was helping to unload a wagon of sawn lumber, but two even younger men were doing most of the work.

"I am looking for a doctor," she said abruptly. "Do you know of any doctors among the workmen here?" The man she spoke to dropped the armful of planks and hastily snatched off his hat.

"Sure an' it is that I do not, Marm," he answered, the Irish in his speech as unmistakable as his cheerful countenance. "Is it unwell that you are, then? If you wish to rest for a bit, then I will search one out for you, sure as my name is Seamus O'Doyle!"

That was why he looked so familiar, Margaret thought – she had met him before, the messenger who had brought them news of San Jacinto, the ebullient Irishman who all but acted out the parts of the story.

"I thank you so much," Margaret answered with relief, and a smile so open that it brought an answering smile from him, "but it is for my husband. He has a weak chest and I fear that he may soon have the consumption of the lungs unless I find a doctor that will treat him."

"Ah, so that's the way of it." Seamus O'Doyle nodded his head, quite sympathetically. "Then I shall help you find such, if there is to be found. Sure it is there is a doctor among us, there is ivry other sort. An' some of them not a' gentlemen, Marm, if ye don't mind a word o' warning. Paddy – you an' Andrew, finish unloadin' th' wagon, I have an errand fer th' lady." He clapped his hat upon his head again, and offered her his elbow with as much assurance as if he had been a lord.

"Thank you," Margaret laid her hand in the crook of it, oddly reassured. "And we have met before, Mr. O'Doyle, after San Jacinto, when you brought the word to us of our great victory. I am Mrs. Horace Vining; we were camped near Harrisburg, waiting to know if we had a country still."

"Aye," Seamus O'Doyle's face brightened, as happy as a boy with a new toy. "And here I was thinking that yer ladyship was one I knew familiar! Oh, that was a proper glorious ride indade, bringing word to all. Near to as grand as buildin' a grand new city to be the crown of Texas!"

"It is fine work, indeed," Margaret answered sedately, as Seamus O'Doyle carefully led her to the next building site. She had been thinking hard, assessing Mr. O'Doyle and what little had been said of him by those folk who knew him, before coming to a decision. "My father has long lived in Waterloo and we often thought of it as being in the farthest wilderness. There is another matter, as well as our need of a doctor. My husband cannot work to support us, I have resolved to begin taking boarders, but only those of good character – honest, hardworking men, neither drunkards nor wastrels. I would be grateful to you if you could refer such to us. My father's house is only a little removed from here, in a fair situation upon that hill where he planted apple trees. I am accounted to be a fair cook," and she took a deep breath, "but our situation is such that I must ask for payment in advance." Seamus O'Doyle's eyes rounded slightly, with astonishment and no small amount of pity.

"I know how that is," he said, at last. "And perhaps 'tis a good thing to be considering, what with the Legislature planning t'meet in December. A good roof, a foine cook, and a fair sity-ation; that is a treasure an' no mistake, Marm. It's a one such as I value meself. So count me in – although to be fair, I do loike a taste o' the creature now an' again, but ne'er to excess. The thing o' it being, Marm, my own purse is as empty as yours. If I may barter work for m'keep, would yourself consider that?"

"I would," Margaret answered, cautiously. "What do you do for a living, Mr. O'Doyle?"

"Carpentry, o' course," he answered. "Woodwork, if ye loike. I've me own tools. They do say," and he looked quite smug, "that Seamus O'Doyle could build a mansion hisself, an' ivry stick o' foine cabinetry in it, out o' a wagonload o'wood."

"Could you?" Margaret mused. "That would serve very well, indeed. As yet I have no other rooms than the back and front porch of Papa's house. A roof over and a floor under, but all open to the air. Would it be a very great trouble for you to wall them in, and put windows and doors where needed, for I assure you Mr. O'Doyle, they will be needed before winter."

"No trouble a'tall, Marm," Seamus O'Doyle beamed. "No trouble at all. I'd see what I could do for ye, in exchange for six months room and board. Subject to negotiation o' course," he added hastily. "An' I will pass the word to any foine gentlemen that I know, o' course. That's settled, Marm – a doctor for his lordship, now."

Margaret remained terribly grateful to Seamus O'Doyle that day, and to the good fortune that had led her to speak to him first, for he was as good as his word. He conducted her all among the workers, up one side of a muddy street stretching from the riverside to the top of a steep hill which he said had been settled upon to be the site of the capitol building itself, asking of every group of men if they might know of a doctor. Most men replied no, but a teamster with five brace of mules hitched to a heavy-laden wagon spit a stream of tobacco juice into the mud – courteously, on the far side of his wagon from Margaret, and answered, "There's a doctor come from Galveston, I heard tell, a friend of Mr. Schoolfield the surveyor."

"D'ye know where we might find him," Seamus O'Doyle asked, while Margaret echoed, "And do you know his name that we might ask after him, or of his dress and appearance?"

The teamster spat again, and said, "Brown coat, gold spectacles – a real city gent, by the name of Williamson. Dr. Williamson. Kinda absent-minded, they keep having to fetch him back from wherever he has wandered off to."

"We'll find him ourselves, if need be," Seamus O'Doyle answered, with energetic good cheer, "wherever he has wandered off to – for he has a new patient now, and no less than the husband of this good lady."

They continued their progress along the tangle of half-built offices and places of business without any result for some little time, but Margaret was not discouraged: there was a doctor, somewhere in this tangle. Seamus O'Doyle would help her to find him, and his tireless optimism was a tonic. He talked all the while, a veritable torrent of words – of what the city would be like, and what a beautiful situation, how he himself had come from Wexford as a child and how he and his family had eventually drifted to New Orleans, and he had come to San Felipe two years before the war. He had hoped for a grant of land, but ruefully confessed to not being enough of a man of substance to qualify for one.

In spite of herself, Margaret was amused, especially when he said, "I do not think I'll make meself a grand fortune in land, Marm, save for a city plot or two, but I do know this; most folk wish for comfort, a bit o' good fellowship, an' a full plate after a good day's work. And I'm thinkin', Marm – you would be in a good way to providin' that. But I am also after knowin' – if I might be so for'ard, presumin' on your indulgence – th' management of it all, that will be hard work, and it will not be fittin' for a lady of a foine establishment to do all hersel'."

"And what are you suggesting that I do?" Margaret asked, for he was quite right – it would amount to a lot of work; cooking, cleaning and laundry.

He beamed cheerily at her, and answered, "See, Marm, I have some friends at Beeson's Landing; the Moylan sisters, Hetty and Morag. Their brother Frankie – his given name was Fergus but everyone called him Frankie – died a bit ago. Fell into the river at flood, and drowned, so they say. A great sorrow to us all, y'see, for he was a jolly man, niver a bad word for any! He had a little dram shop, just by the ferry landing, but he had a partner in it and now him, with the black heart o' him, he wants to marry Morag. A bit of a child she is still but she will not have him, an' Hetty, bless her lion's heart, she will not permit it either. So there they are; they would leave Beeson's if they could, but have no place to go. See, Marm," and Seamus O'Doyle looked at her very earnestly, "you will be needin' a proper staff, if y'are to do this in a proper manner. Hetty an' Morag, they'll work for wages an' a place to live. Mother Mary an' Joseph bless them both – they've no place to go where they'll feel safe – but they would come here, on my word so they would. Their father and mine were cousins, y'see, back in Wexford, and so I'm bound m'self to look after them if friendship w' Frankie wasn't enough."

"I can't afford to pay wages, until I have the house properly set up," Margaret answered, but she had already considered the wisdom of his suggestion. "But if they are in desperate need of home and refuge, then I would welcome them gladly."

"And they would be grateful, so they would," Seamus O'Doyle beamed again, "And you would not regret it, for they are accustomed to work in an establishment of hospitality, of the daycent sort, o'course."

"Then say to them, when next you see them," Margaret answered, "that they may come and work for me."

Chapter 20 – *A Woman of Business*

Feeling as breathless if she had just been rescued from a runaway carriage, Margaret agreed to pay wages to Seamus O'Doyle's cousins, only afterwards considering that perhaps she was rash in doing this sight unseen – and moreover, that she was putting a considerable amount of trust in a man she had just met. Upon further consideration as he continued with her, searching among the muddy, clamorous work-site that would become their queen city, she concluded she was right to do so. There were people, Margaret reasoned, who just seemed right, as solid as a piece of oak, fair and straight and true – no matter what their appearance, station or speech might be. Harry Karnes was one of these, so was the Burnett's Negro servant, Hurst.

They searched the other side of the vast expanse of mud that Seamus O'Doyle said would one day be a splendid promenade from the riverside to the capitol building, asking for the doctor, or for directions to where the surveyors might be camped.

"If we do not find him," Margaret said at last, as they walked down towards where they had begun, "I will ask at the Harrell's. They had built some houses with a stockade around – perhaps the doctor and the surveyors have settled in there."

"Sure that I am, the doctor will be close by the workings," Seamus O'Doyle answered, with a grin, "that will be where th' need for him will be. We should seek him there, Marm."

"You should continue with your own work, Mr. O'Doyle," Margaret urged him. "I am needlessly taking you from it."

"No, Marm. No one dare to say that once having begun Seamus O'Doyle will not finish," he answered firmly and Margaret allowed him to conduct her further down along the scattering of buildings under construction – still, however feeling somewhat guilty. At the next place, however, when Seamus O'Doyle inquired after the elusive Dr. Williamson, a man cutting notches in the corners to set logs one atop another paused long enough to jerk his bearded chin towards the next establishment under construction and say, "He's there, sure enough. Tell that clumsy fool Jem that when the Doc is done, he'd better get back to work, or I'll hold back his wages for the week."

"For shame!" Margaret exclaimed. The man looked at her for a full moment,

"Well, ma'am, he'll be takin' better care where he swings that ax next time, won't he? I'm paying wages for work, not picking wildflowers."

The place where the doctor might be at work was one of those roofed with canvas, a careless assembly of planks and logs, and half-open to the outside. A man lay groaning on a tall table, which had been assembled out of some lengths of plank laid over a pair of barrels. A quantity of fresh blood was pooled underneath the table, darkening at the edges where it had soaked into the dust – blood that appeared to have lately gushed from a deep gash across his leg, above his knee. His trousers were lowered down to around his ankles, but the long tails of his shirt covered all the rest, except for around his knees and lower thighs, fish-belly pale save for the blood-oozing gash. Margaret hastily averted her eyes, not so much from the nakedness, but the sight of the second man, unconcernedly probing the wound with a slender silver instrument, the blood from it splashed past his wrists. He was a tall man, whom a stovepipe black beaver hat made even taller, although he had laid his brown coat aside and worked in his shirtsleeves. There was a bottle of whiskey at his elbow, a wad of lint, and some linen torn into neat strips.

"Oh, Marm, perhaps you'd best step away," Seamus O'Doyle groaned, upon seeing this, and Margaret replied, crisply, "I'm a married woman, Mr. O'Doyle. It's not like I would see anything here that I have not seen before."

She spoke louder than she had intended, for the man with the probe in his hand looked up from his work, just as Seamus O'Doyle asked, "Is it Dr. Williamson, then?" The man nodded, distractedly, saying, "Yes, yes. Hold still, will you, Jem Burnside? Is that a woman with you?"

"Yes," Margaret answered, with a gasp of relief. "We – that is – I have been looking for a doctor. My husband is terribly ill, and he has coughed up blood and so we feared . . ."

"Quite rightly," Dr. Williamson nodded, although with an absent air. He was looking in Margaret's direction, but not as if he were looking at her. Margaret wondered for one awful moment as if he were blind. He was an older man, about forty, with strong, blunt features which looked as if they had been carved out roughly with a hatchet, and disconcertingly pale blue eyes. "Would you mind terribly, madam, if I asked you to thread a needle for me? I have misplaced my glasses, you see." He peered towards her, earnestly. "I cannot see without them. Would you be so kind?"

"Yes, please ma'am!" the man lying on the makeshift table moaned. "For the love of the almighty, I am half-dead for wanting this over and done!"

"I will do that," Margaret answered, wondering if she and Seamus O'Doyle had somehow wandered into a madhouse, "if you will tell me where to find your thread and needle."

"In my bag," Dr. Williamson answered. "Which is somewhere around here." He looked at the instrument in his hand with an air of vast puzzlement. "I know that I brought it with me."

"It's at your feet, sor, so it is indeed." Seamus O'Doyle pointed it out, and the Doctor looked down, much relieved.

"Why, so it is. There is a needle-case in the bottom, and a paper of silk threads. The largest needle and the heaviest of the threads, if you would be so kind; you needn't knot the end. This is surgery, not fine embroidering."

"Fine embroidery," gasped the doctor's patient, "that would be something to show the boys."

"I do plain stitching only, Jem," Dr. Williamson answered, with a complete lack of humor. Margaret opened the doctor's leather valise and began searching inside. She had expected to find a jumble within, but it was as tidy as her own mending basket, with small pockets or loops of tape sewn within the lining to hold various items. Margaret had no idea of what they might be, save that some rather looked like scissors. She found the needle-case, and the thread, heavy black silk twist – which appeared already cut to lengths. She threaded the largest of the needles, in accordance with Dr. Williamson's request, and he took it from her hand with a mumble of thanks. Margaret swallowed against an uprush of bile as he calmly sank the needle into the flesh at the edge of the oozing gash and again into the flesh opposite; it seemed to meet as much resistance as sewing heavy canvas. He drew the thread almost to the very end, before knotting the tail of the thread to the other end, pulling gently to ease the gashed flesh together.

"My scissors, please?" the doctor asked; Margaret seemed to have been nominated as assistant surgeon, for Seamus O'Doyle had gone as white as a linen sheet. She found the scissors easily enough, but Dr. Williamson said, "If you would give them to me with the handles first. Thank you." He took four or five stitches, loosely drawing the sides of the gash close, but not together, and cutting the needle and thread free, as soon as he had completed the stitch. "It must drain, you see," he said by way of explanation to no one in particular. "I'm finished," he added to Jem Burnside, who left off gritting his teeth and raised himself up on one elbow to survey the doctor's handiwork on his leg.

"I could use a good pull from that," he said, pointing at the bottle of whiskey, but Dr. Williamson tipped the bottle and splashed the last of the contents over the gash, as the injured man howled.

"Actual consumption of this rotgut is not medically advised, Jem," Dr. Williamson answered, austerely, "as I believe that mistaking this for a good drink was precisely how you came to this predicament in the first place."

"I wouldn't mind a drop o' the creature, m'self," Seamus O'Doyle commented, and he shook his head, wryly. "I canna stand the sight o' blood, Marm, save in the heat of battle, loike – turns me that light-headed."

"Fortunate that you are not in the practice of medicine," Dr. Williamson said, with a magisterial air. He was meanwhile padding the stitched gash with lint and wrapping it all tightly with bandages, while his patient groaned. "Now, you should abjure drinking while committing acts of carpentry with sharp tools. Consider it a lesson learned, hey?" He looked at Margaret, as if surprised to see her still standing there. "I don't suppose you could mend his trousers?" he asked tentatively, and Margaret answered, "Certainly not!" Then she thought to soften that refusal. "I am keeping a boardinghouse, Doctor. I would have to charge extra for mending clothes. But I came to find you because I fear that my husband is deathly ill." She hastily averted her eyes from the sight of Jem Burnside sliding carefully down from the makeshift table and hoisting up his trousers. Meanwhile, Dr. Williamson was wiping off his hands on a towel, and rolling down his shirtsleeves.

"So you were saying." The doctor made a hastily grab at his hat, as if suddenly reminded of conventional gentlemanly manners. "Mrs. . . . ."

"Vining," Margaret answered, "Mrs. Horace Vining." The doctor was not looking at her, but rather into his hat. He was not as old as he first appeared, although the light brown hair under his hat was hazed with grey, reminding Margaret of the color of frost-killed grass.

"Oh, there they are," He pulled out a pair of gold-framed spectacles, and unfolding them, perched them upon his nose. "Much better. Henry Williamson, Doctor of Medicine and Phrenology. Your husband may be consumptive? I should examine him, to better make my own diagnosis."

"I would not be able to pay you at once for his care," Margaret blurted, relieved at having found a doctor, especially one who seemed agreeable, if tolerably absent-minded. "That is, I am intending to take in boarders – but I cannot pay you until I have sufficient wherewithal."

"I am sure that we can make an arrangement." Dr. Williamson's eyes, much magnified behind the lenses of his spectacles, were at once oddly innocent, and mild. "Good money is such a dear commodity; I am accustomed to being paid in goods. But not livestock, I beg you. I was paid with a good laying hen once. Endlessly troublesome, although the eggs were most welcome . . . where is your husband, Mrs. Vining? Not far, I hope?"

"In my father's house, on top of the hill, there." Margaret pointed out the chimneys of Papa's house. It was now to be seen clearly, since so many trees had been felled.

"A good brisk walk," the doctor answered. "Best attend to my next patient, then. Good day, Mr. Burnside – eschew alcohol when next you are cutting timber poles, hey?"

Behind her, she heard Seamus O'Doyle murmuring, "Save us, he's a better carpenter with a drop or two in him. Not my equal, though, but tolerable." Then he added, in a louder voice, "Having found the doctor, Marm, I'll go to me own work, now. But I shall pay a visit, as soon as may be, and show what Seamus O'Doyle may do. And ye won't forget about Hetty and Morag, then?"

"I will not," Margaret answered, and Seamus O'Doyle tipped his hat again to her and sauntered away.

She and Dr. Williamson did not speak much to each other during the walk back up the hill to Papa's house, nestled among the apple trees. Margaret was grateful for his silence, after the loquacious Mr. O'Doyle. The relief in her oldest son's eyes as she and the doctor walked towards the house was also a tonic; they trusted her so! Margaret resolved to do all that she could, to be worthy of that trust. The mound of corn shucks had grown in her absence.

"I've brought the doctor, children," she said to them, as she climbed up the steps to the porch. "You've done very well and I have already found a boarder for us, and we may soon have word of many more – so we will need lots of dried shucks for mattresses, as many as there are in Opa's field."

"What will Opa say, Mama?" Horace asked, and Margaret smiled bravely.

"Probably nothing welcoming," she answered, "but your Opa said that I should have the management of his house. I intend to manage it as I see best, whether Opa favor it or no. Go on with the shucking, and spread out the finest ones to dry well."

"Yes, Mama," they chorused, and as she went into the house with Dr. Williamson following, he observed, "You are a woman of strong will and firm decision, I see. Which is well; if your husband is consumptive, the care of your family will fall to you, even if his affliction is forced into abeyance."

"I know that, doctor," Margaret replied; although she had only that day begun to consider how she might do so. Her husband still lay in a feverish sleep, but wakened at once when Margaret laid a gentle hand on his shoulder and whispered, "Dearest – I have found a doctor. The city is not even built yet, and yet we have a doctor already . . . is not that a wonderful thing?"

"Daisy-mine." He clasped her hand, and looked at her with eyes that were unnaturally bright, but then he began to cough. Dr. Williamson set down his bag on the foot of the bed, and fished his glasses out from the lining of his hat.

"Let me assemble my stethoscope, and allow me to listen to your lungs." He was already looking at Race with complete absorption. The stethoscope was a curious device, wrought of fine wood and ivory; a small bell-shaped cup on one end and an ear-piece on the other, connected by a flexible tube covered in silken braid. "If you would be quiet now – just try and breathe." Margaret watched every movement, and both of their faces, trying to ascertain what the doctor might be thinking, as he moved the ivory cup across Race's chest, listening with fierce attention at every moment, as Race breathed painfully, in and out. "Now, from the back," Dr. Williamson said. "Breathe again." Race loosened his nightshirt, letting it fall from his shoulders, and again Dr. Williamson moved the ivory cup across his upper back. When he had finished, he looked at them both, with a somber expression.

"I detect some strictures in the lungs, indicative of phthisis," he said at last. The ivory and wooden stethoscope lay in his hands, like some strange musical instrument. "How long have you had a productive cough, Mr. Vining?"

"This time?" Race coughed again, "At least a week, Daisy-mine?"

"Ten days," Margaret assisted him to re-fasten his nightshirt, and set two pillows behind him so that he could lie propped up, as it seemed to make breathing easier. "But the first time he coughed up blood was this morning."

"Have you often been afflicted with ailments of the lungs and chest?" Dr. Williamson asked, and listened carefully as Race outlined the story of his childhood frailty and his consumptive mother, how the state of his health forced him to leave Boston for more temperate climes.

"Had you been ill since coming to live in Texas?" the doctor asked, and Margaret answered swiftly, "On two occasions before this time, but this is the first time he has coughed blood."

"And what has your treatment been, thus far?" the doctor asked, and Race smiled wearily.

"That is a question for my wife," he answered, "concerning her potions of foul-tasting herbs; her remedies also include breathing steam from camphor-drops in boiling water, and warm blankets. They have usually had the desired effect of restoring me to something resembling good health, until now."

"I would continue with them," Dr. Williamson continued with grave courtesy. "Plenty of rest, fresh air, as long as it is not unbearably cold outside, absolute cleanliness. Consumption is a disease compounded by poverty, overcrowding, and the miasma of cities. May I have further words with you, in private?" He sent a rather embarrassed look at Margaret.

"I will be on the porch, doctor," she said. It was too early to begin preparations for the evening meal. Instead, she took the bolt of mattress ticking and her sewing box and went to sit on the porch where her sons were still industriously shucking corn.

"What are you doing, Mama?" Johnny asked, coming to lean on her knee, as she measured out two and a half lengths of ticking, spreading her arms wide twice and then measuring from the end of her hand to the middle of her chest. She measured that length against a second, then cut carefully with her scissors straight across, before answering, "Mattresses, Johnny – see, I must make several more, sew them together while the corn shucks dry. When I am finished, we will stuff them with shucks and then we shall have pallets for our boarders to sleep upon."

"Why, Mama?" he asked, as she measured out two more and she answered, "Because this will be a fine establishment, and too good to have our guests sleep rolled up in blankets on the floor."

"Where will they sleep, Mama?" Horace asked with deep interest, and Margaret said, "On the back porch, for now."

What had it come to, that she was talking to her children about her plans and even feeling something of comfort in doing so! It was not as if they could give her wise counsel and advice, but the exercise of putting her thoughts into words and saying them out loud and sharing them with someone; that was where the comfort lay. "That will only be at first. As soon as I can afford it, and before the weather turns cold, then we shall have a carpenter come and make walls, so that there will be rooms across the back."

"And what is this? What are you are planning with my house, M'grete?" That was Papa's voice, and Margaret started a little. Papa had obviously overheard what she had said. He stood, glowering at them all, a heavy basket of harvested corn over his shoulder. He set it down with a thump, as Margaret answered with a calm assurance that she certainly did not feel, "To expand it, Papa. I am going to take in boarders. When profits allow, I will expand the roof even farther. I must support my children, after all, and the husband who gave them to me. He was a soldier for Texas, as were you and my brothers. Does that present a difficulty for you, Papa?"

"It does, girl," Papa replied, his face dark with wrath. "For it is my house."

"But you have given the management of it over to me, Papa," Margaret replied. "And taking in boarders is the only way that I may continue doing so in decency. Otherwise, I shall have to leave, taking my husband and the boys to another place. Perhaps we should return to Gonzales. You did say that I could order the household in the way that Mama did, and in the way that I thought best?" She met Papa's eyes levelly. "This is what I think best, Papa – and you would have meals, clean sheets and a well-ordered household, if I choose to remain." It was on the tip of her tongue to mention that Papa had the money from the sale of the land, and she had nothing, but that might move

Papa to consider hiring a housekeeper to see to his comforts; no, best not bring that thought to his mind. Papa had always depended upon Mama to see to his comforts and the management of his house. In his mind, she realized in a quicksilver flash of insight – that was merely what he accepted as his due, one of the purposes of marriage. He would no more consider paying for his rightful due than he would frequent some light woman . . . Margaret quickly wrenched her mind out of that thought path. She would go on seeing to those matters, as her duty to blood, family, and marriage vows led her. She met her father's hot blue-eyed glare with calm assurance, and to her inner relief, the anger melted into rueful amusement.

"You're right, girl, so I did," and he chuckled, appreciatively. "Said you would have the running of it, didn't I? You're the clever one, M'grete, as clever as your brother now, taking me at my own words and turning them to your use. So – you are planning to wall in the back, and settle them all on pallet-beds? Then what?"

"I shall expand the house, Papa," Margaret answered. "I would add more rooms, and even a proper upstairs. I have already arranged for a carpenter," she added, seeing that Papa was about to say something. "And the carpenter has women kinfolk who might come to Austin to help me with the housekeeping." Another careful tread on the porch, and a gentle clearing of his throat brought her attention to Dr. Williamson, who had just emerged.

"I see that you found a doctor," Papa rumbled. Margaret set aside her sewing and sprang to her feet. "Now you have a means to pay his fees, eh, girl?"

"What of my husband's condition?" she demanded, paying no mind to Papa's jab. The doctor blinked vaguely behind his spectacles.

"I bring neither good news nor bad, Mrs. Vining," he answered, "regarding Mr. Vining's condition, which I regard as frail. He is not now in any particular peril – but his constitution is not equal to his intellect or will, and he will require careful nursing if he is to recover any semblance of health."

"I expected as much," Margaret answered, while Papa up-tilted the bushel basket, empting the harvested cobs onto the pile that the boys had managed to diminish. He nodded brusquely at Dr. Williamson and stumped away, the empty basket over his shoulder, while the doctor cleared his throat again.

"You should continue with the remedies you have been using to treat your husband. They have been efficacious, in some small degree. At any rate, they bring comfort and do no harm, which is what Hippocrates commanded." The doctor fumbled with his hat and his glasses, while Margaret waited for him to continue. "He is resting now, most peacefully. About the fee for my visitation

. . . I would accept terms, contingent upon the success of your enterprise. And I have noted that this house has a most pleasing situation. It would suit my domestic needs very nicely, Mrs. Vining, especially considering my current lodging . . . if you would consider me as a boarding guest. It is quiet, you see. And I have no great skill as a cook."

"We have not set up properly for guests," Margaret answered, "but yes, I would be honored to provide lodgings for you, Doctor – if you could but allow us to complete preparations."

"Oh, of course." The doctor replaced his hat on his head, his countenance appearing much cheered. "I shall look forward, with happy anticipation to joining your household in a guest capacity. Mr. Vining possesses the largest library that I have seen since coming to Texas. One of my motivations for raising the matter of boarding is that I should dearly love to explore it. With Mr. Vining's permission, of course," he added hastily, and Margaret extended her hand to him. He bowed over it tentatively, as if not quite sure of his skill in courtly courtesies, barely brushing the back of it with his lips. "Then I will return in a week, Mrs. Vining. If you have need of my medical expertise before then, I may be found at the place where you and Mr. O'Doyle came upon me this very day practicing surgery."

Margaret murmured some words of polite leave-taking, hardly aware of her lips forming them as her mind was racing so far ahead. Two paying guests in one day, and how many more would Seamus O'Doyle find for her before the week was out? The doctor had reassured her that Race was not so ill, and Papa had consented to her plans. She settled to work then and there, feeling that her future was within her grasp, running a coarse seam along the woven selvages of the striped ticking, hardly caring that her stitches were hasty and long, as long as the shredded corn shucks remained within.

She had finished two of the mattress covers by evening, and worked long into the night on another, working by lantern-light. Within days, she had done three more, and to her astonishment and barely concealed pleasure, Papa had constructed half-a-dozen rough bedstead frames from lengths of cedar and woven strips of rawhide between, so that the pallets would not rest upon the floor. Eagerly the boys filled ticking sacks with dried corn shucks while she sewed the opening closed, and then they all lugged the filled ones around to the back porch to lay upon the rough cots, neatly lined up with their heads against the house wall. Margaret closed her eyes, envisioning her guest room when completed – how neat, tidy and welcoming it would be for the right sort of gentleman boarder come to town for the legislative session. If Seamus

O'Doyle could rough-wall-in the porch before winter brought cold winds and icy rain, that would be all to the good . . . and then Margaret snapped open her eyes: she would need bed linen for all these additional beds.

Her husband rested comfortably after Dr. Williamson's visit. His cough continued to produce some blood, although in decreasing amounts. Margaret took comfort from this. However, she did ask him about that which the doctor had wished to discuss privately. Her husband sighed deeply.

"He wished to caution me about sharing the connubial bed, Daisy-mine – should my condition worsen in any degree. He warned me that you or the boys might also be at risk of becoming consumptive. You and they maintain such a robust state of good health, I would not wish to selfishly imperil it."

"Oh," Margaret answered, suddenly unsettled by this revelation; she had never considered any such thing as maintaining a bed apart from Race, save for that brief time in Gonzales when he had been desperately ill. "I . . . I do not think I would care to do so – unless you would rest easier by my absence. I do not fear the consumption for myself, any more than I fear childbirth."

"Brave Daisy," Race answered, smiling in approval. "I would miss your fond company in the small hours of the night; we will disregard the good doctor's counsel, in this matter, at least."

She began to hem sheets and pillowcases, having no liking for using the best linen – that of Mama's weaving, adorned with embroidery which she and Oma Katerina had wrought long ago in Pennsylvania. Better to have plain and practical stuff, made from mill-woven muslin. For blankets, there were plenty of the coarse-woven Mexican blankets, brought to the markets in Bexar and sold everywhere. Margaret aired them thoroughly and folded them with sachets of dried verbena tucked into the folds so that they would not smell so much of sheep and the dye-vats. At the end of the week, Dr. Williamson came trudging up the hill to Papa's house with his medical bag in one hand, a carpetbag in the other, and a boy following after, leading a mule with two small trunks balanced on either side of the pack saddle. With her heart in her throat for apprehension, lest the doctor think the quarters on offer were too mean or lowly, Margaret showed him through the house to the porch.

"I shall have a wall built to enclose this before winter comes," she offered, and the doctor looked around with the air of vague surprise which she would come to know as typical of him. "And I shall serve meals daily in the porch at the front of the house or in the kitchen when the weather becomes cold. I hope you don't mind that this presently looks out upon the barn and the vegetable patch . . ."

265

"Does it?" Dr. Williamson searched for his glasses, finding them in his hat. "I hadn't noticed. At any rate, it is a tidier prospect than my previous quarters, and a view of a garden is supposed to be most restful to contemplate. I will be most content here, Mrs. Vining. I shall take the bed on the end, if no other guest has chosen it." He delved into his hat again, finding a little leather purse secreted in the hatband. The purse jingled faintly: the doctor opened it and took out several Mexican silver half-real coins. "I think this shall be sufficient for the time being. At some point, when your enterprise has become profitable, Mrs. Vining, then deduct my fee for treating Mr. Vining from my account." Margaret took the reals from his hand – the coins felt solid, heavy and of worth – and thanked him, thinking that keeping a boardinghouse could not be so very hard, if the boarders were generous and easy-tempered gentlemen such as the doctor and Seamus O'Doyle.

Two weeks following the eventful day when she had decided to keep boarders, Seamus O'Doyle appeared, at the reins of a freight wagon, heavy laden with sawn lumber and heavier timber beams. Two women came with him seemingly clinging to each other, and looking around with wide-eyed apprehension as Seamus O'Doyle handed them down to the ground.

"Mrs. Vining," he called out to her, as she came to the door with a tin plate in one hand and a towel in the other. "I have brought a foine stock o' lumber, intendin' to do what needs doing; a palace this shall be when Seamus O'Doyle's work is done! Here are my cousins, the sisters Moylan. Morag, child, a curtsy to 'er ladyship would not be amiss . . . an' this is Miss Hetty." The second Moylan sister was tall, rawboned, and older than the first, who appeared little more than a child; they both had blue eyes, but Morag's hair was ink-black and her features were fine and pale. Morag murmured a barely audible greeting to Margaret and stood nervously clutching a bundle in her hands and looking at the ground. Her older sister's face was splattered with pale freckles and her hair was of a faded carroty hue. She looked to be a blunt and practical woman, as plain and wholesome as a loaf of good bread. Hetty took Margaret's hand in her own strong one, knotted with hard work and as callused as a man's.

"Seamus says that you've started a boardinghouse," she remarked abruptly. "Aye, and he tells me that you'd be after a cook and a maid of all work, as no one woman may do it alone, Marm. Hetty, he says – it's a sity-ation made for you, so take up your trash an' trunk, an' come wi' me to the crown city o' Texas, where they'll be more men o'property an' high station then there're be rooms befittin' – an' says Seamus, there's jist th'place fer ye both." Seamus stood back, beaming impartially upon them all, and laughed when Hetty continued, in tones of dark disapproval, "You have no' loaned him money, Marm?"

"No," Margaret answered. "Rather, he is loaning me his labor and assistance."

"Hetty, me darlin'," Seamus laughed outright, "I am by way of bein' an' investor. Aye, that's the right o' th' matter. I am investin' this wagon o' lumber in Mrs. Vining's house by way o' ensurin' my own comfort, an' your future. Now, if you may, Marm – show me the place, an' Seamus O'Doyle will make of it somethin' foine indade!"

He hoisted down his box of tools from the wagon and tied up the horse team to the rails around the corral that Papa had for his own stock, chattering eagerly all the while, as happy as one of her sons anticipating a Christmas gift. And he did indeed seem to look upon the improvement of the house as a rare treat, whistling gaily between his teeth as he took out a folded measuring rule and a piece of chalk from among his tools. He seemed almost to forget his two cousins in his happy absorption of the prospect at hand. The two women – or rather, woman and girl followed attentively after Margaret.

"I thought for now, you would sleep in the loft with my two boys," Margaret ventured, "The ladder to it goes from the parlor, next to where my husband and I sleep," she added. Young Morag appeared very much relieved, and Seamus O'Doyle added jovially, "An' a proper an' fit staircase will we have, very soon, Morag my dear," and he went on expounding on what he could build and improve while Margaret and Hetty exchanged a wry and affectionately understanding glance.

"Oh, that Seamus," Hetty remarked, "w' his plans! Truly, Marm, I think your house needs little improving."

"'Tis grand, aye," Morag barely whispered. Margaret relished Morag's approval and the businesslike way that Hetty looked around at the kitchen and the store of smoked meats, of apple quarters drying on swags of string on the sunniest part of the porch, at barrels of corn meal and hominy, and crocks of honey in the larder-cupboard.

"I can not say that I was not worrit," Hetty said at last, and with palpable relief on her face, "when Seamus spoke t' Morag an' I – but I am not worrit now, no, not a'tall." The smile lightened her plain and bony features. "Foir he is a good lad, and a foine friend. We'll be happy to stay an' work for ye, so we will, an' thank Seamus every day for his kindness."

Yes, the best of friends, Margaret thought – *but not a lad, rather a knight-errant, a knight-errant with a carpenter's toolbox, riding to the rescue of ladies in peril. Could there be anything in the world more gallant or humble?*

It was mid-morning; she showed Hetty and Morag where to take their bundles and small trunk up to the loft. Morag immediately made friends with Horace and Johnny. Margaret could hear their voices, as they showed Morag their favorite places around the farm, while she and Hetty sat on the front porch, companionably hemming pillow-slips and talking, talking so long that the sun stood well above the apple trees – how had the time passed so swiftly – now it was well-past time to begin preparing the midday meal! Margaret felt a curious kinship with her almost immediately; a kinship which – as they talked through that morning of hemming pillow cases and bed sheets – she felt was reciprocated. Twice-blessed, that chance which had brought her to speak to Seamus O'Doyle on that fateful day, she thought with a sense of relief and gratitude. Oddly enough, Hetty reminded her of Maggie Darst – and oh, the comfort of speaking to another woman! How long it had been, how much she had missed those fond conversations with Maggie or Mama or Mary Millsaps. As loving and dear as a husband, brothers, and sons could be – a woman's heart was an alien thing to them, a mystery and a puzzlement, a land as unexplored as the plains of the Llano – and to a man, freighted with as much peril! Yet to another woman, that knowing was as comfortable and familiar as her own kitchen hearth.

At last, Margaret clapped her hands to her own mouth, saying, "Oh, my – I have not talked to another woman in so long! You must forgive me; I never thought that I could chatter so!"

"'Tis like meat and drink," Hetty replied, "an' so have I taken pleasure for myself, Marm." She set down her own sewing for a moment, and looked around, her plain and freckled face aglow with contentment. "For it seems, that we – Morag an' myself – that we have come to a blessed home. An' I am resolved to stay as long as you have need o' me . . . however long that might be."

Chapter 21 – *Out of the Llano*

"I'm going to town," Margaret announced to Hetty, on a winter midmorning some months after the Moylan sisters had come to live in Austin. Hetty looked up from the trough of bread she was kneading. It was a fair and warm day outside. The fire burned hot in the new patent iron stove, heating the old kitchen unbearably, even with the window shutters over the newly-enlarged windows and the door stood open wide to catch a breath of fresh air. "Mrs. Eberly has told me of a man who builds fair furniture, and might have some bedsteads and a chest of drawers for sale, but she did not tell me his name,"

"Perhaps her ladyship wished to keep such knowledge for herself, for the advancement of her own establishment." Hetty turned the great mass of dough. "I do no' think that anyone can build finer furniture than Seamus." Her forehead was beaded with perspiration from her efforts, and the breast of her dress and half-moons of the fabric under her arms were darkened with it.

Margaret shook her head. "But Mr. O'Doyle is off again, not to return for many a week. And there are so many come to town for the Legislature, seeking a quiet room and a comfortable bed to lie in of a night. I should hate admitting we do not have any comfortable beds. After all," Margaret added, "there are so many that they are paying any price just to roll up in their blankets on the floor of a handy tavern."

"Bein' they have been drinking there all the evening after adjourning for the day," Hetty snorted, "most men would find that convenient, I am sure!"

"So they would," Margaret answered equably, "but as for our house, we will only offer our rooms to the best and most gentlemanly of them . . . men such as Mister Hattersley."

"That plaguey Englishman!" Hetty returned, "with his turned-up nose and his la-te-dah manners. There's no good to come of his loike, Marm. Butter wouldn't melt in his mouth, but take my word on it, he's lookin' around, seeing what he can get from the situation. Dinna trust him a lick, Marm, and that's my advice to ye!"

"Yes, Hetty – I will take that into consideration." Margaret took down a large basket from a peg on the beam which bisected the kitchen, and stifled a small sigh. That was one of the things that no one had ever said about the business of running a boardinghouse – of that effort put into listening to complaints, and patiently soothing down the various ruffled feathers. Hetty, blunt and outspoken to a fault, worked her fingers to the bone with the cooking for Margaret's enlarged household, while Morag labored over the laundry and the housekeeping. In three months, since taking over the management of Papa's house she had acquired nearly a dozen boarders. True to his word, Seamus O'Doyle had made four fine rooms by walling in the front and back porches, and four more by extending the sleeping loft, and adding a pair of dormer windows and a stairway. But it meant a greater quantity of work than she had expected, even after installing her one splurge – the iron cook stove. No, she must have patience with the Moylan sisters and the gentleman boarders, Margaret reminded herself yet once again. Speaking calm and fair words was the least part of her work.

Austin had grown beyond being able to support more than one or two boarding houses and hotels. And she might very well loose Morag yet, to a decent proposal of marriage; it had not escaped Margaret's notice that Morag – who had begun to overcome her timidity in the safety of Margaret's house – had admirers of a Sunday afternoon, bashful young men come to pay their respects after early morning Mass. Margaret could very well see how their brother's old business partner might have wanted to pursue marriage, even over Morag's reluctance. As a chaperone, Hetty guarded her younger sister with the ferocity of a mother wolf, but Margaret did not doubt that Morag would eventually come to them both with the hand of some tongue-tied young swain firmly held in hers. *We wish to marry, Marm, sister*, Morag would say. This was Texas, where women were few and men were many. The young man would first look at his boots and then draw his courage up and look them in the eye, and promise to worship Morag with his body and endow her with all his worldly goods. He would build her a fine little log house somewhere – if not in Austin, then in Gonzales or Brazoria and Margaret would need to hire another girl to do the laundry and housekeeping.

"Sufficient unto the day," Margaret told herself, and stepped out of the kitchen into one of the new rooms – the room next to the kitchen where her family and the boarders were accustomed to take meals, walled in from the original porch but still open and airy, with tall windows which looked out on the apple trees and the valley where the little settlement of Waterloo had once been. Now the house rambled along the brow of the hill, framed by the apple trees, the extended verandahs spreading out like the wings of a bird. The new rooms were bright with fresh plaster, and when the takings afforded it, she intended to have glass to let light in for all of the windows, not just the front parlor and the dining room. She had also begun to think of adding another wing to the end of the house, three rooms up and three down, with another long verandah all the way around, and she spent those few minutes of leisure which she had in poring over Vitruvius and considering how best to position the windows in the new wing. She stepped into the doorway of the next of the new rooms, where Race lay on the daybed with an opened book in his lap.

"I'm going into town," she said, seeing that his eyes were open. It wrung her heart to see him so thin and frail, as insubstantial as something made from glass. He had lost flesh and strength after the latest bought of illness, and only now was recovering something of his previous vigor. Poor Bucephalus was growing fat with idleness; if Dr. Williamson did not borrow him now and again, the horse would have gotten no exercise at all. Only Race's eyes were the same, the clever grey-hazel of them, and the wicked curve of his lips as he smiled for her, and only for her. "Are there any books that you are longing to read, that I should search out for you?"

"I am content, Daisy my own," he answered, and coughed a little. "Mr. Hattersley loaned some volumes from his own collection to me. I took no little pleasure in his copy of *Sketches by Boz*. Such a very amusing writer. I look forward to his next book with happy anticipation."

"You will teach Horace and Johnny this afternoon?" Margaret tied her plain straw bonnet over her head and leant down for a kiss. "They should behave very well after spending the morning doing chores for Papa."

"Indeed," Race laughed, a laugh which ended in a cough into his handkerchief, while Margaret attempted to keep the worry from her countenance, watching his poor bony shoulders shaking like a spavined horse. At last the spasm passed. He took the hand and the cloth in it from his face, crumpling it so swiftly she could not see if he had coughed up blood. No, she should not unman him by hovering over his every move like a nervous wet-nurse. He may have recovered something of his former health, but Margaret had come to accept the fact that nothing would change the eventual outcome of his illness, whether he coughed blood or not.

He continued upon recovering his breath. "Your father is a very demon for work, Daisy-mine. The boys should be very attentive, knowing that otherwise they would be slaving away like a nigra in a cotton patch."

"The garden needs to have the muck dug in," Margaret replied, in faint reproof, "and we are not gentry – too good to dirty our hands with the work that keeps us fed."

"I know it well," he answered, with a wry twist to his mouth. "It's the very damnation. I should be doing the work proper for a man, for you and the boys, instead of lying around, being coddled."

"Coddled, nothing," Margaret answered crisply, and she leaned down to kiss him again, "Besides you do the work of a man very well. Well enough for me, husband."

"So I do," he brushed her cheek with his lips, and his dear pale hand touched the apron over her belly very gently.

"I'll tell the boys you shall want them for a lesson," she added, as she straightened up. Now he said, "They will be very glad to hear that. But don't tire yourself by walking far, Daisy-mine."

"I won't." She smiled over her shoulder as she went out the door. She was more than seven months gone in pregnancy, and still barely showing under the tight lacing and full skirts of a dark calico dress made in the latest fashion. Margaret was glad that had never shown much until the very last weeks. There was too much work to be done, that work which had made the house fair for her family, and relieved Race of the necessity of taxing his strength by making a living. She could earn a living for them all, and a fine one at that! But Race – he would always be frail, that's what Doctor Williamson had said, blinking vaguely over his spectacles. Her husband did not have a constitution equal to his will, or his intellect.

On the new verandah, she paused and surveyed her domain – or at least those portions of it visible from the dooryard; the line of winter-bare apple trees opposite, and the pasture for the cows beyond it. It was warm in the sunshine, but chill in the shadows. It had been a mild winter so far. Around the side of the house, Jamie played with a pile of corn cobs under the shelter of the oak tree. He was standing them in the soft ground, pretending they were soldiers in ranks. Horace and Johnny worked in the vegetable garden under Alois Becker's stern eye, digging in the well-rotted stable muck.

"Lessons this afternoon, boys," she called to them, and Papa straightened with a grunt of effort.

"They will not have finished digging in the muck," he grumbled, and Margaret answered, "Tomorrow, Papa. They will finish tomorrow." She was rewarded by the faces of Horace and Johnny brightening at her words, even as her father scowled. But he did not offer an argument. Margaret could not decide if that pleased her or not – that her father yielded to her authority so easily. She walked briskly down the footpath, thinking that Race was right. Something crumbled within her father after her mother's death and Rudi's and crumbled even farther when the state offered money for his land. He had given up the farm, taken the money paid for it and just remained under the old roof, as if the spring that propelled the mechanism within him had broken or run out.

She would like to ask him what he intended to do with all the money that had been paid to him by the state if he did not intend to buy more land elsewhere. Papa had bid on some town lots – that she knew – but what he intended to do with them Margaret did not know. On the whole, Margaret decided that she did not really care. Renting rooms to boarders brought in sufficient for herself and Race and the boys; if Papa involved himself in the enterprise he would doubtless demand to make decisions about it, and frankly, Margaret cringed at the thought. Of late, Papa had all the charm and tact of a hungry bear newly waked from hibernation, and his anger had become so easily provoked. Now and again she feared that he might strike someone, in a fit of uncontrolled rage. Better he stay at work in the garden or in the evenings glowering by the fire, rather than driving the boarders out of the parlor of an evening. That day that Papa refused to pay for a doctor to attend on her husband was a final straw for Margaret. After that, whatever Papa did for himself was a matter of indifference to her.

At the rise in the path, Margaret paused to look down at town; such a place it was now, with the new frame capitol building rising like a sea-reef on the top of a hill, framed by the new main avenue. No, it was not such a grand place as Boston or any of the long-established cities back east which Race recalled to her and the boys. This city, whose avenues and noble facades would spread over what had been her father's fields and pastures, was still new and raw. The grand avenue was a muddy expanse, frequented by many pigs wallowing in the deeper puddles, through which heavy wagons and horsemen threaded their way. It heartened Margaret to think of all that had been accomplished in a few years, and what would be done in the future. At the same time she was rather saddened to think of all those glades of trees where Rudi and Carl had hunted for deer and gathered pecans, being cut down and made into houses. New people coming to Austin would never know how beautiful it was when the Beckers first settled, and when Margaret and Race and the children had come back after the war. No latecomer would ever recall how in the mornings the mist rose from the river and twined itself around the hills and the trees, and the sun came up and turned all to pearl, while every leaf-edge glittered as if trimmed with tiny diamonds.

Margaret straightened her back, looped the handle of her basket a little more securely on her arm, and walked on; she did not have all day to stand and admire the scenery. She wanted to be at home while Race tutored the boys. She loved to watch them all together, loved them all with fierce devotion, these wonderful small creatures who came from the commingling of hers and his flesh; like and yet unlike their parents.

They had begun to build a timber sidewalk along the fronts of some stores and saloons along Congress Avenue, linking one with another. The shop owners made a half-hearted effort at keeping slops and garbage from being thrown out the front of their establishments, so she did not need to pick her footing quite so carefully. She was looking at a selection of books in the front window of the newly opened print shop, wondering if there were any among them that Race had not yet read, as a straggle of horsemen came around the corner at a fast trot; a dozen or twenty rowdy and ragged young men with unkempt locks of hair falling around their shoulders. Shouting and whooping like Indians, they halted their horses across Congress Avenue in front of Simpson's General Mercantile and the haberdashery next to it and shouldered their way in.

"Oh, my," Margaret remarked as the proprietor emerged from his doorway, "Who are they?"

"No one you should fear, Mrs. Vining," he answered gallantly. "I suppose it is only Captain Hardeman's Ranger Company, returned from a long scout into the north. They do appear the veriest ruffians and gypsies – since they have been so very long in the wilderness."

"They look as wild as any Indian," Margaret answered. She spoke a little longer with him, then took her leave and continued along the sidewalk. She looked across the street, to where the Ranger's horses, still laden with pistol and rifle scabbards, had been left carelessly tied to porch posts and railings. One or two Rangers had already emerged, their arms full of new clothes; she noted particularly one young man for his untrimmed mop of fair hair, as pale as her own. If it weren't for that, she would have thought him an Indian scout, a Lipan Apache perhaps, for he was wearing moccasins and a brief kilt with a sheathed knife stuck through his belt, leather leggings below, and a shirt above which appeared to be more rag than a garment. The fair man turned his head to call back into the haberdashery, and at that very moment Margaret saw his countenance in profile and thought how oddly familiar he looked – *like Papa when he was young* – and in the next breath she recognized him. She picked up her skirts in one hand, heedless of the mud of Congress Avenue and hurried across, crying breathlessly, "Carl! Carl! Where have you been, all this time! Why did you never write to us?"

Her stays pinched her sides, and the lump of the child underneath her heart cramped her breathing; by the time she gained the other side of the street, she could only gasp. She drank in the sight of her brother with greedy eyes, realizing with a shock that he had grown even taller, had filled out across the shoulders. There was nothing left of the boy he had been, save about the eyes, calm and as blue as the sky behind his head. He held a pile of new clothing under one arm, and was fiddling with the reins of his horse with the other hand.

"Hullo, M'grete," he answered, and half-shrugged. "Couldn't think of anything to say at first. Then I just sort of forgot."

"Forgot!" Margaret cried, indignantly. "We were so worried, never knowing if you were safe, where you were! What were you thinking?"

"Guess I wasn't." He looked briefly regretful. "You shouldn't have worried, M'grete. The fellows and I look out for each other, pretty much."

"You should have known that I would worry, little brother." Margaret realized abruptly that they had been speaking English to each other, as if the childhood language of German was something they had long since left behind. She put her arms around him, heedless of the basket on her arm, or the pile of clothes in his, feeling a new sense of shock that he had grown so tall. This was not like taking one of her sons into her arms. This was like embracing her husband; a man, rather than a child. "You must come home with me this instant," she whispered in German. "I won't have it any other way – and where else would you go?" She stepped back, as he half-shrugged in reluctance.

"Oh, me and the fellows would stay someplace," he ventured. "I said we look after each other."

"Then your special friends should come with you," Margaret commanded. "I keep a boardinghouse now, so there would be room," and when he still looked as if he would hesitate, she added in her sternest tone, "Carl, Mama would not have it that you would pass by and never set foot under our roof."

"Papa wouldn't give a pigs arse if I did or not," her brother answered, in a tone so flat that all the emotion had been squeezed out of it like water wrung out of a piece of laundering. "Assuming the old bast – the old man is still alive."

"So he is," Margaret retorted. "But Papa does not command my household, and he does not speak for Race and I." She reached up and cupped her brother's cheek in her hand – yet another moment of astonishment, feeling the prickle of his beard stubble against her palm. "And we want you to come home, little brother – this very instant. Bring your horse, and your fine fellows but most of all, bring yourself. We have missed you, very much. And," she looked at him with a sharper eye. "Whatever happened to your shirt, Carl? It looks like it was used to put out a fire."

"It was," her brother answered, diffidently. "Well, in a way. I fell into a campfire."

"Clumsy of you, little brother – falling into your own campfire."

"Not ours. Some Penateka raiders had a little camp in a little draw, away out beyond the San Saba, out in the Llano country. I was scouting them out from the top of the bluff and the edge of it gave way underneath me."

"I imagine they were surprised," Margaret observed, after a moment.

"They were," her brother agreed, with a cheerful expression on his face. "And then they were dead. Good luck for me, I didn't lose hold on Jack's carbine in the fall or my knife."

"That was indeed fortunate, little brother," Margaret replied, dryly. "So. Gather your friends, tell them where to go and give them my invitation. I will wait out here and walk with you, then."

"Not letting me out of your sight, then?" Carl looked very amused.

"Of course not," Margaret agreed. "I know you all too well."

They walked together, mostly in companionable silence, with Carl trailing his horse after them and carrying his new clothes in a flour sack over his shoulder.

"Waterloo is very much changed," Margaret observed once. "I'd think you would scarce recognize it, after having been away all this time."

"It's a town now," Carl shrugged. "And towns are all alike. Just in different ways. Same businesses, same buildings. Same stink of privies and wood smoke, same mud, same places to get drunk a bit. Maybe different roofs on them. Tile or shingles. Different language in the streets, different music. That's all."

"You sound like you prefer the wilderness better," Margaret observed. "Out there, like a wild Indian."

"I do so," her brother answered, his blue eyes unreadable. "It's harsh, but fair. Live or die, win or lose. It's uncomplicated."

"I see." Margaret thought on it for a moment. "I think you have spent too much time out there, little brother. And besides, you need your hair cut and maybe remember what it is to be a civilized man."

"A civilized man?" his voice shocked her, with the depth of bitterness in it. "Papa would call himself civilized. General Santa Anna, and his gold-braid officers, they called themselves civilized, too. And they told us lies, as they led us all away to be lined up and slaughtered. Me, I think I prefer the Comanche. They don't pretend to be anything other than what they are, not just when the occasion suits and everyone is looking at them."

"Then let someone like Race recall it to you," Margaret answered, after a moment. She looked sideways at his face. "He carries honor and gentility within him, no matter where he is or whatever the circumstances, even out here in the wilderness."

"So he does," her brother laughed. Seemingly the bitterness was only momentary. "He brought Boston with him, didn't he, Margaret? All that book-learning and fine manners; Race Vining would be a gentleman wrapped in a buffalo robe in the middle of the Llano. Jack reminds me of him."

"Jack?" Margaret queried gently. That was the second time that name was mentioned. "I do not know that name – do we know of him? Is he one of your comrades in Captain Hardeman's company?"

"No," Carl shook his head. "We were enlisted together in Deef Smith's company first. He's from Tennessee. His right moniker is John Hays. You'd like him, Margaret. He talks so soft and looks so young, everyone takes him for a harmless boy; but he fights like the devil, and he has the devil's own luck. I'm proud to call him my friend."

"You should bring him to stay with us," Margaret replied, but her brother shook his head.

"No, he's left the company. They made him the district surveyor for Bexar and he is already gone." Margaret looked sideways at her brother, again feeling that sense of disjointedness that she also must look up. He spoke with affection of this Jack whose name was really John Hays, and she wondered if he would soon be following this friend of his to Bexar. She thought with a sudden acute memory of the fight over the little cannon at Gonzales, and of how the news of General Cos' advancing army flew around to all of the American settlements. Papa had told them how Rudi was all for haring off towards the excitement in Bexar. Carl now had the same longing to follow after; Margaret hoped that if it were so, that this Jack Hays might have better sense – and he might do a better job of looking after her little brother than Rudi had managed to do. Then she thought of the ragged Rangers and their dusty horses, hung with rifle scabbards and fresh from another long scout into the Llano, and admitted – *probably not.* But at the very least, Carl had three years of that adventurous experience under his belt, and looked to have thrived upon it, no matter how ragged his clothes were. Perhaps this Jack Hays was better able to guard himself and her brother and his fellows when they ventured into harm's way, out beyond the frontier, into the endless rolling grasslands of the Llano country.

They began to climb the path up the last hill below the house, Margaret puffing slightly from the pressure of her stays and the bulge of the child below her ribs. Without a pause in his stride, her brother switched the flour sack to his other shoulder and set his arm around her waist. He felt solid, like a tree trunk. Such a comfort to lean on strength, Margaret thought, involuntarily. How wonderful if Carl would decide to stay home for this while. She needed him, this was his home. Papa was old and tired, Race was ill and tired – and the boys would not be grown for years.

"How long are you intending to stay?" she asked, and regretted that she sounded the least bit plaintive.

"Not long," her brother answered, and smiled at her with that particular sweetness that had ever been a part of him. "Long enough to congratulate Race, at least. Do Horace and Johnny want a brother, or would the two of you prefer a daughter?"

"I hope for a girl, as they have already a small brother." Margaret sounded breathless, even to herself. "Jamie – we named him Jamie, as you would know if you came home oftener."

"Home," Carl echoed, as they came to the top of the footpath. "Is it? You tell me it is a boardinghouse now, rooms for all. It's bigger than it used to be, that I can see." At that very moment, they crossed between the rows of apple trees, those trees which had been particularly bountiful this last harvest. The branches had drooped under the weight of apples, apples russet or yellow, or pippins the color of the pale green-glass beads that the Indians loved so dearly. Here was the vegetable garden, with the turned soil brown and rich with all the well-rotted stable muck dug into it. And there stood Papa, glowering at them both from under the brim of his planter hat, droplets of perspiration rolling down his countenance. For a frozen moment, he and Carl just stood stock still and staring at each other. Before Margaret could catch her breath and say a word, Papa took off his hat and swiped his shirt-sleeve over his forehead.

"About time you came back," he growled. "Put the damned horse away in the stable and get to work. The boys have gone for lessons and the muck doesn't dig itself in."

"It'll have to, today," Carl answered, mildly.

"Not if you want to eat a meal under my roof, you insolent young pup!" Alois Becker gripped the hoe handle as if he held a club, and he glared angrily at his younger son. Margaret held her breath. Carl had never openly defied Papa. Even after he came back after Goliad, he had done as Papa ordered, obeyed every time, as he was bid to do this or that, to cut hay, or harrow the cornfield. She had something of that old standing-aside feeling, the same feeling that she did as a child when she watched Mama and Papa; that they were not kin of hers but she was a stranger, and seeing them as such. She saw that Papa was old, his face gouged with the deep lines that care and hard labor out-of-doors had put there. He reminded her still of a golden lion, but gone shabby and with failing strength, and for that she pitied him; Papa had never been a bad man. Papa was blunt, and said what he thought, never considering how it sounded to people. Or how it might hurt them, terribly, which Margaret thought must be the worst of Papa's tragedies.

"Papa, he will eat with the boarders," Margaret looked between them. "He is just home from the Llano, of course he will eat under our roof." Carl had taken his supporting arm from around Margaret; standing now a little aside, she saw how very alike they were; the same height, the same broad fair features, but Carl was young. He was a lion as well, but strong and tempered by three years as a Ranger, and his expression was unreadable.

"I'll eat outside, and unroll my blankets under the apple trees. Is the stable still where it always was?" Carl's voice was mild, perfectly level. Without another word he nodded courteously towards Margaret and walked away towards the corner of the house, leaving her feeling as if she had just fallen from a height and had the breath knocked out of her.

"You should not have said that, Papa," she chided him, with a soft voice, as Mama had so often done. "He has just come home, we have not heard a word from him in three years, and this is the welcome you give your only son?"

"Would that it was his brother!" Alois raged, with both his hands white-knuckled, as they gripped the hoe-handle. "Did it not impugn your mother to think so, I would doubt that he was of my begetting at all!"

"Papa!" Margaret was shocked, shocked into speaking what she had often thought but never voiced. "How could you even think such a wicked thing as that? He has always been a good son to you, and loyal and obedient! He looked to you always for affection and respect, even as you spurned him in order to make much of Rudi! And that was from his very earliest childhood – you were not fair with him, Papa, you never had a kind word!"

"Fair!" her father's face reddened with anger. "Fair? What in this world is fair, hey? Prattle to me of fairness, after I have buried a true son and a loving wife! The world has taken away all I cared for most and left me with a whey-faced simpering fool and a useless, cowardly idiot of a boy and now you would bid me be kind to that – that –" His lips twisted, as if there was no word vile enough that be could bring himself to say, before Margaret. "The devil take that!" he finally spat, and turning with the hoe gripped in both hands, he stumbled away from Margaret towards the stand of apple trees. Margaret watched him go; his shoulders were shaking, as if he was racked with grief, and she supposed he was, at that. Papa's words had long since lost the power to hurt her in any way – and now it seemed that they had also lost much of their power to affect her little brother as well. *Poor Papa*, she thought, as she crossed the yard to the back of the house, *to be so wrecked with grief over Rudi and Mama that he had no consideration for those children left to him.* In the very deepest recesses of her own heart, Margaret knew that she would long outlive Race – and knew also that she would grieve long. But she would not be destroyed by it, that grief would not poison her life. And she was struck by a flash of perception, as she climbed the back steps; Papa was such a proud man. He would never come to acknowledge that he had treated his younger son so unfairly, never admit his own guilt. *Poor Papa*, she thought to herself, *trapped in the very pit that he had dug for himself.*

"My brother has returned," she said to Hetty, through the open doorway. "I have told you of my younger brother, who went with Colonel Smith's Ranger company? He will dine with us tonight."

"Mother Mary and Joseph," Hetty dusted off her floury hands on her apron, "and will he be remaining long? And what does th' old Sir think of that, if I may be so bold to ask? He should be proud and pleased to have the lad home at last, I would say."

"No, I think not," Margaret answered, and Hetty's face went somber, as she looked at Margaret. Margaret had talked of her brothers to Hetty, of them as children, and how Rudi died among Fannin's men, of how his final act in life had been to save Carl. What else that Hetty had deduced from those reminiscences Margaret couldn't begin to guess.

"Oh, but I do see the way of it, Marm," she answered, with surprising shrewdness. "Like two toms in a sack, or old Master D'Arcy up at the Hall when Mam was a girl; two sons he had, couldn't do enough for the older and finally the youngest jined John Company's Army and went off to India. And when the older lad died of the typhoid when he was on his way to Dublin to buy a horse, Master D'Arcy must swallow his pride and write to the younger and ask for his return. He didn't come back, o'course, or so my Mam told the tale – he was happy enough where he was, not that any blamed him. Old D'Arcy was bitter and proud and ate his supper in grand style, wi' a pair of footman at the back of his chair even when it was just himself alone wi' his dogs. The younger boy married a Raja's daughter, if ye can believe that, and built a palace along the Hoogly with a hundred rooms. That's the river at Bombay, y'see, or perhaps Calcutta. Anyway, Marm," Hetty added, with another dusting of her hands, "you and the young Sir and the boys will be happy enough, and it's not like your brother married a Comanche princess –

there'll be nothing to keep him away from home, then. Will there, Marm?"

"No," Margaret answered, after divining the sympathy and the meaning behind Hetty's spate of words. "But nothing much to keep him here, I'm afraid."

"What a pity, then, Marm," Hetty said and patted Margaret's shoulder, comfortingly. "I shall set another place, for sure and shall he be sleeping in the boarder's quarters?"

"No, I think we should put a pallet on the floor of the boy's room for him," Margaret answered. She went to tell Race and the boys that Carl had finally returned, finding Race sitting with Jamie in his lap, reading the *Iliad* to the older boys while Jamie slept. Waving shadows from the afternoon sun shining through the branches outside wove a moving tapestry on the scrubbed pine floor. Margaret paused in the doorway, drinking in the sight of that domestic contentment, taking fierce satisfaction in knowing that through her work she had made it possible; these clean, white-washed walls, un-smudged with smoke from an open fire, the tall windows with glass in them, not scraped gut or oiled paper, the comfortable furniture – frontier make, of rough wood and padded with leather – but comfortable none the less. The room was sparingly ornamented with those few cherished bits of china or glass from the East, Race's bookshelves filled with his beloved volumes, the rag rug that she had braided herself, of scraps dyed with indigo in shades of blue, and best of all it sheltered her husband and her children.

At that moment, Race looked up from the *Iliad* and observed, "Daisy-mine, you are early returned. I thought you would be hours, among the delights offered among the emporia of our sweet little metropolis."

"Carl has come home," she answered. "I doubt that he will stay for long."

"Ah," Race looked thoughtful. "I would not, were I him and knowing your fathers' nature. So does Father Becker know of the prodigal's return?"

"Yes. He took his horse to the stable, after he had words with Papa."

Race whistled, softly, "I can imagine his temper, Daisy-mine. And what Father Becker said in return. Go – you two, go to the stable and help welcome your uncle home. After a talking-to by your grandfather, your uncle will be glad of soft words and a warmer welcome. Go, now."

"Yes, go on," Margaret added her encouragement, as Horace and Johnny scrambled down from where they sat on either side of their father on the day-bed. She stood a little aside as they raced each other out of the parlor doorway, and came to sit on the side of the daybed. She reached out and gently tousled Jamie's head – such soft curls, as fine and delicate as a chick's down, and then Race captured her hand.

"So," Race ventured at last, "the worm finally turns. The things that Father Becker had to say when Carl returned to the land of the living; were as cruel as anything I'd expect to hear from my worst enemy. That I might come to have such words for young Jamie . . ." Race shook his head. "It passes belief, Daisy-mine. He was never that harsh before, was he?"

"No, never," Margaret answered, "although he seemed more like to be indifferent. It was only when Carl returned alone from La Bahia that he became bitter, as if Papa took it as an insult to him, to the memory of Rudi, that Carl should be alive and Rudi dead."

"Daisy-mine, it has also come to me that Father Becker never recovered from his madness in the field at San Jacinto." Race looked thoughtful.

"You had never said that he was mad them, only that he fought like a man possessed," Margaret answered, and Race smiled briefly.

"So we did. There was a certainty to that fight, and most of us held on to possession of our senses, even in running forward. But Father Becker fought in a fury – like a berserker in a frenzy of rage, heedless of all around him save that enemy before him, and then the next, and the next after that. He was a glutton for the killing of Mexican soldiers." Race's eyes were suddenly haunted. "After we broke their line, Father Becker did not re-load his musket but used the butt of it like a club. His arms were wet to the shoulder with blood. The last was a boy, a drummer boy, maybe an ensign. Father Becker beat him down, like a man chopping down a tree, even as the lad was trying to surrender. We – Bo Lamar and I, we were shouting to him to leave off, but it was as if he didn't hear us. Not until the Mexican boy's head was as smashed as a pot run over by a wagon wheel. Father Becker dropped to his knees and began to howl, like a wolf. He could not speak sensibly, but he pointed at the hunting coat the Mexican boy had over his shirt and stock. It looked like one of ours, for the Mexicans do not affect such fashion – and the color and cut of the one Rudi wore. We knew that their poor soldiers often looted our slain of their clothing. I know not if it was truly Rudi's coat, but I think Father Becker believed so."

"Oh," Margaret said only, and clasped her hands around Race's fingers. "I had thought Papa's grief over Mama and Rudi had changed his temper so. I had not considered . . ." Childish voices came from outside the sunny parlor, and quiet footsteps attended by the patter of lighter and faster ones. Race looked from her face to the door, smiling in genuine welcome.

"You look well, lad – welcome home! I see that rangering agrees with you. And you should have many stories to tell the boys, then."

Carl had changed into the new clothes, Margaret saw – stiff and still in store-creases. He had not put off the moccasins or his belt with the sheathed hunting-knife, and he ducked his head coming through the door. There was a brief look of shock on his face, there and gone in a flash, so that Margaret almost thought she had not seen it. But her brother had ever been good at guarding his expression.

"Not all of them," he flashed a brief grin. "Some aren't fit for company. You look like a gentleman of leisure, Race!"

"I lift nothing heavier than a book," Race answered in the same tone. "The winters here have got to my poor old chest, at last. Some years later than the snows and cold of Boston would have gotten to it, or so Doctor Williamson avers. I am more content than I ever thought I could be, at any rate. Sit, and tell me of where you have been, and what you have seen?"

"I will leave you two gentlemen, then." Margaret arose, "I must attend to matters in the kitchen, since I am not a lady of leisure . . . no, don't rise for me, Race, you'll disturb Jamie."

As she went around the door, she heard her brother say, "This cub, and yet another on the way? You could give my sister a rest, now and again!"

"Mine own Marguerite manages it all very well," she heard Race say, imperturbably; this amused her, as it provided evidence of the old teasing affection between the two. In hallway, she paused to look out of the door that gave onto the garden. Yes, Papa had returned to digging in the muck, his back towards the house. It came to Margaret that he looked bent, old and diminished, and again she felt that flash of sympathy, as well as the sure knowledge that there was no way that Papa might ever find comfort. He would never reconcile with his younger son, or accept that Rudi and Mama had been so cruelly taken from him – and there was nothing that Margaret could do or say. Papa was just there, like the disintegrating stump of the biggest post oak tree, the one that Papa and Rudi had felled to make one of the sill-beams for their house. The stump defied removal, being too large to dig out. It still sat at the end of the row of apple trees; something to be walked around, now and again – but otherwise an object of no particular importance.

"Hetty," Margaret called into the kitchen. "Have you begun the pies for supper? If you have not already, then I will start them. My brothers were always very fond of apple pie. Carl will try to eat a whole one himself, I think."

Chapter 22 – *The Head of Her Household*

From where she sat at the head of the table, Margaret surveyed her household at supper with considerable satisfaction; a table of plain and sturdy make, spread with a cloth of unbleached homespun, and set with ordinary tin tableware and simple pottery plates – but she took pride in everything being was as clean as could be, and the serving dishes overflowed. The dining room had once been half of the front porch, now walled in as the back had been, creating a pleasant room with tall, airy windows, and plaster covering the logs and planks that had formed the walls. Her supper table was much changed, and sometimes she thought of that simpler table and familial company with regret. The boys, with Hetty and Morag and Papa, had eaten supper in the kitchen – Papa because he cared nothing for the company, the boys because they were bound early for bed, and Hetty and Morag because they must serve supper while Margaret and Race presided over the table.

With Hetty's help, she set an enviable table, a bounty of good things – a succulent dish of smoked ham, cut into generous pink slices and spiced with coarse brown sugar and whole cloves, squash baked to tender softness, whole potatoes boiled with onion, cabbage spiced with pepper, butter, and tiny slips of crisp smoked bacon, and an array of pickles and preserves – preserves to spread on Hetty's excellent biscuits, hot from the oven. Hetty was a genius with beaten biscuits. They were delicately flakey; the napkin-lined basket in which they resided on the table never failed to be taken away by a proudly smiling Morag empty of everything but a few forlorn crumbs. Margaret observed with a sharpened eye towards the quality of her hospitality, for so much depended upon that! At times, she thought she walked upon a knife-edge, depending upon the satisfaction of boarding gentlemen who might very easily go anywhere else – and whose bad report of her establishment might well spell disaster to her enterprise. Margaret paid careful attention to the conversation at table, and in the old log-walled parlor now set aside as the boarders' parlor. Her stock in trade was comfort, good cooking, cleanliness, and genteel conversation. She might ably control three of these qualities, but the fourth element commanded her rigorous attention.

Mr. Hattersley, the Englishman – who had, he said, come to Texas to start a newspaper, was deep in conversation with a gentleman from San Augustine, who also intended launching a newspaper; John Ford, he was called – he had come late to Texas but made up for lost time by serving in the army, and then settling in San Augustine as a doctor and when that palled, qualifying in law. It seemed that the practice of law was also proving tedious to John Ford.

Margaret liked him, for himself – for John Ford was tall and outspoken, with a head of hair as red as any Irishman, and passionate in his opinions. He had amusing, if slightly stomach-churning disputations with Dr. Williamson on matters medical. On those occasions, Margaret had been obliged to step in and turn the conversation back into more conventional and less painfully descriptive channels. But on this evening, Dr. Williamson was engaged in the perusal of a medical journal propped up against the vinegar cruet and a small bottle of jam, serenely oblivious to the conversation flowing all around.

It seemed that Mr. Hattersley – so urbane and cultured that Margaret sometimes felt like an unschooled child when conversing with him – now felt that enthusiasms were embarrassingly provincial things. He turned from Mr. Ford to speak with Race, at his customary seat at the other end of the table. Margaret took fond satisfaction from that: Her husband was assured of constant and stimulating company, of intelligent conversation on those topics of most interest to him. Such were the benefits of running a boardinghouse in the new capital city of Texas, a guarantee of a constant stream of interesting men and fascinating conversation for Race! And he was the equal to Mr. Hattersley in intellect and education, of that Margaret was certain, observing their comfortable conversation from the length of the table away.

Her eyes briefly rested on Carl, sitting at Race's elbow. He ate as if he had not sat down to a good meal since he left home, silent and efficient. He spoke a few words when questions were asked of him; his answers appeared to be dragged forth with the greatest reluctance, like a weed with a long taproot. Margaret could barely conceal her amusement. Hearing that Carl had just returned from beyond the Llano with Captain Hardeman's company, Mr. Hattersley left off wondering aloud when the author of *Sketches by Boz* would bring forth another book and turned his attention towards her brother.

"So you have been out beyond the San Saba River," Mr. Hattersley ventured. "Is not that where the Spaniards established a mission, in the expectations of taming the wild Indians – and inducing them to work in the vast silver mines they expected to find? 'Pon my soul, it's as much as a white man's life is worth to set foot in the place!" Carl's reply was an inarticulate mumble, as he helped himself to another biscuit.

"I understand the roving Comanche bands have made any establishment of authority beyond the Llano and San Saba all but an untenable proposition," Mr. Hattersley persisted. Carl had his mouth full. He merely shrugged, while Mr. Hattersley continued, "I trust that your government – those gentlemen of whom a fair representation is around this table – ensure that at the least you are well-armed and supplied for such daring incursions." That elicited another mumble from her brother, accompanied by a shrug, as Mr. Hattersley continued, "For your own self, sir, do you have a favorite weapon in these violent affrays, one which you have ever found most reliable?"

Carl swallowed his last mouthful of biscuit, finally making a reply which Margaret could hear at the other end of the table. "Yep – this one." He unsheathed the hunting knife that hung at his belt, the knife so comfortable to his hand, Margaret thought, that it must be a part of himself. He reversed the blade, and dropped it flat on the tabletop. It was a wicked long thing, brass-backed, with the curved point that Jim Bowie had made such a fashion, and a hilt of cow-horn smoothed and scored to provide a good grip – a knife that was all but a sword.

"That's what they call a real Arkansas toothpick!" John Ford exclaimed, slapping the tabletop in amused approval, while Mr. Hattersley regarded the knife with an expression which mixed fascination and disbelief.

"Good god, sir – what a weapon! I am amazed that the weight of such a trinket does not render it nearly impossible to use!"

Carl said clearly, "I use it easy enough. Last time – two months ago, in the country north of the Clear Fork. Three Comanche finished off clean, one got away. He left a blood trail that a blind man could follow." He took that deadly knife in one hand, and calmly carved off a large slab of apple pie with it, cleaning the crumbs of crust and fruit off the blade with the other and licking his fingers. "I didn't take their scalps 'r ears, though. Jack said that would be right uncivilized." He sheathed the knife while Margaret briefly closed her eyes. Race and John Ford were laughing; either in frank amusement at what Carl had said, or the expression of horror on Mr. Hattersley's face, as her brother went back to eating apple pie.

The evenings turned chill after the sun set in a smear of gold and orange cloud. Margaret had become accustomed to one last survey of her extended household, the last of her many duties before she withdrew to hers' and Race's room and prepared for bed. Horace was almost asleep, Jamie had been fast asleep for hours; only Johnny remained awake for her nighttime visit.

"You have said your prayers, then?" she whispered, as Johnny flung his arms around her neck in a drowsy embrace. The boys had a bed to sleep in now, rather than pallets on the floor. However, the pallet-bed she had Morag put out for her brother was unoccupied.

"Yes, Mama," Johnny answered, and closed his eyes as she tucked the quilts back around him. She dropped another kiss on Horace's forehead, lightly caressed Jamie's fair head – he was all but buried under the covers.

"Where is your uncle, then?" she asked; her son replied drowsily, "He's still downstairs, Mama."

Their room now boasted a dormer window, closed with shutters against the cold night air; light left the room with the candle in the tin holder that she carried in her hand. She could hear men's voices from downstairs; it sounded like John Ford's voice. She tapped on the other door at the top of the tiny landing, and Hetty answered from within. Opening the door, she saw that Morag sat on the bed they shared, both of them in nightgowns. Hetty ran a comb through Morag's long dark hair; she looked as sleepy as the children.

"Goodnight, then," she bade them. "Rest well, Morag – laundry in the morning." Morag made a face; Margaret and Hetty laughed companionably. Downstairs in the kitchen, Hetty had already laid out one end of the table for breakfast, the other with what she would need to begin preparing for it. Papa snored from behind the curtain drawn around his bed in the corner. He stubbornly refused to move into another room; Margaret often wondered if he resisted taking one of the new rooms – which she would have given him freely – out of a preference for the way his house used to be, or if he wished her enterprise to have one more room available. Most of the boarders had already retired for the evening, although Dr. Williamson still sat in the old parlor, deeply absorbed in his medical journal in the golden pool of light cast by the single lamp, while John Ford and Mr. Hattersley debated the question of the Cherokee – had Chief Bowls really plotted against the government of Texas with agents of Mexico, and if so, was the treatment of his tribe entirely justified? Margaret sighed a little; as she understood it, General Sam had been a friend to that tribe always, but Bo Lamar trusted them rather less.

"He has made enemies where only indifference existed before," Mr. Hattersley was saying, while John Ford stubbornly shook his head and insisted, "Conniving with the agents of Mexico, sir – that is unforgivable!"

"Excuse me, gentlemen," Margaret ventured, and both of them sprang at once to their feet, although Dr. Williamson remained engrossed in his reading, "I am about to bar the outside door – and have you seen my brother?"

"That young spark?" John Ford chuckled. "I do b'lieve, Miz Vining, he has gone to bed."

"Nay, for I saw him go outside," Mr. Hattersley added, and Margaret clicked her tongue in mild annoyance. She was about to bar the door from the inside for the night; although there was no need to fear Indian raids and brigands – not with so many in the house and the city itself nearby – she could not sleep knowing that the door was all but open during the hours of darkness.

She stepped from the front of the house, walking a little way into the dooryard, carrying the candle and sheltering it with her hand against the night breeze. The moon was up and nearly full; a pearly shape half-veiled by an edge of steel-colored clouds. Custom, and the passage of iron-edged wheels had established a wagon-drive around the side of the house towards the barn and outbuildings; she hesitated before venturing very far. Surely Carl could not have slipped away to town at this hour. She recalled how he had often taken a blanket and slept outside the house during those uncomfortable months following upon his return.

She hesitated; the great cypress tree that he and Rudi favored – was long gone, being on that part of property that Papa had sold, and having been cut down for lumber by the new owner. Just as she had decided to return to the house, she sensed a furtive moment from the deep shadows underneath the nearest apple tree, and heard a single brief metallic click. There was a darker shadow under the tree, a roll of blankets spread on the ground, and a man-shaped shadow topped with a mop of pale hair, leaning on one elbow. The candlelight trapped a gun-metal gray reflection, as her brother lowered the long-barreled pistol, which he had aimed at her, seeing only another faceless shadow against that small light from her candle, and that which leaked from the house windows behind her, and the pale moon overhead.

"Carl!" she exclaimed, "it's only me! Why are you out here when there is no need for it? We set a place for you in the boys' room. I told you that Papa does not command my household!"

"Sorry, M'grete," her brother answered, ruefully. "Your house it may be, but I can't belong."

"Don't be ridiculous, Carlchen, of course you belong here!" Margaret stooped under the lower branches, and a night-cooled twig stroked her cheek as she knelt clumsily, setting the tin candlestick on the ground beside where Carl had spread out his bedroll. Was this the tree she had sat under when she decided to use the management Papa's house for her needs and Race's? "Papa made it clear months ago – the governance of his house is in my hands; who eats at the table and sleeps in the rooms, the decision is entirely mine to make. You saw he did not eat at the table with us. Papa – I believe he has grown old. He has no real stomach for dictating the lives of his children. Let it go, Carlchen. Come inside. I had Morag make up another bed in the boy's room."

"It's not Papa, M'grete," Carl's voice in the darkness sounded infinitely sad, terribly adult. "It's me. I don't belong here any more. It's a civilized place, and I'm still . . . out there. The walls and the roof over my head choke me, M'grete. I can't breathe proper; the air inside smells different. I have to see the stars up there. I have to know that I'm not . . . I'm not cornered. I must have a way out, M'grete, or I can't sleep."

Margaret regarded her brother in the darkness, wondering where the confident, affectionate little boy that he had once been had gone away to. The Mexicans at Goliad had killed a part of Carl as efficiently as they had killed Rudi. Perhaps Papa's cruelty had done something of that killing. She remembered holding hands with her brothers as they fell asleep, on the night that Papa came back to San Felipe from Bexar and they were frightened of death because the Comanche had murdered Papa's hired man, and Rudi had seen all of that but the actual death. It was an ache in her heart, knowing that holding Carl's hand in the dark could not be of reassuring comfort any more.

"Well then," she answered, her voice as tender as if she had spoken to her sons, "sleep out here if you wish, Carlchen – but be careful about whom you aim that pistol at, if you are only half awake. You might kill one of my boarders and each one of them is money in the purse to me, besides being good friends to my husband. Are your warm enough? Do you wish another blanket, for it may be colder still in the morning?"

"No, M'grete. I am warm enough," he answered. By the sound of his voice she knew he was smiling. "That Englishman. I might take aim at him, just to put a fright in him. I wouldn't shoot him, really. He just talks too much."

"I think you have become too much of a wild Comanche Indian yourself," Margaret answered, as she got to her feet, feeling very much the weight of the baby. It put her off-balance. She must lean against the tree for support as she groped for the candle-holder. "Carlchen, what will you do with yourself now? Tomorrow and tomorrow, for all the days that you have of life?"

"I don't know," her brother replied thoughtfully. "But first I think I will go to Bexar. Jack – my friend that I spoke of – has asked me. He went to be surveyor for the district, but he talked of raising a company of Rangers. I'm very good at rangering, M'grete. Everyone speaks well of me – Hardeman promoted me to sergeant. And I have a good horse and a good rifle. Someday I might be able to live inside a house again. But not now; I need to breathe."

"As you wish it, little brother," Margaret pulled her shawl closer around her. "But promise me this one thing. When you leave again – come to us, to Race and I – and say 'goodbye.'"

"I will, M'grete."

"Promise, little brother. And tell us where you are going, and in whose company!"

"I will, M'grete," he said again, and Margaret sighed; perhaps he would come and tell them when he was away again, but she would not hold her breath on it. Carl had become a will-o'-the-wisp, accountable to no one but himself. She returned to the house, and bolted the door. She bid goodnight to the three men still in the boarder's parlor; in their own little room beyond, her husband sat up in bed, reading a book by the light of the last lamp. He looked up and smiled as she sat on the edge of the bed, and with an effort reached down to unlace her shoes.

"Mine own General Daisy, come from a last patrol of her command." Race smiled fondly. "I take it that all is well?" As ever, her own heart turned over in her breast at the sight of his smile. She had been so afraid for him, afraid for their own future, afraid of what would happen to the boys if Race died of the consumption and she was left widowed and alone. Now there was a space to breathe; she had that in common with Carl – wanting room to breathe free in a sphere where she had confidence in her own control.

She flashed a returning smile at her husband. "You may," she answered, and turned to shedding her stockings. With a sigh, she pressed her hands to the small of her back, for there was an ache there. Suddenly she was very tired, a weariness that went straight to her bones and sapped every scrap of energy. She felt that she barely had the strength to take off her dress and take her nightgown from the hook beside the bed. She sat on the bed with it in her hands. "I have barred the door for the night, dearest. Carl has chosen to sleep outside, under a tree . . . again. Dr. Williamson cannot be distracted from his book. Mr. Ford and Mr. Hattersley are going at it in the parlor. It sounds as if they will be talking for hours. They never tire of politics, which makes it very wearisome for all. Oh dear, what a long day. And it's laundry day tomorrow. Just recalling that makes me tired!"

"Shush, then, dearest General Daisy." Race set aside his book. "You spent too much of your strength today. Shush." he laid his fingers on her lips. "Not another word. Here, let me loosen your laces. Is that better, now?"

"Oh, yes," Margaret drew a deep breath into her lungs, and laughed as the baby inside of her kicked as if turning to stretch, to press tiny knees or elbows against the soft container of her body. She drew her nightgown on, and Race lifted the bedclothes so that she could slide her clumsy self in between them "Oh, she has the fidgets tonight! Please little Marie, let me sleep, babykins. I promise not to walk so far tomorrow."

"She?" Race pulled her into his arms, curled with her back to him, spoon-fashion, as his hands gently sought out and caressed the shape of the child within her belly. "Very strong and emphatic for a daughter, Daisy-mine. I think another son, a strong-willed stubborn one like Jamie."

290

Margaret groaned; this was a discussion revived with each child since Johnny. She wished for a daughter, hoped each confinement would reward her with one. Race proclaimed himself extravagantly content with sons and took every indication – that she carried high or low, that the child was active in her womb or quiescent – as proof positive that she would bear yet another.

"Sleep baby, sleep," she sang softly, and closed her hands over Race's gentle ones. "Your father is watching the sheep . . . your mother is shaking the little tree, sweet dreams to fall down upon you and me . . ."

"Sweet dreams indeed, mine own Daisy," Race whispered, "Sleep now, and rest as long as you wish. Peter will be slumbering in a very short time."

"Marie," Margaret yawned. "The baby is Marie."

"Peter," Race insisted, his arms cradling her close. "Peter – for my cousin who fought with Washington, God rest him." Margaret would have disputed for a little longer, but she was so tired; a great wave of sleep washed over her and pulled her down into its depths. The last she was aware of was her husband gently stroking her belly and telling Peter to go to sleep.

Her husband was right – the baby was another son, born a month and three weeks later, as the first blue norther of winter lashed the roof with torrents of rain, and leaden skies pressed as close as a pot lid. The labor went as easily for Margaret as it usually did; attended by Hetty, with Dr. Williamson looking in, peering vaguely over his spectacles. This time, she might take a little more rest, for Hetty had rule of the kitchen and Morag of the household labor that once had fallen entirely to Margaret. She could hold the new child to her, admiring at leisure the perfect little fingers and toes, on hands and feet which seemed two sizes larger than the rest of him. Peter had the promise of being another like Jamie, the promise of height and Saxon-fair hair. Margaret so wished that Carl might have remained longer but he had gone to Bexar within days. He had come to bid them farewell this time, with which Margaret must be content. She had extracted a promise from him to write now and again.

"I would not want to hold my head underwater until he does," she had observed to Race, who laughed and shook his head. They were in the parlor, Margaret resting on the daybed with baby Peter in the cradle at her side.

"He has the wanderlust in him, Daisy-mine, as did I at his age. I had the excuse of my weak chest to indulge my taste for travel – though some thought I should have settled down. It took me several years to tire of it for good and all . . . your brother, though. He may acclimate himself to living within four walls again, but I don't think he will ever willingly settle in a city or town. And if there is one thing that Texas has more of, it is wilderness as compared to town. I am content with what I have now, Daisy-mine. I am sure that Carl will come to domesticity eventually and hold it in the same affection as I. We have been married for . . . how long now?"

"Ten years," Margaret answered, "going on eleven." As she said that, a cold prickling feeling ran down her spine, a feeling that she was watching the last few grains of sand pour from the glass. Ten years and one of happiness with her husband – that is what the witch-woman had promised on her twelfth birthday. Those years, weeks and days – were all but spent. Over that time, she had schooled herself to not think of the matter. She told herself once again that Race had recovered; with Dr. Williamson's care and the shelter and income from Papa's house under her rule he would continue to improve. His affection was a constant upon which she depended; she could not bear the thought of having it withdrawn from her by death or distance.

"What is the matter, Daisy-mine?" Race asked with sudden concern, for he was sensitive to her expressions and conversation.

"Nothing," she answered. "Iis just past time to nurse the baby." She pressed her hands to her breasts, which did truly ache, for they were full and being so always pained her.

Winter passed, and spring came on; the rains were soft, not icy cold as in winter. The river ran high in spring flood, swelling past the cypress-lined banks, Just as Margaret felt she could not endure another grey and dreary day of dripping skies and mud, the clouds parted, dissolving into scatterings of pure white. Papa's apple trees burst into their own pure clouds of blossom. Margaret had a letter from Carl – only a few lines saying that he was in Captain Hays' company of Rangers in Bexar, he was well, and he could be reached with a message sent to Lawyer Maverick's house in the Plaza Mayor. Margaret cherished this brief missive not for any literary qualities, but as a promise that Carl showed some inkling of mature responsibility when it came to upholding the ties of family – and that he had not entirely forgotten his letters. Margaret passed off her recollection of the witch-woman's prophecy as a queer fancy as spring came on, for Race's health improved with the return of warm weather. The witch-woman had been wrong, she thought. It was only a strange fancy, although it had given her comfort now and again. But it was only a fancy. The company of his sons and the addition of baby Peter to their number made a tonic better than anything Dr. Williamson could have devised. As she went about her duties – the cooking and preparation of dainties for the table, overseeing the care of the boarder's rooms – those fears sank conveniently to the back of her memory, assisted by the very number of her household duties and obligations. Until on a clear spring afternoon a she was reminded of them again, as a thunderbolt striking from a clear blue sky.

Horace and Johnny had their lessons with their father on that afternoon. Margaret nursed the baby, while Jamie played quietly on the floor with a dozen corn-doll soldiers that Morag had made to amuse him, dressing them in scraps of dark cloth, and folding little cocked hats for them out of stiff paper. When Peter had his fill, she would have to go to the kitchen and assist Morag with supper, so Margaret relished these few moments with her husband and the boys. It had amused Margaret very much to see her son playing with his soldiers, pretending to drill them, and assigning them daring missions. Jamie's play-war today involved taking books from the bottommost shelves to build a fortified enemy castle and sending his little army to storm the gate and blow it all up.

"Jamie, be careful with Papa's books!" Margaret chided him, as her son toppled the tallest book-tower with a happy shout and several volumes fell to the floor with their covers spread wide and their pages bent. Peter was nearly done with his nursing; Margaret took him from her breast, closed the front of her shift and her dress, and hastily held him up to her shoulder to burp. In the meantime, Jamie had gleefully sent another book-tower crashing. This would not do, although Race had barely glanced up from where he sat with the older boys at the parlor table. Margaret put Peter in the cradle, and knelt to begin rescuing books from the floor and careless childish hands. He had so many more books now, she thought, with deep satisfaction – books brought from the East when he had been Bo Lamar's emissary, books that he had from friends since his return, so many books that the newest were unfamiliar to her. Because of her business, she had not the time to explore them as she once had done. She picked up one, two, three books, carefully straightening their pages, and restoring them to the bookshelf, but the fourth one fell open in her hands as she took it from the floor – a calf-leather duodecimo of Lovelaces's poems, one of those brought back from Boston on his last visit. Race was very fond of Lovelace's verses, she recollected, though to her mind most of them were trifles, meant to flatter men and women long-dead and little known. Idly, she turned to the flyleaf before replacing it with the others; someone had inscribed it. She read the words written there in a woman's elegant hand, read them three times over, as her breath and blood seemed to freeze within her.

For my dear husband Horace at Christmas, a gift from your loving wife, Annabelle Saltinstall Vining, Boston, December 1837.

She did not cry out – she could not move, for it seemed as if the very world had shattered around her. Her thoughts scrambled like mad, frantic things. Christmas – three years ago, when Race had returned to the East. He spent a Christmas with his family in Boston – he had written a letter about it. *Loving wife, Annabelle Saltinstall Vining* – but was not she his loving wife, for these last eleven years? Who was this woman, giving books with fond inscriptions in them to her dear husband Horace? She closed the book with trembling fingers. Another Horace, also with a loving wife – but why would her own husband possess a volume intended for another?

Now she knew how Carl must have felt that day in the parlor when Mr. Vanderpole took his leave and Papa said those thoughtless, cruel words ' . . . *you should have known Rudolph, my oldest son. He was such a promising boy, worth three of this one . . .*' He appeared as if he had been struck a blow so hard that he was beyond feeling pain, and now Margaret knew that beyond-pain feeling as well. In the daze of her own agony and bewilderment, she was hardly now aware of anything within the little parlor but herself and the book in her hand, the book that spelled the end . . . the end of everything. She knew as surely as she knew anything, that whatever explanation, whatever rationale and reason Race had for that damning inscription that her unthinking trust in him – and the assurance she had in her own judgment – had been slaughtered in a moment. Nothing between them would ever be the same.

"Daisy-mine?" Now his voice echoed hollowly in her ears. "Daisy, what is the matter? You look as if you had seen a ghost."

She forced herself to turn and look at him, feeling as if she was looking at a stranger from an impossible distance. *How very well he does that*, she thought, *such a convincing pretense of concern. We were all fooled – all of us, my family, my friends, and I.* She held out the book wordlessly, and in turn his own countenance went deathly pale as horrified realization flooded in upon him. And there went her last frail hope that the book belonged truly to another named Horace. It was his, a volume of one of his favorite poets – the book could belong to no other.

"Boys . . . lessons are over for today. Take Jamie outside for a little while and see if your grandfather wants help with the chores." Both Horace and Johnny's faces fell, at those words, but they gathered up Jamie's corn-shuck soldiers and departed the small parlor – although Margaret could see clearly from the windows that they did not seek out their grandfather but instead went to play under the apple trees. A harsh silence fell in the room, broken only by the voice of Hetty in the kitchen, telling Morag to pour the cream off the milk pans which had been sitting all morning, and churn a fresh making of butter for supper. Feeling as if she were in a dreadful dream, Margaret laid the book on the table in front of Race and went to close the door. She could not bear any longer to look at his face. Bright motes of dust floated and swirled in the light, slanting in through the glass window.

"Who is she?" she asked at last. Her voice in her own ears sounded calm, proud and even. "Annabelle Saltinstall . . . who claims your name . . . is she indeed your wife?" Race met her gaze firmly, although a hectic flush rose in his face.

"She is," he answered. "And has been so legally and in the eyes of society, ever since we married in the summer of 1822. Our mothers were related . . . third cousins, I think, as well as being girlhood friends. It was expected. We had known each other since dame-school days, I think. She is . . . a very fine woman. I would feel very considerable fondness for her on that account. I am sorry, Daisy-mine. I did not know that she had inscribed that book. I received it from her on my last visit to Boston, and never glanced at it again."

"You married her." Margaret felt as if she would vomit, saying those words, wondering how he could justify what he had done with such a lack of shame or remorse, "Feeling such fondness towards her, as you say. And then you married me, saying nothing to me or to my father of previously engaged affections. Do you have anything in you of honor, or respect for womanhood . . . or towards me, to whom you have professed such words of love? I have been your loving wife for eleven years. I have borne you four sons, kept your household, and seen to your interests for that long, nursed you in sickness, rejoiced with you in health, shared your bed, been otherwise faithful in all things to you and you alone above all other men. Yet it seems that I have been mistaken in this. I have done all of this under false pretenses – I have loved you and only you, while you were the lawful wedded husband of another woman – and she still living! Is there anything you can give me as a reason, any justification you can make for the insult of having made me . . . into a concubine, in the disguise of honorable marriage?" Her throat hurt, she burned with a white-hot rage, seeing that he flinched at every one of her words, as though a bullet went home. "And our sons – by this you have made them into bastards, brought about all of our ruin!" In a tiny corner of her mind, she marveled at how angry she was that she would use such a word, a word that men used when they spoke to each other in contempt or anger, but should never pass the lips of a genteel woman. "What did you think would happen? That I – and they would never find out?"

"Yes," Race answered quietly. He met her gaze directly. "I did think so. Forgive me, Daisy – I did but think that you and the boys need never know. She – Annabelle, that is – would never leave Boston. And my home has been in Texas. I thought . . ."

"You did not think!" Margaret cried. "You did not think at all! Other men have left wives to come west, but they had the decency to divorce them before making another life for themselves and taking another woman to their bed! Shall I name them? General Sam, for one, Colonel Bowie for another, and god knows how many other lesser men – are you no better than they?"

"I could not divorce her," Race answered again, still oddly calm in the face of Margaret's fury. "Although I did not love her as a husband. I have known that for years, Daisy-mine. But she has been a friend to me since childhood and her family is very old and important. I could not inflict the shame of a divorce upon her or our daughter."

"You daughter?" Margaret whispered; sour bile rushed into the back of her mouth. "You . . . have . . . a daughter. A daughter with your wife in Boston?" Now she felt as if she really would vomit; she pressed her fingers to her lips. They felt icy, like lumps of ice.

"Her name is Sophie." Race met her eyes, and it seemed that his face softened at the mention of her. "She is just nineteen now. She married last year, to the heir of a fine old Boston family. The scandal of a divorce would have killed all of her hopes, her hopes of a good marriage and a happy life. I couldn't bear to do that, so help me God, Daisy-mine."

"And of our hopes?" Margaret whispered. "And of my life, and our sons? Am I a person less vulnerable to scandal, and is the future of our boys of less value? What consideration do we have in your eyes – any at all, husband? Or have I been a camp-follower all this time, a draggle-taggle gypsy with a pack of brats, following after a man who throws her some money now and again?"

"Daisy-mine!" Race sprang out of his chair at last, his composure finally breached by those stinging words. "No – I swear to you, no. Do not think such an ugly thing of yourself or of me! I can explain myself, you must understand!" He made as if to take her hands, pull her into an embrace, but she stepped back, striking his hand away from her.

"Don't you dare touch me!" she cried, "Don't you dare." She pulled away, her hands balled into fists. She wanted at once to strike him . . . and then at once, she wanted away. Just away. "I must think," she said, schooling herself to calm. "I must go and think. Do not follow me." She darted past him, yanked open the door to the little parlor. Her bonnet and shawl hung from a peg in the entryway – she snatched them up as she fled from the house, past Hetty gaping in the kitchen doorway with her hands covered in flour. She thought that Race called after her once, as she ran.

Chapter 23 – *A Life Apart*

Margaret ran as if pursued by wild Indians, ran until her heart pounded wildly and her corsets pinched her ribs and left her breathless, hardly knowing where she ran until she stumbled and fell awkwardly to her knees. Her bonnet fell back, held only by its ribbons around her throat. She heard something in her garments tear, as she scrambled to her feet again. She was unaware that she was weeping, until she felt the wetness of tears on her face; was there a place to reach, if she could only run fast enough, far enough to escape the pain of betrayal – a betrayal which pierced her like a spear though the heart?

She leaned herself against the trunk of a tree, gasping. She had come down through Papa's property and a good way along the track which led along the river, once a deer path and a hunting trail for Joseph Harrell and her brothers – now printed with iron wheels and the hoofs of horses until it had become a fairly presentable road, meandering along the side of the Colorado. The river flowed as smooth as mirror-glass, upstream from the ford. The city was at her back, as was Papa's house; all Margaret knew was that she did not want to be seen, or to look at people, not now – not strangers or friends – and most of all, not at the face of that man she had thought of as her husband until a bare quarter-hour ago. She wanted to be alone and to think. Surely someone might see her if she remained on the track. Ahead of her, distant and around the bend, she heard a horse neigh and the faint musical jingle of bridle-chain or a rider's spurs. Someone ahead of her on the river-trace, and there might yet be someone following after, she thought, with a rising sense of panic. She gathered her shawl around her, casting around frantically for a refuge; the riverbank, a gentle slope where an irregular line of cypress trees dipped their knobby knees into the water. The other way was too steep, and thickly strewn with brambly thickets. In a moment the horseman ahead would be in sight, in sight of her. Margaret fled towards the river, wading up to her shoe-tops in new green grass and old river-drift. Her trailing shawl caught on a broken branch, jerking it off her shoulders and out of her hands with the speed of her passage. With a sob she turned, and wrenched it free of the branch – oh, she would be a fright to see, but Margaret cared nothing save for being out of sight, at the river's edge and screened by a sheltering cypress tree.

The riverbank was a tumble of stones, of hard-packed earth anchored by cypress-roots and trunks, some which had been dislodged and pulled to ground level in floodwaters decades past. Beyond was the water – no farther then. Margaret sank onto the nearest branch; surely she was out of sight here; her dress was green and her shawl of a woolen plaid, in soft colors – greens and grays and browns; surely no one would notice her, if she remained quiet and still. Here at the river, quiet and still – she would look at the river and think. Think about what had happened, what Race had done, what would happen now . . . and how she should speak of it to him and to others . . . and how she must feel. Margaret dropped her face into her hands and began to weep, silently. What was to be done, when a whole fissure ran through your world, across your life, seeming to destroy it utterly? Where to begin, in making things whole again – if they could ever be made whole? This was worse than the burning of Gonzales and Mama dying in the runaway scrape, worse than Papa refusing to pay a doctor. She wept, her tears dropping onto the skirt of her dress, oblivious of anything beyond her own hurt.

Just when she thought there were no more tears to be had, that she was as empty of them as a hollow gourd, there was a quiet step on the grass and river-gravel close at hand, and a deep masculine voice, which ventured tentatively, "Ma'am, I see that you are distressed – is there some manner in which I might be of assistance to you? And do not ask me to go away, for I will not leave a lady alone out here. Even this close to our town, there is a danger of Indians and other brigands."

Margaret sat up; the voice sounded at once familiar – not one of the boarders, or their neighbors. She blinked her eyes clear.

"Mrs. Vining is it – of Gonzales? I thought as much; Houston does not forget a face or a friend."

It was indeed General Sam, his craggy, lively face seeming to be only a little more aged than when he had held Susanna Dickinson's hand and wept as she told them all what had happened to their friends within the Alamo. Margaret choked – she could not speak for a moment. She made a little gesture with her hand, and the General swept aside the coattails of his long riding coat and sat down on the same log a little and respectful way apart from her. His horse was tied up to another tree some distance removed. He took a clean white handkerchief from his coat and put it in her hand, waiting courteously while she composed herself and blew her nose.

"It is nothing," Margaret began on a sob, her voice shaking but steadying as she continued, "Or rather, nothing to anyone else but me, sir. I have been made aware of a matter which affects my marriage, of an aspect to it which affects me most grievously. I have only just now been told of this matter. I do not wish to make a public show of my feelings to any at all, so I must beg for your discretion. I fear that the scandal of it will reflect badly on us, aside from the pain that it has caused to me. And I do not know what to do. I must think of what to do, but I cannot . . ." Her eyes threatened to overflow again.

"Ah. I see, Mrs. Vining," General Sam answered warmly. "I am sorry to hear of this. It's a tragedy, sure enough – anything that makes a woman weep so! I would make a promise then that I will hold whatever you choose tell me in strictest confidence, and also, if you bid me so, to dismiss this encounter from all but our memory."

Margaret turned the handkerchief – a very large and fine cotton one – to a dry spot and wiped her eyes; curiously she did feel some comfort at his words, or perhaps she was done with crying.

The General continued. "I recollect when we first met in Gonzales, your husband was the schoolteacher, and the owner of a fine black horse! One of my good friend Deef Smith's peerless scouts." For a moment, the General himself seemed almost overcome. "The best and bravest, that was our gallant Smith. And your husband served in his company. Yes, now I recollect him very well. Bit of a dandy, an Easterner, too – so you have come here, now?"

"My father has – had property here, when it was Waterloo," Margaret answered, hiccupping slightly. "And then my husband became so ill, he could not open a school and teach as he once did. I made my father's house into a boardinghouse."

"Ah!" the General exclaimed. "That is what brought your name so very readily to my mind: Mrs. Eberly mentioned your establishment to me." Now he looked at her with thoughtful concern, and his voice was most particularly kindly. "So, this is to do with you and your husband – you did say it was to do with your marriage, and scandal, and a matter most painful to you? I shall not pry for any details, Mrs. Vining. I am one who has essayed twice into the lists of matrimony and emerged more battered than most. Whatever has happened in your particular instance – it is not the business of Houston, or any other. If there is a piece of advice that you would allow me to give, it is this only: Scandal is a thing which may be faced down. It may even be kept small, if you and your husband keep your nerve and refuse to give fuel to it. This means," and he took her hand, "that you and your husband must talk, arriving at a solution mutually agreeable – and then never speak of the circumstances to any, not even your closest and most dear. No justification, no blame, no recriminations; none must ever pass your lips. Thus, scandal dies, deprived of nourishment, although it is a hard oath to keep. I speak from bitter knowledge, Mrs. Vining."

"For myself, I'd not favor my husband to go to Indian Territory and crawl into a whiskey keg to kill a scandal," Margaret answered before she thought, and to her mixed amazement and horror at her outspoken words, the General cracked a great delighted laugh, and patted her hand.

"There is that," he answered, cheerfully. "I'd not recommend that particular course of action to all; but it depends on circumstances and inclination, of course. Miss Allen was a lady beyond reproach. We were badly matched in marriage and how bruising that mistake turned out to be for the both of us! Miss Diana Rogers was also a fine woman, of whom the only ill that could be said is that she didn't wish to come to Texas with me and so our marriage ended. I'll say no more." His countenance turned most particularly earnest; Margaret did not doubt that his next words were a reflection of General Sam's most heartfelt beliefs. "No honest gentleman should take up arms against a woman, Mrs. Vining, no matter what the provocation. And your husband is a gentleman."

"That he is, in some respects," Margaret answered, although her heart ached still with the feeling of betrayal. "I should return to our house, but I came here to compose myself, to think of what I should do."

"To a beautiful place, a balm for a sickened and weary soul," General Sam agreed. "Well chosen, indeed! Can there be anything more soothing to look upon than the woods and water, the sunset dying over yonder far bank; what a painter could make of this, eh? Reminds me of Tennessee – such a beautiful place is our Texas! Lamar would deafen us all, singing the praise of this aspect. Contemplate it at your leisure, Mrs. Vining. I have no pressing duties upon me. I would see you safely returned to your house," he added with an earnest and fatherly expression. "For in spite of all assurances I am far from convinced that this place is entirely safe as a capitol city of our Texas, or for a woman of good character to be unescorted within its environs."

"And you might also be afraid I would throw myself into the water from despair?" Margaret returned, "and prevent it by remaining guardian at my elbow?" From the way that his eyebrows went up, she knew that shot of hers had hit home, but he answered, fair and forthrightly.

"I did entertain such a concern upon seeing you from afar, but not upon having conversation with you and recalling our previous exchanges. You do not seem to Houston to be one to fall into such a pit of black despair that you would consider ending it all. I am not infallible, of course – but I hope that in my lifetime I have acquired an excellent sense of judgment regarding the characters of men, and women alike. You, Mrs. Vining – you are a fighter, resolved on your course to the bitter end, and you will never give up. I recollect seeing you at Groce's Crossing, with your wagons and your women friends, and all of your children around you; no, Mrs. Vining, in the midst of despair you were stalwart and unbowed. Remember – the darkest hours of night come just when dawn is about to break." Margaret blew her nose again;

oddly enough, the General's bracing words of confidence in her own abilities and character had proved to be comforting. She looked at him through her eyelashes; he was about Papa's age, she thought – only there was something vital in him that would never be wearied by age or defeat. In that she was reminded of Opa Heinrich, dead these long years ago in Pennsylvania. What a pity that Papa could never have offered the same sensible comfort and regard, as General Sam did! She thought of how wisely General Sam had sworn young Davy Darst into his army – and then sent him on detachment to care for her wagon. That had been a very judgment of Solomon!

Now, he was patting the pockets of his coat again, emerging with another handkerchief, "Ah – dear Mrs. Eberly; she sees to the laundry so carefully I am always well-equipped with handkerchiefs. Another stalwart daughter of Texas – no, give me the other." And with perfect composure, he took the dampened handkerchief and rose from the log seat. She watched as he rinsed it clean in cool river water, although he sank to the ankles of his riding boots in the mud at rivers' edge, and brought it to her so that she might wash her face, and dab cool water on her eyes. She had no glass to see herself in, but she put her bonnet on again and thought about facing her husband, and the words that General Sam had said to her. The heartbreak, the anger and despair were still there, still stabbing cruelly – but she felt armored against them now.

"Thank you," she turned to the General as he offered her his arm. "You have been very kind. I should not delay you about your business."

"My duty," he answered very firmly, "as well as my pleasure, Mrs. Vining. Think nothing of it." So he walked with her to the edge of Papa's property, to where they could look up and see the apple trees, clad in white clouds of bloom that all but hid the house and Morag with Peter in her arms and her older sons running after. Peter was howling. The boys came running down the hillside towards her, shouting gleefully to each other and to Morag that they had found her, that Mama was here.

"Miss Hetty sent us to find you," Horace explained with a sideways look at General Sam. "She said that you had gone for a walk, but it's time to start supper now, and did you want her to do sweet potatoes or plain? And there's been another gentleman to see about a room, but Papa shut the door to the little parlor and didn't want to speak to anyone. Where were you, Mama? We couldn't find you anywhere until now," he added plaintively, as Morag caught up, flushing pink from breathlessness.

"You were away, Marm – and the baby is hungry!" Margaret took the screaming infant from her; Jamie was tugging at her shawl and babbling a hundred questions, while Johnny stared like an owl at the General and looked as if he would like to start sucking his thumb again. The ache in Margaret's heart eased a little; whatever came of this, she had the boys, and would always be assured of their love.

"I wanted to sit by the river for a bit, and think about things," she answered, hoping that she sounded casual, and Horace asked, "What did you want to think about, Mama?"

"About potatoes for dinner," she answered. "And I met General Houston on the track and thought I should ask him to sup with us also . . . if you would," she added hastily, for General Sam was grinning like a boy. "This is General Houston, the hero of San Jacinto."

"I remember," Horace brightened, and put out his hand, with all the gravity of a young man much older, "I'm Horace Templeton Vining, sir. I am pleased to make your acquaintance."

"A pleasure," the General rumbled, and Horace gravely introduced his brothers, adding that Jamie wanted to be a soldier someday. Jamie burned with excitement upon being introduced to a real general, as Horace solemnly affirmed that he had seen General Sam marching at the head of a real army, with cannons and cavalry and all, while Morag stared, so awestruck that she could hardly speak.

"Indeed," General Sam answered, and looked towards Margaret with a wryly humorous expression. "Your lad will make a fine soldier, I am certain – all of them will! Fortunately, our situation in Texas is not quite so perilous these days as they were formerly. We can allow our recruits time to acquire considerably more seasoning. Now I find myself not only envious of the horse that your husband possesses, but his family and his residence! " He bowed over Margaret's hand, and ruffled Jamie's hair, "Alas, I have a previous engagement, and Mrs. Eberly is exacting, as regarding mealtimes. But I insist that you should consider me as a friend, Mrs. Vining – and call upon me, if you should ever need good counsel or the help of a friend."

"I shall," Margaret answered; and recalled with a shiver one of the other things the witch-woman had said all those years ago; *"Joy an' sorrow, will you have, an' always friens . . . some o'dem pow'ful men . . . .eben do dey some o'em will nebber know yo heart."* It seemed that General Sam was already one of those friends, for there was certainly not a more powerful man in Texas. As Race had often observed, the government was a sack full of tomcats and General Sam most certainly the largest and wiliest of them. Now he took his leave with courtesy, and she hitched Peter more comfortably in her arms, for he had stopped his wailing. The boys were excited beyond words to have made the acquaintance of the General.

As they walked towards the house, Morag spoke up, as shy as ever. "He were ever so pleasant a man, Marm . . . an' he were so cordial to us, for such a great a man as they say."

"He is a great man," Margaret answered, "but one should ever expect perfection from him, or any who are held to be great. But there is one curious quality in him, Morag. He is a man who likes women."

"Oh, Marm – all men like women!" Morag answered, comfortable enough now with Margaret that she could show her exasperation, and Margaret smiled; to think she was once that young, that she thought she knew all there was to know about the matters of men and women.

"Morag dear, there are men who marry and treat their wives well out of duty and custom, but who save their closest friendships and confidences for their friends, who are most usually other men. Then there are men who are confirmed bachelors, who want little to do with women anyway. Finally, there are men who truly like women as a general rule, who have respect for the female as a sensible and intelligent and interesting person. I think General Sam is one of those . . . he has a generous consideration for those of our sex who are elevated to his friendship. That is the best kind of man." Margaret sighed, wistfully. For a time, she had thought herself the luckiest of women, wed to one such.

"But they do say," Morag answered after a moment, "that General Sam does drink something awful."

"So I have been told also," Margaret said, "and it is a flaw – but as human flaws can go, not such an awful one. I think I would rather trust a man of great stature with a flaw or two, recognizing that they are human after all."

She held the baby particularly close to her for comfort and reassurance as she climbed the stairs to the house, nodding respectfully to those three or four boarders taking their ease upon the verandah. Peter was quiet now, but munching on his fist in a way that meant he was still hungry and not in the least appeased. To her relief no one seemed to think anything odd had taken place that afternoon, and the boys were chattering excitedly about having met General Houston himself. In the kitchen, Papa was sitting at his place in the corner mending a bit of harness, careless of Hetty preparing the evening meal. Hetty lifted up her head from peeling potatoes.

"Oh, Marm – I had to start the potatoes, so I did, an' thin the babe began to cry, and Himself could not say when you would return."

"Very good, Hetty, plain potatoes are what I would have done." The door into the little parlor was still closed fast – no, there would be no time for a private talk. She went to their little room off the old parlor to sit in the rocking chair to nurse Peter and to consider General Sam's advice. The pain of knowing that Race was married – was still married – to someone else had diminished to a dull ache; now she must work out how best to live with it, to carry on with her life and the work of the household. She was dreading to meet Race's gaze over the supper table. How much of what he had said to her over the years of their marriage was based on a lie? *Yet*, Margaret acknowledged to herself, *some of this was my own doing. I was a child, when I began believing that he was intended to be mine – and I went on believing it so strongly that I never questioned that belief or anything of what he said or did which might have planted a doubt. Well, I am a child no longer, and I shall put away a belief in childish things such as a witch-prophecy!*

She rocked Peter until he fell asleep, while long evening shadows crept across the garden and the farmyard just outside the window, and the parlor clock musically chimed the quarter hours around. It was suppertime, time to face the household and her husband with a serene face, a watchful eye and tactful words. For the rest of the evening, she felt as if she moved through the careful steps and gestures of a slow dance, the ritual of presiding over the supper table, while Morag brought out each dish from the kitchen. Race emerged from the front parlor at the moment when the boarders were gathering; Margaret was aware that he exchanged the usual pleasantries with them. Fortunately, the conversation over supper was general, and much taken up with the matter of Mexican incitement of the Cherokee and the dreadful failure of peace talks with the Comanche. News had just arrived from Bexar that there had been an attempt by the Comanche tribes, come to a parley there, to extort a higher ransom for white captives than had been already agreed to. Margaret, without being particularly interested in the details, learned that the State peace commissioners had given orders that the Comanche chiefs be detained until the captives were returned, as previously agreed. Thereupon the chiefs and their escorting warriors had flung themselves with their knives and arrows upon the soldiers and the peace commissioner, and it all had devolved to a vicious and running fight through the streets of Bexar.

"Did any of Captain Hays' company take part?" she asked at once; it appeared not, which removed her greatest reason for concern. But the men at table continued talking; a single white captive had been returned, a girl of fourteen who had been infamously treated and mutilated by her Comanche captors, at which Margaret lost most of her remaining interest and all of her appetite. She excused herself as soon as she could graciously do so, to help

Morag in the kitchen with the cornmeal pudding that was for the sweet. Then she helped Hetty and Morag with the dishes, although Hetty looked at her very keenly: she had not often left the supper table this early.

"Are ye' feelin' ill, Marm?" Hetty asked, and Margaret answered, "A little – the gentlemen were speaking of Miss Lockhart, and the degrading manner in which she was tormented by her captors all this year long. They say the other captives were burned alive. I could not bear to hear any more and so I left the table."

She saw the boys to bed still chattering excitedly about General Sam, and made her usual rounds, drawing in the main door latch and closing the shutters. She found her customary routine to be wondrously calming. The door to their little room was closed; she laid her hand on the latch and opened it, rejoicing that her hands were steady and her countenance serene. He sat on the edge of their bed in his shirtsleeves, as if he had been waiting for her. He met her eyes as she stooped to tuck a blanket a little more firmly around the sleeping baby and then sat in the rocking chair, with her hands folded in her lap like a good and obedient schoolgirl.

"We must talk," she said, levelly, "about how you came to marry two wives, and what must be done about it." He relaxed in some infinitesimal degree, no doubt relieved that she was being calm, and looked down at the floor.

"Daisy-mine, I never intended for you to know, and for this to harm what we have together in any way." He sounded perfectly wretched, but Margaret was implacable, steeled by the vision of her sons' innocent faces, of baby Peter asleep in the cradle by her knee.

"But now I do know," she answered, "and it has harmed us, regardless of intent. The children are harmed, for they are by-blows to your own kin. And I am harmed, for I would be seen by respectable society as a willing concubine; a faithful mistress – but not your rightful wife in the eyes of the law. For my own curiosity, I would like to know how this came about, and what you intend doing to mend it – if anything might be done to mend it at all!"

"Then hear me out, Daisy-mine. I am shamed, for having acted knowingly, and knowing that social condemnation will fall unjustly upon you, who are entirely blameless. I will make it up to you; I promise on my honor and my life . . . I will make it up to you. I beg you to listen and understand; perhaps then you might look on me more kindly. For god's love, Daisy, we have been heart and soul for eleven years. There was never a night we spent apart that my last waking thought was of anything but you! I would not have lived to this day without your loving care. Daisy, do not look upon me so unkindly, I beg you! In my own eyes, you are my true wife!"

"But not in the eyes of the law or society." Margaret's own anger was abated somewhat by Race's protestations. "Oh, have no fear – I have resolved to never speak of this with any but you. I was told by one who should know that scandal eventually dies, without idle chatter to lend it fuel. So tell me, then – husband – again, how did you come to have one wife in law and another in your heart?"

Race sighed heavily, and took her hands within his. After a moment, he answered,

"As I began to say – Annabelle and I had always known each other. Our mothers fondly assumed that we were meant to wed, and in truth we did not have any objections. Neither of us had attachments to another; I had sufficient residual income to support a family . . . as soon as was practical, we were married with the blessings of both our families and commenced a life together. I swear to you, Daisy-mine, I thought we were happy, she with me and I with her. Our life was agreeable and full of contentment, or so I thought, not having any particular experience of true married bliss. Annabelle was affectionate towards me – yet even having so little knowledge of life as I did at the time – I did note that she did not seem to enjoy marital intimacies, but I thought nothing of it. She was a well-brought up young lady; who would have expected wanton eagerness in the marriage bed or out of it? But she was agreeable enough, at first – until after our daughter was born. She . . . had a difficult confinement. The doctors advised . . . we slept apart from then on. Within months our marriage dwindled to mere companionship, to an acceptance of different interests. When I in turn became ill and was advised for the sake of my good health to take up residence in a warmer clime, Annabelle declined to depart Boston. She was adamant; her family and friends were all there, all the society that she knew or ever wanted to know. There was only the empty form of a marriage left at that point, only our daughter to tie us together. I could have taken Sophie and departed; I would have been within my legal rights to do so, I suppose. But it seemed a cruel thing to do to a woman who had never given me grounds for complaint, to take her one child from her; I am not heartless, Daisy-mine, you know that! We parted as friends; I left her and Sophie well provided for in Boston and went in search of a healthier clime with the understanding that we should have our own lives. Should she ever have evinced a desire to marry another, I would have obliged, though it would have caused a scandal. But she did not – she was happy with a position in Boston society."

"I see," Margaret interjected. "She desired the position and advantageous benefits of a wife, but without the pleasures or any of the burdensome duties. A marriage made in Boston? A bit different from a marriage made in Texas! Does she keep a large doll in the form of a man, to prop in a chair and sit opposite of an evening? A being to talk to which does not require an answer? Does she also have a large pillow to put in the bed to sleep next to at night?"

"Stop it," Race's composure snapped. "Stop it, Daisy-mine, this is petty and unworthy of you!"

"Unworthy?" Margaret retorted, and she felt the angry color rising in her face. "I shall be the judge of what is unworthy for me, husband – and He who is the judge of us all might also have something to say." She made an effort to calm herself – after all, it was she who had demanded that they talk and for Race to explain. "Do continue . . . you had departed Boston, with the agreement that you should each lead a separate life from each other. When did you decide that your separate life ought to include another wife?"

"When I grew lonely of my own company of an evening and tired of a bachelor establishment, shared with no one else," Race answered, and there was a bleak timbre to his voice. "The memory of her grew remote to me, as I made my life in Texas – establishing my school, relishing the company of new friends. She wrote but infrequently, and in time I came to think of her letters as nothing but a momentary interruption of my life. When I first returned to Boston after some years, her manner towards me was of a cordiality more befitting a distant relation, barely recollected – and I perceived that her lack of interest in my doings more than matched my own in hers. Only a mutual interest in our child bound us in any way."

"Your daughter," Margaret interjected. Race smiled, a melancholy smile.

"Yes, Sophie; she was then about the age that Jamie is now. I flatter myself that she had something of the same charming fearlessness about her . . . but her mother discouraged me from taking an interest in her, fearing – I believe – that I might draw the child's affections." Race sank his face into his hands, rubbing his eyes. "I could not remain in Boston; the child was happy there with her mother. What could I do? When she was old enough to make her debut into society, the least that I could do was to stand aside and not damage her reputation, or her chance to make a fine marriage. Our lives were so separate . . . it just fell out that way. Annabelle and her life in Boston; what was there to stop us from having a life of our own in Texas? It seemed to be the most expedient manner for all of us to reach for some few crumbs of happiness." He dropped his face into his hands again, and when finally he spoke again, his voice seemed wracked by tragedy and hopelessness. "Dear God, Daisy-mine, I could not think of any other way. Forgive me!"

"Oh, my dear," Margaret answered, moved by Race's very real distress, but not so moved that she could entirely set aside her own lingering anger and shame. "You were gallant beyond words in protecting the honor of your daughter and her future happiness, but couldn't you see the hazard in the path you chose for my honor? Didn't you realize you had made a choice, in not choosing? You only put off making a decision and now the choice at hand has only been made crueler. Now you must betray her, or me – and by extensions your sons, and the life here that your work and mine has made for them." She did and did not want to touch him, torn between wanting to comfort him in his distress and to strike back in some way against his duplicity by holding herself implacably apart. But she had loved him well for the larger portion of her life, girl and woman; her affection for Race was only deeply shaken, not destroyed utterly. She set her hands on his, and he clung to them desperately for some moments.

"Daisy-mine, I know it plain now," he finally said, still crushing her hands between his, as he raised his face to meet her gaze. "I should have done it long before – for all I hold dearest in life, I should have. I will make the journey to Boston and tell my wife – tell Annabelle that now we must be divorced. Sophie is happily wed; there is no more reason to delay, save my own sloth and disinclination."

"It is a long journey," Margaret answered quietly, "And a difficult one. I fear for your health should you arrive in winter – since it is almost summer."

"No, no," Race shook his head. "I would take ship from Galveston to New Orleans, and from New Orleans to New York; it would not be so strenuous a journey. And I would not stay any longer than to consult with a good man of law. I believe Annabelle would agree to a separation. My sister Minnie – she will talk to her, as they are good friends." He already appeared more cheerful, and yet Margaret, regarding him, felt something of that 'standing aside' feeling that she had often felt as a child, watching her parents as though they were strangers to her. He had revived, being somewhat assured that she would not abandon him; he seemed like one of the boys, like Johnny or Jamie, distraught over some small injury, yet sunny and smiling within minutes of her administering to a scraped knee or a bumped head. And with a pang, she realized that now she might always be standing a little apart from her husband, ever holding back from that intimacy which they had once shared.

Chapter 24 – *The Sack of Cats*

The perception that she stood a little apart, watching herself and her husband from a distance, persisted with Margaret. On the surface of things, all was as it had been before; they spoke affectionately to each other, of the same matters and in the same words they had always used. At night they slept as they always had when they were together, tucked spoon-fashion into the curve of each others' bodies, although Margaret was wakeful more often than not, staring into the darkness and hearing his breathing. She had one of her 'thinks' such as she had rarely indulged in since she was a child. Why did she feel so distant from Race, now? It seemed like the opposite of falling in love; that she was falling into indifference. Her thoughts kept circling unbidden, back to the moment of Race telling her about his wife and daughter in Boston. That was when something snapped, set anger smoldering within her like the coals in the heart of a dead fire, smothered in grey ash, but underneath it all . . . still burning. She loved him still, hoped that she showed with every gesture and soft word that she did, and wished with every fiber of belief that she might someday come back to loving him with the same whole-hearted devotion . . . but there was a barrier set now between them which should not have been there. When she regarded him, or slept with his arms about her at night, listened to his words – all conspired to remind her of that pain, the humiliation and anger. Perhaps, she thought wistfully as she made preparations for his long journey back to Boston, the weeks and days apart might allay some of those feelings. Procuring a divorce from his wife in the East might put things back to what they should have been. When he returned, perhaps her anger would have burned down to a layer of grey ash which the winds would blow away.

She laid out his best clothes, and saw that he had a sufficiency of well-mended shirts and laundered handkerchiefs. This time Race meant to travel to Galveston in a borrowed trap, accompanying Dr. Williamson, so that he could take more than just what could be packed in saddlebags. A merchant's wagons and a company of Rangers were returning to Bexar from Austin – all intended to travel together for safety in these unsettled times. On the evening that Race's journey east was first discussed at the boarder's supper-table, Dr. Williamson looked up from perusal of a medical circular with the vaguely baffled expression of a person discovering something usual in the surroundings but being too well-mannered to make a mention of it.

"I am intending to travel to Galveston to visit my sister within a few weeks," he ventured, blinking behind his spectacles. "If you wish to travel with me, I would welcome the company." He left unsaid what was plain to Margaret, that Race's worsening bouts of illness over the last two years had put a long journey on horseback out of the question – and to have a doctor accompany him would be welcome indeed. Silently, Margaret blessed the good doctor for his tact and the fortunate coincidence of his journey.

She packed the old tin trunk full of Race's clothes for the journey, adding a few of his favorite books. In the top of the trunk there was a wooden tray for toilet articles and hairbrushes; on the morning of his departure, Margaret added those last personal things. There still remained room for a coat or a blanket, folded small. Without knowing why she did so, Margaret took from the bride-chest at the foot of their bed one of those red blankets that Mama had woven of unraveled Mexican wool. She held it to her for a moment, recalling how she had sewn the binding around the edges, after persuading Mama that she should give it to the schoolmaster as a gratitude-gift. How innocent she had been, assured in her conviction that she would marry him! She laid the blanket over the top of the clothes, added the wooden tray and closed the trunk. Snapping the latches closed had the sound of finality to it, like closing the lid of a coffin.

Just then, Race put his head around the doorway, asking, "Is everything packed, Daisy-mine?" He was smiling, his coat over his arm and hat in hand; the boys clamoring their affectionate farewells. "Dr. Williamson is just bringing the trap around."

"Hetty has packed a basket for you," Margaret answered. "Bread and ham, dried-apple pie, enough that you need not worry about the fare wherever you will spend the next few nights." She went to his arms for an embrace willingly enough, tasting his kiss upon her lips and thinking that he was too thin; she could feel the bones beneath his clothes. She took his face between her hands. He still looked like the young schoolteacher of San Felipe, not having thickened with age in body or features, but there were lines at the corners of his eyes which had not been visible before and those lines which creased his cheeks when he smiled were scored a little deeper.

"Have a care for yourself," she said, briskly, "return as soon as you can, for we who love you will be missing you every day that you are in Boston."

"My dearest Daisy," he answered, and then he was gone from her arms, and young Horace and Doctor Williamson were helping him to carry out the tin trunk to the waiting trap. Hetty stood with the covered basket in her hands, giving it to young Horace who staggered under the weight, laughing breathlessly as he handed it up to his father. Then the trap lurched as Dr.

Williamson snapped the reins over the teams' backs, and rolled away, leaving Margaret standing on the verandah, waving as the trap vanished down the hill.

As soon as it was out of sight, but for a brief boil of dust, she dropped her hand, feeling curiously unmoved by Race's departure. Hetty glanced towards Margaret with an odd expression on her face, saying, "Ah, the pity of it, Marm – you'll be missing him then, will ye?"

"I shall," Margaret answered, "but he will write to us, and I will cherish his letters nearly as much as I cherish his presence." She was still wondering why she did not feel the aching sense of loss that she had always felt, nothing of the dread of that first night of sleeping alone in their bed tonight, and all the nights after, until he returned.

Hetty shot her a very odd look, before saying, "Ach, he will be returnin' soon enough – for a taste o' my biscuits, right enough!"

She gave Margaret's hand a comforting squeeze as she went inside; Margaret watched the final settling of the powder-fine dust, wondering if Hetty had not divined something in her own demeanor and words. Hetty was another woman, not a child like Morag, and had been long enough in Margaret's household to sense certain undercurrents of emotion. But Hetty was wise enough to let them pass in silence, for which Margaret was grateful.

Upon being told that Race was traveling to the East, Papa had only grunted and said, "He's off again, M'grete? Hardly be missed then. All he's ever been good for around here is siring four whelps on you and eating at my table."

"My table, Papa," Margaret had corrected him, so long accustomed to Papa's ill-humor that she could barely bring herself to the point of being offended by it. That night, when she lay down in their bed and pulled the quilt and blankets over herself, she felt only the smallest pang upon noting the emptiness in the place where he was accustomed to lie at her side, at hearing only her own breathing, and that of Peter, fast asleep in the cradle. *I said only that we who loved him would long for his return,* Margaret thought; *I did not say that I loved him. Does that make a difference, I wonder?* Against her expectations, she slept well and deeply that night, and for most nights thereafter, save when Peter fussed to be nursed.

He wrote two letters to her, before departing Texas; one from Bexar, where he had planned to seek out Carl. But Jack Hays' company of Rangers was out on patrol; having only just departed was not expected to return for weeks, if not months. Rumors of raids by Comanche warriors in the wake of the abortive peace talks and the fight at the Council House had the whole district on edge. Race contented himself with a visit to the widow of his old friend and comrade, Don Esteban Menchaca, and seeing for himself that young Porfirio – now a bold and lively boy of about ten years of age – was well, and growing to resemble his father. Alas, Race added, he was as devoted to horses as his father and uncle had been, he could not read or write nearly as well as young Horace. He also noted, with much sadness, that feelings among the Anglo element, especially those new-come to Texas, ran very strongly against all Mexicans, even those who had fought and shed their own blood against the *Centralistas* of Lopez de Santa Anna. It was a tragedy, her husband wrote with much passion. These new Texians no longer gave honor to such like Juan Seguin, to whom such respect was rightfully and abundantly due. In consequence, Juan had become embittered; he had endured instead a flood of insult from those latecomers who had not marched shoulder to shoulder with him at San Jacinto, or affected not to know of how faithfully he and his *Bexarenos* had performed yeoman's service as a rearguard to Sam Houston's retreating army. Race waxed indignant, and Margaret set his letter aside, recalling how Race and the Menchaca brothers, with Juan Seguin and Almaron Dickinson, had talked the politics of the day, sitting in the breezeway of their house in Gonzales – Centralists and the Federalists, and questions about the tax policies of the customs agent at Anahuac – with the feeling that the time before that war had indeed been a very long time ago.

Race's second letter came from Galveston, carried back to her by Dr. Williamson. He had taken passage to New Orleans, from there to take another passage to New York – or if there was good and reliable steamship service up the Mississippi, to avail himself of an inland route. Margaret hoped not – it would still be a grueling and slow journey, not without its own dangers. Race sounded well, and optimistic in his letters, and when Margaret pressed Dr. Williamson, he only took off his glasses, and blinked at her.

"The sea air was most revivifying. I advised Mr. Vining to take the sea passage to New York, as being much less taxing. He was in good spirits, when we departed." For a moment, she thought the doctor would say more, but seemed to reconsider. He polished the lenses of his glasses, and replaced them, repeating, "In excellent good spirits, my word upon it, Mrs. Vining."

In midsummer, she received a third letter from Race, sent from New Orleans; a short note, reiterating his determination to remain in Boston only as long as it might take to institute divorce proceedings, and then return with all speed. He asked that she kiss the boys and the baby for him, and to see that Horace and Johnny continue with the lessons he had left them, for he would return with more books and did not wish to discover they had fallen behind in his absence. Margaret folded the letter very small and tucked it into the bottom of her bride's chest, where she kept all of his writings to her. She expected his next letter to come postmarked from Boston, knowing that it would take many weeks, even months. She wrote in answer to him, sending her own letters to the address of Race's sister Minnie in Boston, thinking that she – of whom Race had ever spoken of with affection – would be discreet and careful with them.

After the letter from New Orleans, she did not receive another. At first, she did not worry, but as the branches of the apple trees bent ever lower under the weight of russet, pink and yellow-gold fruit, she began to be uneasy.

"Have you not heard a word from Himself, at all?" Hetty asked, with a sidelong look, as she and Margaret made apple butter, one afternoon. Only that very day, Horace had asked, with a worried look, "Wouldn't Papa have been in Boston now for weeks, Mama?" and Margaret had to confess that it was so: Race's ship would have made harbor in New York.

"Perhaps his last letter was lost," she said. "Perhaps the ship carrying it sank, and it will take time for another letter to get here."

That answer contented her son, who looked melancholy and answered, "I do miss Papa – he was supposed to be home before winter, wasn't he?"

"Yes, he is," Margaret answered. "He promised so, and your Papa keeps his promises."

Each day of that troubled summer, which brought a post to Austin or a messenger carrying letters with none for Margaret from her husband, she felt hope dying a little within her. Every day without a message from him, renewing the assurances that he had made convinced her that he had chosen to remain in Boston and redoubled her fears: every memory of trustful affection came to her with a seed of doubt already planted. He had done that which presented the least trouble for him once – might he have chosen to do so again, once returned to his home and the comforting ease of life in the East? She often turned from these troubling thoughts to worries about the household, and about what was happening in Texas with a sense of relief.

The troubles with the Comanche worsened; the fight at the Council House in Bexar had set the Penateka afire with a thirst for revenge, for blood, fire, and plunder. Although, as John Ford had pointed out, with cynical humor – the Penateka Comanche in that humor were only a degree or two more hostile than they had been before, so it was difficult to see any difference. Margaret, Hetty, and Morag were warned, over and over again, not to venture much beyond the farmyard alone. Papa often went about his chores with a musket slung over his shoulder and the Spanish pistols thrust through his belt. Armed guards accompanied those who ventured much beyond the cluster of log houses clustered around the intersection of Congress Avenue and Pecan Street, and now and again patrolled along the river, searching for trail sign indicating that a war party might have passed nearby. Many who had come to establish businesses or a home for their families while they attended to governmental matters chose to return to their old homes in the settled country for fear of Comanche raids and the isolation on the far frontier. Margaret recalled what General Sam had said about Austin not being safe – a new city here had been Bo Lamar's vision, not shared by General Sam; Margaret did not know if General Sam truly believed so, or if he and Bo Lamar merely took opposite sides over a bone of contention because it was their nature. All the same, the number of residents had shrunk by more than half since the Legislature had finished meeting; many remaining in town chose to sleep at night in Bullock's Inn, or in the sturdy log outbuildings. Papa and Seamus O'Doyle had made stout shutters to cover the new, longer windows, and saw they were tightly secured at night. Once again, Papa's cattle and Bucephalus were locked in the stable at night, the stable door being secured with a chain and padlock. The few gentlemen boarders left – Dr. Williamson, Seamus O'Doyle, and Mr. Hattersley the Englishman, slept at night with loaded armaments close by and within reach all that long summer and into autumn. During the first weeks of August, Margaret often noted a smudge of low cloud hanging in the southern sky, clouds that she suspected might be smoke for the similarity it bore to the smoke of burning towns that she had seen on the journey from Gonzales to Harrisburg during the war.

"It's a right Comanche moon, they say," Seamus O'Doyle remarked, in mid-August, upon looking out the dining room window and seeing the pale mother-of-pearl disc rising above the tree line, hanging in the twilight sky like a distant lantern. "'Tis a good thing to be makin' a fort o' the house. There's talk o' a great party of Indians come out of Comancheria, goin' down the Guadalupe Valley like wolves on a sheepfold, so many that the Rangers daren't give battle."

"Who told you this?" Margaret asked, for rumors had been swirling all summer, "And what else did they tell you?" The dining room was quieter, with only herself, the three boarders, and her oldest son. That summer, Margaret began allowing Horace to sit at the table for supper since he was of an age to have the benefit of listening to the adults talk – or at least, Mr. Hattersley and Mr. O'Doyle talk; Dr. Williamson customarily brought a book to the table and propped it against the cruet-stand. Now Horace sat at the foot of the table, in the place that Race had taken, listening with wide eyes and barely venturing a word unless spoken to.

"A carter from Gonzales," Seamus O'Doyle answered, "who was expecting to collect a shipment o' gentleman's fittings at Linnville – a shipment for Robinson's emporium in Bexar, but as he was almost to Victoria he was warned away by one of Cap'n Burleson's boys. The Injuns are on the warpath, he says. They have swept through Victoria on their way to the coast; it's the losin' o' your hair to continue. So he turned away, and took a load of goods for the French Legation's foine establishment instead."

"A foine establishment?" Mr. Hattersley raised his eyebrows, and mocked Seamus O'Doyle's turn of speech. "God save us, the Comte de Saligny is going to build a palace. I can only imagine how a gentleman of *le Francais* must suffer, living in a log cabin with the pigs running in and out – let alone the sufferings of his *chef du cuisine*!"

"You'd dine with him, readily enough," Seamus O'Doyle retorted, without any heat, "for the sake of his foine table – and the clarry in his cellar, wouldn't ye just, ye heretical Protestant?"

"But he does not actually have a cellar, you bog-trotting heathen," Mr. Hattersley replied. "Only some packing cases filled with straw. I have to say, though – it doesn't harm the taste of the claret."

"Gentlemen," Margaret said, in soft warning; although Mr. Hattersley and Seamus O'Doyle got on very well and exchanged ruderies with each other like a pair of schoolboys, she thought such remarks were not a good example for her son, or added anything to the tone of conversation at her table.

"Not a comte," Dr. Williamson swam up to the surface of the conversation. "His name's Dubois – just a jumped-up secretary. And a snob, as well." He withdrew into his book, as abruptly as he had emerged from it.

"Aye, I would no'mind havin' the buildin' of that foine establishment," Seamus O'Doyle sank back into his chair, musing thoughtfully. "But as for settin' a table – I do no' think that any nobleman's table can boast the like o' Miss Hetty's biscuits."

"What of the Comanche war party," Margaret asked. "Which your carter friend had heard of – did he have any else to say?"

"I regret, no' much else," Seamus O'Doyle replied, "Save that Cap'n Burleson an' Cap'n Caldwell had sent word to all Ranger companies, to rally together at Plum Creek, two day's ride to the south of here – he bein' of the opinion that the Injuns would return by that way."

"We should take special care then," Margaret said, although she could not honestly think of any care to be taken that her household had not already performed. She could not recall any time when the Comanche had attacked a town straight on; they preferred to attack with overwhelming numbers, striking an isolated homestead, harassing a farmer in his fields, or a traveler on a lonely road, looking for horses, loot, and human captives. "Especially at night. I believe we are safe, within these walls – we are well-armed and from this hill, we would have warning if they approach during the day."

"Niver happen, Marm," Seamus O'Doyle answered, gallantly. "Fir as many as they are said to be, a blind man will know they are coming. And the Old Sir, he built well when he placed this house here, Marm, so he did. Still, we should keep a watch, now, so we should. They say that the Army has gone to jine wi' Cap'n Burleson. Or at least their officer – and what kin ye do w'out an officer, then?"

"Mama?" That was young Horace, from the other end of the table, a bit startled at the sound of his own voice and fearful but trying to hide it. "What will we do if the Injuns come?"

"We shall defend ourselves," Dr. Williamson answered, unexpectedly emerging from his book again, and looking kindly at young Horace over his spectacles. "That is, if they are hostile of course."

"Aye," Seamus O'Doyle added. "A stout redoubt we may make o' this house – if you and your brothers, Miss Hetty, Miss Morag, and your mother may re-load for us, we'd make a brave show 'ginst any foe. Th' doctor, th' Old Sir, Mr. Hattersley, an' mysel'. Not to worry, boyo. 'Tis only makin' plans we are. To be prepared and forewarned – that is half the battle won! 'Tis how we won at San Jacinto now, didn't we just, for I was there, and so was yer faither now; we were prepaired and so we gained glory everlastin'!"

"We've heard the story," Mr. Hattersley commented, with mild yet cutting sarcasm, "over and over again."

"Aye," Seamus O'Doyle answered, "an' so I have told so, again an' again; a brave story, an' one yet worthy of bein' told, again an' again. We live by our stories, man – such of our stories that we may tell, are a light in the dark places, a guide to our stumbling feet."

"More stumbling than most," Mr. Hattersley yawned ostentatiously and Margaret interjected, "I do enjoy Mr. O'Doyle's accounts, especially hearing of San Jacinto; I have never forgotten how he brought us the good news."

"See, then?" Seamus O'Doyle beamed. "We need stories, as much as bread an' drink. Never fear, there's niver an' end to th' stories I may tell."

Mr. Hattersley groaned and theatrically sank his face into his hands, but all at the table laughed in good humor, and even young Horace's face brightened with the reassurance which the men's words had offered to them. Margaret's own heart warmed at the conviviality in that lamp-lit room, and proper womanly affection towards those three gentlemen who took the time to reassure her son and herself, in the absence of husband and father.

The rumors continued to fly regarding the Comanche raid deep into the heart of the settled country. Those men, neighbors and friends who were members of a mounted militia company, vanished from town. Margaret took her bedding and Peter's cradle to the upstairs of the house, that part which Papa had built as sturdily as a blockhouse. For a time Papa and the boarders took turns for one of them in turn to stay awake throughout the night. Mr. Hattersley allowed as that he did not mind, as he often sat up long into the night working on his book. They passed a week of nervous days, until the morning that Jamie came running into the kitchen, afire with excitement.

"Mama!" he shouted, "There's men on horses coming up from the river!"

"Comanche?" Margaret caught Jamie to her in one arm. They were alone in the house; the boarders had their daily business to attend, and Papa was out in the barn with Horace and Johnny, piling cut summer hay into the loft. Morag gasped and dropped the wooden spoon that she had been stirring the cornmeal pudding with, splattering hot batter across the stovetop.

"Saints preserve us," Hetty cried, turning as pale as the milk that she had been skimming the new-risen cream from. "Morag, child – take the baby upstairs now, I'll find the Old Sir and –" Jamie fought his way down from Margaret's grasp, saying with a great deal of boy-impatience,

"No' Injuns, Mama – white men!" he cried, as Margaret heard the distant thundering, the hooves of many horses. Of course, Jamie would run from the house at once, and Margaret hastened after him, lifting the skirts of her dress to her knees. The horses pounding up the hill were within sight, spilling into the farmyard, whooping and shouting to each other. There were only a dozen or so, Margaret realized – but they were making enough noise for twice their number; dust-covered men on dust-covered horses, all powdered thickly with the same layer of black, sooty dust. The sweat dripping from them made muddy black rivulets on their hides, and the men's faces so dirty that it was difficult to tell what race they were, let alone recognize any. A tall man on a tall grey horse took off his hat and waved at her, shouting, "M'grete! Food, if you have any and can bring it out at once!"

"Carl!" Margaret shrieked, for it was indeed her brother – an exuberant grin and a flash of white teeth in an infamously dirty face. "What are you doing!"

"Chasing Comanche!" he shouted back. "They broke and ran at Plum Creek! We're chasing a party back towards the Llano. They're running with all the loot they took away. We'll catch them yet, but we need food, and our horses need water! Bring it quick – Jack's gone ahead, we must catch him up before long!"

"Cap'n Yack!" shouted a man at her brother's side, a man with the braids of an Indian, flopping over his bare shoulders as he exuberantly waved a musket in one hand, "Cap'n Yack, he ride into hell, no? An' we ride too – Cap'n Yack, he no fear the debbil, no do we!"

"The devil, he fear Hilario!" Carl shouted back to the Indian rider, "and the Comanch fear the Tonkaways, when the Tonkaways ride with Cap'n Yack! Hurry with the food, M'grete, we cannot wait!"

Standing in his stirrups, he reached into the branches of the nearest apple tree, for the last of the harvest within reach. Laughing, he plucked an apple from those remaining on the higher branches, another and another, throwing them deftly to the hands of the other riders, until they, whooping like Indians themselves, rode among the trees and snatched apples for themselves. Hetty, who had run from the house at Margaret's side, ran back into it, shouting for Morag to bring whatever they had in the larder that could be eaten cold and out of the hand. Margaret looked for Jamie, fearing he could be trampled in the rush of excited horses. To her horror, Carl had scooped the child from the ground, setting Jamie behind him on the saddle, where he was shrieking with gleeful delight. Hetty materialized at her elbow, a basket of bread and smoke-cured sausages, hastily torn or hacked into pieces and Morag with a water pail and tin dipper.

"Bring him back!" Margaret shrieked at her brother, who was still laughing and hurling apples towards his fellows as his horse danced with impatience. Carl crammed the rest of an apple in his mouth, and heeled the horse away from the tree.

"Aww, M'grete – we were only having fun! It's not every day a little tyke gets to ride with Cap'n Jack's company! I'll have some bread." He let Jamie slip to the ground, and swiftly snatched a handful of bread and sausage from Hetty's basket, which he stuffed into the front of his leather hunting coat. Morag held up a dipper of water for him. "Drink your fill and let's ride, boys! Burning daylight an' Cap'n Jack, he'll not want to chase Comanch himself!"

"What has been going on?" Margaret demanded. "Tell us, for we have had no news for a week and more."

"There is no time," Carl answered, wiping his chin with his coat sleeve, transferring another installation of dust to his face. "Buffalo Hump's Penateka went all the way to Linnville – a thousand warriors with all the tribe trailing after with their trash an' traps. They took horses from Victoria. Sacked

Linnville a'fore burning it to the ground. Our folk took refuge on boats out in the bay. Cap'n Caldwell and Cap'n Burleson worked out that they'd go back to the Llano country near enough by the way they came. So we assembled at Plum Creek and waited. You should have seen 'em, M'grete – so many horses and mules, packed with loot, they were going slow. We sat back, watching them all go past . . . then we came out and chased them all. You never saw such sport, all the warriors going one way, all their pack-beasts the other . . . dust boiled up something awful." He grinned down at Margaret again, and whistled piercingly, two fingers in his mouth. "Beaten fair, M'grete, now just the mopping up! C'mon, boys, we're not letting Cap'n Jack have all the fun!"

He wheeled his horse with a wave and a shout. In another minute they had poured out of the farmyard, leaving the ground broken and cut up with horses' hoofs and littered with apple-cores and a broken branch or two, and Papa coming cautiously from the barn with his musket in hand, the boys following after. It all had taken barely as much as five minutes by the small parlor clock ticking bravely in the sudden silence that had fallen.

"Who were those young ruffians?" he grumbled, upon seeing the dooryard in such disarray; since she had been taking in boarders, Margaret had often reproved him for casually allowing the farm matters to slop around to the front of the house – that being the first thing which guests and possible guests would see!

"My brother and his comrades," Margaret answered, lifting her chin. "They were chasing the Comanche from the fight at Plum Creek, Papa – they could not stop to pass the time of day."

"Mannerless, thoughtless young louts," Papa grumbled, and Margaret answered, "They protect us from Comanche raids – and if they have proper manners or no, it matters little to me and those whom they protect."

That brief encounter with Carl's Ranger comrades had emptied the larder of all of Hetty's baked bread and most of the cured sausage, but Margaret did not begrudge a single mouthful. She fell asleep on her pallet-bed upstairs that night, with the baby curled trustfully next to her, and the older boys mad with hero-worship and envy of Jamie for having sat on Uncle Carl's horse. She hoped with no little longing that perhaps her brother would come back through Austin after they had defeated the last of the Penateka band which had so ravaged the lowlands and Linnville – but he did not. She must be content with a scribbled letter, directed to her from Lawyer Maverick's establishment, a very ill-spelled and scrawled letter which grieved her for the evidence it gave that her brother had taken so little away from those school days in San Felipe and Gonzales.

Chapter 25 – *A Widow and Yet Not*

Winter descended upon them, doubly bitter for Margaret; Race had promised to return well before that time, and she still had no letter from the East explaining his absence or his plans. He had always written before, she recalled with despair, long letters and dispatched often, which made this long silence even more inexplicable. Horace often asked wistfully when Papa would return, until the evening that Margaret cried out, in despair, "I don't know, Horace, I don't know!"

Her son looked at her with his father's clever, grave eyes and asked, "Is he coming back, Mama? At all?" When Margaret answered again that she didn't know, Horace considered her answer with solemn-faced care. He and his brothers were sitting up in their bed, Johnny and Jamie hanging on her answer and looking very anxious.

"I think he must be dead, Mama," Horace said at last, with a mournful expression. Johnny looked as if he might begin to wail and cast himself from the bed into Margaret's lap for comforting. "He would have sent us word, surely. Don't cry, Johnny – Mama will take care of us, and so will Opa and the doctor, and Mr. O'Doyle."

Margaret sat with them a while until Johnny was comforted, before going to her own bed, wondering if her son was right. Surely, Race would not have willingly abandoned his sons to an indifferent world. No, it must be that he had gone from this life, among folk too uncaring or unable to send any word. A thought to break the heart, but easier to bear than thinking he had chosen to remain in the East, forgetting his life and family in Texas as one would put aside a worn-out garment.

In the morning, Margaret rose from the bed in the room which they had shared, and upon opening the shutters, looked out into the farmyard and the tumbled earth of the garden, plowed under until spring. The ground was white with frost, every twig, dead leaf, and blade of grass edged with it. The trees held their winter-bare branches up to the pale sky, flushing pink with dawn. A ghostly mist rose from the ground. Bitter cold stung her cheeks with needles of ice. As she looked upon the winter-world, she felt a curious sense of emptiness, of loss, overtaken by the feeling that the book – the book of this part of her life – was finished, done with and closed. There wasn't even any grieving left to be done. She had spent much of this last year grieving, in doubt and turmoil. The witch-woman had promised eleven years of happiness with her husband, and had spoken true. Now those years were done and spent; of what else had the witch spoken? Friends, a large house, that she would marry again; Margaret winced at the thought of allowing another man into her bed, and those joyful intimacies of the body. To give the care of her heart into another hand, to trust again, without reservation and doubts; oh, no, Margaret thought. Had not she had enough heartbreak from one husband? She must be strong, not a girl chasing after a will-o'-the-wisp of affections. She had her sons to protect. Her children were the world to her. Nothing must be allowed into her life that might harm them or damage their interests and property.

Margaret drew the shutters closed on that frost-sparkling dawn. Peter was drowsily awake and sitting up in the truckle bed that had replaced the cradle; soon, she thought – he would join his brothers in their room, for he was already walking and talking. Margaret acknowledged how she had clung to keeping him as an infant rather than face the months which had passed. It was time now to face her duties bravely as the mother of sons and a woman of property and consequence, rather than the schoolteacher's wife.

"Wake up, my dear little ducking." She lifted him into her arms, and coaxed a smile onto his face – how like her brothers he looked! More than Horace and Johnny, Peter was a true Becker, like Jamie; Saxon-fair, with the promise of height and shy charm. "Breakfast of porridge! Then, if you like, I shall have Morag move your truckle bed upstairs. Would you like to be a big boy and share the room with your brothers? Dear duckling, I think you would like that, wouldn't you?" He clapped his little hands and laughed with glee, and Margaret knew that he would. She hugged him to her one more time.

She was therefore not much surprised, on an afternoon sometime after the new year had arrived, when Dr. Williamson returned from a call in town, with a somber expression on his face, saying, "May I speak to you privately in the parlor, Mrs. Vining? I have received a letter from the East, and it contains bad news."

"The parlor, Dr. Williamson," Margaret said, white-lipped, and feeling a kind of detached sympathy for the doctor. He had a small parcel in his hand, and an unfolded letter – obviously, the letter to which he referred. She and Hetty were kneading bread, bread that must be set to rise in loaves and then baked in the oven. Papa had just brought in an armful of well-cured oak logs to bring the oven to the proper temperature. At the worst time of all, a message from the East had finally arrived – but why to Doctor Williamson? He was such a kind man, she thought – and must be in such dread of what he must say to her now.

She hastily wiped flour from her hands, and hung up her apron. "Hetty, as soon as you are finished with the bread, will you and Morag fetch the boys?"

"I will that, Marm," Hetty answered, looking from her face to Dr. Williamson's; no surprise, no curiosity in her expression. "Go on then, Marm – I'll see to the bread."

Margaret led the way to the front parlor, the room that Race had made into his library, and drew the door closed. She settled herself into the chair where he had been wont to sit when teaching the boys, and silently gestured the doctor to another. The room was cool; no fire burned in the fireplace, but it seemed warm from the sunshine pouring through the tall windows, painting oblongs and squares of pale gold on the scrubbed oak floor. Dr. Williamson sat himself down, facing her, across the parlor table.

"I regret that I must bring you this news, Mrs. Vining," he said at last, "but I have had a letter from Boston, from an old friend of mine, bearing news that Mr. Horace Vining succumbed to consumption while under his care."

"When?" Margaret's voice came out as in a whisper. She had more than half-expected this news, had expected to hear such for months, but to hear it now, for a certainty . . . the door on her marriage – or what had appeared to be a marriage – had well and truly closed.

"In the early part of December last," Dr. Williamson answered. "He was attended for months since arriving in Boston by the finest doctors there and from New York, according to my friend. It was to no avail. When we parted in Galveston in the spring," Dr. Williamson's composure seemed to waver, although his eyes were fixed earnestly upon Margaret, "I entertained doubts with regard to your husband's health and his fitness for the continued journey, but he brushed aside my misgivings. He was most insistent, saying that the business he had to conduct in Boston was of such gravity that he must not brook the least delay. He was . . . unbending in his determination, Mrs. Vining. I could not dissuade him. Confirmation of my medical judgment in Mr. Vining's case gives me no satisfaction. I will regret to the end of my days that I was not able to dissuade him from carrying out his plans. I spent much time in trying to persuade him of the wisdom of returning home. To no avail – there are no words to adequately express my sorrow at your loss, Mrs. Vining. I regret being of such poor comfort."

"I have the comfort of my sons, and our home and friends," Margaret answered. "Of which you are one. My husband . . . was always of the notion that he would not live long, and I would be left to raise our sons as best I could. You need not fear that I should be desolate with grief, Dr. Williamson. I have been in expectation of this day for some time. It's just," she looked down at her hands, for the first time feeling tears coming to her eyes, her fragile composure wrecked, as they began to spill down her cheeks. "I thought that he and I would be together . . . his last words would be to me."

"I am assured by my correspondent that his family, especially his sister, Miss Vining – took exemplary care of him." Doctor Vining patted his coat and vest pockets, searching for a handkerchief. He pulled one forth, but it was a crumpled calico one, prodigiously unclean, and he thrust it back with an expression of embarrassment on his kindly, blunt features. In the midst of her tears, Margaret felt like giggling at his discomfiture, before her heart was stabbed with a sudden and unexpected sense of loss and anger at the unfairness of it all. Oh, how cruel of fate! Race had claimed to love her; insisted that she was the wife of his heart, yet it must have been the duty of his lawful wife to tend him in his last hours. Margaret thought herself done with grieving, to have become acquainted and well-accustomed to Race's absence in all these months. *No,* she told herself – *I must be strong enough to set this aside now. I must tell the boys now.* She lifted her head to see that Dr. Williamson still regarded her anxiously, fidgeting with a small parcel – a packet wrapped in a sheet of paper and sealed with ribbon and a blob of bright red wax; wax as red as blood.

"This enclosure was entrusted to my friend by Miss Vining with instructions to be forwarded to you. She impressed upon him the need for absolute discretion. Miss Vining is apparently a most formidable lady."

"She is, or so my husband always assured me that she was," Margaret steadied her voice with an effort as Dr. Williamson rose from his chair and placed the slender parcel in her hands. "I know that no one truly relishes bearing such sad news to another, but I thank you for taking the burden of it upon yourself."

The doctor fumbled at his pockets again, apparently in search of his spectacles, which he unfolded and put on, meanwhile stammering, "I am . . . that is . . . it is no burden, Mrs. Vining – or one that might be cheerfully born, if it were any other such tidings. If it is a matter of import to you . . . than it is no burden for me. I will . . . then leave you to compose yourself."

At her nod, he fled, closing the parlor door behind him. Margaret sat in silence, looking at the sealed packet for some minutes. The seal broke easily, and she spread the sheet of thick paper open. There was not much inside – five letters, and a note folded in half. To her dismay and horror, she recognized her own handwriting on two of them; the letters she had sent to Race in the summer. The seals were broken – they had been read by someone. Margaret unfolded the note, which began curtly, without a salutation:

My dear brother informed me privately, some weeks after his return, of the alliance that he had contracted with you and of his purpose in returning to Boston. I could not in good conscience and good honor keep the promise of silence he had requested of me. To obtain a divorce is unthinkable, the shame unbearable for his lawful spouse and child. I sought the council of our older brothers, and our family lawyer, who agreed; we could not be a party to this final unspeakable humiliation of our blood and to those whom we have held in affection for so many years. My brother arrived home already mortally-ill of that consumptive affliction which has blighted so much of his life, and was confined to a sickbed for the remainder of his time on earth. It required very little effort on our various parts to thwart his wishes with regard to his intentions. Indeed, I was the only person to whom he confided his deep affections toward your person.

He repeatedly entreated me to believe your innocence in this entanglement, and of your noble character and devotion . . . Alas, I am duty-bound to consider first those ties of affection to my sister-in-law, and niece, ties which are of a long-standing nature and reinforced by the laws of the land. However, you must not think I am without pity for your sad situation. I have made a private provision, with the approval of my surviving brothers. A bank draft is enclosed, which should enable you to live in some comfort and to raise up your sons in some honorable profession.

Finally, I would implore you, as a condition of accepting this provision, that if you cannot readily take for yourself and your sons another surname than that of Vining, that you now and forever refrain from advertising any connection whatsoever to the Vinings of Boston and Beacon Hill. I believe such a course will spare both your family and ours mutual embarrassment over such a reckless and ill-conceived connection.

Yours in mutual sorrow,
Minerva Templeton Vining

Margaret first crumpled the note; was this to be one last and final humiliation for her? Anger and indignation dried her tears. The Vinings of Boston, indeed! Against her inclination, she recalled one of Race's tales from the ancient Romans, the response of the new-made general of no particular family to a patrician who disparaged him for his lack of noble ancestors: *The honor of my family begins with me, that of yours ends with you!* She opened the second missive, unsealed but scribed on heavy paper. *Ah,* she thought – *the honor of the Vinings, at such a cost. Well, then – the honor of the Vinings of Texas begins with me, with my sons. That of the Vinings of Boston . . . ends, and how shabbily! Of Race's surviving brothers, one is childless, the other fathered only daughters. Let them have their precious name and their empty, loveless honor! I am the daughter of Alois Becker, who resettled his family three times until he found his right place. My brothers fought for their friends and Texas – can I do any less for my sons? General Sam honors me with friendship, thinking that I am a stalwart woman, unbowed, one who would fight to the bitter end. So – let them see how a daughter of Texas fights for those whom she loves!*

She flattened out the note from Minerva, and folded it within the bank-draft. If she were truly a proud woman, she would burn the lot – but caution whispered in her ear. No, the draft – and in such an amount! That was a thing to be saved, against reversals of fortune. Horace was but ten, Peter little more than a baby – who knew what the future would hold? She broke the seal upon the final enclosure, and her heart felt as if it had turned over in her breast; this was but a single sheet, and in Race's hand, but a few sentences raggedly-written, as if he barely had strength to hold the pen.

My dearest and most-beloved Daisy
You are in my thoughts always and forever, from now until the ending of all things. Forgive me my failures, and think upon me always with kindness and enduring love,
Your husband of the heart,
R

Margaret held the paper carefully, as if it were something with delicate wings, like a butterfly, as if something of it would brush off on her fingers. *At the end, perhaps his last thoughts were of us,* she thought. *And that is a kind*

325

of balm, a comfort to consider – not that these few words will ever erase my memories of what happened between us this year just past. She folded Race's last missive and laid it with the rest, folding the paper wrapping around it all, and gathering up the crumbs of sealing wax out of the habit of tidiness in her house. Eleven years of happiness she had been promised by the witch-woman; and she had that and a year of sorrow too. Love and joy, sorrow and grief, many friends – but from this day forward, very few of them would truly know her heart.

Coda – *Deep in the Heart*

"A dream," Margaret smiled at her grandson, touched as always by his resemblance to his father and grandfather; a wiry and hazel-eyed boy, a Vining to the very core of him. "But a pleasant dream. When I look back, many of the years after that day seem like a lovely dream, as when your father was a baby and we all lived in Gonzales together." Such a long time ago that was, Margaret reflected; and it seemed as if those memories were of a distant age, since she was the only one left alive to cherish them. "So many of them I have outlived!" she exclaimed, and her grandson looked up from his toy soldiers, arrayed in marching order on the hearth rug.

"Who, Gran'mere?" he asked, his eyes alive with curiosity.

"All of them," she answered. "My own Mama and Papa, both my husbands, my brothers, too, although I was older than Rudi and Carlchen. I have even outlived General Sam, and who would have thought that?"

"You look as if you are crying, Gran'mere," Horrie observed. "Are you sad? Why are you sad – is it because you are lonely?"

"I am a little sad," Margaret admitted. She would not admit to Horrie that one of those unspoken sorrows was that she had also outlived three of her sons; the dying throes of the Confederacy might ensure that she would survive Peter as well, although not by very much. "Because I am the only one left to remember. But I am not lonely – you are here to listen to my stories."

"I like your stories, Gran'mere." Horrie came and leaned confidingly against the side of her bed. "They're real! Better than books."

"So they are, Little One," Margaret smiled. "And perhaps I should tell you another one today, before I am too tired."

"Yes, Gran'mere," Horrie smiled at her, with the lively, intelligent eyes of his Grandfather Race, in a face which would someday be the very likeness of his. "If you tell me all of your stories, then I will remember them for you – and then no one will forget them, ever!"

"Devious Little One," Margaret returned the smile. "Is there one you would like to hear, most especially?"

"I'd like to hear about how Gran'pere escaped from the Perote prison," Horrie answered, and hitched himself up onto the tall bed, to curl on top of the covers, with his head on Margaret's shoulder. Margaret clicked her tongue, chidingly.

"He did not escape, Little One – he was let go . . ."

327

Notes: Early Texas, the Alamo, and More

It sometimes seems that in writing about 19th century Texas, a stop at the Alamo is almost obligatory – and in that I am no exception. It is the keystone of the Texian Iliad; fascinating because of the appeal of the characters and the situation involved. Even with the mythic qualities dialed down a couple of notches, the Alamo is nearly irresistible to the writer of historical fiction. I was able to fight against the impulse to do an Alamo novel with this book to some degree – but one just can't get far away when it comes to writing about the time and place. No matter what construction can be put on the characters and motivation of those involved, their decision to remain and hold against an overwhelming force, in a crumbling mission compound which they had been urged over and over again to leave – it resonates. Whether the stand at the Alamo was for ideals or friendship, patriotism, or even simply personal pride, that is the stuff of which legends have been made since the last stand of the Spartans at Thermopylae.

On visualizing the character of the triad of men who earned fame everlasting in their defense of that half tumbled-down old mission, I have relied very much on William O. Davis' *Three Roads to the Alamo* for a distillation of their characters and their back-stories. It seems obvious to me from this account and others that William Barrett Travis appeared to his contemporaries in life as a hothead, imperishably self-important, and a serious pain. But he could write, and when it counted he could organize, lead, and inspire – qualities that were called for in the situation that he found himself. James Bowie, possessed of a dark and violent glamour as well as a distinctly shady past, emerges as a Texian version of Lord Byron; mad, bad, and dangerous to know. David Crockett, former U.S. senator and all around personality, emerges as the most personally congenial of the three. He may not have wholly grasped what he was getting himself and his Tennessee comrades into when he appeared at the Alamo gates in the spring of 1836, but he conducted himself as bravely as could be expected. They could have left – but they did not.

Since all of those with firsthand knowledge of what happened during the 14-day siege have long since died, either in the fighting around the old mission or long after, conjectures about what really happened are based upon an assortment of accounts. Most of these were written long afterwards, are extremely sketchy, or strongly biased – or some combination of all three. Historians and historical novelists must carefully pick a way among them – and make our own best guesses, according to our lights. Regarding the siege

328

and the resolution of it, as having a bearing in this volume: Travis did give his signet ring to Angelina Dickinson, as a keepsake, tying it around her neck on a piece of string during the final hours of the siege and Crockett and one John McGregor of Nacogdoches did have wild competitions as to who could make the most noise, with violin and bagpipes as a means of lifting morale.

Generally, I have preferred to concentrate upon those characters who were second or third-rank spear-carriers; most particularly those volunteers who had taken part in the "Come and Take It Fight" – that Lexington Green moment of the Texas War for Independence which kicked off the open rebellion against Mexican authority. Many of the participants in that encounter later became members of the Gonzales Ranging Company, which six months later answered Travis's plea for help in the early spring of 1836. Many more individual volunteers from throughout the Anglo-Texan settlements who came to Gonzales in response to calls for assistance would later become prominent, either in the leadership cadre of the War, during the decade of the Republic, or in the tumultuous decades afterwards.

Early Texas was a small place – people knew each other, had family, friends, or interests which drew them together. They still know each other. Texas and those places which on first glance appear to be large cities, are thickly webbed with personal and familial connections. It is so today, and was even more so in the early days. I found Victoria Frenzel's *Gonzales* – a compendium of biographies of participants in the various actions of that period – to be extremely helpful, as well as the website *Sons of DeWitt Colony Texas*. The *Sons* website is a veritable goldmine of information on early Texas, Gonzales, as well as settlers and their families.

Regarding the battle of Gonzales, fought over that tiny and all-but-useless cannon – it did, as Race Vining observed – appear as an anticlimax, and a slightly farcical one at that. But those citizens of Gonzales in 1835 had no more idea of what the future boded than my neighbors do, in this unsettled year of 2010. That's the way of it – is it a grand gesture or a faintly ridiculous one? How would it all end? What looked like a bit of an anticlimax in the watermelon field in September of 1835 would become deadly serious within six months.

Those names given for those participants in the "Come and Take It" fight, as well as those officials and residents of Gonzales, and those members of the Gonzales Ranging Company, are real, as are those of their wives, children and neighbors. I have made up most of the conversations between characters, although not any of the events and incidents. The circumstances of the first moments of rebellion, centering on the disputed little cannon, are taken from contemporary accounts. The incident of John King and his son William exchanging places in the Ranging Company as they departed actually happened, although tradition has it occurring as the Company rode past John King's property on their way to the Alamo.

These settlers were not newly-arrived hotheads and filibusterers from the United States; or adventurous single men, looking for a fight and any fight going, as many American volunteers seem to have been initially. The older members of the Gonzales Ranging Company were men of family, with relatively well-established ties in the community. They had businesses, families, and homes and little inclination for extraneous fights that would put all of that at risk. The settlers of Gonzales had done well out of their cordial relationship with the Mexican establishment; they were the farthest west of the Texian settlements, having settled on an entrepreneurial land grant made in good faith. Men like John-Will (John William) Smith, Erastus "Deef" Smith – and James Bowie – among others, had all married into local families in San Antonio. They did not rebel hastily and without thought. They were moved to it gradually, in a long slow buildup of dissatisfaction with the Mexican central government which finally exploded into open rebellion. I have tried to make clear that gradual process which took place over a period of about five years, a process which took in such small events as the unprovoked beating of Jesse McCoy and the imprisonment of Stephen F. Austin . . . a gradual drip-drip-drip of political oppression and objection, until a stark choice between rebellion or submission became unavoidable.

That portion of present-day Texas settled by the Anglo-Texians encompassed about two-thirds of the eastern-most and arable coastal lands. Because of the danger from raiding Comanche Indians, and the distance from Mexico, all but the southwestern part of the state proved to be uninviting to Spanish and later Mexican entrepreneurs, in spite of every official inducement. East and north of present-day Texas – that was all Texian. Of those settled regions deep within Texas, only the area around San Antonio and Goliad, and Nacogdoches in East Texas have long-time historical association with official Spanish/Mexican establishment – and Nacogdoches was soon officially abandoned. To Spain and to Mexico in succession, Texas was a far-distant frontier, a dangerous but beautiful and potentially rich place. It was technically within their possession, and yet . . . they could not induce any but the most desperate, ambitious and heavily subsidized of their citizens to go there, to bring their families and to establish businesses. Only Martin de Leon, at Victoria, a handful of hapless Irish settlers at San Patricio, and a number of Mexican ranchers – cattlemen, shepherds and horse traders along the band between the Nueces and the Rio Grande seemed to find settlement in Texas at all enticing. By the 1820s, much of the Texas coastal lowlands were a vacuum, just waiting to be filled.

What is sometimes given fairly short shrift in the popular accounts is how the war for Texas' independence was deeply rooted in the Centralist-Federalist schism in the Mexican political factions of the early 19th century. The settlers and the industries brought by Stephen Austin, Green DeWitt, and other entrepreneurs were welcomed by newly independent Mexico. It appeared that under the Constitution of 1824, Mexico would evolve into a nation very much resembling the United States as it then was; a federation of fairly independent states and localized authority, elected by free citizens – not a top-down, authoritarian, centrally-governed nation, where all power and control was vested in Mexico City. When Antonio Lopez de Santa Anna ended the debate by assuming dictatorial powers to himself and voiding the Constitution of 1824, Texas was not the only state to rebel, and the Anglo-Texians were not the only rebels. Liberal Mexican politicians and local office-holders like Lorenzo de Zavala and Juan Seguin had good reason to join with their Anglo neighbors in Texas, especially as Lopez de Santa Anna brutally crushed rebellion in other Mexican states. Looking at it from that aspect, the Texas War for Independence was a logical outgrowth of a bitter civil war within Mexico. Sometimes it was not all about us.

Returning to various incidences in this book; Susanna Dickinson did not depart with her husband as I have described here. She left Gonzales to join him in Bexar some weeks later. I had made mention in Chapter Nine of Texian volunteers flocking into Gonzales in the fall of 1835, and some of them being dangerous and disreputable men. Accounts are sketchy, but it appears from some of them that the Dickinson house was broken into. It is hinted that Susanna may have been assaulted; in any case, she insisted on joining her husband in Bexar, rather than remain in Gonzales alone.

As much as I tried, I could not find out exactly where she was interviewed by General Houston when she returned to Gonzales with Lopez de Santa Anna's message, and so have settled on the Hunter's hotel, which would have been conveniently close to where the gathering volunteers for the relief of the Alamo would have been camped on Military Square. Gonzales was torched that evening, as described, as Sam Houston began his long retreat east, sheltering and training the only military force that Texas possessed. Mary

Millsaps and her children were inadvertently left behind in the evacuation. But young Davy Darst, (David Sterling Hughes Darst) did not enlist in Sam Houston's army at the age of fifteen, or fight at San Jacinto, although his father, Jacob Darst had taken him to the site of the "Come and Take it" fight sometime in the weeks or months afterwards and impressed upon him the location and importance of those particular events of late 1835. Given the circumstances of the time, boys of that age did enlist eagerly; no doubt many more wished they could have done so. William King and Galba Fuqua were both 16 years of age and John Gaston 17 when they rode with Gonzales Company to the aid of the Alamo garrison.

The miserable conditions of the 'runaway scrape' as described were not exaggerated; in fact, they may have been even worse for many families, who had only bare moments in which to pack up a few things and depart. Many families did bury those valuables that they could not take with them. It was the rainiest spring in many decades, making matters equally difficult for the refugees, Sam Houston's army, and the Mexican Army. Those Texas rivers which would have been easily fordable in any other year proved to be nearly impassible in early 1836. The battle of San Jacinto was truly won in eighteen minutes; a single charge by Sam Houston's thinly ranked army overwhelmed the larger one of Lopez de Santa Anna: the accounts by Seamus O'Doyle and Race Vining are accurate descriptions of what happened. It would have seemed a miracle – and still sometimes seems so today.

Finally, the life-story of Margaret Becker Vining, and her involvement in the signal events of the Republic of Texas will be continued in *Deep in the Heart*, which will be available in December, 2011. Sample chapters and essays about significant historical events will be available through my website and blog, at www.celiahayes.com.